Accolades for
THE GLASS BOOKS of the DREAM EATERS

"Furiously entertaining...utterly succeeds...thrilling."
—*Boston Globe*

"Sometimes books, like cakes, can be built upon recipes. In the
case of *The Glass Books of the Dream Eaters* by Gordon Dahlquist,
that would be one part history, two parts fantasy, three parts deft
plotting and skilled narrative, and about 17 heaping cupfuls of
suspense...and the result is one marvelous confection of a
book...which serves to keep the reader from doing anything else
but, well, read. It makes Dahlquist's tome seem infinitely shorter
than it is. I...found that it took only three days to finish. The
newest Harry Potter took me four. Make of that what you will."
—*Philadelphia Inquirer*

"This is a plump English tea cake of a book: messy, studded with
treats, too big and too rich to finish in just one sitting."
—*Entertainment Weekly*

"A combination of science fiction, dark fantasy, thriller and gothic
horror, this novel is as flat-out fun, engaging and funny as any tale
of mystery and imagination I can recall.... The dialogue is wry,
the descriptions clever and the complicated plot advances as
smoothly as a patrician's pocket watch.....At more than 700
pages, this one ends too quickly." —*Cleveland Plain Dealer*

"*The Glass Books of the Dream Eaters* has a clever conceit with a
foundation of literature as fantasy.... Dahlquist may have created
a literary character in Miss Temple, whose resolve to be of one
mind between dream and reality also holds the book together."
—*Kansas City Star*

"Carr[ies] the reader on a mind-twisting odyssey . . . *The Glass Books of the Dream Eaters* is sweeping, highly original and absorbing . . . well worth the investment." —*Dallas Morning News*

"Fantastic . . . I was in seventh heaven . . . somewhere between Dickens, Sherlock Holmes and Rider Haggard." —Kate Mosse, author of *Labyrinth*

"A kinky, atmospheric look at Victorian England." —*Washington Post*

"Oh, this guy is goo-ood! The most original thing I've read in years: deftly executed, relentlessly inventive and with a trio of the most unusual and engaging heroes who ever took on a sinister cabal out to rule the world by means of sex and dreams." —Diana Gabaldon, author of *Lord John and the Brotherhood of the Blade*

"*The Glass Books of the Dream Eaters* is a big, fat, rich-as-whipped-cream, tart-as-balsamic-vinegar novel that begins like an old-fashioned romance and turns into a wildly imaginative near fantasy with more than a little violence and a climax that will knock your socks off—and promise a sequel, too. . . . [Dahlquist is] fiction's new golden boy—he really is a richly talented storyteller with a terrific gift for offbeat but recognizable and wonderfully likable characters. . . . The writing is as chewy and delicious as a nougat, the story gains speed with every page . . . and the whole reading experience is (as I seem driven to say) as satisfying as a feast." —*Sullivan County Democrat*

"Sometimes sly, other times full-frontally in your face, the author's inventive detail beggars inventory. . . . A marvelous revival of old-fashioned theatrical melodrama with some contemporary zip. . . . As a storyteller he's awfully good. . . . The author imparts to the book a tremendous amount of energy. . . . Builds to a smashing climax. . . . A major confection with serious undertow." —*Locus*

THE GLASS BOOKS

of the DREAM EATERS

•VOLUME ONE•

Gordon Dahlquist

BANTAM BOOKS

THE GLASS BOOKS OF THE DREAM EATERS, VOLUME 1
A Bantam Book

PUBLISHING HISTORY
Bantam hardcover edition of Volumes 1 and 2 published September 2006
Bantam trade paperback edition / January 2009

Published by Bantam Dell
A Division of Random House, Inc.
New York, New York

Book design by Glen M. Edelstein

Library of Congress Catalog Card Number: 2006040740

Bantam Books and the Rooster colophon are registered trademarks
of Random House, Inc.

ISBN 978-0-553-38585-4

Printed in the United States of America
Published simultaneously in Canada

www.bantamdell.com

BVG 10 9 8 7 6 5

Time spent in an imaginary city calls forth a startling array of generosity and patience. To these people, places, and events this book is indebted, and to each I offer my thanks, grateful for the opportunity to do so.

Liz Duffy Adams, Danny Baror, Karen Bornarth, Venetia Butterfield, CiNE, Shannon Dailey, the Dailey family, Bart DeLorenzo, Mindy Elliott, Evidence Room, *Exquisite Realms,* Laura Flanagan, Joseph Goodrich, Allen Hahn, Karen Hartman, David Levine, Beth Lincks, Todd London, the Lower East Oval, Honor Molloy, Bill Massey, John McAdams, E. J. McCarthy, Patricia McLaughlin, *Messalina,* David Millman, Emily Morse, New Dramatists, Octocorp@30th & 9th [RIP], Suki O'Kane, Tim Paulson, Molly Powell, Jim and Jill Pratzon, Kate Wittenberg, Mark Worthington, Margaret Young.

My father, my sister, my cousin Michael.

THE GLASS BOOKS of the DREAM EATERS

ONE

Temple

From her arrival at the docks to the appearance of Roger's letter, written on crisp Ministry paper and signed with his full name, on her maid's silver tray at breakfast, three months had passed. On that morning, her poached eggs steaming their silver bowl (gelatinous, gleaming), Miss Temple had not seen Roger Bascombe for seven days. He had been called to Brussels. Then to the country house of his infirm uncle, Lord Tarr. Then he had been required at all hours by the Minister, and then by the Deputy Minister, and finally by a pressing request from a cousin desperate for discreet advice about matters of property and law. But then she found herself in the same tea shop as that same cousin—the over-fed, over-wigged Pamela—exactly when Roger was said to be soothing her distress. It was quite clear that Pamela's only source of disquiet was a less than ready supply of buns. Miss Temple began to feel tremulous. A day went by with no word at all. On the eighth day, at breakfast, she received the letter from Roger regretfully severing their engagement, closing with the politely expressed desire that she take pains to never contact nor see him in any way for the complete remainder of her days. It contained no other explanation.

Such rejection had quite simply never occurred to her. The manner of dismissal she barely noticed—indeed, it was just how she would have done such a thing (as in fact, she had, on multiple galling occasions)—but the fact of it was stinging. She had attempted to re-read the letter, but found her vision blurred—after a moment she realized she was in tears. She dismissed the maid and unsuccessfully attempted to butter a slice of toast. She placed the toast and her knife carefully on the table, stood, and then walked rather hurriedly to her bed, where she curled into a tight ball, the entirety of her small frame shaking with silent sobs.

For an entire day she remained indoors refusing all but the most bitter Lapsang Soochong, and even that watered down (without milk *or* lemon) into a thin, rusty beverage that managed to be both feeble and unpleasant. In the night she wept again, alone in the dark, hollow and unmoored, until her pillow was too damp to be borne. But by the next afternoon, her clear grey eyes ringed red and her sausage curls lank, waking in pallid winter light (a season quite new to the warm-blooded Miss Temple, who judged it objectively horrid), the bedding tangled about her, she was once more determined to be about her business, and brisk.

Her world had been changed—as she was willing to admit (she had a young lady's classical education) did happen in life—but it hardly meant she was obliged to be docile, for Miss Temple was only docile on the most extraordinary occasions. Indeed, she was considered by some a provincial savage if not an outright little monster, for she was not large, and was by inclination merciless. She had grown up on an island, bright and hot, in the shadow of slaves, and as she was a sensitive girl, it had marked her like a whip—though part of that marking was how very immune from whips she was, and would, she trusted, remain.

Miss Temple was twenty-five, old to be unmarried, but as she had spent some time disappointing available suitors on her island before being sent across the sea to sophisticated society, this was not necessarily held against her. She was as wealthy as plantations could make her, and sharp-witted enough to know that it was natural for people to care more for her money than for her person, and she did not take this point of materialist interest to heart. Indeed, she took very little to heart at all. The exception—though she found herself now hard-pressed to explain it, and though lacking explanations of any kind vexed her—was Roger.

Miss Temple had rooms at the Hotel Boniface, fashionable but not ridiculous, consisting of an outer parlor, an inner parlor, a dining room, a dressing room, a sleeping room, a room for her two maids, and a second dressing and sleeping room for her aged Aunt Agathe, who lived on a small plantation-derived stipend, and who generally alternated between meals and slumber but was enough respected to be a suitable chaperone, despite her lack of attention. Agathe, whom Miss Temple had only first met upon her disembarkation, was acquainted with the Bascombe family. Quite simply, Roger was the first man of reasonable status and beauty to whom Miss Temple had been introduced, and being a young woman of clarity and loyalty, she found no further reason to search. For his part, Roger gave every impression of finding her both pretty and delightful, and so they were engaged.

To all accounts it was a good match. Roger's expressed opinion aside, even those who found Miss Temple's directness difficult would admit to her adequate beauty. They would also happily admit to her wealth. Roger Bascombe was a rising figure in the Foreign Ministry, cresting the verge of palpable authority. He was a man who looked fine when well-dressed, displayed no flagrant vice, and who possessed more chin and less stomach than any the Bascombes had produced in two generations. Their time together had been brief but, to Miss Temple's experience, intense. They had shared a dizzying variety of meals, strolled through parks and galleries, gazed deeply into each other's eyes, exchanged tender kisses. All of this had been new to her, from the restaurants and the paintings (the scale and strangeness of which prompted Miss Temple to sit for several minutes with a hand pressed tightly over each eye), the variety of people, of smells, the music, the noise, the manners and all the new words, and further to the particular strength of Roger's fingers, his arm around her waist, his kindly chuckle— which even when she felt it came at her expense she strangely did not mind—and his own smells, of his soap, his hair oil, his tobacco, his days in meeting rooms amidst piles of thick documents and ink and wax and wood varnish and felt-topped tables, and finally the, to her mind, devastating mixture of sensations she derived from his delicate lips, his bristling side whiskers, and his warm searching tongue.

But by Miss Temple's next breakfast, though her face was blotched and swollen about the eyes, she met her eggs and toast with customary ferocity, and met the maid's timorous gaze just once with a narrow peremptory glance that served as a knife drawn across the throat of any speech, much less consolation. Agathe was still asleep. Miss Temple had been aware (from the husky, insistent, violet-scented breathing) that her aunt had lingered on the opposite side of her door through the day of her (as she now thought of it) Dark Retreat, but she wanted no part of that conversation either.

She launched herself out of the Boniface, wearing a simple but frankly quite flattering green and gold flowered dress, with green leather ankle boots and a green bag, walking crisply toward the district of expensive shops that filled the streets on the near bank of the river. She was not interested in actively buying anything, but had the idea that looking at the assembled goods of the city—of the world—making their way from so many different lands to this collection of shops might serve as a spur to new thinking about her own new state of affairs. With this in mind, she found herself eager, even restless, moving from stall to stall, her eyes roving without lingering over fabrics, carved boxes, glassware, hats, trinkets, gloves, silks, perfumes, papers, soaps, opera glasses, hairpins, feathers, beads, and lacquered items of all kinds. At no point did she actually stop, and sooner than she had imagined possible Miss Temple found herself on the district's other side, standing at the edge of St. Isobel's Square.

The day above her was a cloudy grey. She turned and retraced her steps, gazing still more intently into each exotic display, but never—if she herself were a fish—finding the item that would hook her attention into place. On the Boniface side again, she wondered exactly what she thought she was doing. How, if she was with clarity embracing her new sense of loss and redefinition, did nothing—not even an especially cunning lacquered duck—generate interest? Instead, at each object, she felt herself driven onward, prey to some nagging urge she could not name, toward some unknown prize. That she had no conscious idea what this prize might be irked her, but she took comfort from the implication that it did exist, and would be potent enough to alert her when it came into view.

So, with a resolute sigh, she crossed back through the shops for a third time, her attention entirely elsewhere, confident, as she crossed the square toward the nest of monumental white stone buildings that made up the government Ministries, that her interest was—in a word—disinterested. The matter lay not so much with the perceived faults of her own person, if any, nor the perceived superiority, if any, of a rival (whose identity she was, out of idle curiosity alone, in the back of her mind trying to guess), but merely that her own case was the best example at hand. Or was it the only example? Still, it did not mean she was *troubled* by it, or that she'd no perspective, or that for any future affections of the now-beyond-her Roger Bascombe she would give two pins.

Despite these absolutely rational thoughts, Miss Temple paused upon reaching the center of the square, and instead of continuing on to the buildings where Roger was undoubtedly even now at work, she sat on a wrought-metal bench and looked up at the enormous statue of St. Isobel at the square's center. Knowing nothing of the sainted martyr and in no way devout, Miss Temple was merely disquieted by its vulgar extravagance: a woman clinging to a barrel in surging surf, clothes torn, hair wild, ringed by the flotsam of shipwreck, with the water about her churned to froth by a roiling tangle of serpents that wrapped around her flailing limbs, coiled under her garments and wound across her throat even as she opened her mouth to cry to heaven—a cry one saw to be heard by a pair of angels, winged, robed, and impassively gazing down from above Isobel's head. Miss Temple appreciated enough the size of the thing and the technical achievements involved, but it nevertheless struck her as coarse and unlikely. Shipwreck, as an island girl, she could accept, as she could martyrdom by snakes, but the angels seemed fatiguingly presumptuous.

Of course, as she looked into the unseeing stone eyes of the forever serpent-beset Isobel, she knew she could have scarcely cared less. Her gaze finally followed her true interest, toward the nest of white buildings, and so, quickly, she formed a plan, and with each step of that plan, a perfectly sound justification. She accepted that she was forever divided from Roger—persuasion and reunion were no part of her aims. What she sought, what she in fact required, was information. Was it strict rejection alone—that Roger would rather be alone than be burdened with her? Was it a matter of personal ambition—that she must be shunted aside in favor of promotion and responsibility? Was there simply another woman who had supplanted her in his affections? Or was there something else that she could not presently imagine? They were all equal in her mind, of neutral *emotional* value, but crucial as far as Miss Temple's ability to situate herself in her new loss-inflected existence.

It would be simple enough to follow him. Roger was a man of habits, and even when his hours of work were irregular he would still take his mid-day meal, whenever he did take it, at the same restaurant. Miss Temple found an antiquarian book shop across the street where, as she was obliged to purchase something for standing so long watching through its window, she on impulse selected a complete four-volume *Illustrated Lives of Sea Martyrs*. The books were detailed enough to warrant her spending the time in the window, apparently examining the colored plates, while actually watching Roger first enter and then, after an hour, re-emerge, alone, from the heavy doors across the street. He walked straight back into the Ministry courtyard. Miss Temple arranged for her purchase to be delivered to the Boniface, and walked back into the street, feeling like a fool.

She had re-crossed the square before her reason convinced her that she was not so much a fool as an inexperienced observer. It was pointless to watch from *outside* the restaurant. It was only from inside that she could have determined whether or not Roger dined alone, or with others, or with which particular others, with any of whom he might have shared significant words—all crucial information. Further, unless he had merely thrown her over for his work—which she doubted, scoffing—she was like to learn nothing from observing his working day. It was after work, obviously, that any real intelligence would be gathered. Abruptly, for by this time she was across the square and in the midst of the shops, she entered a store whose windows were thick with all shapes of luggage, hampers, oilskins, gaiters, pith helmets, lanterns, telescopes, and a ferocious array of walking sticks. She emerged some time later, after exacting negotiations, wearing a ladies' black traveling cloak, with a deep hood and several especially cunning pockets. A visit to another shop filled one pocket with opera glasses, and a visit to a third weighed down a second pocket with a leatherbound notebook and an all-weather pencil. Miss Temple then took her tea.

Between cups of Darjeeling and two scones slathered with cream she made opening entries in the notebook, prefacing her entire endeavor and then detailing the day's work so far. That she now had a kind of uniform and a set of tools made everything that much easier and much less about her particular feelings, for tasks requiring clothes and accoutrements were by definition objective, even scientific, in nature. In keeping with this, she made a point to write her entries in a kind of cipher, replacing proper names and places with synonyms or word-play that hopefully would be impenetrable to all but herself (all references to the Ministry were to "Minsk" or even just "Russia", and Roger himself—in a complex train of thought that started with him as a snake that had shed his skin, to a snake being charmed by the attractions of others, to India, and finally, because of his still-remarkable personal presence—became "the Rajah"). Against the possibility that she

might be making her observations for some time and in some discomfort, she ordered a sausage roll for later. It was placed on her
table, wrapped in thick waxed paper, and presently bundled into
another pocket of her cloak.

Though the winter was verging into spring, the city was still
damp around the edges, and the evenings colder than the length-
ening days seemed to promise. Miss Temple left the tea shop at
four o'clock, knowing Roger to leave usually at five, and hired a
carriage. She instructed her driver in a low, direct tone of voice, after assuring him he would be well paid for his time, that they
would be following a gentleman, most likely in another carriage,
and that she would rap on the roof of the coach to indicate the
man when he appeared. The driver nodded, but said nothing else.
She took his silence to mean that this was a usual enough thing,
and felt all the more sure of herself, settling in the back of the
coach, readying her glasses and her notebook, waiting for Roger to
appear. When he did, some forty minutes later, she nearly missed
him, amusing herself for the moment by peering through the
opera glasses into nearby open windows, but some tingling intu-
ition caused her to glance back at the courtyard gates just in time
to see Roger (standing in the road with an air of confidence and
purpose that made her breath catch) flag down a coach of his own.
Miss Temple rapped sharply on the roof of the coach, and they
were off.

The thrill of the chase—complicated by the thrill of seeing Roger
(which she was nearly certain was the result of the task at hand and
not any residual affection)—was quickly tempered when, after the
first few turns, it became evident that Roger's destination was
nowhere more provocative than his own home. Again, Miss
Temple was forced to admit the possibility that her rejection might
have been in favor of no rival, but, as it were, immaculate. It was
possible. It might even have been preferable. Indeed, as her coach

trailed along the route to the Bascombe house—a path she knew so well as to once have considered it nearly her own—she reflected on the likelihood that another woman had taken her place in Roger's heart. To her frank mind, it was not likely at all. Looking at the facts of Roger's day—a Spartan path of work to meal to work to home where undoubtedly he would, after a meal, immerse himself in still more work—it was more reasonable to conclude that he had placed her second to his vaulting ambition. It seemed a stupid choice, as she felt she could have assisted him in any number of sharp and subtle ways, but she could at least follow the (faulty, childish) logic. She was imagining Roger's eventual realization of what he had (callously, foolishly, blindly) thrown aside, and then her own strange urge to comfort him in this sure-to-be-imminent distress when she saw that they had arrived. Roger's coach had stopped before his front entrance, and her own a discreet distance behind.

Roger did not get out of the coach. Instead, after a delay of some minutes, the front door opened and his manservant Phillips came toward the coach bearing a bulky black-wrapped bundle. He handed this to Roger through the open coach door, and then in turn received Roger's black satchel and two thickly bound portfolios of paper. Phillips carried these items of Roger Bascombe's work day back into the house, and closed the door behind him. A moment later, Roger's coach jerked forward, returning at some pace into the thick of the city. Miss Temple rapped on her coach's ceiling and was thrown back into her seat as the horses leapt ahead, resuming their trailing surveillance.

By this time it was fully dark, and Miss Temple was more and more forced to rely on her driver that they were on the right path. Even when she leaned her head out of the window—now wearing the hood for secrecy—she could only glimpse the coaches ahead of them, with no longer a clear confidence about which might be Roger's at all. This feeling of uncertainty took deeper hold the longer they drove along, as now the first tendrils of evening fog began to reach them, creeping up from the river. By the time they stopped again, she could barely see her own horses. The driver leaned down and pointed to a high, shadowed archway over a great staircase that led down into a cavernous gas-lit tunnel. She stared at it and realized that the shifting ground at its base, which she first took to be rats streaming into a sewer, was actually a crowd of dark-garbed people flowing through and down into the depths below. It looked absolutely infernal, a sickly yellow portal surrounded by murk, offering passage to hideous depths.

"Stropping, Miss," the driver called down and then, in response to Miss Temple's lack of movement, "train station." She felt as if she'd been slapped—or at least the hot shame she imagined being actually slapped must feel like. Of course it was the train station. A sudden spike of excitement drove her leaping from the cab to the cobblestones. She quickly thrust money into the driver's hand and launched herself toward the glowing arch. Stropping Station. This was exactly what she had been looking for—Roger was doing something *else*.

It took her a few desperate moments to find him, having wasted valuable seconds gaping in the coach. The tunnel opened into a larger staircase that led down into the main lobby and past that to the tracks themselves, all under an intricate and vast canopy of ironwork and soot-covered brick. "Like Vulcan's cathedral." Miss Temple smiled, the vista spreading out beneath her, rather proud of so acutely retaining her wits. Beyond coining similes, she had the further presence of mind to step to the side of the stairs, use a lamp post to perch herself briefly on a railing, and with that vantage use the opera glasses to look over the whole of the crowd— which her height alone would never have afforded. It was only a matter of moments before she found Roger. Again, instead of immediately rushing, she followed his progress across the lobby to a particular train. When she was sure she had seen him enter the train, she climbed off of the railing and set off first to find out where it was going, and then to buy a ticket.

She had never been in a station of such size—Stropping carried all traffic to the north and west—much less at the crowded close of a working day, and to Miss Temple it was like being thrust into an ant-hill. It was usual in her life for her small size and delicate strength to pass unnoticed, taken for granted but rarely relevant, like an unwillingness to eat eels. In Stropping Station, however, despite knowing where she was going (to the large blackboard detailing platforms and destinations), Miss Temple found herself shoved along pell-mell, quite apart from her own intentions, the view from within her hood blocked by a swarm of elbows and waistcoats. Her nearest comparison was swimming in the sea against a mighty mindless tide. She looked up and found landmarks in the ceiling, constellations of ironwork, to judge her progress and direction, and in this way located an advertising kiosk she had seen from the stairs. She worked her way around it and launched herself out again at another angle, figuring the rate of drift to reach another lamp post that would allow her to step high enough to see the board.

The lamp post reached, Miss Temple began to fret about the time. Around her—for there were many, many platforms—whistles fervently signaled arrivals and departures, and she had no idea, in her subterranean shuffling, whether Roger's train had already left. Looking up at the board, she was pleased to see that it was sensibly laid out in columns indicating train number, destination, time, and platform. Roger's train—at platform 12—left at 6:23, for the Orange Canal. She craned her head to see the station clock—another hideous affair involving angels, bracketing each side of the great face (as if keeping it up with their wings), impassively gazing down, one holding a pair of scales, the other a bared sword. Between these two black metal specters of judgment, Miss Temple saw with shock that it was 6:17. She threw herself off the lamp post toward the ticket counter, burrowing vigorously through a sea of coats. She emerged, two minutes later, at the end of an actual ticket line, and within another minute reached the counter itself. She called out her destination—the end of the line, round-trip—and dropped a handful of heavy coins onto the marble, pushing them peremptorily at the ticket agent, who looked beakily at her from the other side of a wire cage window. His pale fingers flicked out from under the cage to take her money and shoved back a perforated ticket. Miss Temple snatched it and bolted for the train.

A conductor stood with a lantern, one foot up on the stairs into the last car, ready to swing himself aboard. It was 6:22. She smiled at him as sweetly as her heaving breath would allow, and pushed past into the car. She had only just stopped at the top of the steps to gather her wits when the train pulled forward, nearly knocking her off her feet. She flung her arms out against the wall to keep her balance and heard a chuckle behind her. The conductor stood with a smile at the base of the steps in the open doorway, the platform moving past behind him. Miss Temple was not used to being laughed at in any circumstance, but between her mission, her disguise, and her lack of breath, she could find no immediate retort and instead of gaping like a fish merely turned down the corridor to find a compartment. The first was empty and so she opened the glass door and sat in the middle seat facing the front of the train. To her right was a large window. As she restored her composure, the last rushing view of Stropping Station—the platform, the trains lined up, the vaulted brick cavern—vanished, swallowed by the blackness of a tunnel.

The compartment was all dark wood, with a rather luxurious red velvet upholstery for the bank of three seats on either side. A small milk-white globe gave off a meager gleam, pallid and dim, but enough to throw her reflection against the dark window. Her first instinct had been to pull off the cloak and breathe easily, but though Miss Temple was hot, scattered, and with no sense of where she was exactly going, she knew enough to sit still until she was thinking clearly. Orange Canal was some distance outside the city, nearly to the coast, with who knew how many other stops in between, any one of which might be Roger's actual destination. She had no idea who else might be on the train, and if they might know her, or might know Roger, or might in fact be the reason for the journey itself. What if there were no destination at all, merely some rail-bound assignation? In any case, it was clear that she had to find Roger's location on the train or she would never know if he disembarked or if he met someone. As soon as the conductor came to take her ticket, she would begin to search.

He did not come. It had already been some minutes, and he had only been a few yards away. She didn't remember seeing him go past—perhaps when she entered?—and began to get annoyed, his malingering on top of the chuckle making her loathe the man. She stepped into the corridor. He was not there. She narrowed her eyes and began to walk forward, carefully, for the last thing she wanted—even with the cloak—was to stumble into Roger unawares. She crept to the next compartment, craned her head around so she could peer into it. No one. There were eight compartments in the car, and they were all empty.

The train rattled along, still in darkness. Miss Temple stood at the door to the next car and peered through the glass. It looked exactly like the car she was in. She opened the door and stepped through—another eight compartments without a single occupant. She entered the next car, and found the exact same situation. The rear three cars of this train were completely unoccupied. This might explain the absence of the conductor—though he still must have known her to be in the rear car and if he had been polite could have taken her ticket. Perhaps he merely expected her to do what she was doing, moving ahead to where she should have been in the first place, if she hadn't been so late to reach the train. Perhaps there was something she didn't know about the rear cars, or the etiquette on this particular trip—would that explain the chuckle?—or about the other passengers themselves. Perhaps they were in a group? Perhaps it was less a journey and more of an excursion? Now she despised the conductor for his presumption as well as his rudeness, and she moved forward in the train to find him. This car as well was empty—four cars!—and Miss Temple paused at the doorway into the fifth, trying to recall just how many cars there were to begin with (she had no idea) or how many might be normal (she had no idea) or what exactly she could say to the conductor, upon finding him, that would not reveal her complete ignorance (she had no immediate idea). As she stood thinking, the train stopped.

She rushed into the nearest compartment and threw open the window. The platform was empty—no one boarding, and no one leaving the train. The station itself—the sign said Crampton Place—was closed and dark. The whistle blew and the train— throwing Miss Temple back into the seats—lurched into life. A chill wind poured through the open window as they gathered speed and she pulled the window closed. She had never heard of Crampton Place, and was happy enough not to be going there now—it struck her as desolate as a Siberian steppe. She wished she had a map of this particular line, a list of stops. Perhaps this was something she might get from the conductor, or at least a list she could write down in her book. Thinking of the book, she took it out and, licking the tip of the pencil, wrote "Crampton Place" in her deliberate, looping script. With nothing else to add, she put the book away and returned to the corridor and then, with a sigh of resolve, stepped into the fifth car.

She knew it was different from the perfume. Where the other corridors were imbued with a vague industrial mixture of smoke and grease and lye and dirty mop-water, the corridor of the fifth car

smelled—startling because she knew them from her own home—
of frangipani flowers. With a surge of excitement, Miss Temple
crept to the nearest compartment and slowly leaned forward to
peer into it. The far seats were all occupied: two men in black topcoats and between them a woman in a yellow dress, laughing. The
men smoked cigars, and both had trimmed and pointed beards,
with hearty red faces, as if they were two examples of the same
species of thick, vigorous dog. The woman wore a half-mask made
of peacock feathers that spread out over the top of her head, leaving only her eyes to pierce through like gleaming stones. Her lips
were painted red, and opened wide when she laughed. All three
were gazing at someone in the opposite row of seats, and had not
noticed Miss Temple. She retreated from view, and then, feeling
childish but knowing nothing else for it, dropped to her hands and
knees and crawled past, keeping her body below the level of the
glass in the door. On the other side, she carefully rose and peered
back at the opposite row of seats and froze. She was looking directly at Roger Bascombe.

He was not looking at her. He wore a black cloak, closed about
his throat, and smoked a thin, wrapped cheroot, his oak-colored
hair flattened back over his skull with pomade. His right hand was
in a black leather glove, his left, holding the cheroot, was bare. At
a second glance Miss Temple saw that the right gloved hand was
holding the left glove. She also saw that Roger was not laughing,
that his face was deliberately blank, an expression she had seen
him adopt in the presence of the Minister or Deputy Minister, or
his mother, or his uncle Tarr—that is, those to whom he owed
deference. Sitting against the window, the seat between them unoccupied, was another woman, in a red dress that flashed like fire
from beneath a dark fur-collared cloak. Miss Temple saw the
woman's pale ankles and her delicate throat, like white coals beneath the flaming dress, flickering in and out of view as she shifted
in her seat. Her darkly red mouth wore an openly provocative wry
smile and she puffed at a cigarette through a long black lacquered

holder. She also wore a mask, of red leather, dotted with glittering studs where the eyebrows would be, and then—Miss Temple noted with some discomfort—forming a gleaming tear, just ready to drop from the outer corner of each eye. She had obviously said whatever the others were laughing at. The woman exhaled, a deliberate stream of smoke sent to the other row of seats. As if this gesture were the conclusion of her witticism, the others laughed again, even as they waved the smoke from their faces.

Miss Temple stepped clear of the window, her back flat against the wall. She had no idea what she ought to do. To her right was another compartment. She risked a peek, and saw the far seats occupied with three women, each with a traveling cloak wrapped around what seemed to be, judging from their shoes, elegant evening wear. Two wore half-masks decorated with yellow ostrich feathers while the third, her face uncovered, held her mask on her lap, fussing with an uncooperative strap. Miss Temple pulled her own hood lower and craned to see that the other seat held two men, one in a tailcoat and one in a heavy fur that made him seem like a bear. Both of these men wore masks as well, simple black affairs, and the man in the tailcoat occupied himself with sips from a silver flask, while the man in the fur tapped his fingers on the pearl inlaid tip of an ebony walking stick. Miss Temple darted back. The man in the fur had glanced toward the corridor. In a rush she scampered past Roger's compartment, in open view, and through the connecting door to the previous car.

She shut the door behind her and crouched on her hands and knees. Interminable seconds passed. No one came to the door. No one entered in pursuit, or even curiosity. She relaxed, took a breath, and brought herself sharply to task. She felt out of her depth, beyond her experience—and yet, frankly, Miss Temple had no confirmation why this must be true. Despite being assailed with sinister thoughts, all she had definitely learned was that Roger was attending—without obvious pleasure, nor anything more evident than obligation—an exclusive party of some kind,

where the guests were masked. Was this so unusual? Even if to
Miss Temple it was, she knew this did not figure, so much was
strange to her sheltered life that she was no objective judge—had
she been in society for an entire season, this kind of entertainment
might seem, if not so routine as to be dull, at least a known quantity. Further, she reconsidered the fact that Roger was not sitting
next to the woman in red, but apart from her—in fact, apart from
everyone. She wondered if this was his first time in their company.
She wondered who this woman was. The other, in yellow with the
peacock feathers, interested her much less, simply for having
been so vulgarly receptive to the more elegant woman's wit.
Clearly the men were unconcerned about hiding their identities—
they must all know each other and be traveling as a group. In the
other compartment, all being masked, perhaps they didn't. Or perhaps they did know each other but were unaware of it *because* of
the masks—the whole pleasure of the evening would lie in guessing, she realized, and in remaining hidden. It struck Miss Temple
as perhaps a great deal of fun, though she knew that her own dress,
if fine for the day, was nothing to wear to such an evening, and
that her cloak and hood, though they protected her identity for
the moment, were nothing like the proper party mask everyone
else would have.

Her thoughts were interrupted by a clicking sound from the
other corridor. She risked a look and saw the man in the fur—
quite imposing when not seated, nearly filling the corridor with
his wide frame—stepping out of Roger's compartment and closing
the door behind him. Without a glance toward her, he returned to
his own. She sighed, releasing a tension she had been unable to
fully acknowledge; he had not seen her, he was merely visiting the
other compartment. He must know the woman, she decided, even
though he could have stepped into the compartment to speak to
any person in it, including Roger. Roger saw so many people in his
day—from government, from business, from other countries—and
she realized with a pang how small her own circle of acquaintance

actually was. She knew so little of the world, so little of life, and here she was cowering in an empty train car, small and ridiculous. While Miss Temple was biting her lip, the train stopped again.

Once more she dashed into a compartment and opened the window, and once more the platform was empty, the station shuttered and dark. This sign read Packington—another place she had never heard of—but she took a moment to enter it into her notebook just the same. When the train began to move again she closed the window. As she turned back to the compartment door she saw that it was open, and in it stood the conductor. He smiled.

"Ticket, Miss?"

She fished her ticket from her cloak and handed it to him. He took it from her, tilting his head to study the printed destination, still smiling. In his other hand he held an odd metal clamping device. He looked up.

"All the way to Orange Canal, then?"

"Yes. How many more stops will that be?"

"Quite a few."

She smiled back at him, thinly. "Exactly how many, please?"

"Seven stops. Be the better part of two hours."

"Thank you."

The clamping device punched a hole in the ticket with a loud snapping sound, like the bite of a metal insect, and he returned it to her. He did not move from the door. In response, Miss Temple flounced her cloak into position as she met his gaze, claiming the compartment for herself. The conductor watched her, glanced once toward the front of the train and licked his lips. In that moment she noticed the porcine quality of his heavy neck, particularly how it was stuffed into the tight collar of his blue coat. He looked back at her and twitched his fingers, puffy and pale like a parcel of uncooked sausages. Confronted with this spectacle of ungainliness, her contempt abated in favor of mere disinterest—she no longer wanted to cause him harm, only that he should leave.

But he wasn't going to leave. Instead, he leaned closer, with a feeble kind of leer.

"Not riding up with the others, then, are you?"

"As you can see, no."

"It's not always safe, a young lady alone..." He trailed off, smiling. The conductor persisted in smiling at all times. He fingered the clamping device, his gaze drifting toward her well-shaped calves. She sighed.

"Safe from what?"

He did not answer.

Before he could, before he could do anything that would cause her to either scream or feel still more galling pitiful disdain, she raised her open palm to him, a signal that he need not answer, need not say anything, and asked him another question.

"Are you *aware* where they—where *we*—are all going?"

The conductor stepped back as if he had been bitten, as if she had threatened his life. He retreated to the corridor, touched his cap, and turned abruptly, rushing into the forward car. Miss Temple remained in her seat. What had just happened? What she'd meant as a question the man had taken as a threat. He must *know*, she reasoned, and it must be a place of wealth and influence—at least enough that the word of a guest might serve to cost him his position. She smiled (it had been a satisfying little exchange, after all) at what she had learned—not that it was a surprise. That Roger was attending in a subordinate position only reinforced the possibility that representatives from the upper levels of government might well be present.

With a vague gnawing restlessness, Miss Temple was reminded that she was actually getting hungry. She dug out the sausage roll.

Over the next hour there were five more stops—Gorsemont, De Conque, Raaxfall, St. Triste, and St. Porte—every name going into her notebook, along with fanciful descriptions of her fellow travelers. Each time, looking out the window, she saw an empty platform and closed station house, with no one entering or leaving the train. Each time also she felt the air getting progressively cooler, until at St. Porte it struck her as positively chill and laced with the barest whiff of the sea, or perhaps the great salt marshes she knew to exist in this part of the country. The fog had cleared, but revealed merely a sliver of moon and the night remained quite dark. When the train started up again, Miss Temple had at each station crept into the corridor and carefully peered into the fifth car, just to see if there was any activity. Once she had a glimpse of someone entering one of the forward compartments (she had no idea who—black cloaks all looked the same), but nothing since. Boredom began to gnaw at her, to the point that she wanted to go forward again and get another look into Roger's compartment. She knew this to be a stupid idea that only preyed upon her because of restlessness, and that further it was times like these when one made the most egregious mistakes. All she had to do was remain patient for another few minutes, when all would be clear, when she could get to the very root of the whole affair. Nevertheless, her hand was in the act of turning the handle to enter the fifth car when the train next stopped.

She let go of it at once, shocked to see that all down the corridor the compartment doors were opening. Miss Temple ducked back into her compartment and threw open the window. The platform was crowded with waiting coaches, and the station windows were aglow. As she read the station sign—Orange Locks—she saw people spilling from the train and walking very near to her. Without closing the window she darted back to the connecting door: people were exiting from a door at the far end, and the last person—a man in a blue uniform—had nearly reached it. With a nervous swallow and a flutter in her stomach, Miss Temple stepped silently through the door and rapidly, carefully, padded down the corridor, glancing into each compartment as she passed.

All were empty. Roger's party had gone ahead, as had the fur-coated man.

The man in the blue uniform was also gone from view. Miss Temple picked up her pace and reached the far end, where an open door and a set of steps led off the train. The last people seemed to be some yards ahead of her, walking toward the coaches. She swallowed again. If she stayed on the train, she could just ride to the end and take the return trip easily. If she got off, she had no idea what the schedule was—what if the Orange Locks station were to close up like the previous five? At the same time, her adventure *was* continuing in the exact manner she had hoped. As if to make up her mind, the train lurched ahead. Without thinking Miss Temple leapt off, landing with a squawk and a stumble on the platform. By the time she gathered herself to look back, the train was racing by. In the doorway of the final car stood the conductor. His gaze was cold, and he held his lantern toward her the way one holds a cross before a vampire.

The train was gone and the roar of its passage faded into the low buzz of conversation and the clops and jingles and slams of the travelers climbing into their waiting coaches. Already full coaches were moving away, and Miss Temple knew she must decide immediately what to do. She saw Roger nowhere, nor any of the others from his car. Those remaining were in heavy coats or cloaks or furs, a seemingly equal number of men and women, perhaps twenty all told. A group of men climbed into one coach and a mixture of men and women piled into two more. With a start she realized that there was only one other coach remaining. Walking in its direction were three women in cloaks and masks. Throwing her shoulders back and the hood farther over her face, Miss Temple crossed quickly to join them.

She was able to reach the coach before they had all entered, and when the third woman climbed up and turned, thinking to shut the door behind her, she saw Miss Temple—or the dark, hooded figure that Miss Temple now made—and apologized, situating herself farther along on the coach seat. Miss Temple merely nodded in answer and climbed aboard in turn, shutting the door tightly behind her. At the sound, after a moment to allow this last person to sit, the driver cracked his whip and the coach lurched into motion. With her hood pulled down, Miss Temple could barely see the faces of the other passengers, much less anything out the window—not that she could have made sense of what she might have seen anyway.

The other women were at first quiet, she assumed due to her own presence. The two across from her both wore feathered masks and dark velvet cloaks, the cloak of the woman to the left boasting a luxurious collar of black feathers. As they settled themselves in the coach, the one to the right opened her cloak and fanned herself, as if she were over-hot from exertion, revealing a dress of shimmering, clinging blue silk that seemed more than anything else like the skin of a reptile. As this woman's fan fluttered in the darkness like a night bird on a leash, the coach filled with perfume—sweet jasmine. The woman sitting next to Miss Temple, who had preceded her into the coach, wore a kind of tricorn hat rakishly pinned to her hair, and a thin band of cloth tied over her eyes, quite like a pirate. Her wrap was simple but probably quite warm, made of black wool. As this was not as sumptuous, Miss Temple allowed herself to hope she might not be so out of place, as long as she kept herself well concealed. She felt confident her boots—cunningly green—if glimpsed, would not make her look out of place.

They rode for a time in silence, but Miss Temple was soon aware that the other women shared her own sense of excitement and anticipation, if not her feeling of terrible suspense. Bit by bit they began making small exploratory comments to one another— first about the train, then about the coach or about each other's clothing, and finally, hintingly, at their destination. They did not at first address Miss Temple, or indeed anyone in particular, merely offering comments in general and responding the same way. It was as if they were not supposed to be talking about their evening at all, and could only proceed to do so by degrees, each of them making it tacitly plain that they would not be averse to bending the rule. Of course Miss Temple was not averse in the slightest, she just had nothing to say. She listened to the pirate and the woman in silk compliment each other on their attire, and then to both of them approve of the third woman's mask. Then they turned to her. So far she had said nothing, merely nodding her head once or twice in agreement, but now she knew they were all examining her quite closely. So she spoke.

"I do hope I have worn the right shoes for this cold an evening."

She shifted her legs in the tight room between seats and raised her cloak, exhibiting her green leather boots, with their intricate lacing. The other three leaned to study them, and the pirate next to her confided, "They are most sensible—for it will be cold, I am sure."

"And your dress is green as well...with flowers," noted the woman with the feathered collar, whose gaze had moved from the shoes to the strip of dress revealed above them.

The woman in silk chuckled. "You come as a Suburban Rustick!" The others chuckled too and, so bolstered, she went on.

"One of those ladies who live among novels and flowered sachets—instead of life itself, and life's gardens. The Rustick, and the Piratical, the Silken, and the Feathered—we are all richly disguised!"

Miss Temple thought this was a bit thick. She did not appreciate being termed either "suburban" or "rustick" and further was quite convinced that the person who condemns a thing—in this case novels—is the same person who's wasted most of her life reading them. In the moment, as she was being insulted, it was all she could do not to reach across the coach (for it was an easy reach) and take sharp hold of the harpy's delicate ear. But she forced herself to smile, and in doing so knew that she must place her immediate pride in the service of her adventure, and accept the more important fact that this woman's disdain had given her a costume, and a role to play. She cleared her throat and spoke again.

"Amongst so many ladies, all striving to be most elegant, I wondered if such a *costume* might be noticed all the more."

The pirate next to her chuckled. The silken woman's smile was a little more fixed and her voice a bit more brittle. She peered more sharply at Miss Temple's face, hidden in the shadow of her hood.

"And what is your mask? I cannot see it . . ."

"You can't?"

"No. Is it also green? It cannot be elaborate, to fit under that hood."

"Indeed, it is quite plain."

"But we cannot see it."

"No?"

"But we should like to."

"My thinking was to make it that much more mysterious—it being in itself, as I say, plain."

In reply the silken woman leaned forward, as if to put her face right into the hood with Miss Temple, and Miss Temple instinctively shrank back as far as the coach would allow. The moment had become awkward, but in her ignorance Miss Temple was unsure where the burden of *gaucherie* actually lay—with her refusal or the silken woman's gross insistence. The other two were silent, watching, their masks hiding any particular expression. Any second the woman would be close enough to see, or close enough to pull back the hood altogether—Miss Temple had to stop her in that very instant. She was helped, in this moment, by the sudden knowledge that these women were not likely to have lived in a house where savage punishment was a daily affair. Miss Temple merely extended two fingers of her right hand and poked them through the feathered mask-holes, straight into the woman's eyes.

The silken woman shot back in her seat, sputtering like an

over-full kettle coming to boil. She heaved one or two particularly whingeing breaths and pulled down her mask, placing a hand over each eye, feeling in the dark, rubbing away the pain. It was a very light touch and Miss Temple knew no real damage had been done—it was not as if she had used her nails. The silken woman looked up at her, eyes red and streaming, her mouth a gash of outrage, ready to lash out. The other two women watched, immobile with shock. Again, all was hanging in the balance and Miss Temple knew she needed to maintain the upper hand. So she laughed.

And then a moment after laughing pulled out a scented handkerchief and offered it to the silken woman, saying in her sweetest voice, "O my dear... I *am* sorry...," as if she were consoling a kitten. "You must forgive me for preserving the... *chastity* of my disguise." When the woman did not immediately take the handkerchief Miss Temple herself leaned forward and as delicately as she could dabbed the tears from around the woman's eyes, patiently, taking her time, and then pressed the handkerchief into her hands. She sat back. After a moment, the woman raised the handkerchief and dabbed her face again, then her mouth and nose, and then, with a quick shy glance at the others, restored her mask. They were silent.

The sounds of the hoofbeats had changed, and Miss Temple looked out of the coach. They were passing along some kind of stone-paved track. The country beyond was featureless and flat—perhaps a meadow, perhaps a fen. She did not see trees, though in the darkness she doubted she could have had they been there—but it did not *seem* like there would be trees, or if there had been once, that they had been cut down to feed some long-forgotten fire. She turned back to her companions, each seemingly occupied with her own thoughts. She was sorry to have ruined the conversation, but did not see any way around it. Still, she felt obliged to try and make amends, and attempted to put a bright note in her voice.

"I'm sure we shall be arriving soon."

The other women nodded, the pirate going so far as to smile, but none spoke in reply. Miss Temple was resilient.

"We have reached the paved road."

Exactly as before, all three women nodded and the pirate smiled, but they did not speak. The moment of silence lengthened and then took hold in the coach, each of them sinking deeper, as the air of solitude intruded, into her own thoughts, the earlier excitement about the evening now somehow supplanted by an air of brooding disquiet, the exact sort of gnawing, unsparing unrest that leads to midnight cruelty. Miss Temple was not immune, especially since she had a great deal to brood about if she were to shift her mind that way. She was keenly reminded that she had no idea what she was doing, where she was going, or how she would possibly return—and indeed, more than any of these, what she would return *to*. The stable touchstone of her thoughts had disappeared. Even her moments of satisfaction—frightening the conductor and besting the silken woman—now struck her as distant and even vain. She had just formed the further, frankly depressing, question "was such satisfaction always at odds with desire?" when she realized that the woman in the feathered cloak was speaking, slowly, quietly, as if she were answering a question only she had heard being asked.

"I have been here before. In the summer. It was light in the coach . . . it was light well into the evening. There were wildflowers. It was still cold—the wind is always cold here, because it is close to the sea, because the land is so flat. That is what they told me . . . because I was cold . . . even in summer. I remember when we reached the paved road—I remember because the movement of the coach changed, the bouncing, the rhythm. I was in a coach with two men . . . and I had allowed them to unbutton my dress. I had been told what to expect . . . I had been promised this and more . . . and yet, when it happened, when their promises began to be re-

vealed...in such a desolate locale...I had goosebumps everywhere." She was silent, then glanced up, meeting the eyes of the
others. She wrapped her cloak around her and looked out the window, smiling shyly. "And I am back again...you see, it gave me
quite a thrill."

No one said a word. The clattering hoofbeats changed once
more, drawing the coach onto uneven cobblestones. Miss
Temple—her mind more than a little astir—glanced out the window to see that they had entered a courtyard, past a large, tall iron
gate. The coach slowed. She could see others already stopped
around them, passengers piling out (adjusting cloaks, putting on
hats, tapping their walking sticks with impatience), and then a first
glimpse of the house itself: splendid, heavy stone, some three tall
stories high and without excessive ornament save for its broad windows, now streaming out welcoming golden light. The entire effect was of a simplicity that, when employed on such massive scale,
bespoke a hard certainty of purpose—in the same way as a prison
or an armory or a pagan temple. She knew it must be the great
house of some Lord.

Their coach came to a halt, and as the last person in Miss
Temple took it upon herself to be the first person out, opening the
door herself and taking the coachman's large hand to aid her descent. She looked up to see, at the end of the courtyard, the entrance to the house, double doors flung open, servants to either
side, and a stream of guests disappearing within. The massive
splendor of the place amazed her, and she was again assailed by
doubt, for surely once inside she would have to remove her hood
and cloak and be revealed. Her mind groped for a solution as her
eyes, brought back to their task, scanned the milling crowd for a
glimpse of Roger. He must already be in the house. Her three companions were all out of the coach and had begun walking toward
the doors. The pirate paused for a moment, looking back, to see if
she was with them, and in another sudden decision Miss Temple

merely gave in answer a small curtsey, as if to send them on their way. The pirate cocked her head, but then nodded and turned to catch up with the other two. Miss Temple stood alone.

She looked about the courtyard—was there perhaps some other way inside?—but knew that her only hope, if she wanted to truly discover what Roger was doing and why, in service to this, he had so peremptorily thrown her over, was to present herself at the grand entryway. She fought the urge to run and hide in a coach, and then the urge to just put things off long enough to record her most recent experiences in the notebook. If she must go in, it was better to go in at the proper time, and so she forced her legs to take her with a sureness of step that her racing heart did not share. As she got closer she moved among the other coaches, whose drivers were being directed by grooms toward the other side of the court-yard, more than once causing her to dodge rather sharply. When her path was finally open, the last of the other guests—perhaps her three companions?—had just cleared the entryway and vanished from her view. Miss Temple lowered her head, throwing more shadow over her face, and climbed the stairs past footmen on ei-ther side, noting their black livery included high boots, as if they were a squadron of dismounted cavalry. She walked carefully, rais-ing her cloak and her dress high enough to climb the stairs without falling, but without being so vulgar as to expose her ankles. She reached the top of the stairs and stood alone on a pale marble floor, with long, mirrored, gas-lit hallways extending before her and to either side.

"I think perhaps you're meant to come with me."

Miss Temple turned to see the woman in red, from Roger's car. She no longer wore her fur-collared cloak, but she still had the lac-quered cigarette holder in her hand, and her bright eyes, gazing fixedly at Miss Temple through the red leather mask, quite belied their jeweled tears. Miss Temple turned, but could not speak. The

woman was astonishingly lovely—tall, strong, shapely, her pow-
dered skin gleaming above the meager confines of the scarlet dress.
Her hair was black and arranged in curls that cascaded across her
bare pale shoulders. Miss Temple inhaled and nearly swooned
from the sweet smell of frangipani flowers. She closed her mouth,
swallowed, and saw the woman smile. It was very much how she
imagined she had so recently smiled at the woman in blue silk.
Without another word, the woman turned and led the way down
one of the mirrored halls. Without a word Miss Temple followed.

Behind, she heard a distant buzz, of movement, of conversation, of
the party itself—but this was fading before the sharp report of the
woman's footfalls on the marble. They must have gone fifty
yards—which was but half the length of the hall—when her guide
stopped and turned, indicating with her outstretched hand an
open door to Miss Temple's left. They were quite alone. Not
knowing at this point that she could do anything else, Miss
Temple went into the room. The woman in red followed, and shut
the heavy door behind them. Now there was silence.

The room was spread with thick red and black carpets which
absorbed the sound of their passage. The walls were fitted with
closed cabinets, and between them racks of hooks, as if for clothing, and a full-length mirror. A long, heavy wooden work table
was shoved against one wall, but Miss Temple could see no other
furniture. It looked like some kind of attiring room, for a theatre,
or perhaps sport, for horseback riding, or a gymnasium. She imagined a house of this size might well have its own anything it
wanted, if the owner was so inclined. On the far wall was another
door, not so fancy, set into the wall to look at first glance like one
of the cabinets. Perhaps that led to the gymnasium proper.

The woman behind her said nothing, so she turned to face her,
head inclined so as to shadow her face. The woman in red wasn't
looking at Miss Temple at all, but was fitting another cigarette into

her holder. She'd dropped the previous one on the carpet and ground it in with her shoe. She looked up at Miss Temple with a quick ghost of a smile, and strode over to the wall, where she jammed the new cigarette into one of the gas lamps and puffed on the holder until it caught. She exhaled, crossed to the table and leaned back against it, inhaled, and exhaled again, gazing at Miss Temple quite seriously.

"Keep the shoes," the woman said.

"Beg pardon?"

"They're quaint. Leave the rest in one of the lockers."

She gestured with the cigarette holder to one of the tall cabinets. Miss Temple turned to the cabinet and opened it; inside, hanging from hooks, were various pieces of clothing. On the hook right in front of her face—as if in answer to her fears—was a small white mask, covered in closely laid small white feathers, as if from a dove or a goose or a swan. Keeping her back to the woman in red, she threw off her hood and tied the white mask into place, weaving the strap beneath her curls, pulling it tight across her eyes. Miss Temple then shucked off her cape—glancing back once to the woman, who seemed to be smiling with wry approval of her progress—and hung it on a hook. She selected what seemed to be a dress from another hook—it was white, and silken—and held it out in front of her. It wasn't a dress at all. It was a robe, a very short robe, without any kind of buttons or sash, and quite thin.

"Did Waxing Street send you?" the woman asked, in a disinterested, time-passing tone.

Miss Temple turned to her, made a quick decision, and spoke deliberately.

"I do not know any Waxing Street."

"Ah."

The woman took a puff of her cigarette. Miss Temple had no idea whether her answer had been wrong—whether there had been a right or wrong answer—but she felt it was better to tell the truth than to guess foolishly. The woman exhaled, a long thin stream of smoke sent toward the ceiling.

"It must have been the hotel, then."

Miss Temple said nothing, then nodded, slowly. Her mind raced—what hotel? There were hundreds of hotels. *Her* hotel? Did they know who she was? Did her own hotel supply young women as guests to luxurious parties? Did any hotel do such a thing? Obviously so—the mere question told her that—yet Miss Temple had no idea what this meant as far as her own disguise, what she ought to say or how she was expected to behave or what this exactly implied about the party, though she was beginning to have suspicions. She looked again at the wholly inadequate robe.

She turned to the woman. "When you say *hotel*—"

Her words were cut off brusquely. The woman was grinding out her second cigarette on the carpet, and her voice was suddenly annoyed.

"Everything is waiting—it's quite late. *You* were late. I have no intention of serving as a nursemaid. Get changed—be quick about it—and when you're presentable, you can come find me." She walked directly toward Miss Temple, reached out to take hold of her shoulder—her fingers surprisingly hard—and spun her so her face was half-way into the cabinet. "This will help you get started—given the fabric, think of it as an act of mercy."

Miss Temple squawked. Something sharp touched the small of her back, and then shifted its angle, driving upward. With a sudden ripping sound, and a simultaneous collapse of her garment, Miss Temple realized that the woman had just sheared through the lacings of her dress. She whirled around, her hands holding it to her bosom as it peeled away from her back and off of her shoulders. The woman was tucking something small and bright back into her bag, crossing to the small inner door, and jamming a third cigarette into her holder as she spoke.

"You can come in through here."

Without a further glance at Miss Temple the woman in red opened the door with impatience, paused to get a light from the nearest wall sconce, and strode from view, pulling the door behind her so it slammed.

Miss Temple stood, at a loss. Her dress was ruined, or at least ruined without immediate access to new lacing and a maid to tie it up. She pulled it off of her upper body and did her best to shift the back section around so she could see it—fragments of green lacework were even now tumbling to the floor. She looked at the door to the hallway. She could hardly leave like this. On the other hand, she could hardly leave in her corset, or in the pitifully gossamer silk robe. She remembered with relief that she did still have her cloak, and could surely cover any less than decorous attire with that. This made her feel a little better and, after a moment of steady breathing, she was in less of a hurry to escape, and began to wonder once more about the woman, the party, and of course, never far from her thoughts, Roger. If she could return to fetch her cloak at any time and simply put it over her corset or ruined dress, then what was the harm in perhaps investigating further? On top of this, she was now intrigued by the reference to the hotel—she was determined to find out if such things happened at the Boniface, and how other than by continuing could she pursue her brave plan? She turned back to the cabinet. Perhaps there were other things than the robe.

There were, but she wasn't sure if she was any more comfortable at the thought of putting them on. Several items could only be described as undergarments, and probably from a warmer climate than this—Spain? Venice? Tangier?—a pale silken bodice, several sheer petticoats, and a pair of darling little silk pants with an open seam between the legs. There was also another robe, similar to the first, only longer and without any sleeves. The ensemble was all white, save for the second robe, which had a small green circle embroidered repeatedly as a border around the collar and the bottom hem. Miss Temple assumed this was why she was allowed to keep her shoes. She looked at her own undergarments—shift, petticoats, cotton breeches, and her corset. Except for the corset, she didn't see too much of a difference between what was in the cabinet and the items on her body—save for the former being made of silk. Miss Temple was not in the habit of wearing silk—and it was only rarely that she was provoked into a choice outside her habits. The problem was getting out of her corset and then back into it, without assistance. She felt the silken pants between her fingers and resolved to try.

Her fingers tore behind her at the knotwork of the corset, for now she was concerned about taking too long, and did not want anyone coming in to collect her when she was half-naked, and once she was free of it—and taking deeper breaths than she was used to—she pulled the corset and her shift over her head. She pulled on the silk bodice, sleeveless, with tiny straps to keep it up, and tugged it into place over her bosom. She had to admit that it felt delicious. She pushed her petticoats and breeches down to the floor and, balancing on one foot and then the other, kicked her shoes free of them. She reached for the little pants, feeling a strange thrill at standing in such a large room wearing nothing but the bodice, which did not stretch below her ribs, and her green ankle boots. Stranger still, pulling on the pants, was how she felt somehow even more naked, with the open seam along her delicate curls. She ran her fingers through them once, finding the exposure both exquisite and a little frightening. She removed her fingers, sniffed them by habit, and reached for the silken petticoats, holding them open and stepping through the circle one foot at a time. She pulled them up, tied them off, and then reached again for her corset.

Before she put it on, Miss Temple stepped in front of the large mirror. The woman who stared back was unknown to her. It was partially the mask—the experience of looking at herself in a mask was extremely curious, and not unlike running her fingers along her open pants. She felt a tingle crawl down her spine and settle itself right among her hips, a ticking restless hunger. She licked her lips, and watched the woman in the mask of white feathers lick hers as well—but this woman (her pale arms bare, her legs muscular, throat exposed, roseate nipples at plain view through the bodice) licked them in quite a different way than seemed normal to Miss Temple—though once she saw that image, its sensation was, as it were, taken into her, and she licked them again as if some transformation had indeed been made. Her eyes glittered.

She dropped the corset back into the cabinet and put on the robes, first the shorter one with sleeves, and then over it the larger, almost like a tunic, with the borders of green embroidery, which did in fact have several hooks to keep it closed. She looked at herself again in the mirror, and was happy to see that together the two layers of robe provided enough of a barrier for decency. Her arms and lower legs were still semi-visible through their single layers, but the rest of her body, though suggested, could not in any detail be seen. As a final precaution, because she had not fully lost her sense of place or perspective, Miss Temple fished in the pocket of her cloak for both her money and her all-weather pencil, which was still rather sharp. Then she knelt on alternating knees, stuffing the money into one boot and wedging the pencil into the other. She stood, took a couple of steps to test comfort, closed the cabinet, and then walked through the inner door.

She was in a narrow unfinished hallway. She walked a few paces in gradually growing light and reached a turn where the floor slanted up toward the bright light's source. She stepped into glaring light and raised a hand to block it, looking around her. It was a kind of sunken stage—above and around it rose a seating gallery pitched at a very steep angle, covering three sides of the room. The stage itself, what she took for playing space, was taken up with a large table, at the present moment flat but with a heavy apparatus underneath, which, she assumed from the large, notched curve of steel running the length of the table, could tilt the table to any number of angles, for better viewing from the gallery. Behind the table, on the one wall without seating, was a common, if enormously large, blackboard.

It was an operating theatre. She looked to either side of the table and saw holes that dangled leather belts, to restrain limbs. She saw a metal drain on the floor. She smelled vinegar and lye, but beneath them some other odor that prickled the back of her throat. She looked up at the blackboard. This was for teaching, for study, but no mere man of science could afford such a home. Perhaps this Lord was their patient—but what patient would want an audience for his treatment? Or patron to some medical prodigy—or himself a practicing amateur—or an interested spectator? Her flesh was chilled. She swallowed, and noticed something written on the board—she hadn't seen it from the entrance because of the light. The surrounding text had been erased—indeed, half of this word had been erased—but it was easy to see what it had been: sharp block printing, in chalk, the word "ORANGE."

Miss Temple was startled—indeed, she may have squeaked in surprise—by a throat being cleared on the far side of the stage, from shadow. There was an opposite rampway rising up from the floor she hadn't seen, hidden by the table. A man stepped into view, wearing a black tailcoat, a black mask, and smoking a cigar. His beard was elegantly trimmed, and his face familiarly ruddy. It was one of her two dogs from the train, who had been sitting across from Roger. He looked at her body quite directly, and cleared his throat again.

"Yes?" she asked.

"I have been sent to collect you."

"I see."

"Yes." He took a puff on the cigar but otherwise did not move. "I'm sure I'm sorry to make anyone wait."

"I didn't mind. I like to look around." He looked again, frankly examining her, and stepped fully up from the ramp into the theatre, raising his cigar hand above his eyes to block the light. He glanced over the gallery, to the table, and then to her again. "Quite a place."

Miss Temple adopted, without difficulty, a knowing condescension. "Why, have you never been here?"

He studied her before answering, then decided not to answer, and stuck the cigar into his mouth. With his hand free, he pulled a pocket watch from his black waistcoat and looked at the time. He replaced the watch, inhaled, then removed the cigar, blowing smoke.

Miss Temple spoke again, affecting as casual an air as possible.

"I have always found it to be an elegant house. But quite . . . particular."

He smiled. "It is that."

They looked at each other. She very much wanted to ask him about Roger, but knew it wasn't the time. If Roger was, as she suspected, peripheral, then asking for him by name—especially a guest in her strange position (as much as she did not fully understand what that was)—would only arouse suspicion. She must wait until she and Roger were in the same room and—while both were masked—try to engage someone in conversation and point him out.

But being alone with anyone was still an opportunity, and despite her terrible sense of disquiet and unease, in order to try and provoke this canine fellow further, she let her eyes wander to the blackboard, looking fixedly at the half-erased word, and then back to him, as if pointing out that someone had not fully done their job. The man saw the word. His face twitched in a quick grimace and he stepped to the board, wiping the word away with his black sleeve, and then beating ineffectually on the sleeve to get rid of the chalk smear. He stuck the cigar in his mouth and offered her his arm.

"They *are* waiting."

She walked past the table and took it, bobbing her head as she did. His arm was actually quite strong and he held hers tightly, even awkwardly, as he was so much taller. As they walked down the ramp into darkness, he spoke, nodding his head back to the theatre. "I don't know why they had you go through there—I suppose it's the shortest way. Still, it's quite a sight—not what you'd expect."

"That depends," Miss Temple answered. "What do *you* expect?"

In response, the man only chuckled, and squeezed her arm all the harder. Their ramp made a turn just like the other had, and they walked on level ground to another door. The man pushed it open and thrust her deliberately into the room. When she had stumbled several steps forward he came in behind and closed the door. Only then did he let go of Miss Temple's arm. She looked around her. They were not alone.

The room was in its way the opposite of where she had changed clothes, for just as it was on the opposite side of the theatre so it must be used for an opposite kind of preparation—an entirely different kind of participant. It felt like a kitchen, with a flagged stone floor and white tiled walls. There were several heavy wooden tables, also fitted with restraints, and on the walls various bolts and collars, clearly meant for securing the struggling or insensible. However, and strangely, one of the wooden tables was covered with an array of white feather pillows, and on the pillows sat three women, all wearing masks of white feathers and white robes, and each of them dangling their naked calves off of the table, the robes reaching just below their knees. All of their feet were bare. There was no sign of the woman in red.

No one was speaking—perhaps they'd gone silent at her arrival—and no one spoke as her escort left her where she was and crossed to one of the other tables, where his companion, the other dog-fellow, stood drinking from a flask. Her escort accepted the flask from him, swallowed manfully, and returned it, wiping his mouth. He took another puff from his cigar and tapped it against the edge of the table, knocking a stub of ash to the floor. Both men leaned back and studied their charges with evident pleasure. The moment became increasingly awkward. Miss Temple did not move to the table of women—there wasn't really room, and none of the others had shifted to make any. Instead, she smiled, and pushed her discomfort aside to make conversation.

"We have just seen the theatre. I must say it is impressive. I'm sure I don't know how many it will seat compared to other such theatres in the city, but I am confident it must seat plenty—perhaps up to one hundred. The notion of so many attendees in such a relatively distant place is quite a testament to the work at hand, in my own opinion. I should find it satisfying to be a part of that endeavor, however much as a tangent, even as a distraction, even for only this evening alone—for surely the fineness of the facility must parallel the work done in it. Do you not agree?"

There was no reply. She continued—for this was often her experience in public conversation and she was perfectly able to press on, adopting the pose of the knowing veteran.

"I am also, of course, happy for any excuse to be wearing so much silk—"

She was interrupted when the man with the flask stood and crossed to the far door. He took another nip and stuffed the flask into his tailcoat as he walked, then opened the door and closed it behind him. Miss Temple looked at the remaining man, whose face in the interval had gone even redder, if that were possible. She wondered if he were in the midst of some kind of attack, but he smiled passively enough and continued to smoke. The door opened again and the man with the flask poked his head through, nodded to the man with the cigar, and disappeared from view. The man with the cigar stood and, smiling once more at them all—the gaze of each woman following him closely—crossed to the open doorway. "Any time you're ready," he said and walked out, closing the door behind him. A moment later Miss Temple heard the distinct sharp click of that door being locked. Their only path led back to the theatre.

"You've kept your shoes," said one of the women, on the right.

"I have," said Miss Temple. It was not what she wanted to talk about. "Have any of you been *in* the theatre?" They shook their heads no, but said nothing more. Miss Temple indicated the restraints, the bolts, the collars. "Have you looked at this room?" They blandly nodded that they had. She became almost completely annoyed. "He has locked the door!"

"It will be fine," said the woman who had spoken before. Miss Temple was suddenly caught up—did this voice seem familiar?

"It is merely a room," said the woman in the middle, kicking at one of the leather restraints hanging near to her leg. "It's not what it is used for *now.*"

The others nodded blankly, as if no more needed saying.

"And what exactly would *that* be?" demanded Miss Temple.

The woman giggled. It was a giggle she'd heard before too. It was from the coach. This was the woman who'd let the men unbutton her dress. Miss Temple looked at the other two—seeing them in such different apparel, such different light—were they the pirate and silken woman whose eyes she had poked? She had no idea. She saw that they were smiling at her too, as if her question had indeed been very foolish. Were they drunk? Miss Temple stepped forward and grasped the woman's chin, tilting her face upwards—which she passively, strangely, allowed—and then lowered her own face to the woman's mouth and sniffed. She well knew what alcohol—particularly rum—smelled like, and its squalid influence. The woman wore perfume—sandalwood?—but there was another odor that Miss Temple did not recognize. It was not alcohol, or indeed anything she had smelled before—nor, further, did the odor emanate from around the woman's mouth (again occupied with giggling), but higher on her face. The odor was vaguely mechanical, almost industrial, but it wasn't coal, nor rubber, nor lamp oil, nor ether, nor even burnt hair, though it seemed adjacent to all of these unpleasant smells joined together. She could not place it—not in her mind, nor on the woman's body—was it around her eyes?—behind the mask? Miss Temple released her and stepped away. As if this were a signal to all three of them, they hopped off the table as one.

"Where are you going?" Miss Temple asked.

"We are going in," said the one in the middle.

"But what have they told you? What will happen?"

"Nothing will happen," said the woman on the right, "save everything we desire."

"They are expecting us," said the woman on the left, who had not yet spoken. Miss Temple was certain it was the woman who had arrived wearing the blue silk dress.

They pushed past her to the door—but there was so much more to ask them, so much more they could say! Were they invited guests? Did they know of any hotel? Miss Temple sputtered, dropping for the moment her condescending pose, crying to them all, "Wait! Wait! Where are your clothes? Where is the lady in red?"

All three erupted into stifled laughter. The one in front opened the door, and the one in the rear dismissed Miss Temple with a derisive flip of her hand. They walked out, the last closing the door behind them. There was silence.

Miss Temple looked around her at the cold, menacing room, her early confidence and pluck having quite ebbed away. Obviously, if she were bold, the path to full investigation lay up the dark ramp and into the theatre. Why else had she met the challenge of changing clothes, of formulating questions, of coming *all this way*? At the same time, she was not a fool, and knew enough that this room and the theatre, this party—all legitimately disquieting—could well pose a keen danger to both her virtue and her person. The outside door was locked, and the men outside that locked door horrid. The room held no cabinets or alcoves in which to crouch concealed. She pointed out to herself that the other women—who must know more than she—were unconcerned. The other women might equally be whores.

She took a breath, and chided herself for so brusque a judgment—after all the women had been finely dressed. They might be unchaste, even slatternly, they might indeed be here by way of some hotel—who knew the complications of another's life? The true question was whether this must lead perforce to a situation beyond her skills to manage. There were great gaps in Miss Temple's experience—which she would freely acknowledge, when pressed—that were only generally filled in with equally great swathes of inference and surmise. About many of these things she nevertheless felt she had a good idea. About others, she preferred to find pleasure in mystery. In the matter of the strange theatre, however, she was determined that no gaps, so to speak, should be filled at all.

She could at least listen at the door. With care she turned the knob and opened the door perhaps an inch. She heard nothing. She opened it a bit wider, enough to insert her head through the gap. The light looked the same as before. The other women had only just gone out—she could only have dithered for the space of a minute. Could it be that the crowd was so soon in hushed concentration? Was there already some ghastly tableau on display? She listened, but heard nothing. Peering around the corner, however, just gave her the glaring light in her eyes. She crept forward. She still heard nothing. She lowered herself to a crouch, then to her hands and knees, all the while gazing up the ramp at an uncomfortable angle. She saw and heard nothing. She stopped. She was at the point where any further movement would reveal her to the gallery—she was already fully visible from the stage, had anyone been there to see her. She shifted her gaze to the table. There was no one upon it. There was no one at all.

Miss Temple was extremely annoyed, if also relieved, and further, more than a little curious as to what had actually happened to the three women. Had they merely gone out the other side? She resolved to follow them, but happened in crossing the stage to glance up again at the blackboard, the glaring light now out of her eyes. In the same block letters, someone had inscribed, "SO THEY SHALL BE CONSUMED." Miss Temple visibly started, as if someone had blown in her ear. The words had definitely not been there before.

She whirled around to the gallery seats again, looking for anyone hiding on their hands and knees. There was no one. Without delay she continued across to the first ramp and down it, rounding the corner to the door. It was closed. She put her head to the door and listened. She heard nothing—but this meant nothing, the doors were thick. Tired as she was of unnecessary stealth, she again turned the knob with excruciating patience and opened it just enough to peek through. She widened the opening, listened, heard nothing, and widened it again. Still nothing. Annoyance getting the best of her, Miss Temple opened the door completely, and gasped with shock.

Strewn across the floor were the tattered, savaged remains of her hooded cloak, her dress, her corset, and her undergarments— all slashed beyond repair, nearly beyond recognition. Even her new notebook had been destroyed—pages torn out and scattered like leaves, the binding snapped, the leather cover pitted and gashed. Miss Temple found herself shaking with outrage, and with fear. Obviously she had been discovered. She was in danger. She must escape. She would follow Roger another time, or she would engage professional operatives, men who knew their business—stout fellows who would not be so easily tricked. Her efforts had been ridiculous. They might well be her undoing.

She crossed to the wall of cabinets. Her own clothing was destroyed, but perhaps one of the others held something she could use to cover herself. They were all locked. She pulled with all her strength, to no avail. She looked around for anything to force the cabinet doors, to pry them open, but the room was bare. Miss Temple released a cry of guttural frustration, an unexpectedly plangent whine—which when she heard it herself, with a certain shock, made clear the true extent of her desperate position. What if she were discovered and her name made known? How could she distinguish herself from any of these other similarly clad women? How could she face Roger? She caught herself. Roger! It was exactly the thing to restore her resolve. The last thing she wanted was to be in any way subject to his scrutiny—the very thought of it filled her with rage. *He* filled her with rage. In that moment she despised Roger Bascombe and was newly determined to get free of this horrid predicament and then, at her leisure, dedicate herself to ruining him utterly. And yet, even in the act of imagining that ruin, and herself sneering in triumph above him, Miss Temple felt a stab of pity, of proprietary concern for what the foolish man had managed to become involved in—what depravity, what danger, what career-destroying scandal was he here so blithely courting? Was it possible he did not understand? If she were to somehow speak to him, could she apprise him of his peril? Could she at least divine his mind?

Miss Temple walked to the hallway door and opened it. The hallway seemed empty, but she craned her head out as far as she could, listening closely. One way took her back to the front, to the thick of the party and directly past—she assumed—other guests, servants, *everyone*. It would also take her to the coaches, if in her present costume she were able to get out of the house without being discovered, exposed, ridiculed, or worse. The *other* way took her deeper into the house, and deeper into danger but also deeper into intrigue. Here she might legitimately hope to find a change of clothing. She might find an alternative route to the coaches. She might even find more information—about Roger, about the woman in red, about the Lord in residence. Or she could find her own destruction. While Miss Temple posed the question to herself as one of "running away" versus "bravely pushing on" it was also true that going deeper into the house, though more frightful as a whole, served to postpone any immediate confrontation. If she were to go back to the entrance she was certain to run into servants at least. If she went forward anything at all might happen—including an easy escape. She took one more look toward the great entrance, saw no one, and darted in the opposite direction, moving quickly and close to the wall.

She came to three successive doors on her side and one across the mirrored hall, all of which were locked. She kept walking. Her shoes seemed impossibly loud on the tiled floor. She looked ahead of her to the end of the hallway—there were only two more doors before she'd have to turn around. Another door across the hall—she glanced backwards again and, seeing no one, dashed across to it. The handle did not budge. Another look—still no one—and she trotted back to the other side, and up to the last door. Beyond it, the hallway ended in an enormous mirror that was inset with panes and posts to look like one of the great windows that faced out from elsewhere in the house—only the view here was ostentatiously and pointedly turned inward, as if to confide that (frankly, behind doors) such an interior view was truly the more important. To Miss Temple it was chastening, for she saw herself reflected, a pale figure skulking on the border of opulence. The earlier pleasure she'd felt upon seeing herself so masked was not wholly absent, but tempered with a better understanding of a risk that seemed to be its twin.

At the final door her luck changed. As she neared it, she heard a muffled voice and sounds of movement. She tried the knob. It was locked. There was nothing else for it. Miss Temple squared her shoulders and took a deep breath. She knocked.

The voice went silent. She braced herself, but heard nothing—no steps to the door, no rattle of the lock. She knocked again, louder, so that it hurt her hand. She stepped back, shaking her fingers, waiting. Then she heard quick steps, a bolt being drawn, and the door snapped open a bare inch. A wary green eye stared down at her.

"What is it?" demanded a querulous male voice, openly peeved.

"Hello," said Miss Temple, smiling.

"What the devil do you want?"

"I'd like to come in."

"Who the devil are you?"

"Isobel."

Miss Temple had seized the saint's name on instinct, from nerves—but what if it gave her away, if there were another Isobel who was known to be somewhere else, or didn't look anything like her, some fat blotchy girl who was always in a sweat? She looked up at the eye—the door had not opened a jot farther—and desperately tried to gauge the man's reaction. The eye merely blinked, then quickly ran up and down her body. It narrowed with suspicion.

"That doesn't say what you want."

"I was directed here."

"By whom? By *whom*?"

"Whom do you think?"

"For what purpose?"

Though Miss Temple was willing enough to continue, this was going *on,* and she was acutely aware of being so long visible in the hallway. She leaned forward, looked up to the eye, and whispered, "To change my *clothing*." The eye did not move. She glanced around her, and back to the man, whispering again. "I can hardly do so in the *open air...*"

The man opened the door, and stepped away, allowing her to enter. She took care to scamper well past his possible grasp, but saw that he had merely closed the door and indeed stepped farther away. He was a strange creature—a servant, she assumed, though he did not wear the black livery. Instead, she noted that his shoes, though they had once been fine, were scuffed and clotted with grime. He wore a white work smock over what looked to be a thoroughly simple and equally worn brown shirt and pants. His hair was greasy, smeared back behind his ears. His skin was pale, his eyes sharp and searching, and his hands black as if they had been stained with India ink. Was he some kind of printer? She smiled at him and said thank you. His reaction was to audibly swallow, his hands worrying the frayed hem of his smock, and then study her while breathing through his open mouth like a fish.

The room was littered with wooden boxes, not as long or deep as a coffin, but lined with cushioning felt. The boxes were open, the tops haphazardly propped up against the wall, but their contents were not apparent. In fact, they all seemed empty. Miss Temple took it upon herself to glance into one of them when the man snapped at her, traces of spittle lancing into the air with his vehemence.

"Stop that!"

She turned to see him pointing at the boxes and then, his thoughts shifting, to her, her mask, her clothing.

"Why did he send you here? Everyone's supposed to be in the other rooms! I have work to do! I can't—I won't be the butt of his jokes! Hasn't he done enough to me already? Hasn't his lap-dog Lorenz? Do this, Crooner! Do that, Crooner! I have followed every instruction! I am just as responsible for . . . my own designs—one momentary, regrettable lapse—I have agreed to every condition—submitted utterly, and yet—" He gestured helplessly, sputtering at Miss Temple. "This *torment!*"

She waited for him to stop speaking and, once he did, to stop huffing like an ill-fed terrier. On the far side of the room was another door. With a serious nod and a respectful dip of her knee, Miss Temple indicated this door and whispered, "I will trouble you no further. If you-know-who *does* happen to question me, I will make plain that you were solely focused on your task." She nodded again and walked to the door, very much hoping it was not a closet. She opened it and stepped into a narrow hallway. Shutting the door behind her, Miss Temple sagged with relief against the wall.

She knew there was no time to rest and forced herself on. The hallway was an unadorned servants' corridor, allowing swift, undisturbing passage between vital parts of the house. With a surge of hope, Miss Temple wondered if it might lead her to the laundry. She padded as softly as her boots would allow to the door at the far end. Before turning the knob, she noticed a metal disk the size of a coin fixed to the door with a tiny bolt. She swiveled it to the side and revealed, set into the wood, a spy hole. Obviously this was so a careful servant could be sure not to interrupt his master with an untimely entrance. Miss Temple fully approved of this engine of discretion and tact. She stood on her toes and peeked in.

It was a private closet, luxurious in size, dominated by a large copper bath. On a table sat an array of bathing implements— sponges, brushes, bottles, soaps, and stacks of folded white towels. She saw no person. She opened the door and crept in. Immediately, she lost her footing—her heel skidding on the wet tile floor—and sat down hard on the floor in an awkward, spraggling split. A sharp ripping sound told her the outer robe had torn. She froze in place, listening. Had anyone heard? Had she actually yelped? There was no answering sound from beyond the open closet door. Miss Temple gingerly stood. The floor had been liberally splashed with water, a number of used towels dropped without care on the floor, crumpled and soaked. She carefully leaned over and dipped her fingers into the bath. It was tepid. No one had been in the tub for at least thirty minutes. She dabbed her fingers on one of the towels—no servant had been in the room either, or all would have been cleared and swabbed. This meant that either the occupant was still there, or that the servants had been warned away.

It was then that Miss Temple noticed the smell, drifting in from the room beyond. She probably hadn't detected it immediately because of the residue of flowered soaps and oils, but as soon as she had taken a step toward the door her senses were assailed with the same strange unnatural odor she had found on the masked woman's face, only now much stronger. She put a hand over her nose and mouth. It seemed a mixture of ash and burnt cork perhaps, or smoldering rubber—she wondered suddenly what burning glass smelled like—yet what were any of those smells doing in the private quarters of a country mansion? She poked her head out of the bathing closet and into a small sitting room. A quick glance took in chairs, a small table, a lamp, a painting, but no source of new clothing. She stepped across to the far doorway leading out, which was when she heard the noise.

Heavy footsteps, approaching nearer and nearer. When they had practically reached her—when she was just about to bolt back to the closet—the footsteps stumbled and Miss Temple heard the distinct screech and crash of something heavy being knocked into something else, which in turn toppled to the floor and shattered. She flinched to see a spray of China blue glass jet through the open doorway past her feet. A pause. The footsteps resumed, again lurching, and faded away. Miss Temple risked a peek around the corner. At her feet were the scattered remains of an enormous vase, the lilies that had been inside, the broken marble pedestal it had rested upon, and an end table knocked askew. The room held a large canopied bed with all its linen stripped away. Instead, the bed held three wooden boxes, identical to those the strange servant had opened in the room off the hall. These too were open and lined with felt—orange felt, as she now fully took in, recalling the word on the blackboard. The boxes were all empty, but she picked up one of the discarded lids and saw that letters—also in orange—had been stenciled on the wood: "OR-13." She looked at the other two lids and saw that they had in turn been stenciled "OR-14" and "OR-15." She snapped her head up to the archway. The footsteps had returned, careening even more recklessly. Before Miss Temple could do a thing to hide there was a thicker, meaty crash, and then another silence.

She waited, heard nothing, and crept to the archway. The smell was even stronger. She gagged, holding part of her sleeve across her nose and mouth. This was another sitting room, more fully furnished, but with every item covered by a white cloth, as if this part of the house were closed. On the floor, poking from behind a white-shrouded sideboard, were a pair of legs: bright red trousers with a yellow cord on the outside seam, stuffed into black boots. A soldier's uniform. The soldier did not move. Miss Temple dared to step into the room and look at him fully. His coat was also red, draped with golden epaulettes and frogging and he had a thick black moustache and whiskers. The rest of his face was covered by a tight red leather mask. His eyes were closed. She did not see any blood—there was no immediate indication that he had hit his head. Perhaps he was drunk. Or overwhelmed by the smell. She poked the man with her foot. He did not stir, though she saw from his gently moving chest that he lived.

Wadded up in his hands—and perhaps tripping on this had been his difficulty—was a black cloak. Miss Temple smiled with satisfaction. She knelt and gently prized it free, and then stood, holding it open before her. There was no hood, but it would cover the rest of her very well. She smiled again with cunning and knelt at the man's head, carefully unfastening his mask and then peeling it away from his face. She let out a gasp. Around his eyes the man bore what looked like a strange brand, an impression on the skin, as if a large pair of metal glasses had been pressed into his face and temples. The flesh was not burned, but discolored a visceral shade of plum, as if a layer of skin had been rubbed away. Miss Temple examined the other side of his mask with distaste. It did not seem fouled or bloody. She wiped it on one of the white chair covers. It left no stain. Still, it was with distrust that she pulled off her own white mask and exchanged it for the red. She then pulled off her white robes and wrapped herself in the black cloak. There was no mirror, but she still felt as if she had regained some of her footing. She stuffed the discarded things into the sideboard and made her way to the next doorway.

This was quite large, clearly the main entrance to this suite of rooms, and it opened directly onto a crowd of finely dressed guests moving purposefully past her down a large, well-lit corridor. A man noted Miss Temple's appearance in the doorway and nodded, but did not pause. No one paused—in fact there seemed to be some hurry. Happy not to be causing alarm, Miss Temple stepped into the moving mass and allowed herself to be swept along. She was mindful to hold her cloak closed, but otherwise had leisure to study the people around her. They all wore masks and elegant evening wear, but seemed a variety of types and ages. As she shuffled along several others nodded or smiled to her, but no one spoke—in fact, no one was speaking at all, though she did sense an occasional smile of anticipation. She was convinced that they were all going toward something that promised to be wonderful, but that very few, if any, of them actually knew what it was. As she looked ahead and behind, she saw it was really no great group in the corridor—perhaps forty or fifty. Judging from the number of coaches at the front of the house, this was but a fraction of those attending the party. She wondered where everyone else was, and how they had explained the absence of this group. Further, where were they going? And how long was the corridor? Miss Temple decided that whoever laid out the house was unhealthily fixated with *length*. She stumbled abruptly into the person ahead of her—at this point a short woman (which was to say, of her own height) in a pale green dress (a color similar to Miss Temple's own, she noted with a pang) and an especially ingenious mask made from strings of hanging beads.

"Oh, I am so sorry," Miss Temple whispered.

"Not at all," the woman replied, and nodded at a gentleman in front of her, "I trod on *his* heel." They were stopped in the hall.

"We are stopped," observed Miss Temple, trying to keep up the conversation.

"I was told the stair is quite narrow, and to be careful with my shoes. They never build for ladies,"

"It is a terrible truth," agreed Miss Temple, but her gaze had shifted over their heads, where indeed she saw a line of figures winding their way up a spiral staircase, fashioned of bright metal.

Her heart leapt in her throat. Roger Bascombe—for it could be no one else, despite the plain black mask across his eyes—was even as she watched moving around the upper spiral, and for the moment facing her directly. Once more, his expression was guarded, his hand tapping impatiently on the rail as he climbed, one step at a time, other guests immediately above and below him. He so disliked the crush of a crowd—she knew he must be miserable. Where was he going? Where did he *think* he was going? Then all too brusquely Roger had reached the top, a narrow balcony, and disappeared from sight.

Miss Temple turned her gaze to the people around her—she had shuffled another few steps forward, her thoughts fully awhirl—and realized the woman in green had been whispering. "I'm sorry," Miss Temple whispered back, "I was suddenly distracted with excitement."

"It is very exciting, isn't it?" confided the woman.

"I should say it is."

"I am feeling quite girlish!"

"I am sure you speak for everyone," Miss Temple assured her, and then blithely wondered, "I did not expect so many people."

"Of course not," answered the woman, "for they've been very careful—the hiding of this group within the larger function, the subtlety of our invitations, the concealment of identity."

"Indeed." Miss Temple nodded. "And what a cunning mask you have."

"It *is* very cunning, is it not?" The woman smiled. By this time she had taken a half-step back so she could walk next to Miss Temple and they could speak lower without attracting the attention of others. "But I myself have been intending to compliment your cloak."

"Ah, well, that is kind of you to say."

"Rather *dramatic*," the woman muttered, reaching to touch a border of black ribbon edging the collar that Miss Temple had not noticed. "It looks almost like a soldier's."

"Is that not the fashion?" Miss Temple smiled.

"Indeed"—here the woman's voice went lower still—"for are *we* not soldiers now, in our own way?"

Miss Temple nodded, and spoke in quiet solidarity. "My feeling is the same."

The woman met her gaze significantly, and then ran her eyes quite happily over the cloak. "And it is quite long—it covers you completely."

Miss Temple leaned closer. "So no one will know what I am wearing."

The woman smiled wickedly and leaned in closer still. "Or if you are wearing anything at all . . ."

Before Miss Temple could respond they were at the foot of the staircase. She gestured for the woman to go first—the last thing she wanted was for these impulsive words to prompt her companion to look under her cloak from below. As they rose, she looked down—there were only a scattered dozen people still in the corridor. Then she swallowed—for behind them all, advancing slowly, almost as if to herd them like sheep, was the woman in red. Her gaze fell across Miss Temple, who could not suppress a flinch, and then slid past her toward the balcony. Miss Temple kept climbing and was soon around the other side of the spiral, out of sight. When she once more rotated out into the open she steeled herself to merely face upward into the green woman's back. The nape of her neck prickled. It was all she could do not to look, but she held to her will, resisting the destructive urge—sure she'd been discovered. Then the green woman stopped—there was a delay above them. Miss Temple felt fully exposed, as if she wore no cloak and no mask, as if she and the woman in red were alone. Again, she sensed that gaze boring into her and distinctly heard those footfalls she remembered from the mirrored hall. The woman was coming closer…closer…she had stopped directly below. Miss Temple looked down—and for a terrible flashing moment met that pair of glittering eyes. Then, an infinitesimal shift, and the woman was looking—or trying to look, partially blocked by the step she was standing on—up her cloak. Miss Temple held her breath.

The woman above her climbed on, and Miss Temple followed, aware that as she moved her cloak by necessity opened around her feet, but she was unable to look down again to confirm if the woman had recognized her, or had merely examined her along with all the others. Three more steps and she was on the balcony, walking across it and through a small, dark door. Here the woman in green paused, as if to suggest they continue together, but Miss Temple was now too frightened of exposure and wanted to hide alone. She nodded to the woman, smiling, and then walked deliberately in the opposite direction. It was only then she actually perceived where she was.

She stood in an aisle that ran along the top of the steeply raked gallery, looking down at the operating theatre. The gallery itself was largely full, and she forced herself to search for an empty seat.

On the stage she saw the man from the train, the very large man in the fur coat—no longer wearing the coat, but still fingering his silver walking stick. He glared up at the gallery, impatiently waiting for people to situate themselves. She knew how bright the light in his eyes actually was, that he could not see, but nevertheless felt his gaze restlessly pass over her, hard as a rake across gravel, as she stepped to the far aisle. She dared not stray from the upmost row—the lower one sat, the more visible one was from the stage— and was relieved to find an empty seat three places in, between a man in a black tailcoat and a white-haired fellow in a blue uniform with a sash. As each was some inches taller than she, Miss Temple assured herself that she was less visible between them—though what she felt was fully trapped. Behind her, she knew the woman in red must have entered. She forced her gaze to the stage, but what she saw didn't help her fears in the slightest.

The powerful man extended his hand into the shadow of a rampway and pulled it back, now gripping the pale shoulder of a masked woman in white silk robes. The woman walked carefully, blinded by the light, allowing the man to guide her. He then— with no ceremony at all—hoisted her with both hands into a sitting position on the table, legs dangling. He scooped up her legs and pulled them around to the table front, rotating her. He was obviously speaking to her, too low for anyone else to hear, for with a shy smile she lay back on the table, and shifted her body to be properly in the center. As she did this, the man matter-of-factly positioned each of her ankles to opposite corners of the table and threaded a leather belt around them. He tightened the belts with a sharp tug and let the slack drop. He moved up to her arms. The woman said nothing. Miss Temple was unsure which of the three women was on the table—perhaps the pirate?—and while she was trying to guess, the man bound the woman's arms. Then, carefully, he cleared away her elegantly curled hair and threaded another belt across her pale, delicate throat. This was also tightened, in a firm but not so muscular manner, leaving the woman completely secured. The man then stepped behind her and took hold of a metal handle, like that of a pump. He pulled it. The machinery answered with a percussive snap, loud as a gunshot, and the top of the table lurched upwards, rotating toward the gallery. Three more snaps and the woman was perhaps half-way to being vertical. He released the handle and walked off the stage into shadow.

The woman had no particular expression, aside from a bland smile, but this could not disguise the fact that her legs were shaking. Miss Temple risked a glance over the shoulder of her neighbor, back toward the door, and quickly turned her eyes back to the stage. The woman in red stood directly in the doorway, as if on guard, glancing idly across the crowd as she worked a new cigarette into her holder. Miss Temple's only other escape would be to vault onto the stage and rush down a rampway, which was hardly possible. Restlessly, she looked across the crowd herself, trying to find some idea, some new avenue. Instead, she found Roger, directly in the center of the gallery, sitting between a woman in yellow—she must be the laughing woman from his train compartment—and, of all things, an empty seat. It must be the only empty seat in the theatre. Somewhere behind her, Miss Temple smelled burning tobacco. She was certain that seat belonged to her scarlet nemesis— but what could explain the connection of that woman and Roger Bascombe? Was she some diplomatic figure—or a mysterious courtesan, or decadent heiress? Simply by collecting Miss Temple at the door, she proved herself part of whatever the crowd had here gathered to watch. Roger had been with her on the train—but did that mean he knew what they'd see as well? But then, with a sudden stab of doubt, Miss Temple wondered instead if the seat *she* occupied had been the woman's—but what could she possibly do now?

The powerful man returned to the light, now bearing in his arms another of the white-robed women. This was certainly the one in blue silk, for her long hair was undone and trailed down toward the floor. He walked to the center of the stage, in front of the table, and cleared his throat.

"I believe we are ready," he began.

Miss Temple was surprised at his voice, which far from being harsh or commanding, was faint, almost a rasp, if still in a bass register. It emerged from his throat like something scarred, no longer whole. He did not raise his voice either, but relied on others to pay attention—and his bearing was such that his audience did so completely. He cleared his throat again and lifted the woman in his arms, as if she were a text he would expound.

"As you can see, this lady has become fully subject. You will understand that no opiates nor other coercive medicines have been employed. Further, while she seems quite helpless, this is merely what has become her preferred state. It is hardly a necessity. On the contrary, a high level of responsiveness is perfectly within her grasp."

He swung the woman's body in such a way as to lift the upper half and sweep her legs into position beneath it, dropping her feet to the floor. He then stepped away, releasing his grip. The woman tottered, her eyes still glassy, but she did not fall. Without warning he slapped her sharply across the face. A gasp rippled across the gallery. The woman reeled, but she did not go down—on the contrary, one of her own arms shot out toward the man's own face, ready to strike. He caught her hand easily—he had clearly expected her blow—and then slowly lowered her arm to her side and released it. She did not move to swing again, and in fact her staid manner was as if the slap had never occurred. The man looked up into the gallery as if to acknowledge this, and then reached again toward the woman, this time putting his powerful hand around her throat. He squeezed. The woman reacted violently, clawing at his fingers, slapping at his arm, then kicking at his legs. The man held her at arm's length and did not waver. She could not reach him. The woman's face was red, her breath labored, her struggles more desperate. He was killing her. Miss Temple heard a murmur of shock from the uniformed man next to her—a murmur echoed elsewhere in the crowd—and felt him shift in his seat, as if he was going to stand. Anticipating this exact moment of protest, the man on stage released his grip. The woman staggered, her breath a series of ragged whoops—but her struggles soon abated. At no time did she refer to the man. After a minute or so regaining her strength, she stood once more with a placid stance and blank expression, exactly as if he were not there at all.

Again, the man looked up at the gallery, registering his point, and then stepped behind his subject. In a swift movement he flipped up the back of her robes and plunged his hand beneath them, deliberately digging. The woman stiffened, wriggled, and then bit her lip—the rest of her facial features consistently blank. The man remained behind her, his unseen fingers working. His expression remained impassive—he might have been repairing a clock—as before him the woman's breathing deepened, and her posture subtly shifted, leaning forward and placing that much more of her weight on her toes. Miss Temple watched, rapt—she knew what access the woman's silken pants would provide and exactly where he was occupied—as the slow arc of accelerating pleasure took hold on the woman's face—an audible gasp, a blush spreading over her throat, her clutching fingers. Again, abruptly, the man removed his hand and stepped away, taking a moment to wipe his fingers on the back of her robes. For her part, once he was clear, she immediately relaxed into her passive stance and expression. The man snapped his fingers. Another man stepped from the shadows—Miss Temple saw he was her own canine escort from earlier—and took the woman's hand. He led her down the rampway and out of sight.

"As you see," the man on stage continued, "the subject is both highly responsive and content to remain within her self. Such are the *immediate* effects, along with varying degrees of dizziness, nausea, and narcolepsy. It is why, during these early stages, supervision—protection—is of vital concern." He snapped his fingers again and from the opposite rampway emerged the second canine escort, guiding the last of the three women in white. She was led to the powerful man, walking perfectly normally, where she curtsied. He took her hand from the escort (who departed the stage) as she straightened, and turned her to face the gallery. She curtsied again.

"This lady," the man went on, "has been our subject for three days. As you see, she remains in complete control of her faculties. More than this, she has been *liberated* from strictures of thought. She has in these past three days embraced a *new method of life*."

He paused for his dramatic words to register fully, and then continued, a note of dry disdain audibly rising in his voice.

"Three days ago, this woman—like so many others, like so many others here this evening, I presume—believed herself to be in *love*. She is now positioning herself, with our assistance, to be in *power*." He paused and nodded to the woman.

As she spoke, Miss Temple recognized the low voice of the woman in the feathered cloak. Her tone was the same as when she told the story of being with the two men in the coach, but the cold dreamy distance with which she spoke of herself gave Miss Temple chills.

"I cannot say how I was, for that would be to say how I was a child. So much has changed—so much has become clear—that I can only speak of what I have become. It's true I thought myself to be in love. In love because I could not see past the ways in which I was subject, for I believed, in my servitude, that this love would re-lease me. What view of the world had I convinced myself I understood so well? It was the useless attachment to another, to *rescue*, which existed in place of my own action. What I believed were solely consequences of that attachment—money, stature, re-spectability, pleasure—I now see merely as elements of my own unlimited capacity. In these three days I have acquired three new suitors, funds for a new life in Geneva, and gratifying employment

I am not permitted"—here she shyly smiled—"to describe. In the process I have happily managed to acquire and to spend more money than I have hitherto in my entire life possessed."

She had finished speaking. She nodded to the gallery, and took a step backwards. Once more the escort appeared, took her hand, and walked her into darkness. The powerful man watched her exit, and turned back to his audience.

"I cannot give you details—any more than I would provide details about any of you. I do not seek to *convince,* but to offer *opportunity.* You see before you examples of different stages of our Process. These two women—one transformed three days since, the other just this night—have accepted our invitation and will benefit accordingly. This third...you will watch her transformation yourselves, and make your own decisions. You will bear in mind that the severity of the procedure matches the profundity of this *transformation.* Your attention—along with your silence—is quite the limit of what I ask."

With this, he knelt and picked up one of the wooden boxes. As he crossed with it to the table, he casually pried the top back with his fingers and tossed it aside with a flat clatter. He glanced at the woman, who swallowed with nervousness, and placed the box onto the table, next to her leg. He pulled out a thick layer of orange felt, dropped it onto the floor, and then frowned, reaching into the box with both hands, performing some adjustment or assembly. Satisfied, he removed what looked to Miss Temple like an overly large pair of glasses, the lenses impossibly thick, the frames sheathed in black rubber, trailing hanks of copper wire. The man leaned across the woman's front, blocking her from view, and tossed her white mask to the side. Before they might know her identity, he lowered the strange piece of machinery onto her open face, tightening it with short powerful movements of his hands that caused the woman's legs to twitch. He stepped back to the box. The woman was breathing hard, her cheeks were wet, the sleeves of her robe balled up in her fists. The man removed a wickedly toothed metal clamp, attached one end to the copper wire, and secured the other inside the box to something Miss Temple could not see. Upon his doing this, however, the thing inside the box began to glow with a pallid blue light. The woman caught her breath and grunted with pain.

In that exact moment, Miss Temple did the same, for a sharp stabbing sensation pricked her spine directly between the shoulders. And as she turned her head to see the woman in red was no longer in the doorway, she felt from her other side that woman's breath in her ear.

"I'm afraid you must come with me."

Throughout their passage from the darkened gallery, across the balcony, and down the stairs themselves, the woman had maintained the pressure of her pinpoint blade, convincing Miss Temple not to call out, pretend a faint, or even to trip her adversary so she might fly over the railing. Once they had reached the long marble corridor, the woman stepped away and tucked her hand back into a pocket—but not before Miss Temple could note the bright metal band across her fingers. The woman glanced up to the balcony, to make sure no one had followed, and then indicated that Miss Temple should lead the way back down the corridor toward the rest of the house. Miss Temple did so, desperately hoping for an open door she could dash through, or the intervention of some passer-by. She already knew that there were other guests—that the events in the operating theatre were hidden from outside eyes within the larger gathering taking place in the whole of the house. If she could only reach *that* collection of people, she was certain she would find aid. They passed several closed doors, but Miss Temple's journey to the staircase had been so focused on the people around her that she had little memory of anything else—she'd no idea where these might go, or even if one of these doors might be where she had entered. The woman drove her ahead with sharp shoves past any landmark where she thought to linger. At the first of these offensive gestures, Miss Temple felt her sense of propriety to be fully overwhelmed by her fear. She was frankly terrified what was going to happen to her—that she could be so subject to abuse was just another sign of how low she had fallen, how desperate her straits. At the second shove, a rising level of annoyance was still nevertheless overborne by her own physical frailty, the woman's weapon and obvious malice, and the knowledge that, as she could certainly be accused with trespassing and theft, she had no legal ground to stand on whatsoever. At the third such shove, however, Miss Temple's natural outrage flared and without thinking she whipped round and swung her open hand at the woman's face with all the strength in her arm. The woman pulled her head back and the blow went wide, causing Miss Temple to stumble. At this the woman in red chuckled, insufferably, and once more revealed the device in her hand—a short vicious blade fixed to a band of steel that wrapped across her knuckles. With her other hand she indicated a nearby doorway—by all appearances identical to every other in the corridor.

"We can speak in there," she said. Glaring her defiance quite openly, Miss Temple went in.

It was yet another suite of rooms, the furniture covered with white cloths. The woman in red closed the door behind them, and shoved Miss Temple toward a covered divan. When Miss Temple turned to her, eyes quite blazing, the woman's voice was dismissive and cold.

"Sit down." At this, the woman herself stepped over to a bulky armchair and sat, digging out her cigarette holder and a metal case of cigarettes. She looked up at Miss Temple, who had not moved, and snapped, "Sit down or I'll find you something *else* to sit on— *repeatedly.*"

Miss Temple sat. The woman finished inserting the cigarette, stood, walked to a wall sconce and lit it, puffing, and then returned to her seat. They stared at each other.

*   *   *

"You are holding me against my will," Miss Temple said, out of the hope that standing up for herself had prompted this conversation.

"Don't be ridiculous." The woman inhaled, blew smoke away from them and then tapped her ash to the carpet. She studied Miss Temple, who did not move. The woman did not move either. She took another puff, and when she opened her mouth to speak, smoke came out along with her words.

"I will ask you questions. You will answer them. Do not be a fool. You are alone." She looked pointedly at Miss Temple and then, shifting her voice to a slightly more dry tone of accusatory recitation, began in earnest. "You arrived in a coach with the others."

"Yes. You see, I am from the hotel," Miss Temple offered.

"You are not. It will not aid you to lie." The woman paused for a moment, as if trying to decide her best course of questioning. Miss Temple asserted herself.

"I am not afraid of you."

"It will not aid you to be stupid either. You came on the train. How did you know what train to take? And what station? Some person told you."

"No one told me."

"Of course someone told you. Who are your confederates?"

"I am quite alone."

The woman laughed, a sharp scoffing bark. "If I believed that, you'd be headfirst in a bog and I'd be done with you." She settled back into her chair. "I will require names."

Miss Temple had no idea what to say. If she simply made up names, or gave names that had nothing to do with the matter, she would only prove her ignorance. If she did not, the risk was even greater. Her knee was trembling. As calmly as she could, she put a hand on it.

"What would such a betrayal purchase me?" she asked.

"Your life," answered the woman. "If I am kind."

"I see."

"So. Speak. Names. Start with your own."

"May I ask you a question first?"

"You may not."

Miss Temple ignored her. "If something were to happen to me, would this not be the most singular signal to my confederates about the character of your activities?"

The woman barked again with laughter. She regained control over her features. "I'm sorry, that was so very nearly amusing. Please—you were saying? Or did you want to die?"

Miss Temple took a breath and began to lie for all she was worth.

"Isobel. Isobel Hastings."

The woman smirked. "Your accent is...odd...perhaps even fabricated."

As she was speaking in her normal voice, Miss Temple found this extremely annoying.

"I am from the country."

"What country?"

"This one, naturally. From the north."

"I see..." The woman smirked again. "Whom do you serve?"

"I do not know names. I was given instructions by letter."

"What instructions?"

"Stropping Station, platform 12, 6:23 train, Orange Locks. I was to find the true purpose of the evening and report back all I had witnessed."

"To whom?"

"I do not know. I was to be contacted upon returning to Stropping."

"By whom?"

"They would reveal themselves to me. I know nothing, so I can give nothing away."

The woman sighed with annoyance, stubbed out her cigarette

on the carpet, and rummaged for another in her bag. "You've some education. You're not a common whore."

"I am not."

"So you're an *un*-common one."

"I am not one at all."

"I see," the woman sneered. "Your expenses are paid by the work you do in a *shop*." Miss Temple was silent. "So tell me, because I do not understand, just who are you to be doing this kind of . . . 'investigation'?"

"No one at all. That is how I can do it."

"Ah."

"It is the truth."

"And how were you first . . . recruited?"

"I met a man in a hotel."

"A *man*." The woman sneered again. Miss Temple found herself studying the woman's face, noting how its almost glacially inarguable beauty was so routinely broken by these flashes of sarcastic disapproval, as if the world itself were so insistently squalid that even this daunting perfection could not stand up against the onslaught. "What *man*?"

"I do not know him, if that is what you mean."

"Perhaps you can say what he looked like."

Miss Temple groped for an answer and found, looming out of her unsettled thoughts, Roger's supervisor, the Deputy Foreign Minister, Mr. Harald Crabbé.

"Ah—let me see—a shortish man, quite neat, fussy actually, grey hair, moustache, polished shoes, peremptory manner, condescending, mean little eyes, fat wife—not that I saw the wife, but sometimes, you will agree, one just *knows*—"

The woman in red cut her off.

"What hotel?"

"The Boniface, I believe."

The woman curled her lip with disdain. "How *respectable* of you . . ."

Miss Temple continued. "We had tea. He proposed that I might do such a kind of task. I agreed."

"For how much money?"

"I told you. I am not doing this for money."

For the first time, Miss Temple felt the woman in red was surprised. It was extremely pleasant. The woman rose and crossed again to the sconce, lighting a second cigarette. She returned to her seat in a more leisurely manner, as if musing aloud. "I see . . . you prefer . . . leverage?"

"I want something other than money."

"And what is that?"

"It is my business, Madam, and unconnected to this talk."

The woman started, as if she had been slapped. She had been just about to sit again in the armchair. Very slowly, she straightened, standing tall as a judge over the seated Miss Temple. When she spoke, her voice was clipped and sure, as if her decision had already been made, and her questions now merely necessary procedure.

"You have no name for who sent you?"

"No."

"You have no idea who will meet you?"

"No."

"Nor what they wanted you to find?"

"No."

"And what *have* you found?"

"Some kind of new medicine—most likely a patent elixir—used on unsuspecting women to convert them to a lifetime spent in the service of corrupted appetites."

"I see."

"Yes. And I believe *you* are the most corrupted of them all."

"I'm sure you are correct in every degree, my dear—you have much to be proud of. Farquhar!"

This last was shouted—in a surprisingly compelling voice of command—toward a corner of the room blocked from view by a draped changing screen. Behind it Miss Temple heard the sound of a door, and a moment later saw her escort from before emerge, his complexion even redder, wiping his mouth with the back of a hand. "Mmn?" he asked; then, making the effort to swallow, did so, and cleared his throat. "Madam?"

"She goes outside."

"Yes, Madam."

"Discreetly."

"As ever."

The woman looked down at Miss Temple and smiled. "Be careful. This one has *secrets*." She walked to the main door without another word and left the room. The man, Farquhar, turned to Miss Temple.

"I don't like this room," he said. "Let's go somewhere else."

The door behind the screen led them into an uncarpeted serving room with several long tables and a tub of ice. One of the tables held a platter with a ravaged ham on it, and the other an array of open bottles of different shapes. The room smelled of alcohol. Farquhar indicated that Miss Temple should sit in the only visible chair, a simple wooden seat with no padding, a high back, and no arms. As she did, he wandered over to the ham and sawed away a chunk of pink meat with a nearby knife, then skewered the chunk on the knife and stuck it into his mouth. He leaned against the table and looked at her, chewing. After a moment he walked to the other table and leaned against it, tipping a brown bottle up to his teeth. He exhaled and wiped his mouth. After this moment of rest, he continued drinking, three deep swallows in succession. He put the bottle on the table and coughed.

The door on the far side of the room opened and the other

escort, with the flask, stepped in. He spoke from the doorway. "See anything?"

"Of what?" Farquhar grunted in reply.

"Fellow in red. Nosing about."

"Where?"

"Garden?"

Farquhar frowned, and took another pull from the brown bottle.

"They saw him out front," continued the other man.

"Who is he?"

"They didn't know."

"Could be anybody."

"Seems like it."

Farquhar took another drink and set the bottle down. He nodded at Miss Temple.

"We're to take her out."

"Out?"

"Discreetly."

"Now?"

"I expect so. Are they still occupied?"

"I expect so. How long does it take?"

"I've no idea. I was eating."

The man in the door wrinkled his nose, peering at the table. "What is that?"

"Ham."

"The drink—what's the drink?"

"It's...it's..." Farquhar rummaged for the bottle, sniffed it. "Spiced. Tastes like, what's it...cloves? Tastes like cloves. And pepper."

"Cloves make me vomit," the man in the doorway muttered. He glanced behind him, then back into the room. "All right, it's clear."

Farquhar snapped his fingers at Miss Temple, which she understood to mean that she should stand and walk to the open door, which she did, Farquhar following after. The other man took her hand and smiled. His teeth were yellow as cheese. "My name is Spragg," he said. "We're going to walk quietly." She nodded her agreement, eyes focused on the white front of his dress shirt, stained with a thin spatter of bright red blood. Could he have been just shaving? She pulled her eyes away and flinched as Farquhar took her other hand in his. The two men glanced at each other over the top of her head and began to walk, holding her firmly between them.

They made directly for a pair of glass double doors, covered with a pale curtain. Spragg opened the doors and they stepped out into a courtyard, footfalls rustling onto gravel. It had become cold. There were no stars, nor any longer palpable moonlight, but the courtyard was ringed with windows that threw out a general glow, so it was easy enough to see their path, winding among shrubbery and statues and great stone urns. Across, in what must be another wing of the house, Miss Temple fancied she could see the movements of many people—dancing perhaps—and hear the faint strains of an orchestra. This must be the rest of the party, the main party. If only she could break free and run across to it—but she knew that while she might stamp on the foot of one of her escorts, she could not do it to both of them. As if they knew her thoughts, both men tightened their grip on Miss Temple's hands.

They guided her toward a small darkened archway, a passage running between wings of the house, for gardeners or others having no acceptable business indoors. It allowed the three of them to skirt the main party completely, as well as the main entrance to the great house, for when they had emerged on the other side, Miss Temple found herself at the large cobblestone courtyard where the coaches were waiting, and where she had so long ago—so it seemed—arrived.

She turned to Farquhar. "Well, thank you, and I am sorry for the inconvenience—" but her attempts to extricate her hand were of no avail. Instead, Spragg gave her right hand to Farquhar to hold as well, and stalked off to where a small knot of drivers huddled over a hot brazier. "I will go," insisted Miss Temple. "I will hire a coach and leave, I promise you!" Farquhar said nothing, watching Spragg. After a moment of negotiation, Spragg turned and pointed to an elegant black coach, and began walking to it. Farquhar pulled Miss Temple to join him.

Farquhar looked at the empty driver's seat. "Who's up?" he asked.

"Your turn," answered Spragg.

"It isn't."

"I drove to Packington."

Farquhar was silent. Then, with a huff, he nodded at the coach door. "Get in then."

Spragg chuckled. He opened the door and climbed in, reaching out with both of his meaty hands to collect Miss Temple. Farquhar huffed again and hoisted her up, as if her weight meant very little. As Spragg's hard fingers grabbed her arms and then her shoulders, Miss Temple saw her cloak fall quite away from the rest of her body, giving both men lurid views of her silken underthings. Spragg pushed her roughly onto the seat across from him, her legs awkwardly splayed and her hands groping for balance. They continued to stare as she collected the cloak tightly around herself. The men looked at each other. "We'll get there soon enough," Farquhar intoned to Spragg. Spragg merely shrugged, his face an unconvincing mask of disinterest. Farquhar closed the door of the coach. Spragg and Miss Temple gazed at each other in silence. After a moment, the coach swayed with the weight of Farquhar climbing up into the seat, and after another moment, leapt forward into life.

"I heard you mention Packington," Miss Temple said. "If it is convenient, you may leave me off there, where I can meet the train with little trouble."

"My goodness." Spragg smiled. "She's a *listener*."

"You were not exactly whispering," replied Miss Temple, not liking his tone—in fact, not liking Spragg at all. She was annoyed with herself for not managing her cloak when she entered the coach. Spragg's gaze was positively crawling across her without shame. "Stop looking at me," she finally snapped.

"Oh, what's the harm?" He chuckled. "I saw you earlier, you know."

"Yes, I saw you earlier as well."

"Earlier than that, I mean."

"When?"

Spragg picked a bit of grime from under his thumbnail. "Did you know," he asked, "that in Holland they've invented glass that works like a mirror on one side, and a clear picture window on the other?"

"Really. Well, how do you beat that for cleverness?"

"I don't think you do." Spragg's smile widened further into satisfaction, if not outright malice. Miss Temple blanched. The mirror where she'd changed her clothes, where she put on the feathered mask and licked her lips like an animal. They had watched her through all of it, watched her together, as if she were an Egyptian vaudeville.

"My Lord it's hot in here." Spragg chuckled, tugging at his collar.

"I find it quite cold, actually."

"Perhaps you'd like a drink to warm you up?"

"No thank you. But may I ask you a question?"

Spragg nodded absently, digging in his coat for the flask. As he sat back and unscrewed the cap, Miss Temple felt the coach shift. They had left the cobblestones for the paved road that must lead to the border of the estate. Spragg drank, exhaling loudly and wiping his mouth between pulls. Miss Temple pressed on. "I was wondering . . . if you knew—if you could tell me—about the other three women."

He laughed harshly. "Do you want to know what *I* was wondering?"

She did not answer. He laughed again and leaned across to her. "*I* was wondering . . ." he began, and placed his hand on her knee. She swatted it away. Spragg whistled and shook his hand, as if it were stinging. He sat back and took another pull on the flask, and then tucked it away in his coat. He cracked his knuckles. Outside the coach was darkness. Miss Temple knew she was in a dangerous spot. She must act carefully.

"Mr. Spragg," she said, "I am not convinced we understand one another. We share a coach, but what do we really know about the other person? About what advantage that person can offer—advantage, I must point out, that may remain secret from other interested parties. I am speaking of money, Mr. Spragg, and of information, and, yes, even of *advancement*. You think I am a wayward girl without allies. I assure you it is not the case, and that it is indeed you who is more in need of *my* assistance."

He looked back at her, impassive as a fish on a plate. In a sudden movement, Spragg leapt across the coach and fully onto her body. He caught up both her hands in his and blocked her kicking legs with the bulk of his middle, crushing them to her so she could not swing with any force. She grunted with the impact and pushed against him. He was quite strong, and very heavy. With a quick jerk he adjusted his grip so that one of his large hands held both of hers, and with his free hand ripped at the ties of her cloak, tearing it away from her. Then the hand was pawing her body as it had never been touched before, with a crude insistent hunger—her breasts, her neck, her stomach—his mauling touch so rapidly invasive that her understanding lagged behind the spasms of pain. She pushed against him with all of her strength, with such a desperate exertion that she was gasping, her breath now coming in sobs. She had never in her life known that she could struggle so, but still she could not move him. His mouth lurched closer and she turned her head to the side, his beard scratching her cheek, the smell of whisky suddenly overwhelming. Spragg shifted again, wedging his bulk between her legs. His free hand took hold of an ankle and roughly pushed it up, forcing her knee toward her chin. He let go, doing his best to pin it in place with his shoulder, and dropped his hand between her thighs, pulling apart her petticoats. Miss Temple whined with fury, thrashing. His fingers tore the silk pants, blindly stabbing her delicate flesh, digging deeper, catching her with his ragged nails. She gasped with pain. He chuckled and drew his wet tongue across her neck.

She felt his hand leave her, but sensed through the movements of his arm that it was occupied elsewhere—with loosening his own clothing. She arched her back to throw him off. He laughed—he *laughed*—and shifted his grip from her wrists to around her throat. Her hands fell free. He was choking her. His other hand was back between her legs, pushing them apart. He pressed his body nearer. In a moment of clarity, Miss Temple recalled that the leg bent awkwardly against her chest wore the shoe which held her sharpened all-weather pencil. It was within her reach. She desperately groped for it. Spragg leaned away from her, allowing himself the pleasure of looking down between them—at the spectacle of their bodies— one hand choking her, the other wedging her thighs apart. He was about to thrust himself forward. She drove the pencil deep into the side of his neck.

Spragg's mouth opened with surprise, the hinges of his jaw twitching. His face went crimson. Her fingers were still gripping the pencil and she wrenched it free, ready for another blow. Instead, this released a thick pulsing jet of blood that sprayed like a fountain across her body and onto the walls of the coach. Spragg gasped, groaned, rattled, jerking like a puppet above her. She kicked her way free—she was screaming, she realized—everything wet and sticky, blood in her eyes. Spragg dropped with a thud between the seats. He thrashed for another few moments and became still. Miss Temple held the pencil, breathing hard, blinking, covered in gore.

She looked up. The coach had stopped. She groaned aloud with dismay. She heard the distinct crunch of Farquhar jumping down from the driver's seat. With a sudden thought she threw herself on top of Spragg's leaden body and pawed at his coat, trying to locate the pockets in the dark, hoping he had a knife, a pistol, any kind of weapon. The latch turned behind her. Miss Temple wheeled and, bracing her legs, threw herself forward just as Farquhar pulled open the door. She cannoned into his chest, flailing with the pencil, screaming. His hands came up instinctively to catch her, and she stabbed over them at his face. The tip of the pencil ripped deeply into Farquhar's cheek, dragging an ugly gash, and then snapped. He howled and flung her away. She landed heavily and rolled, the breath knocked from her body, her knees and forearms stinging from the gravel. Behind her, Farquhar was still howling, mixed with inarticulate curses. She crawled to her hands and knees. She looked at the broken stub in her hand and let go of it with an effort. Her fingers felt tight and strange. She wasn't moving quickly enough. She needed to be running. She looked back at Farquhar. One side of his face seemed split in two: the lower half dark and wet, above it almost obscenely pale. He was silent. Farquhar had looked into the coach.

He reached into his coat and removed a black revolver. With his other hand he fished out a handkerchief, flapped it in the air to open it, and then pressed it against his face, wincing at the contact. When he spoke, his voice was run through with pain.

"God damn . . . God damn you to hell."

"He attacked me," Miss Temple said, hoarsely. They stared at each other.

She very carefully shifted her weight so she could straighten up, sitting on her heels. Her face was wet and she kept having to blink. She wiped her eyes. Farquhar didn't move. She stood, which took a bit of an effort. She was sore. She glanced down at herself. Her underthings were ripped apart and soaked with wide scarlet stripes, clinging and torn—she may as well have been naked. Farquhar kept staring at her.

"Are you going to shoot me?" she asked. "Or shall I kill you as well?"

She looked around her. Near her on the ground she saw a jagged stone, perhaps twice the size of her fist. She bent over and picked it up.

"Put that down!" Farquhar hissed, raising the pistol.

"Shoot me," Miss Temple replied.

She threw the stone at his head. He squawked with surprise and fired the pistol. She felt a scorch along the side of her face. The stone sailed past Farquhar and slammed into the coach. This impact, occurring in nearly the same moment as the shot, caused the horses to leap forward. The open coach door smacked into the back of Farquhar's head and spun him off balance toward the advancing rear wheel. Before Miss Temple could quite understand what she was watching, the wheel clipped the man's legs, and with a shocked cry he toppled beneath. The wheel went over Farquhar's body with a hideous snapping sound and he rolled to an awkward stillness. The coach continued away, out of her sight and hearing.

Miss Temple fell onto her back. She stared up into the depthless black sky, growing cold. Her head swam. She could not tell what time had passed. She forced herself to move, to roll over. She vomited onto the ground.

After another set of trackless minutes, she was on her hands and knees. She was shivering, a mass of aches and dizziness. She touched the side of her head, and was surprised to realize she was no longer wearing the mask. It must have come off in the coach. Her fingers traced a raw line above her ear, scored by Farquhar's bullet. Her throat heaved again as she touched it. It was sticky. She smelled blood. She had never known so much blood at a time, to know that it had a smell at all. She could not now imagine ever forgetting it. She wiped her mouth and spat.

Farquhar remained in place on the ground. She crawled to him. His body was twisted and his mouth was blue. With great effort, Miss Temple pulled off his coat—it was long enough to cover her. She found the revolver and shoved it into one of the pockets. She began to walk down the road.

It was an hour before she reached the Orange Locks station. Twice she'd staggered from the road to avoid a coach on its way from the great house, crouching on her knees in a field as it passed. She had no idea who might be in them, and no desire to find out. The platform itself was empty, which gave her hope that the train was still running—as the occupants of the coaches she had seen were gone. Her first instinct was to hide while she waited, and she had curled herself into a shadowed corner behind the station. But she kept catching herself nodding into sleep. Terrified of missing the train if it should come, or of being discovered in so vulnerable a state by her enemies, she forced herself to wait on her feet, until she was weaving.

Another hour passed, and no other coaches had arrived. She heard the whistle of the train before she saw its light, and hurried to the edge of the platform, waving her arms. It was a different conductor who lowered the steps, openly staring as she climbed past him into the car. She lurched into the corridor and bent down for the money in her other shoe. She turned to the conductor— she had lost her ticket with her cloak and her dress—and stuffed a note worth twice the fare into his hand. He continued to stare. Without another word she made her way down toward the rear of the train.

The compartments were all empty, save for one. Miss Temple glanced into it and stopped, looking at a tall, unshaven man with greasy black hair and round spectacles of dark glass, as if he were blind. His equally unkempt topcoat was red, as were his trousers and his gloves, which he held in one hand, a thin book in the other. On the seat beside him was an open razor, lying on a hand-kerchief. He looked up from his book. She nodded to him, and just perceptibly dipped her knee. He nodded in return. She knew that her face was bloody, that she was dressed in rags, and that yet somehow he understood that she was more—or other—than this appearance. Or was it that in this appearance she was revealing her true nature? He smiled faintly. She wondered if she had fallen asleep on her feet, and was actually dreaming. She nodded again and made her way to another compartment.

Miss Temple dozed with one hand on the revolver until the train reached Stropping, early in the morning, the sky still thick with shadow. She saw nothing more of the man in red, nor of any-one she recognized, and was forced to pay three times the usual fare to get a coach to the Boniface, and then to bang on the glass front of the hotel with the revolver to be let in. Once the staff was convinced who she was and allowed her to enter—faces white, eyes wide, jaws gaping—she refused to say another word and, clutching the coat around her body, went directly to her rooms. Inside was warm and still and dark. Miss Temple staggered past the closed doors of her sleeping maids and her sleeping aunt to her own chamber. With the last of her strength she dropped the coat behind her to the floor, tore away the bloody rags and crawled naked but for her green boots into the bed. She slept like a stone for sixteen hours.

TWO

Cardinal

He was called Cardinal from his habit of wearing a red leather topcoat that he'd stolen from the costume rack of a traveling theatre. It had been winter, and he'd taken it because the ensemble included boots and gloves as well as the coat, and at the time he was lacking all three. The boots and gloves had since been replaced, but he had preserved the coat, despite wearing it through all weathers. Though few men in his line of work sought to identify themselves in any way at all, he found that, in truth, those who sought him out—for employment or punishment—would find him even if he wore the drabbest grey wool. As for the name, however ironic or mocking, it did bestow a certain veneer of mission—given his life was a persistent and persistently vicious struggle—onto his itinerant church of one, and though he knew in his heart that he (like everyone) must lose at the finish, the vain title made him feel less through the course of his days like an animal fattened in a pen.

He was called Chang for more immediate reasons, if equally ironic and mocking. As a young man he'd been deeply slashed by a riding crop over the bridge of his nose and both eyes. He'd been blinded for three weeks, and when his vision finally cleared—as much as it was ever going to clear—he was greeted with the blunt scars that crossed and then protruded out from the corners of each eyelid, as if a child's caricature of a slant-eyed menacing Chinaman had been scrawled with a knife over his features. His eyes were thereafter sensitive to light, and tired easily—reading anything longer than a page of newspaper gave him a headache that, as he had learned many times over, only the deep sleep of opiates or, if such were unavailable, alcohol, might assuage. He wore spectacles with round lenses of dark smoked glass in all circumstances.

It was a gradual process by which he accepted these names, first from others, and then finally used them himself. The first time he replied "Chang" when asked his name, he could too easily recall the taunting comments as he waited day after day in the sickroom for his sight to return (it was a name to be always accompanied by a bitter smile), but even those associations seemed more real—more important to carry forward—than an earlier identity marked with failure and loss. More, the names were now a part of his working life—the rest were distant landmarks on a sea voyage, faded from sight and usage.

The riding crop had also damaged the inside of his nose, and he had little sense of smell. He knew abstractly that his rooming house was more objectionable than his own experience told him—he could see the nearby sewers, and knew by logic that the walls and floors had fully absorbed the fetid airs of their surroundings. But he was not uncomfortable. The garret room was cheap, isolated, with rooftop access and, most importantly, in the shadow of the great Library. For the smell of his own person, he contented himself with weekly visits to the Slavic baths near the Seventh Bridge, where the steam soothed his ever red-rimmed eyes.

At the Library, Cardinal Chang was a common sight. It was knowledge that put him ahead of his competitors, he felt—anyone could be ruthless—but his eyes prevented long hours spent in research. Instead, Chang made the acquaintance of librarians, engaging them in long interrogative conversations about their given responsibilities—specific collections, organizational theories, plans for acquisition. He pursued these topics in calm but relentless inquiry, so that eventually—through memory and rigorous mental association—it had become possible for him to isolate at least three-quarters of what he needed without actually reading a word. As a result, though he haunted its marbled halls nearly every day, Cardinal Chang was most often found pacing a Library corridor in thought, wandering through the darkened stacks by memory, or exchanging keen words with a blanching though professionally tolerant archivist as to the exact provenance of a new genealogical volume he might need to consult later in the day.

Before the incident with the riding crop and the young aristocrat who wielded it, Chang had been a long-time student—which meant that poverty did not trouble him, and that his wants, then from necessity and now by habit, were few. Though he had abandoned that life completely, its day to day patterns had marked him, and his working week was divided into a reliably Spartan routine: the Library, the coffeehouse, clients, excursions on behalf of those clients, the baths, the opium den, the brothel, and bill collecting, which often involved revisiting past clients in a different (to them) capacity. It was an existence marked by keen activity and open tracts of ostensibly lost time, occupied with wandering thought, thick sleep, narcotic dreams, with willful nothingness.

When not so pacified, however, his mind was restless. One source of regular consolation was poetry—the more modern the better, as it usually meant a thinner text. He found that by carefully rationing out how many lines he read at a time, and closing his eyes to consider them, he could maintain a delicately steady, if perhaps finally grinding, pace through the whole of a slim volume. He had been occupying himself in such a manner, with Lynch's new translation of the *Persephone* fragments (found in some previously unplundered Thessalonikan ruin), when he looked up and saw the woman on the train. He smiled to think of it, as he lay just awake on his pallet, for the lines he'd been reading at the time— "battered princess / that infernal bride"—had seemed to exactly illustrate the creature before him. The filthy coat, the blood-smeared face, her curls crusted and stiff, her piercing grey eyes—a meeting of such beauty and such spoilage—he found it all perfectly impressive, even striking. He had decided at the time not to follow, to allow the incident its own distinction, but now he wondered about finding her, remembering (with a stirring of lust) the lines fallen tears had traced down her cheeks. After consideration, Chang decided he would ask at the brothel—any new whore so covered in blood would certainly have *someone* talking about her.

The grey light from his window told him that he had slept later than usual. He rose and washed his face in the basin. He dried himself vigorously on an old towel and decided he could go another day without shaving. After a moment of indecision, he decided to swirl a mouthful of salt water around his teeth, spat into his chamber pot, pissed in the pot, and then ran his fingers through his hair in lieu of a comb. His clothes from the previous day were still clean enough. He put them on, re-knotted a black cravat, tucked his razor into one coat pocket and the slim volume of *Persephone* into another. He put on his glasses, relaxed as even this day's pallid light was dimmed, grabbed a heavy, metal-knobbed walking stick, and locked his door behind him.

It was just after noon, but the narrow streets were empty. Chang was not surprised. Years ago the neighborhood had been fashionable, rows and rows of six-story mansions crowded near the river, but the growing stench of the river itself, the fog and the crime it covered, along with the city's expansion elsewhere into broad landscaped parks had caused the mansions to be sold, each of them cut up into a myriad of smaller rooms, rough unpainted walls thrust between the once elaborate stucco moldings, catering to a vastly different caste of occupants—disreputable occupants such as himself. Chang walked some distance out of his way, north, to find a morning newspaper, and tucked it under his arm unread as he turned back toward the river. The Raton Marine was historically a tavern—and still functioned as such—but during the daylight had taken to serving coffee, tea, and bitter chocolate. In this way it had expanded its role as a place of itinerant business, where men might linger to seek and to be found, in rooms both public and unseen.

The Cardinal took a table inside the main room, away from the glare of the open walkway, and called for a cup of the most dark and acrid South American chocolate. This morning he didn't want to speak to anyone, or at least not yet. He wanted to read the newspaper, and that was going to take time. He spread the front page over his table and squinted so that he could really only make out the largest size of type, sparing his eyes as much unwanted text as possible. In this way he skimmed through the headlines, moving quickly past international tragedies and domestic scandals, the perfidies of weather and disease, the problems of finance. He rubbed his eyes and took a hot mouthful of chocolate. His throat clenched against the bitter taste, but he felt his senses sharpened all the same. He returned to the paper, moving into the inner pages, bracing himself for smaller type, and found what he was after. Chang took another fortifying swallow of his drink, and plunged into the dense column of text.

REGIMENTAL HERO MISSING

Col. Arthur Trapping, commander of the 4th Dragoons, decorated hero of Franck's Redoubt and Rockraal Falls, was reported missing today from both his regimental quarters and his own dwelling on Hadrian Square. Col. Trapping's absence was noted during the formal investiture of the 4th Dragoons as the "Prince's Own", with newly designated responsibilities as a Household Regiment for Palace defense, Ministry escort, and ceremonial duties. Acting for Col. Trapping in the ceremony was the regiment's Adjutant-Colonel, Noland Aspiche, who received the formal charge of duty from the Duke of Stäelmaere, attended by Palace representatives. Despite concerns expressed from the highest levels of government, the authorities have been unable to locate the missing officer. . . .

Chang stopped reading and rubbed his eyes. It told him all he needed to know—or all he was going to learn for the moment. Either the truth was being suppressed, or indeed the facts had somehow remained unknown. He could not believe that Trapping's movements were so much a secret—he'd followed the man easily enough, after all—but any number of things could have happened between then and now to alter what appeared to be the facts. He sighed. Though his involvement ought to have been finished, it was more likely to be merely beginning. It would depend on the client.

He was about to turn the page when another headline caught his eye. A country aristocrat—Lord Tarr, whom he'd never heard of—had been murdered. Chang peered at the text, and learned that the ailing Tarr had been found in his garden, in his nightshirt, with his throat torn out. While there was a chance that he'd been attacked by an animal, it was now suspected that the wound had been brutally enlarged to disguise the deep cross-cut of a blade. Inquiries were pending. Inquiries were *always* pending, Chang thought to himself, reaching for his cup—that was why he had regular work. No one liked to wait.

As if on cue, someone near him coughed discreetly. Chang looked up to see a uniformed trooper—red coat and trousers, black boots, a brass helmet with a horse-tail crest in one hand, the other resting on the hilt of a long saber—standing at the doorway, as if actually entering the Raton Marine would foul his military crispness. Upon getting Chang's attention, the trooper nodded and clicked his heels. "If you'll accompany me, Sir," he deferentially called over to Chang. None of the other customers acted as if they'd heard a word. Chang nodded to the trooper and stood. This was happening more quickly than he'd expected. He collected his walking stick and left the paper for someone else to read.

They did not speak as Chang was led to the river. The bright uniform of his guide seemed to vibrate against their monochrome surroundings of stone paving, grey mottled plasterwork, and black pools of standing fetid water. Chang knew that his own coat had a similar effect, and smiled at the thought that the two of them might be seen as a strange kind of pair—and how much the trooper would loathe such an idea. They rounded a corner and walked onto a stone balcony that overhung the river itself. The wide black water slipped past beneath them, the far bank just visible through the tracings of fog that had either not fully abated from the night or were already beginning to gather. The balcony had been a wharf for pleasure craft and boats for hire when the district was thriving. It had since been left to rot, despite being regularly used for nefarious transactions after nightfall.

As he expected, Adjutant-Colonel Noland Aspiche stood waiting for him, with an aide and three other troopers standing behind, and two more waiting in the trim launch tied up to the stairwell. Chang stopped, allowing his escort to continue on to his commander, click his heels and report, gesturing back to Chang. Aspiche nodded, and then after a moment walked over to Chang, out of earshot from the others.

"Where is he?" he snapped, speaking quietly. Aspiche was a hard, lean man, with receding hair cut close to his skull. He dug a thin black cheroot from his red jacket, bit the tip off, spat, and pulled out a small box of safety matches. He turned away from the wind and lit one, puffing until the flame took. He exhaled a blue plume of smoke and returned his sharp gaze to Chang, who had not answered. "Well? What have you got to say?"

Chang despised authority on principle, for even when veiled by the rubric of practical necessity or the weight of tradition he could not see institutional power as anything but an expression of arbitrary personal will, and it galled him profoundly. Church, military, government, nobility, business—his skin crawled at every interaction, and so though he granted Aspiche his probable competence there was an urge in Chang, rising at the very manner in which the officer bit off the tip of his cheroot and spat, to savage the man with his razor then and there, no matter the consequences. Instead he was still, and answered Adjutant-Colonel Aspiche as calmly as possible.

"He's dead."

"Are you sure? What did you do with the body?" Aspiche spoke moving only his mouth, keeping the rest of his body still—from the back, as his men saw him, he was merely listening to Chang.

"I didn't do anything with the body. I didn't kill him."

"But—we—you were instructed—"

"He was *already* dead."

Aspiche was silent.

"I followed him from Hadrian Square to the country, to the Orange Canal. He met a group of men, and together *they* met a small launch sailing up the canal. From the launch they unloaded a cargo onto two carts, and drove the carts to a nearby house. A great house. Do you know what house that was, near the Orange Canal?"

Aspiche spat again. "I can guess."

"Evidently it was quite an occasion—I believe the given excuse was the engagement of the Lord's daughter."

Aspiche nodded. "To the German."

"I was able to enter the house. I was able to find Colonel Trapping, and with a fair amount of difficulty, I was able to introduce a substance to his wine—"

"Wait, wait," interrupted Aspiche, "who else was there? Who else was with him at the canal? What happened to the carts? If someone else killed him—"

"I am telling you," hissed Chang, "what I am going to tell you. Are you going to listen?"

"I'm contemplating having you horsewhipped."

"Are you *really*?"

Aspiche sighed and glanced behind him at his men. "No, of course not. This has been very difficult—and not hearing from you—"

"I was awake into the early morning. I explained that this was likely to happen. And instead of paying attention you first sent a uniformed man to collect me, and then appeared yourself in a part of the city you can have no decent social or professional business in whatsoever. You might as well have set off fireworks. If anyone has suspicions—"

"No one has suspicions."

"That you know of. I will have to go back to the coffeehouse and give ready money to the five men who saw me so *collected*— to protect the both of us. Are you this careless with the lives of your men in action? Are you this careless with yourself?"

Aspiche was not accustomed to such a tone, but his silence itself was admission of his error. He turned away, gazing back into the fog. "All right. Get on with it."

Chang narrowed his eyes. So far it had been simple enough, but here he was in the dark as much as Aspiche was at least pretending to be. "There were hundreds of people in the house. It was *indeed* an engagement party. Perhaps that is not all it was, but it was certainly that, which created both confusion for me to blend into, and confusion that got in my way. Before the substance could take effect, Colonel Trapping eluded me, leaving the main gathering by way of a back staircase. I was unable to follow directly, and was forced to seek him through the house. When I finally did find him, he was dead. I could not see why. The substance I gave him was not in a quantity to kill, yet he had no marks of mortal violence about his body."

"You're sure he was dead."

"Of course I am."

"You must have miscalculated your poison."

"I did not."

"Well, what do you *think* happened? And you still haven't explained what happened to the body!"

"I suggest that you calm yourself and listen."

"I suggest that you get damned on with your explanation."

Chang let that pass, retaining his even tone. "There were marks on Trapping's face, like burns, around the eyes, but of a regular, precise nature, as if from a brand—"

"A *brand*?"

"Indeed."

"On his *face*?"

"As I said. Further, the room—there was a strange odor—"

"What was it?"

"I cannot say. I have no ability with odors."

"A poison?"

"It is possible. I do not know."

Aspiche frowned, thrown into thought. "All this—it makes no sense," he snapped. "What about these burns?"

"That is my question to you."

"What does that mean?" said Aspiche, taken aback. "I don't have a clue."

They stood in silence for a moment. The Adjutant-Colonel seemed genuinely perplexed.

"My examination was interrupted," continued Chang. "I was again forced to make my way through the house, this time away from pursuit. I managed to lose my pursuers on my way back to the canal."

"All right, all right. What was in those carts?"

"Boxes. Of what I don't know."

"And his confederates?"

"No idea. It *was* a masked ball."

"And this—this *substance*—you don't think you killed him?"

"I know I did not."

Aspiche nodded. "It's good of you to say. Still, I'll pay you as if you had. If he turns up alive—"

"He won't."

Aspiche smiled tightly. "Then you'll merely owe me the job."

He pulled a thin leather wallet from his jacket and handed it to Chang, who tucked it into his coat.

"What happens next?" asked Chang.

"Nothing. My hope is that it's over."

"But you know it isn't," Chang snarled. Aspiche did not reply. Chang pressed him. "Why has there been no further word? Who else is involved? Vandaariff? The Germans? Any one of three hundred guests? You know the answers or you don't, Colonel. You'll tell me what you want to. But someone's hidden your body, and you're going to have to know why. You've come this far—it'll have to be finished."

Aspiche did not move.

As Chang gazed at the man—stubborn and dangerously proud—one of the *Persephone* fragments rose to his mind:

His willful suit, imperious and cold
Pay'd court perfum'd by graves and fetid mold

"You know how to find me . . . discreetly," Chang muttered. He turned and stalked back to the Raton Marine.

Chang had spent the previous three days planning the murder of Arthur Trapping for a fee. It had seemed simple enough. Trapping was the ambitious brother-in-law of Henry Xonck, a wealthy arms manufacturer. To find a position fitting to his newly married status, he had with his wife's money purchased a prestigious commission as commander of the 4th Dragoons, but he was no soldier and his decorations resulted from his mere presence at two provincial engagements. Trapping's actual exploits were limited to consuming heroic quantities of port and a lingering patch of local dysentery. When his regiment was rewarded with a significant change of duties, Trapping's executive officer, the long-suffering Adjutant-Colonel—a professional soldier who, if he were to be believed, didn't desire the command so much for himself, but only to clear the place for any genuinely worthy figure—had taken the quite remarkable step of engaging Cardinal Chang.

Outright assassination was not Chang's usual line, but he'd done murder before. More often, as he preferred to see it, he was engaged to influence behavior, through violence, or information, or both, as necessary. In recent months, however, he'd felt a growing disquiet, as if there were behind his every step the barely audible ticking of a clock, that his life wound toward some profound *accounting*. Perhaps it was a malady of his eyes, a general gnawing anxiety that grew from seeing as much as possible in shadow. He did not allow this lurking dread to influence his movements, but when Aspiche had offered a high fee, Chang saw it as an opportunity to withdraw from view, to travel, to disappear into the opium den—anything until the cloud of foreboding had passed by.

Not that he trusted what Aspiche had told him of the job. There was always more to it—clients always lied, withheld. Chang had spent the first day doing research, digging through social registers, old newspapers, genealogies, and as ever, the connections were there for the finding. Trapping was married to Charlotte Xonck, the middle child of three, between Henry, the oldest, and Francis, as yet unmarried and just returned from a lengthy tour abroad. Though poor Adjutant-Colonel Aspiche might assume that the regiment's rise in stature had been earned by its colonial triumphs, Chang had found that the order to invest the 4th Dragoons as the Prince's Own (or Drunken Wastrel Whoremongering Sodomite's Own, as Chang preferred to think of it) was issued one day after the Xonck Armory agreed to lower terms for an exclusive contract to re-fit the cannons of the entire navy and coastal defenses. The mystery was not why the regiment had been promoted, but why Henry Xonck thought it worth such a costly bargain. Love for his only sister? Chang had sneered and sought out another archivist to badger.

The precise nature of the regiment's new duties was not part of any official document he could find, every account merely parroting what he'd read in the newspaper—"Palace defense, Ministry escort, and ceremonial duties"—which was gallingly vague. It was only after pacing back and forth that it occurred to him to confirm where the announcement had actually been issued. He again dragged the archivist away from his other duties to retrieve the folio of collected announcements, and then saw it on the cover of the folio itself—it was from a Ministry office, but not the War Ministry. He peered at the paper, and the seal at the top. The Foreign Ministry. What business had the Foreign Ministry with announcing—and thus, by inference, arranging—the installation of a new regiment of "Palace defense, Ministry escort, and ceremonial duties"? He snapped at the archivist, who merely stammered, "Well, it *does* say Ministry escort—and the F-Foreign Ministry is indeed one of the, ah, M-M-Ministry offices—" Chang cut him off with a brusque request for a list of senior Foreign Ministry staff.

He'd spent a good hour wandering through the darkened stacks—the staff had conceded access to Chang, reasoning it was less bother to have him out of their sight than in their faces—pushing these rudimentary pieces around in his mind. No matter what else it did, the most important work of the regiment would be under the aegis of the Foreign Ministry. This could only refer to diplomatic intrigues of one kind or another, or internal government intrigues—that somehow in exchange for Xonck's lowered fee, the War Ministry had agreed to put the regiment at the Foreign Ministry's disposal. For Xonck, Trapping would obviously function as his spy, alerting him to any number of international situations that might influence his business, and the rise and fall of the business of others. Perhaps this was reward enough (Chang was unconvinced), but it did not explain why one Ministry would be doing such an outlandish service for another—or why the Foreign Ministry might require its own troops in the first place.

Nevertheless, this much information allowed Chang, after making himself familiar with Trapping's person, the location of his house, his coach, and the regimental barracks, to position himself outside the Foreign Ministry itself, convinced that this was the crucial point of revelation. Such was Chang's way, and while he performed such investigation to better understand what he was engaged with, it's also true that he did it to occupy his mind. If he was but a brute murderer, he could have cut Arthur Trapping down at any number of places, simply by following him until he was isolated in the street. The fact that Chang might well end up doing that very thing in the end didn't alter his desire to understand the reasoning behind his actions. He was not squeamish about his work, but he was well aware that the risk was his, and that a client might always wonder about furthering their own security by arranging things so that Chang too might fall victim to unpleasant circumstance. The more he knew—about the clients and their objects—the safer he was going to feel. In this case, he was keenly aware that the forces involved were far more powerful and vast than Trapping and his bitter Adjutant-Colonel, and he would need to be careful not to provoke their interest. If 'twere done, 'twere best done as invisibly as possible.

On the afternoon of that first day and again on the second, Trapping's coach had taken him from the regimental barracks to the Foreign Ministry, where he had spent several hours. At each evening the coach had taken him to his house on Hadrian Square, where the Colonel remained at home, without any notable visitors. On the second night, as he watched Trapping's windows from the shadow of decorative shrubbery, Chang was startled to see a coach move past, the doors painted with the Foreign Ministry crest. The coach did not stop at Trapping's door, however, but continued on to a house on the other side of the square. Chang quickly loped after it, in time to see a trim man in a dark coat exit the coach and enter the door of number 14, weighed down with several thick satchels. The coach drove away. Chang returned to his surveillance. The next morning at the Library he again consulted the list of Foreign Ministry staff. The Deputy Minister, Harald Crabbé, made his residence at 14 Hadrian Square.

*   *   *

On the third day he'd once again gone to the Ministry, passing his time on the edge of St. Isobel's Square, at a point where he could observe both the coach traffic in front of the building and the intersection where any coach by way of the rear alley would have to exit. By now he'd become familiar with at least some of the Ministry staff, and studied them as they went in and out, waiting for Trapping to arrive. Despite all the suggestions of intrigue around the Colonel, Chang judged the man himself to be a reasonably simple target. If he repeated his pattern of the previous two nights, it would be easy enough to enter through a second-story window (accessible from a drain pipe whose strength Chang had tested the night before) and creep down to Trapping's chamber (whose location he had established from watching the appearance of light in the windows as Trapping climbed to the third floor to sleep). The precise method wasn't settled in his mind, and would depend on the exact circumstances in the room. He would have his razor, but also come equipped with a poison that would, to a careless eye, suggest an apoplexy not unheard-of for a man of Trapping's age. Whether anyone would consider it murder would be one more signifier of the intrigue, and the stakes of Trapping's elevation. Chang was not overly concerned about anyone else in the house. Mrs. Trapping slept apart from her husband, and the servants, if he chose his time correctly, would be far from the room.

He crossed the square at two o'clock and bought a meat pie, breaking it into pieces and consuming them one at a time while he walked back to his position. As he passed the sculpture of St. Isobel, he smiled, his mouth full. The truly hideous nature of the composition—garish sentiment, cloying pathos—never prevented him from finding lurid satisfaction in the image of the saint herself, the coiling serpents swarming across her slippery flesh. It amazed him that such a piece had been erected at public expense

in such an open space, but he found the blithe veneration of something so obviously rank to be a comfort. Somehow it restored his
faith that he indeed had a place in the world. He finished the meat
pie and wiped his hands on his trousers.

At three o'clock, Trapping's regimental coach appeared, empty,
at the alleyway exit, and turned left, heading back to the 4th
Dragoons barracks. The Colonel was inside by way of the rear entrance, and intending to leave by other means. It was four-fifteen
when Chang saw a Ministry coach at the same spot. On one side
of the coach sat Harald Crabbé and in the seat opposite, a splash of
red and gold through the window, sat Arthur Trapping. Chang
dropped his gaze while they passed and watched them go. As soon
as they rounded the corner he sprinted for a coach of his own.

As he expected, the Ministry coach was on its way to Hadrian
Square, and easily followed. What he did not expect was that it
would stop in front of number 14 and that both men would enter,
nor that, when they reappeared some minutes later, their coach
would take them on a direct path northwest of the city. The fog
was growing, and he moved next to his driver to better see—
though his distant vision was at its limit in the falling dusk—
where his quarry took him. His driver grumbled—this was far
beyond his normal reach—and Chang was forced to pay him far
more than he would have liked. He thought of simply taking the
coach for himself, but he trusted neither his own vision nor his
driving skills, besides not wanting to spill any unnecessary blood.
As it was, they were soon beyond the old city walls, and then beyond the sprawl of new building and into the country itself. They
were on the road to the Orange Canal, which went as far as the
ocean, and the coach ahead of them showed no sign of stopping.

They rode for nearly two hours. At first Chang had made his
driver pull back, allowing the other coach to drift to the edge of
sight, but as the darkness grew they were forced to close, being un-

able to see if the other coach should turn from the road. He had followed Trapping initially as merely a continuation of his plan, and then farther at the prospect of isolating him at some vacant place in the country where a murder might be more easily managed. But the farther he went in pursuit, the more wrong-headed it seemed. If he were merely trying to kill the man, he should turn around and try again the next night—simply repeating the plan until he was able to get Trapping alone in his room. The long coach journey with Deputy Minister Crabbé was a matter for intrigue, for Xonck and the War Ministry, and while Chang was certainly curious, he had no idea what he was riding into, and that was always foolish. Aside from these doubting thoughts, he realized he was cold—a bitter wind from the sea had chilled him utterly. He was forming the very words to tell his driver to stop when the man grabbed his shoulder and pointed ahead at a distant knot of torchlight.

Chang ordered him to stop the coach, and instructed him to wait for fifteen minutes. If he had not returned, the man was free to leave him and return to the city. The driver did not argue—he was certainly as cold as Chang, and still bitter over the unexpected length of this particular fare. Chang climbed from the coach, wondering if the man would even wait that long. He gave himself five minutes to make a decision—the last thing he wanted was to be stranded in the darkness, all but blind. As it was, he had to move extremely cautiously. He pulled off his glasses, this being a case where any light was better than none, and tucked them into the inner pocket of his coat. Ahead of him he could see the Ministry coach, waiting among several others. He moved into the grass and toward the torchlight, some thirty yards away, where two figures were walking toward a larger group. Chang crept as close as he dared on the path, and then stepped away from it and crouched, his eyes just clear of the grass to see.

There was a low brisk conversation—it was clear Trapping and Crabbé were late—and what seemed like a perfunctory shaking of hands. As his eyesight grew accustomed to the torches, Chang saw that something was reflecting them—water—and what seemed to have been an abstract mass of shadow resolved itself into an open launch, tied up at the canal. Trapping and Crabbé followed the others along the canal and to what looked like carts (Chang could just make out the wheel tops above the grass). A canvas sheet was pulled back from one cart to show the late arrivals a number of wooden boxes, obviously loaded from the launch. Chang could not make out the faces of any other men, though he counted six of them. The canvas sheet was pulled down again and tied, and the men began to climb onto the carts. At a sharp whip crack, they drove off, away from the coaches, down a road that Chang from his place could not see.

Chang moved quickly after them, pausing to glance into the launch—which told him nothing—and down the road, which was little more than a country path worn through the grass. He thought again about what he was doing. Pursuing the carts meant losing his coach. He resolved himself to being abandoned—worse things had happened to him, after all, and this still might be a perfect opportunity to execute his task. The carts moved much faster than he, however, and soon enough he was walking on his own, alone in the dark. The wind was still cold, and it was at least thirty minutes before he came upon the carts tied up at the kitchen entrance of what looked like a formidable building—though whether it was a dour mansion or a splendid fortress, he could not say. The boxes were gone, as were the men...

Still annoyed from his interview with Aspiche, Chang walked back into the Raton Marine and was relieved to see that everyone who had been present at the trooper's arrival was still there. He stood in the doorway a moment, allowing each person to glance up at him, in order to return those glances with a meaningful nod. He then went around to each man—including Nicholas the barman—and placed a gold coin next to his glass. It was all he could do—and if one of them were to go behind his back, it would at least be seen by others as a broken agreement reflecting poorly on the Judas. He ordered another cup of bitter chocolate and drank it outside. For all practical purposes, he was waiting for Aspiche to do something, but Noland Aspiche was at best a fool who hoped to profit from someone else killing his Colonel, or at worst part of the larger intrigue, which meant he had been lying to Chang from the start. In either case, Aspiche was unlikely to act. Despite the wallet in his coat, Chang was regretting the entire affair. He took a swallow of chocolate and grimaced.

As soon as he'd seen the size of the house, he'd known where he was, for there was only one such dwelling on the coast near the Orange Canal, that of Robert Vandaariff, recently made Lord Vandaariff, the financier whose daughter was famously engaged to a German prince of some small state, Karl-Horst von Somesuch-or-other. Chang couldn't remember—it was in any number of headlines he'd skipped past—but he was quick to realize, as he pushed his gloved hand through the pane of a delicate glass door-way, that he was trespassing into a rather large social occasion, some kind of formal masked ball. He watched from the shadows until he found a drunken guest from whom he could safely wrestle a mask, and then so covered (though again it meant taking off his glasses) moved out in direct search of Trapping. As most of the men were in formal black topcoats, the red-uniformed Colonel was relatively easy to find. Chang himself attracted attention for the same reason—the willfully brazen figure he cut in his usual environment, where intimidation balanced concealment, hardly lent itself to a fancy-dress party in a lavish mansion. But he simply carried himself with the disdainful air of a man who belonged. It amazed him how many people immediately assumed that, because of an unpleasant arrogance, he possessed more rights than they.

Trapping was drinking heavily, in the midst of a rather large party, though it did not seem like he took an active part in the conversation. As he watched, he now realized that Trapping stood between two groups. One gathered around a heavy, balding man to whom all the others deferred—most prominently a young man with thick red hair and an exceedingly well-dressed woman (could this possibly be Trapping's wife, Charlotte Xonck, and the men her brothers Henry and Francis?). Behind this woman was another, whose gown was more demure and who, much like Chang, occupied herself with subtly studying the figures around her—and in this struck him as the figure in the party to most carefully avoid. The other group was made of men, in both formal attire and military uniforms. Chang could not tell if Crabbé was present or not—the masks made it difficult to be sure. As curious as he was to watch such parties gathered around as unimpressive a figure as the Colonel—and to discover *why*—Chang was aware he could not linger. Bracing himself, he strode quite near to them, avoiding eye contact and addressing the servant at the nearby table, calling for a glass of wine. The conversation faded around him as he waited, feeling the impatience of both groups for him to leave. The servant handed him a full glass, and Chang took a swallow, turning to the man next to him—who was, of course, Trapping—fixing him with his gaze. Trapping nodded, then could not help but stare. Chang's scarred eyelids, visible through the mask-holes, gave Trapping pause, for though he could not be certain what he was seeing, he knew something was not quite right. The length of the contact, though, allowed Chang to speak.

"A fine occasion."

"Indeed," answered Colonel Trapping. His gaze had dropped from Cardinal Chang's eyes to his coat, and then to the rest of his garments, which though striking were hardly appropriate for the occasion, or even quite reputable. Chang looked at his own clothes, caught Trapping's eye again and scoffed, chuckling.

"Had to come straight from the crossing. Been riding for days. Still, couldn't miss it, eh?"

"Of course not." Trapping nodded, vaguely mollified, but looking somewhat helplessly over Chang's shoulder, where the rest of his group was drifting distinctly in the other direction to resume their conversation.

"What are you drinking?" demanded Chang.

"I believe it is the same as what you are drinking."

"Is it? Do you like it?"

"It is indeed fine."

"I suppose it is. I suppose it would be, eh? Here's to the host."

Chang touched his glass to Trapping's and tossed off the contents, more or less forcing Trapping to do the same. Before he could move, Chang snatched the glass from him and held them both out toward the servant, barking for more wine. As the servant leaned forward to pour, and as Trapping groped for excuses behind him to leave, Chang deftly dusted a small amount of white powder onto his thumb, and—distracting the servant with a brusque question about a possibly spoiled cork—rubbed it along the rim of Trapping's glass as he picked it up. He handed the glass to the Colonel, and they drank again—Trapping's lips touching the rim of his glass where he'd placed the powder. Once this was done, just as abruptly as he'd arrived, Chang nodded to Trapping and walked out of the room. He'd watch from the margins until the drug took hold.

From there it had quickly gone wrong. The group of men—Crabbé's faction?—finally claimed Trapping from the group Chang guessed to be the Xoncks and walked with him to a rear corner of the room and through a doorway flanked by two men who stood, casually but unmistakably, as sentries. Chang watched his quarry disappear, and looked around for another way, just for one moment catching the eye of Charlotte Xonck's companion, who looked away—not quite quickly enough—in the same instant. He stalked from the main rooms before he attracted any more unwanted attention. It had taken him at least an hour—time spent dodging servants, guests, and what looked to be a growing number of openly suspicious faces—before he finally found himself in a long marbled corridor, lined with doors. It was an exact epitome of his ridiculous situation, and how his decision to risk first entry and then bold exposure to Trapping had utterly failed. By this time Trapping should have been dead, but instead he was most likely shaking off what he would explain to himself as a bit too much wine. Chang had given him only enough of the drug to guarantee his pliability—thinking to drag him into the garden—but now it was just another mistake. He stalked down the corridor, trying the doors as he went. Most were locked, and he was forced to move on to the next. He had perhaps reached the mid-point when he saw, ahead of him at the far end, a crowd begin to emerge from a balcony above, and make its way down a spiral staircase. He lunged for the nearest door. It was open. He dashed through and closed it behind him.

On the floor was Trapping, dead, his face branded—seared? scarred?—but with no immediately apparent cause. Chang detected no wound, nor any blood, any weapon, even another glass of wine that might have been drugged. Trapping was still warm. It couldn't have been long—no longer than thirty minutes, at most—since he had died. Chang stood above the body and sighed. Here was the result he wanted, but in a far more disturbing and complicated manner. It was then that he'd noticed the smell, vaguely medicinal or mechanical—but thoroughly out of place in that room. He had bent down again to go through Trapping's pockets when there was a knock at the door. At once, Chang stood and walked quietly to the next room of the suite and from there into the bath closet, looking for some place to hide. He found the servants' door just as the hallway door was opened, and someone called to Colonel Trapping by his Christian name. Chang was carefully, silently easing the latch behind him when the voice began calling harshly for help.

It was time to get out. The narrow dark corridor led to a strange man in a room—a crabbed, officious creature—surrounded by familiar-looking boxes. The man wheeled at his entry and opened his mouth to shout. Chang crossed the distance to him in two steps and clubbed him across the face with his forearm. The man fell onto a table, scattering a pile of wooden box pieces. Before he could rise, Chang struck him again, across the back of the head. The man smashed into the table and slumped to the floor, groping, gasping damply. Chang glanced quickly at the boxes, which all seemed to be empty, but knew that he had no time. He found the next door and stepped into an even larger corridor, lined with mirrors. He looked down the length and knew that it must lead to the main entrance, which would never do. He saw a door across the hall. When he found that it was locked, he kicked it until the wood around the lock buckled in, and shouldered his way through. This room had a window. He snatched up a side chair and hurled it through the glass with a crash. Behind him there were footsteps. Chang kicked the broken shards free from the panes and leapt through the opening. He landed with a grunt on a bed of gravel and ran.

The pursuit had been half-hearted—for he was near-blind in the night and by all rights any serious attempt should have taken him. When he was sure that they had stopped following, Chang eased into a walk. He had a general notion of where he was in relation to the sea and so turned away from it and eventually struck the rail tracks, walking along them until he reached a station. This turned out to be Orange Canal, and the end of this particular line. He boarded the waiting train—pleased that there *was* a waiting train—and sat brooding until it finally began to move, carrying

him back to the city and, in the midst of that journey, his moment
with the battered Persephone.

At the Raton Marine, he finished his drink and put another coin on
the table. The more he worried over the events of the previous day
and night, the more he berated himself for impulsive nonsense—
all the more that now there was no announcement of Trapping's
death. He felt like going back to sleep for as long as he could, perhaps for days in the opium den. What he forced himself to do instead was walk to the Library. The only new information he had
was the possible association of Robert Vandaariff or his high-
placed prospective son-in-law. If he could explore their connection
to Xonck, or to Crabbé, or even to Trapping himself, he would
then be able to obliterate his senses with a clear conscience.

He walked up the grand steps and through the vaulted lobby,
nodding at the porter, and climbed to the main reading room on
the second floor. As he entered, he saw the archivist he was looking
for—Shearing, who kept all records relating to finance—in conversation with a woman. As he approached, the small gnarled man
turned to him with a brittle smile and pointed. Chang stopped as
the woman turned to face him, and dipped her knee. She was
beautiful. She was walking toward him. Her hair was black, and
gathered behind to hang in curls over her shoulders. She wore a
tiny black wool jacket that did not reach her thin waist over a red
silk dress, subtly embroidered in yellow thread with Chinese
scenes. She held a small black bag in one hand, and a fan in the
other. She stopped, a mere few feet away, and he forced himself to
look at her eyes—past her pale throat and fiercely red lips—which
were fixed upon him with a certain seriousness of manner.

"I'm told your name is Chang," she said.

"You may call me that." It was his customary answer.

"You may call me Rosamonde. I have been directed to you as a
person who might provide me with the aid I require."

"I see." Chang shot a look back at Shearing, who was gawking at them like an idiot child. The man ignored the look entirely, beaming at the woman's splendid torso. "If you'll walk this way"— Chang smiled stiffly—"we may speak more discreetly."

He led her up to the third floor map room, which was rarely occupied, even by its curator, who spent most of his time drinking gin in the stacks. He pulled out a chair and offered it to her, and she sat with a smile. He chose not to sit, leaning back against a table, facing her.

"Do you always wear dark glasses indoors?" she asked.

"It is a habit," he answered.

"I confess to finding it disquieting. I hope you are not offended."

"Of course not. But I will continue to wear them. For medical reasons."

"Ah, I see." She smiled. She looked around the room. Light came in from a high bank of windows that ran along the main wall. Despite the grey of the day, the room still felt airy, as if it were much higher off the ground than its three stories raised it.

"Who directed you to me?" he asked.

"Beg pardon?"

"Who directed you to me? You will understand that a man in my position must have references."

"Of course. I wondered if you had many women for clients." She smiled again. There was a slight accent to her speech, but he could not place it. Nor had she answered his question.

"I have many clients of all kinds. But please, who gave you my name? It is quite the final time I will ask."

The woman positively beamed. Chang felt a small charge of warning on the nape of his neck. The situation was not what it appeared, nor was the woman. He knew this utterly, and strove to keep it in the fore of his mind, but in the same moment was transfixed by her body, and the exquisite sensations emanating from its view. Her chuckle was rich, like the flow of dark wine, and she bit her lip like a woman play-acting the schoolgirl, doing her level best to fix him with her riveting violet eyes, like an insect stuck on a pin. He was unsure she had not succeeded.

"Mr. Chang—or should I say *Cardinal*? Your name, it is so amusing to me, because I have known Cardinals, for I was a child in Ravenna—have you been to Ravenna?"

"No. I should of course like to. The mosaics."

"They are beautiful. A color of purple you have never seen, and the pearls—if you know of them you *must* go, for not seeing them will haunt you." She laughed again. "And once you have seen them they will haunt you all the more! But as I say, I have known Cardinals, in fact a cousin of mine—who I never liked—held such an office—and so it pleases me to see a figure such as yourself hailed with such a name. For as you know, I am suspicious of high authority."

"I did not know."

As the moments passed, Chang became painfully more aware of his rumpled shirt, his unpolished boots, his unshaven face, that his whole life was at odds with the splendid ease, if not outright grace, of this woman. "But you still, forgive my insistence, have not told me—"

"Of course not, no, and you are so patient. I was given your name, and a notion of where you might be found, by Mr. John Carver."

Carver was a lawyer who, through a number of unsavory inter-mediaries, had engaged Chang the previous summer to locate the man who had impregnated Carver's daughter. The daughter had survived the abortion her father—a harsh pragmatist—insisted upon, but had not been seen in society since—apparently the pro-cedure had been difficult—and Carver was especially distraught. Chang had located the man in a seaside brothel and delivered him to Carver's country house—not without injury, for the man had struggled hard once he realized the situation. He left Carver with the wandering lover trussed on a carpet, and did not concern himself further with the outcome.

"I see," he said.

It was extremely unlikely that anyone would associate his name with Carver's unless the information came from Carver himself.

"Mr. Carver has drawn up several contracts for me, and has come to share my confidence."

"What if I were to make it quite clear to you that I have never met nor had any acquaintance with John Carver?"

She smiled. "It would be exactly as I feared, and I must turn for assistance elsewhere."

She waited for him to speak. It was his decision, right then, to accept her as a client or not. She clearly understood the need for discretion, she was obviously rich, and he would certainly welcome a distraction from the unsettled business of Arthur Trapping. He shifted his weight and hopped onto the table top, sitting. He bent his head toward hers.

"I am sorry, but seeing as I do not know Mr. Carver, I cannot in conscience accept you as a client. However, as a man of sympathy, and since you have come all this way, perhaps I can listen to your story and in return provide you with whatever *advice* I am able, if you are willing."

"I would be in your debt."

"Not at all." He permitted himself a small smile in return. At least this far, they understood one another.

"Before I begin," she said, "do you need to take notes?"

"Not as a rule."

She smiled. "It is after all a simple situation, and one that while *I* am unable to answer it doesn't strike me as particularly unanswerable for the man with the proper set of skills. Please interrupt me if I go too fast, or seem to leave anything out. Are you ready?"

Chang nodded.

"Last night there was a gathering at the country home of Lord

Vandaariff, celebrating the engagement of his only daughter to Prince Karl-Horst von Maasmärck—you surely have heard of these people, and appreciate the *degree* of the occasion. I was in attendance, as a school friend—acquaintance, really—of the daughter, Lydia. It was a masked ball. This is important, as you will see later. Have you ever been to a masked ball?"

Chang shook his head. The warning tingle on his neck had by now traveled the whole length of his spine.

"I enjoy them, but they are disquieting, for the masks provide license for behavior beyond the social norm, especially at a gathering this large, at a house this expansive. The anonymity can feel profound, and quite frankly anything can happen. I'm sure I do not need to explain further."

Chang shook his head again.

"My escort for the evening was, well, I suppose you would describe him as a family friend—somewhat older than I, an essentially good fellow whose weak resolve had led him to repeated degradations, through drink, gambling, and foolish, even unnatural, indulgence—and yet through all of this, for our family connection and his, I do believe, essential inner kindness, I was resolved to try and do my part to return him to the better graces of society. Well, there is no way of putting it cleanly. The house is large and there were many people—and in such a place, *even* in such a place, people enter who should not, without invitation, without regard, without any intention beyond, if I may say so, *profit*."

Chang nodded in agreement, wondering exactly when he ought to run from the room, and how many confederates she might have on the staircase below.

"Because—" her voice broke. Tears formed at the corners of each eye. She dug for a handkerchief in her bag. Chang knew he ought to offer her one, but he also knew what his own handkerchief looked like. She found her own and dabbed at her eyes and nose. "I am sorry. It has all been so sudden. You must see people in distress quite often."

He nodded. Distress that he himself *caused*, but he needn't point that out.

"That must be terrible," she whispered.

"One becomes used to anything."

"Perhaps that is the worst thing of all." She folded the handkerchief back into her bag. "I am sorry, let me continue. As I say, it was a large affair, and one was required to speak to many people, aside from Lydia and Prince Karl-Horst, and so I was quite busy. As the evening went on, I realized that I had not seen my escort for some time. As I looked for him, he seemed to be nowhere. I was able to engage the assistance of mutual friends and, as discreetly as possible, we searched the adjoining rooms of the house, hoping that he had merely overindulged in drink and fallen asleep. What we found, Mr. Chang—Cardinal—was that he had been murdered. After conversation with other guests I am convinced that I know the identity of his killer. What I should like—what I should have liked, were you able to accept this task—is for this person to be found."

"And delivered to the authorities?"

"Delivered to me." She met his gaze quite evenly.

"I see. And this person?" He shifted in his seat, ready to leap at her. With the razor at her throat he could force his way past any phalanx of waiting men.

"A young woman. An inch or two above five feet but no more, chestnut hair in sausage curls, a fair complexion, pretty enough in a common style. She wore green boots and a black traveling cloak. Due to the manner in which my friend was killed, it is safe to say that she bore significant traces of blood. She gave her name as Isobel Hastings, but that is undoubtedly a lie."

*   *   *

He had asked other questions after this, but a part of his mind was elsewhere, attempting to make sense of the coincidence. Rosamonde could not say anything else about the woman—she was assumed to be a prostitute of some high stature, otherwise it was not known how she could have entered the house so easily, but Rosamonde had no idea how she had arrived nor how she had escaped. She asked him, as a point of reference, about his usual fee. He told her, and suggested that, again, if he had been able to accept her as a client, they would choose a place to meet or leave word. She looked around her and declared that the Library suited her fine for such a meeting, and that word could be left for her at the St. Royale Hotel. With that she rose and offered him her hand. He felt like a fool but found himself bending over to kiss it. He remained where he was, watching her leave, the stirring vision of her walking away quite matched by the seething disquiet in his mind.

Before anything else, he sent a message to John Carver, asking for confirmation, via the Raton Marine, that his name had been given to a young woman in need. Next, he required something to eat. It had been since the meat pie in St. Isobel's Square the day before, and Chang was famished. At the same time, as he walked down the marble steps outside the Library and into the open air, he was keenly suspicious of having been exposed. He made his way west, toward the Circus Garden and its shops, then stopped at a news kiosk, pretending to look at a racing pamphlet. No one seemed to have followed him from the Library, but this meant nothing—if they were skilled he might have men waiting for him at any particular haunt, as well as his rooming house. He put down the pamphlet and rubbed his eyes.

The food stalls gave him another meat pie—the Cardinal was not expansive in his diet—and a small pot of beer. He finished them quickly and continued to walk. It was nearing four o'clock, and already he could feel the day turning toward darkness, the wind acquiring its evening bite. As Chang saw it, he had three immediate choices: first, back to the Raton Marine to await contact from either Carver or Aspiche; second, stand watch at the St. Royale and find out everything he could about his new client, beginning with her true name; or third, start visiting brothels. He smiled—a rather simple choice, after all.

In truth, it made sense to see the brothels now, for there the business day would have just begun, and his chances were better to get information. The name Isobel Hastings was a place to start, for even if it was false, Chang knew that people grew attached to their disguises, and that a false name used once would most likely be used again—and if it were her true name, then all the easier. He walked back toward the river, farther along the strand, into the decayed heart of the old city. He wanted to visit the lowest of the houses first, before it became too thick with clientele. The house was known as the South Quays because it fronted the river, but also as a joke (for there were no south quays in the city) on the various points of moorage one might consider on the body of a whore. It catered to men of the sea and had a pitiless changeover among its available women, yet it was the best place to look for someone new. The South Quays was a drain that drew down into it all the loose and soiled flotsam of the city.

As he walked, he also regretted giving up the newspaper—he'd have to find another—now wanting to search for this new killing; even another vague reference to Rosamonde's companion as "missing" would at least provide him with a name. A second death on Robert Vandaariff's premises, on such an occasion, certainly added to the financier's reasons for keeping things quiet, though Chang wondered how long Trapping's death could remain so. Chang knew that even if Rosamonde had not actually lied to him, there was more to the story. His own memory of Persephone (which he preferred to Isobel) in the train told him that much. But pursuing Rosamonde's (whoever she actually was) investigation was a way to also pursue the intrigue around Trapping, and keep abreast of his own vulnerability in that regard—for it must mean learning more about the house, the guests, the party, the circumstances. But she had told him nothing about any of that, merely about the woman she wanted found. He clucked his tongue with annoyance as he walked, knowing that his best path to protect himself was also the path most likely to expose his involvement.

When he reached it, Dagging Lane was still empty. This was the rear of the house, whose front overhung the river itself and allowed for easy disposal of those contentious or unable to pay. A large man lounged outside a small wooden door, whose bright yellow paint stood out in a street of dirty brick and weather-stained wood. Chang walked up to him and nodded. The man recognized him and nodded in return. He knocked three times on the door with his meaty fist. The door opened and Chang stepped into a small entryway, cheaply carpeted, and lit with yellow lantern light instead of gas. Another large man demanded his walking stick, which Chang gave over, and then indicated with a practiced leer that he should proceed past a beaded curtain into a side parlor. Chang shook his head.

"I am here to speak to Mrs. Wells," he said. "I will pay for the time."

The man considered this, then walked through the curtain. After a brief interval, which Chang passed by looking at a cheap print framed on the wall (illustrating the intimate life of a Chinese contortionist), the man returned and ushered him through the parlor—past three sofas full of half-dressed, over-painted women, all appearing equally young and equally ravaged in the dim sickly light and who seemed to be generally yawning, scratching themselves, or in several cases, coughing thickly into napkins—and then to Mrs. Wells's own inner room, where the woman herself sat next to a crackling fire with an account book on her knees. She was grey, small, and thin, and in her work as routinely nurturing and dispassionately brutal as a farmer. She looked up at him.

"How long will this take?"

"Not long, I am sure."

"How much were you expecting to pay?"

"I was expecting this."

He reached into his pocket and removed a crumpled note. It was more than he ought to have offered, but the risk in this matter was closer to his person, so he didn't begrudge it. He dropped the banknote onto her ledger book and sat in the chair across from her. Mrs. Wells took the note and nodded at the large man, still standing in the doorway. Chang heard the man leave and close the door, but kept his gaze on the woman.

"I am not in the custom of providing information about my customers—" she began. Her teeth clicked when she spoke—some large percentage were made of white porcelain, which rather hideously showed the true color of those real teeth that remained. Chang had forgotten how much this annoyed him. He raised his hand to cut her off.

"I am not interested in your customers. I am looking for a woman, almost assuredly a whore, whom you may know of, even if you do not employ her directly."

Mrs. Wells nodded slowly. Chang didn't quite know what that meant, but as she did not then speak, he went on.

"Her name may be, or she may call herself, Isobel Hastings. Out of her shoes she is most likely five feet in height, with chestnut hair, in curls. The most salient fact is that she would have been seen early this morning wearing a black cloak and quite liberally—her face, her hair, her person—covered in dried blood. I expect that such a girl returning to your house, or any house, in such a manner—though it is not unheard-of—would have caused remark."

Mrs. Wells did not answer.

"Mrs. Wells?"

Still Mrs. Wells did not answer. Very quickly, and before she could slam the book, Chang darted forward and snatched the banknote away from her. She looked up at him in surprise.

"I am happy to pay for whatever you know, but not for abject silence."

She smiled as slowly and deliberately as a blade being unsheathed. "I am sorry, Cardinal, I was merely thinking. I do not know the girl you speak of. I do not know the name, and none of mine came home so bloodied. I would certainly have heard, and as certainly demanded reparations."

She stopped, smiling. There was more, he saw it in her eyes. He returned the banknote. She took it, placed it in the heavy ledger as a bookmark, and closed the book. Chang waited. Mrs. Wells chuckled, a particularly unpleasant noise.

"Mrs. Wells?"

"It is nothing," she replied. "Merely that you are the third to come asking for this same creature."

"Ah."

"Indeed."

"Might I ask who those others were?"

"You might." She smiled, but did not move, a silent request for more money. Chang was torn. On one hand, he had already paid her far more than he should. On the other, if he attacked her with his razor, he'd have to deal with the two men at the door.

"I believe I have been fair with you, Mrs. Wells . . . have I not?"

She chuckled again, setting his teeth on edge. "You have, Cardinal, and will be so in the future, I trust. These others were less . . . respectful. So I will tell you that the first was this morning, a young lady claiming to be this person's sister, and the second, just an hour ago, a man in uniform, a soldier."

"A red uniform?"

"No no, it was black. All black."

"And the woman"—he tried to think of Rosamonde—"she was

tall? Black hair? Violet eyes? Beautiful?" Mrs. Wells shook her head.

"Not black hair. Light brown. And she was pretty enough— or would have been without the burns on her face." Mrs. Wells smiled. "Around the *eyes,* you know. Such a *dreadful* thing to have happen. Windows to the soul, don't you know."

Chang stalked back to the Raton Marine in a fury. It would have been one thing to learn that he was but one of several out to find this woman, but when he himself was so close to dire exposure in the same affair—whether he'd actually killed Trapping or not, he could just as easily hang for it—it was doubly maddening. His mind was spinning with suspicion. When he reached the Raton Marine it was nearly dark. No word had come from John Carver. Not quite ready to question his client directly, he began walking to the next likely house, near the law courts. This was known as the Second Bench, and was not too far and in a marginally safer location. He could thrash through his thoughts on the way.

As he forced himself to break the parts into discrete elements, he admitted that it was not strange that Mrs. Wells did not know his Persephone. When he had seen her on the train, there was the distinct sense that the image she then made was spectacular—that it was unusual to her, however telling or revelatory, or however large a story lay behind it. Her curls, though bloody and ruined, bespoke a certain care—perhaps the assistance of a servant. This would mean the Second Bench, or even the third house he had in mind, the Old Palace. These respectively offered an escalating class of whore, and served an escalating class of clientele. Each house was a window into a particular stratum of the city's traffic in flesh. Chang himself could patronize the Palace only when he possessed significant cash, and even then solely because of services rendered its manager. The unsavory nature of the South Quays only raised the question of how the other two searchers had found it, or thought to go there. The soldier he could understand, but the woman—her sister? There were, frankly, only so many ways a woman would know of such a place's existence, for the South Quays was nearly invisible to the greater population. That Rosamonde would know of it, for example, he would find more surprising than a personal letter from the Pope. But the others searching *did* know. Who were they, and whom did they serve? And who was this woman they all sought?

This did nothing to support his client's story of her poor murdered friend, who could be no disconnected innocent, but someone about whom other issues—inheritance? title? incrimination?—must be spinning, all of which she had withheld in their interview. Chang cast his mind back to the train, looking into those unreadable grey eyes. Was he looking at a killer, or a witness? And if she *had* killed . . . as an assassin, or in defense? Each possibility altered the motives of those searching for her. That none of them had gone to the police—even if it was at the specific, powerful request of Robert Vandaariff—did not reflect well on anyone's good intentions.

Not that good intentions were any normal part of Chang's life. The Second Bench was his usual choice in brothels, though this had more to do with a desire to balance his financial resources against the likelihood of disease than with any particular merits of the house. Still, he was acquainted with the staff and with the current manager, a fat greasy fellow with a shaved head named Jurgins who wore a number of large rings on his fingers—the very image of a modern court eunuch, it always seemed to Chang. Jurgins affected a jolly manner, though this was pushed aside like a curtain every time money came into the conversation, to be shot back into place once his insistent greed was no longer at the fore. As so many of the place's customers were drawn from business and the law, this mercenary manner was barely noticed, and certainly no cause for offense.

After a few quiet words with the men at the door, Chang was guided into Jurgins's private room, hung with tapestries and lit with crystal lamps whose shades dangled all kinds of delicate fringe, the air so thick with incense that even Chang found it oppressive. Jurgins sat at his desk, knowing Chang well enough to both see him alone and to also keep the door open with a bodyguard at close call. Chang sat in the chair opposite, and removed a banknote from his coat. He held it up for Jurgins to see. Jurgins could not help but tap his fingertips on the desk with anticipation.

"What may we do for you today, Cardinal?" He nodded at the banknote. "A formal request for something elaborate? Something... *exotical*?"

Chang forced a neutral smile. "My business is simple. I am looking for a young woman whose name may be Isobel Hastings, who would have arrived back here—or at another such establishment—early this morning, in a black cloak, and quite covered in blood."

Jurgins frowned thoughtfully, nodding.

"So, I am looking for her."

Jurgins nodded again. Chang met his gaze, and deliberately smiled. Out of a natural sycophantic impulse, Jurgins smiled as well.

"I am *also*"—Chang paused for companionable emphasis— "interested in the two people who have already wasted your time asking for her."

Jurgins smiled broadly. "I see. I see indeed. You're a clever man—I have always said it."

Chang smiled thinly at the compliment. "I would expect them to be a man in a black uniform and a woman, brown hair, well-dressed, with a... *burn* of strange design around her eyes. Would that be accurate?"

"It would!" Jurgins grinned. "He came first thing this morning—he woke me up—and she some time after luncheon."

"And what did you tell them?"

"What I will be forced to tell you, I'm afraid. The name means nothing. And I have heard no news about such a bloody girl, neither from here or any other house. I am sorry."

Chang leaned forward and dropped the banknote onto the desk. "No matter. I did not expect that you had. Tell me about the other two."

"It was just as you said. The man was an officer of some kind—I do not follow the military, you know—and perhaps your own age, quite the insistent brute, not understanding that I was not of his command, if you get me. The woman said the girl was her sister, quite lovely—as you say, except for the burn. Even then, we get people who fancy that kind of thing directly."

"And what were their names—or the names they gave you?"

"The officer called himself *Major Black*." Jurgins smirked at its obvious falseness. "The woman gave herself as a Mrs. Marchmoor." He chuckled with a lurid relish. "As I say, I would have been happy to offer her employment, if not for the delicacy of the occasion, her missing a relative and all."

The Second Bench and the Old Palace were on opposite sides of the north bank, and his path to the Palace took him close enough to the Raton Marine that he decided to stop by to see if Carver had left word. He had not. It was unlike Carver, who fancied himself so important that he kept messengers and runners on hand at all hours—and certainly well into the evening. Perhaps Carver was in the country, which made it less likely that between last night and today Rosamonde could have received his recommendation. It was still possible, however, and he pushed the matter aside until he heard either way. He'd pressed Jurgins for more detail about the officer's uniform—silver facings and a strange regimental badge of a wolf swallowing the sun—and could just return to the Library before its doors shut for the day. Instead, he decided it was important to reach the Palace. In the unlikely case that he did find direct information, he wanted to get it as soon as possible—certainly the major and the sister were there now or had been already. He could easily find the regiment and identify the officer in the morning, if it was still of importance.

Outside the Raton Marine, he paused, and looked at his garments as objectively as possible. They wouldn't do, and he'd have to quickly visit his rooms to change. The Palace was particular about who it allowed in, and if he were to expect further to interrogate its manager then he would have to look close to his best. He cursed the delay and strode quickly along the darkened street—more peopled than before, some nodding to him as he passed, others simply pretending he didn't exist, which was the normal way of the district. Chang reached his door, fishing a key from his pocket, but found when he tried to insert it into the lock that the lock had been dislodged in its frame. He knelt and studied it. A sharp kick had snapped the wood around the bolt. He pushed the door with a gentle touch and it swung open with its habitual creak.

Chang looked up the empty, dimly lit staircase. The building was silent. He rapped on his landlady's door with his stick. Mrs. Schneider was a gin drinker, though this was a bit early for her to be insensible. He tried the knob, which was locked. He knocked again. He cursed the woman, not for the first time, and turned back to the stairs. He advanced quickly and quietly, holding his stick before him in readiness. His room was at the top, and he was used to the climb, striding across each landing with a glance to the doorways, all of which seemed to be closed, the occupants silent. Perhaps the lock had merely been kicked in by a tenant who'd misplaced his own key. It was possible, but Chang's natural suspicion would not rest until he reached the sixth-floor landing... where his own doorway gaped wide open.

With a swift tug Chang pulled the handle out of his stick, revealing a long, double-edged knife, and reversed his grip on the remaining portion in his other hand, allowing him to use the polished oak as a club or to parry. With both hands so armed, he crouched in the shadow and listened. What he heard were the sounds of the city, faint but clear. His windows were open, which meant that someone had gone onto the roof—perhaps to escape, perhaps to explore. He kept waiting, his eyes fixed on the door. Anyone inside would have heard him come up the stairs, and must be waiting for him to enter . . . and they must be getting as impatient as he. His knees were stiffening. He took in a breath and quietly sighed, willing them to relax, and then heard a distinct rustle from the darkened room. Then another. Then a fluttering of wings. It was a pigeon, undoubtedly entering by way of the open window. He stood with disgust and walked to the door.

As he entered, the combination of the darkened room and his glasses left Chang not altogether blind, but certainly in the realm of deep nightfall, and perhaps this deprivation had sharpened his other senses, for as his foot crossed the open doorway he sensed movement from his left side and by instinct—and by his embedded knowledge of the room—threw himself to the right, into a nook between a tall dressing cabinet and the wall, raising the length of his stick before him as he did. The bit of moonlight from the window caught the flashing scythe of a saber sweeping down at him from behind the door. He'd stepped clear of the main blow and stopped the rest of it on his stick. In the same instant Chang drove himself directly back into his assailant. As he did, he thrust the stick across the man's blade—which, in the close quarters, the man was awkwardly pulling back—and so prevented a second blow. Chang's right hand, holding the dagger, shot forward like a spike.

The man grunted with pain and Chang felt the thick, meaty impact—though in the darkness he could not tell where the blow had landed. The man struggled with his long blade, to get the edge or the point toward Chang's body, and Chang dropped his stick to grab the man's sword arm, grappling to keep it clear. With his right hand he pulled the dagger back and rapidly stabbed forward three times more, like a plunging needle, twisting it as he yanked it clear. By the final thrust he felt the strength ebbing from the man's wrist, and he released his grip, stepping away. The man collapsed to the floor with a sigh, and then a choking rattle. It would have been better to question him, but there was nothing for it.

When it came to violence, Chang was realistic. While experience and skill would increase his chances of survival, he knew that the margins for error were tiny and often subject not so much to luck as to a certain authority of intention, or will. In those minute spaces of variability a firm, even grim, determination was crucial, and hesitation of any kind a mortal flaw. Any man could be killed by any other, no matter what the circumstances, and there was always the blue moon chance that a fellow who has never carried a sword will do a thing with it no sane duelist would expect. Chang had in his life dealt out and received all sorts of punishment, and was under no illusion that his skills would protect him forever, or from everyone. In this particular instance, he was lucky that a desire for silence had led his opponent to choose—instead of a revolver—a weapon ridiculously unsuited for assassination in such close quarters. Once he'd missed with his first blow, Chang had stepped within his guard and stabbed home—but the window for action was very narrow. Had Chang paused, dodged farther into the room, or tried to dash back to the landing a second blow from the saber would have mown him down like fresh wheat.

Chang lit the lamp, located the pigeon and—feeling especially ridiculous stepping around the dead body—drove it out of the open window onto the rooftop. The room was not too much of a mess. It had been thoroughly searched, but without the intent to destroy anything and as his possessions were few it would be a brief matter to set things back to rights. He stepped to the still-open door and listened. There was no sound from the stairway, which meant either no one had heard, or that he was indeed alone in the building. He closed the door—the lock had been forced just like the front entrance—and braced the back of it with a chair. Only then did he kneel, wipe the dagger on the man's uniform, and slide it back into the body of his stick. He cast an eye along the length—he'd been fortunate enough to parry the saber on the flat of the blade, and hadn't cracked the wood. He set it against the wall, and looked down at his assailant.

He was a young man, blond hair cropped short, in a black uniform with silver facing, black boots, and a silver badge of a wolf devouring the sun. His right shoulder sported one silver epaulette—a lieutenant. Chang quickly went through the man's pockets, which aside from some small amount of money (which he took) and a handkerchief, were empty. He looked more closely at the body. The first dagger blow had landed just below the ribs from the side. The next three had driven up under the ribcage and into the lungs, judging by the bloody froth at the fellow's mouth.

Chang sighed and sat back on his heels. He didn't recognize the uniform at all. The boots suggested a horseman, but an officer might wear anything, and what young man foolish enough to *be* a military officer wasn't also going to want high black boots? He picked up the saber, feeling the balance of the weapon. It was an expensive piece, exquisitely weighted, and wickedly sharp. The length, the broad curve and flat width of the blade made it a weapon for horseback, for slashing. He'd be light cavalry—not a Hussar by his uniform, but perhaps a Dragoon or a Lancer. Troops for quick movement, reconnaissance, intelligence. Chang leaned over the body and unfastened the scabbard. He sheathed the blade and tossed it onto the pallet. The body he would get rid of, but the sword would certainly be worth something if he needed ready cash.

He stood up and exhaled, his nerves finally easing back to a more normal state of wariness. At the moment a corpse was the last thing he wanted to waste time with settling. He had no clear idea of the hour, and knew that the later he arrived at the Palace the harder it would be to speak to the manager, and the more of a lead his rivals would have upon him. He permitted himself a smile to think that at least one of these rivals would be thinking him dead, but then knew that this also meant that the Major would be expecting word—and undoubtedly soon—from this young agent. Chang could certainly expect another visit, this time in force, in the near future. His room was unsafe until the business was settled—which meant that he'd have to deal with the body now, for he really did not want to leave it unattended—possibly for days. His sense of smell was not *that* bad.

Quickly then, he made himself presentable for the Old Palace: a shave, a wash from his basin, and then a new change of clothes— a clean white shirt, black trousers, cravat and waistcoat—and a quick scrub and polish for his boots. He pocketed what money he had stashed about the room and three books of poetry (including the *Persephone*), and then combed his still-wet hair in the mirror. He balled up his old handkerchief and tossed it aside, then tucked a fresh one and his razor into the pocket of his coat. He opened the window to the roof, stepped out to see if any nearby windows were lighted or occupied. They were not. He returned to the room and took hold of the body under each arm, dragging it onto the rooftop, out to the far edge. He looked over, down at the alleyway behind the building, locating the trash heap piled around the habitually clogged sewer. He glanced around him once more, then hefted the body onto the edge and, checking his aim, pushed it over. The dead soldier landed on the soft pile. If Chang was lucky, it would not be immediately clear whether he had fallen or been murdered in the street.

He returned to his room, collected his stick and the saber, blew out the lamp, and crept back out the window, closing it behind him. It wouldn't lock, but given that the location was known to his enemies, it hardly mattered. He set off across the rooftops. The buildings of this block were directly connected, and his path was simple enough, with only a few slippery stretches of ornamental molding requiring caution. At the fifth building, which was abandoned, he pried open an attic hatchway and dropped down into darkness. He landed easily on the wooden floor, felt for a moment, and located a spot of loose planking. He pulled it back and shoved the saber inside, replacing the plank over it. He might never come back for it, but he had to assume his own room would be searched by more soldiers, and the less they found of their fallen comrade the better. He groped again and found the ladder to the landing below. In a matter of moments, Chang was on the street, still presentable and bound for the Palace, with yet another soul weighing upon his exiled conscience.

The house was named for its proximity to an actual royal residence given over—its fortified walls too out of fashion—some two hundred years ago, which had first been used as a home for various minor Royals, then as the War Ministry, then an armory, a military academy, to finally—and presently—as the home of the Royal Institute of Science and Exploration. While it would seem that such an organization would hardly encourage the nearby thriving of such an exclusive brothel, in fact the various endeavors of the Institute were almost all supported, in competitive fashion, by the wealthiest figures in the city, each striving against the others to finance an invention, a discovery, a new continent, or a newly located star to result in the immemorial attachment of their name to something permanent and useful. In turn, the Institute members strove against each other to attract patrons—the two communities of the privileged and the learned spawning between them an entire district whose economy derived from flattery, favoritism, and the excessive consumption that followed each. Thus, the Old Palace brothel—named, in another anatomical witticism, for perhaps the oldest palace of all.

The entry to the house was respectable and austere, the building itself crammed into a block-long row of identical stiff stackings of grey stone with domed rooftops, the doorway green and brightly lit, the walk from the street leading through an iron gate and past a well-occupied guard's hut. Chang stood so he was clearly seen, waited while the gate was unlocked, and made his way up to the door itself, where another guard allowed him into the house proper. Inside was warm and bright, with music and distant decorous laughter. A fetching young woman appeared for his coat. He declined, but gave her his stick and a coin for her trouble. He walked to the end of the foyer where a thin man in a white jacket hovered at a high rostrum, fitfully scribbling in a notebook. He looked at Chang with an expression that kept just barely to the prudent side of amusement.

"Ah," he said, as if to convey the multitude of comments regarding Chang's person he was, through compassion and kindness, withholding.

"Madame Kraft."

"I am not sure she is available—in fact, I am certain—"

"It is quite important," Chang said, meeting the man's eyes levelly. "I will pay for the lady's time—whatever fee she sees fit. The name is Chang."

The man narrowed his eyes, ran his gaze once more over Chang, and then nodded with a doubtful sniff. He scrawled a few lines on a small piece of green paper, stuffed the paper into a leather tube, and inserted the tube into a brass pipe fixed to the wall. With a gulping hiss, the tube was abruptly sucked from sight. The man turned back to his rostrum, making notes. Minutes passed. The man ignored him absolutely. With a sudden *chonk* the leather tube reappeared from another pipe, shooting into a brass pocket beneath. The man extracted the tube and dug a scrap of blue paper from it. He looked up with a blank expression that nevertheless exuded contempt.

"This way."

*   *   *

Chang was led through an elegant parlor and down a long hallway where the light was dim and the closely patterned wallpaper made the space seem narrower than it actually was. At its end was a metal-sheathed door where the man in white knocked, four times, deliberately. In answer, a narrow viewing slot slid back and then, the visitors having been seen, shot closed. They waited. The door opened. His guide gestured for Chang to enter a darkly paneled room with desks and blotters and ledgers and a large abacus screwed into prominent position on a side table. The door had been opened by a tall man in his shirtsleeves, a heavy revolver holstered under one arm, with black hair and skin the color of polished cherry wood, who nodded him toward another door on the far side of the office. Chang crossed to it, thought it would be polite to knock, and did so. After a moment, he heard a muted request to enter.

The room was another office, but with a single wide desk, across which was spread a large blackboard that had been painted with various columns and inset with strips of wood with holes bored into them, so that colored pegs could be inserted along the columns, cutting each into rows, the whole forming an enormous grid. The blackboard was already scrawled with names and with numbers and dotted with pegs. Chang had seen it before and knew it corresponded to the rooms in the house, the ladies (or boys) at work, and the segments of time in the evening, and that it was wiped and re-written fresh every night of the week. Behind the desk, a piece of chalk in one hand and a moist sponge in the other, stood Madelaine Kraft, the manager—and some said actual owner—of the Old Palace. A well-shaped woman of uncertain age, she wore a simple dress of blue Chinese silk, which set off her golden skin in a pleasant way. She was not beautiful so much as compelling. Chang had heard she was from Egypt, or perhaps India, and had worked her way from the front of the house to her present position through discretion, intelligence, and unscrupulous scheming. She was without a doubt a far more powerful per-

son than he, with high-placed men from all over the land profoundly obligated to her silence and favor, and thus at her call. She
looked up from her work and nodded to a chair. He sat. She
dropped the chalk and sponge, wiped her fingers on her dress and
took a drink of tea from a white china cup to the side of the board.
She remained standing.

"You're here about Isobel Hastings."

"I am."

Madelaine Kraft did not reply, which he took as an invitation
to continue.

"I was asked to find her—a . . . *lady* returning from an evening's
work covered in blood."

"Returning from where?"

"I was not told—the understanding was that the quantity of
blood was singular enough for her to be remembered."

"Returning from whom?"

"I was not told—the assumption being the blood was his."

She was silent for a moment, in thought. Chang realized that
she was not thinking of what to say, but weighing instead whether
or not to say what she was thinking.

"There is the missing man in the newspaper," she said, musing.

Chang nodded absently. "The Colonel of Dragoons."

"Could it be him?"

He answered as casually as he could, "It's entirely possible."

She took another sip of tea.

"You will understand," Chang went on, "that I am being
honest."

This made her smile. "Why would I understand that?"

"Because I am paying you, and your bargains are fair."

Chang reached into his coat for the wallet and extracted three
crisp banknotes. He leaned forward and set them down on the
blackboard. Madelaine Kraft picked up the notes, glanced at the
amount, and dropped them into an open wooden box next to her
teacup. She glanced at the clock.

"I'm afraid there is no great deal of time."

He nodded. "My understanding is that my client desires revenge."

"And you?" she asked.

"First, to know who else is searching for her. I know the
agents—the officer, the 'sister'—but not who they represent."

"And after that?"

"That will depend. Obviously they have already been here asking questions—unless you are involved in this business yourself."

She cocked her head slightly and, after a moment of thought,
sat down behind the desk. She reached over for another sip of tea,
took it, and kept the cup, holding it between her breasts with both
hands, watching him evenly across the desk top.

"Very well," she began. "To begin with, I do not know the name,
and I do not know the woman. No person of my household—or of
my household's acquaintance—appeared in the early hours of this
morning displaying any quantity of blood. I have made it a point
to *ask,* and I have received no such answer. Next, Major *Blach* was
here this afternoon. I told him what I have just told you."

She pronounced the name unlike Jurgins or Wells, as if it was
foreign . . . had he spoken with an accent? The others had not mentioned it.

"And the sister?"

She smiled conspiratorially. "*I* have seen no sister."

"A woman, scars on her face, a burn, claiming to be Isobel
Hastings's sister, a 'Mrs. Marchmoor'—"

"I have not seen her. Perhaps she's still to come. Perhaps she
does not know this house."

"That's impossible. She has been to two other houses before
me, and she would know this one before all the rest of them."

"I am sure that's true."

Chang's mind raced, sorting quickly—Mrs. Marchmoor had

known the other houses, she had bypassed this one—to a swift conclusion: she did not come because she would be *known*.

"May I ask if any women of your household have recently . . . graduated to other situations, perhaps without your consent? With light brown hair?"

"It is indeed the case."

"The type to be searching for a blood-soaked relative?"

"Hardly," she scoffed. "But you said burns across the face?"

"They could be recent."

"They would need to be. Margaret Hooke has been gone four days. The daughter of a ruined mill owner. She would not be known at any lower house."

"Does she have a sister?"

"She doesn't have a soul. Though it appears she's found something. If you can tell me what that is—or who—I'll be kindly disposed."

"You have a suspicion. That's why we're talking."

"We're talking because one of several regular customers of Margaret Hooke is presently in my house."

"I see."

"She saw many people. But anyone wanting to learn what might be learned . . . as I said, there's little time to talk."

Chang nodded and stood. As he turned to the door she called to him, her voice both quiet and more urgent at the same time. "Cardinal?" He looked back. "Your own part in this?"

"Madam, I am merely the agent of others."

She studied him. "Major Blach did ask for Miss Hastings. But he also sought any information about a man in red, a mercenary for hire, perhaps even this bloody girl's accomplice."

He felt a chill of warning. The man had obviously asked Mrs. Wells and Jurgins too, and they had said nothing, laughing at Chang's back. "How strange. Of course, I cannot explain his interest, unless he had been following my client, and perhaps observed us speaking."

"Ah."

He nodded to her. "I will let you know what I find." He stepped to the door, opened it, and then turned back. "Which lady of your house is entertaining Margaret Hooke's customer?"

Madelaine Kraft smiled, her thin amusement tinged with pity. "Angelique."

He returned to the front of the house and collected his stick, then so armed—and untroubled by the staff who seemed to understand that it had been arranged—approached the man in white. Chang saw that he held another small piece of blue paper, and before he could speak the man leaned forward with a whisper. "Down the rear staircase. Wait under the stairs, and then you may follow." He smiled—Kraft's acceptance smoothing the way for his own. "It will provide the additional benefit of allowing you to leave unseen."

The man went back to his notebook. Chang walked quickly past him into the main part of the house, along wide welcoming archways that opened onto variously entrancing vistas of comfort and luxury, food and flesh, laughter and music—to a rear door, watched by another burly man. Chang looked up at him—he was tall himself and found the immediate density of so many taller, broader figures a little tiresome—waited for the man to open the door, and then stepped onto the landing of a slender wooden staircase leading down to a narrow, high passageway of some twenty yards. This basement passage was significantly cooler, moist-aired, and lined with brick. Directly beneath the staircase was a hutch with a door. Chang pulled it open and climbed inside, bending nearly double to fit, and sat on a round milking stool. He pulled the door closed and waited in the dark, feeling foolish.

The interview had raised more questions than it had answered. He knew his conversation with Rosamonde in the map room had been unobserved, so Black must know of him independently—

either from some other informant, from seeing him at the Vandaariff mansion, or, he had to admit, from Rosamonde herself. If Mrs. Marchmoor was also Margaret Hooke, then Angelique was in danger of disappearing as well—though Madelaine Kraft's suspicion had not stopped her from accepting the regular client who might have been the cause. Perhaps this meant that the client was not as important as some other party, or some other power, yet hidden in the shadow—information she hoped Chang could provide. Chang rubbed his eyes. In the course of a day he had placed himself in the shadow of one murder, performed another, and set himself against at least three different mysterious parties—four if he counted Rosamonde—without any real knowledge of the larger stakes at hand. Further, none of this had brought him a step closer to finding Isobel Hastings, who grew more mysterious by the hour.

Despite his racing mind, it was only a minute before he heard the door open and the descending weight of footsteps on the stairs above his head. A man was speaking, but Chang couldn't make out the words over the noise—to his best guess there were at least three people in the party, perhaps more. Finally they were off the stairs and walking away from him down the passage. He cautiously opened the hutch door, and peeked out: the party could only walk single file in the narrow space, and all he could see was the back of the rear figure, an unremarkable-looking man in a formal black topcoat. He waited until they reached the far end of the passage before slowly pushing the door open and extricating himself. By the time he was once more standing at his full height, they had rounded a corner and disappeared. Walking as much as possible on his toes to reduce the sound of his footsteps, he followed at a trot to make up the distance.

At the corner he stopped, listening, and again heard the voice—low and strangely muttering—but not the words themselves, obscured by jingling keys and their fumbling at a lock. He silently dropped to a crouch and then risked edging one eye around the corner—knowing that anyone looking would be less likely to notice an eye at a less-than-normal eye height. The party was some ten yards away, standing in front of a locked, metal-bound door. The man in the rear still stood with his back to Chang, the closer view revealing him to be younger with thin, oak-colored hair plastered flat to his skull. Beyond him Chang could see parts of three other people: a small man in an ash-grey coat bent over the door, attempting to find the right key, a tall, broad-shouldered man in a thick fur, impatiently tapping a walking stick on the floor and leaning down—he was the one muttering—to the fourth person, tucked under his arm like a flower in a grenadier's bearskin: Angelique. Her dress was deep blue, and she did not re-act to whatever the man was saying, gazing without expression at the elegant grey man's hands as he sorted through keys. The lock turned—he'd found the right one at last—and he opened the door, looking back at the others with a trim twitch of a smile. It was Harald Crabbé.

At this the man in the fur snapped open a pocket watch and frowned. "Where in hell is he?" he said, his voice an iron rasp. He turned to the third man and hissed balefully, "Collect him."

Chang darted back around the corner, desperately looking around him for a place to hide. He was fortunate in that, being in a crouch, his eyes naturally looked upwards, and saw a pair of iron pipes, as wide as his arm, running the length of the passage just below the high ceiling. Behind him he heard another voice—Crabbé—interrupt the nearing footsteps of the third man, just at the corner, a step away from discovering Chang.

"*Bascombe.*"

"Sir?"

"Wait a moment." Crabbé's tone changed—clearly now he was addressing the man in the fur. "Another minute. I should rather not give him any insight into our growing displeasure, nor the sat-

isfaction such knowledge would undoubtedly bring. Besides"—
and here his voice changed again, to an awkward sugarish tone—
"his *prize* is with us."

"I am no one's prize," replied Angelique, her voice quiet but
firm.

"Of course you aren't," assured Crabbé, "but he needn't know
that until we're ready."

Chang looked up in horror. At the far end of the passage, above
the staircase, the door was opened. Someone was coming. He was
caught between them. In a surge of strength he took three steps
and jumped, bracing one foot against the wall and thrusting off,
catching the other foot on the opposite side and thrusting again,
higher, so that his outstretched arms could reach the pipes. A pair
of legs were visible descending the stairs. The group around the
corner would hear any second. He pulled himself up, wrapping his
legs around the pipes, and then through sheer force rolled over
above them, so he faced the floor, quickly tucking the ends of his
coat so they didn't hang. He looked down with despair. His stick
was still on the floor, close to the wall, where he'd set it when he'd
peeked around the corner. There was nothing he could do. They
were coming. How long had he taken? Had he been seen? Heard?
A moment later—holding his breath despite his heaving chest—
Chang saw the third man, Bascombe, step around the corner—
standing bare inches from his stick. The footsteps neared from
the other end—louder than he'd thought. It was more than one
person.

"Mr. Bascombe!" one of them shouted, a kind of exuberant
greeting made all the more hearty (or fatuous) by the fact that the
men had most likely been apart for all of five minutes. But the
tone served to announce that they were on an adventure together,
an *evening*—and declare as well who was that evening's guide.
Chang's skin prickled with loathing. He exhaled silently through
his nose. He could not believe they had not seen him—and prepared to drop onto Bascombe, attack the newcomers, then run for

the steps. The pair passed directly beneath. He froze, again holding his breath. One man, a sharp fellow in a crisp black tailcoat, bristling red side whiskers, and long, thick, curled red hair (obviously the man who had called out), supported the shambling steps of another taller, thinner man in a steel blue uniform, capped with a squat, blue-plumed shako, with medals across his chest and tall boots that unmercifully hampered his alcoholic gait. Once they were close enough, Bascombe stepped forward and took the uniformed man's other side, and the three of them vanished around the corner.

Chang stayed above the pipes until he heard the iron door close behind them, then swung himself down to hang by his arms and drop to the floor. He brushed himself off—the pipes were filthy—and picked up his stick. He exhaled, berating himself for being trapped so foolishly. He had only been saved by the uniformed man, he knew, whose stumbling drunken state had diverted attention away from anything else. He thought back to the conversation between the man in fur and Crabbé: which of the two men had they been waiting for—the drunken officer or the hearty fop? And though he resisted the thought—for it led to naught but slow disintegration of his peace—as he walked around the corner and stared at the iron door they'd closed behind them . . . which among them all had laid claim to Angelique?

She'd come from Macao as a child, orphaned when her father, a Portuguese sailor, had died in a knife fight his second day off the ship. Her mother had been Chinese, and her appearance had transfixed Chang from the moment he'd seen her in the main room of the South Quays—where she had found a kind of home after the cruelty of the public orphanage. Exotic beauty and a strangely compelling reserve had elevated her first from that squalid lair to the Second Bench and finally this last year, at the ripe age of seventeen, to the perfumed heights of the Old Palace,

Madame Kraft having purchased her contract for an undisclosed amount. This had effectively placed her beyond Chang's reach. He had not spoken to her in five months. Of course he had barely spoken to her before that—he was not one for speaking in general, and still less to anyone for whom he might possess actual feelings. Though he told himself she was well aware of the special place she held within his—he could not say "heart," for what was that in a life like his (perhaps "panoramic painting" was a more accurate description of the rootless pageant of Chang's existence)—this had prompted no significant words on her part, for no matter her own feelings, she preferred silence as much as he. At first this might have been a question of language, but by now it had become an expression of professional manner, one with a bright smile, pliant body, and impossibly distant eyes. In the devastating moments they'd spent in what passed for intimacy, Angelique was never other than polite and practiced, but always allowed just a glimpse of a boundless inner landscape held firmly in reserve . . . a glimpse that went through Chang's very soul like a fishhook.

He tried the metal door, to no avail, and sighed with impatience. It was an old lock, intended more to delay determined pursuit than prevent it utterly. He groped in his coat for a ring of iron skeleton keys and flipped through them. The second key worked, and he swung the door open slowly—it was well-greased and did not creak—and stepped through into darkness. He pulled the door behind him, leaving it unlocked, and listened. His quarry's pace was slow, not surprising due to the combination of the drunken man and Angelique—her shoes and dress would not be suited to a darkened cobblestone tunnel. Chang followed quietly, stick before him, left hand feeling the wall. The tunnel was not long—judging by the distance just far enough to clear the alley and next block of houses. Quickly Chang tried to place the exact direction—the stairway down, then the passage, the corner, then the dark tunnel, which seemed to have a very gentle curve to the left . . . the block behind the brothel was the outlying wall of the Palace itself—additional buildings for the Institute. Undoubtedly the tunnel had been originally built as a secret bolt-hole from the Palace, perhaps to what was then the house of a mistress, perhaps as a way to escape a mob. Chang smiled to see the usage reversed, but retained his air of caution. He had never been within the walls of the Institute, and had no clear idea what he was going to find.

Ahead, they had stopped. Someone pounded on another iron door, a metallic rapping (the large man's stick?) that echoed sharply through the tunnel. In answer, Chang heard the working of a lock, the shrill ripple of chain pulled through an iron ring, and then the creak of heavy hinges. Orange light bled into the darkness. The party stood at the base of a short stone staircase, and above them an open hatch nearly flush with the ground, as to a cellar. Several men stood with lanterns, offering their hands one at a time as the party members climbed out. They did not close the door—perhaps because they would be bringing Angelique back?—so Chang took the opportunity to slip to the stone steps and crouch low, looking up. Above him, quite ghostly in the moonlight, were the leafless limbs of a tree.

He peeked over the edge and saw that it opened onto a large grassy courtyard between buildings of the Palace. The pool of lantern light moved farther away as the group was guided across the lawn, leaving him very much in shadow. Keeping low, Chang stole from the tunnel—it felt like leaving a crypt—and after them, drifting as he went toward the nearest tree, which gave a more substantial cover. The windows in the buildings around him were dark—he had no idea how much of the Palace the fellows of the Institute actually occupied, or in what manner, so could only hope to remain unobserved. He jogged along to another tree, now even closer to the walls, the thick turf swallowing the sound of his boots. It was easy to see where the party was headed—toward another man with a lantern, who stood marking the entrance to a strange structure at the courtyard's center, apart from and unconnected to any other building.

It was one low story, made of brick, without windows and, as near as Chang could tell, circular. As he watched, the group of six and their guides reached the doorway and entered. The man who had been at the door remained. Chang advanced to another tree, taking more care with any noise. He was perhaps twenty yards away. He waited, still, for several minutes. The guard did not move from the door. Chang studied the courtyard, wondering if he could creep around to the far side of the circular building, in case there might be another door, or a window, or access through the roof. Instead, he eased into a crouch and decided to wait, hoping that the guard would enter or some of the party would come out. The party itself he was still pondering. He did not recognize any of them save Crabbé and Angelique. The man Bascombe was a lackey for either the Deputy Minister or the man in the fur, it was unclear who—just as it was unclear who between those men was the superior power. The final two were a mystery—from his vantage point on the ceiling he could hardly see the face of either man, nor the details of the drunken officer's uniform. Obviously there was some relation to the gathering at Robert Vandaariff's house—Crabbé had been in both places. Had one of them courted Margaret Hooke in the same way as they were courting Angelique—Margaret Hooke who was looking for Isobel Hastings (who had also been at Vandaariff's) and who had the same scarring as the late Arthur Trapping? Her scarring had been recent, just as Trapping's had occurred in the few minutes between his leaving the main reception and Chang finding him on the floor—which at least told Chang that the scarring itself hadn't caused Trapping's death, as the woman had obviously survived. Most important was the disparate nature of the group, gathering for some shared purpose—a purpose that, perhaps only as a tangent, had killed Arthur Trapping and prompted a search for Isobel Hastings. Chang doubted this search was about revenge. His Persephone may indeed have killed Rosamonde's friend—the blood had come from somewhere—but she was being hunted for what she had seen.

The guard turned suddenly, away from Chang, and a moment later Chang himself heard footsteps from across the courtyard. Walking forward into the lantern's glow was a spare man in a long, dark, double-breasted greatcoat with silver buttons and bare epaulettes, his pale head bare, his hands joined behind his back. At the guard's request he stopped several yards away, nodding sharply and clicking his heels in salute. The man was clean-shaven and wore a monocle that reflected the light as he nodded his head, clearly requesting entry and then taking in the guard's refusal. The man exhaled with resignation. He looked behind him and gestured vaguely with his left hand—perhaps at a place where he might be allowed to wait. The guard turned his head to follow the hand. In one swift movement the man whipped his right arm forward, his thumb drawing the hammer of a gleaming black pistol, and aimed the barrel square at the guard's face. The guard did not move, but then very quickly, at the man's brisk, whispered instruction, dropped his weapon to the grass, put down the lantern, and then turned his face to the door. The man snatched up the lantern and placed the pistol against the guard's spine. The guard opened the door with a key and the two men disappeared inside.

They did not close the door either. Chang quickly loped across the lawn toward it and carefully craned his head so he could see in. The entrance led directly to a low staircase that descended several stories on a direct and very steep incline. The building was sunk deeply into the ground and Chang could just see the two figures leaving the stairwell, with only a flickering orange glow bleeding back from the disappearing lantern. Chang glanced around the courtyard, readied his stick, and crept down the stairs, moving slowly, silently, and keeping himself at all times ready to bolt back to the top. Once again he'd placed himself in a narrow corridor at the mercy of anyone appearing above or below him—but if he wanted information, he saw no other way. Just above the lower landing he stopped, listening. He could hear distant conversation, but the words were muddled by the strange acoustics. Chang looked above him. No one was there. He continued his descent.

The stairs opened onto a circular hallway curving away to either side, as if it formed a ring around a great central chamber. The voices were to Chang's left, so he went that way, pressing close against the inner wall to remain unseen. After some twenty yards, moving into a steadily brighter light, he stopped again, for suddenly—as if he had walked through a door—he could hear the voices perfectly.

"I do not care for the *inconvenience.*" The voice was angry but controlled. "He is insensible."

The accent sounded German, but perhaps something else—Danish? Norse? The words were met first with silence, and then the delicate speech of a practiced diplomat, Harald Crabbé.

"Doctor...of course...you must see to your duties—quite understandable, in fact, admirable. You will see, however...the delicacy, the *time* element—that there are requirements—*duties*—in competition. I believe we are all friends here—"

"Excellent. Then I will bid you a friendly good evening," replied the Doctor. In immediate answer came the ringing of steel—a sword being drawn—and the clicks of several guns being cocked. Chang could imagine the standoff. What he could not imagine were the stakes.

"Doctor...," Crabbé continued, with a rising strain of urgency in his voice. "Such a confrontation suits no one—and your young master's wishes, if he were able to make them known—"

"Not my master, but my charge," cut in the Doctor. "His wishes in the matter count for very little. As I said, we will be leaving, unless you choose to kill me. If you do so choose, I promise that I will first blow out the brains of this idiot Prince—which I believe will quite spoil your plans, as well as leaving a powerful father ... angry. Good evening."

Chang heard shuffling steps, and a moment later saw the Doctor, one hand holding up the tottering, insensible man in uniform, and the other occupied with the pistol. Chang retreated with him step for step, keeping out of view of the larger group which he had just glimpsed—Crabbé, Bascombe, the foppish red-haired man (who held the sword), and three guards (who held the pistols). There was no sign of the man in fur, nor of Angelique. As they retreated, no one spoke—as if the situation had progressed beyond words—and soon Chang found himself retreating past the staircase. He considered dashing up, but it would only expose him—they would have to hear his steps and he could not reach the top unseen. It might also be the exact distraction to get the Doctor killed, and right now Chang didn't know if that would be a good thing or not. He still hoped to learn more. The drunken, uniformed man, unless he was very wrong, must be Karl-Horst von Maasmärck. Once more, mysterious connections between Robert Vandaariff, Henry Xonck, and the Foreign Ministry seemed to be dancing just out of reach in his brain. Momentarily distracted with thought, Chang looked up. The Doctor had seen him.

He stood with the slumped von Maasmärck at the base of the stairwell, and had merely glanced down the other end of the corridor as a reflex and been shocked to see anyone, much less a strange figure in red. Chang knew he was beyond the curve of the wall and out of sight to the others, and slowly brought a finger to his lips, indicating silence. The Doctor stared. His skin was pale and the impression he gave nearly skeletal. His hair was ice-blond and shaved on the back and sides of his head in a nearly medieval fashion, long and plastered back in a part on top—though his struggles had broken it forward in lank, white clumps that hung over his eyes. It did not seem, for all his apparent confidence, that the Doctor was a man of action, or necessarily used to waving a pistol.

Chang deliberately backed away from him, keeping eye contact, and made a gesture to indicate that the Doctor should exit—*now*. The Doctor darted his gaze back to the others and began to awkwardly mount the stairs, pulling up the near deadweight of the Prince along with him. Chang retreated farther from view, his thoughts once more askew upon seeing von Maasmärck's face: quite clearly livid with red circular burns around both of his eyes.

The group clustered around the lower door. "Doctor, I am sure we shall see you again," called Crabbé amiably, "and good night to your sweet prince." The Deputy Minister then muttered to the guards near him, "If he falls, take him. If he doesn't, one of you secure the door, and the other follow him. You"—he singled out the guard the Doctor had brought down at pistol point—"stay here." Two of the guards climbed rapidly from sight and one remained, his pistol in hand. Crabbé turned and, with Bascombe and the red-haired fop, disappeared down the hallway whence they'd come.

"It doesn't signify," he said to them cheerfully. "We shall find the Prince tomorrow—in some fashion—and the Doctor may be dealt with at leisure. There is no hurry. Besides"—and here he chuckled, speaking more intimately—"we have another engagement with *nobility*—yes, Roger?"

They passed out of hearing. Chang slowly retreated another ten yards, boxed in again. He would have to attack the guard to get out, or outlast them—assuming that when the party left they would take the guards along. He turned and continued down this half of the corridor, hoping the circle might join on the other side.

Chang advanced with his stick before him in both hands—one on the handle and one on the body—ready to pull it apart at a moment's notice. He had no real idea if he was the hunter or the hunted, but knew that if things went bad he could be fighting several men at once, which was almost always fatal. If the group of men kept their heads, one of them was always presented with an opening, and their lone opponent, no matter how vigorous or skilled, would fall. That man's only option was to attack at as many points as possible and through pure aggression separate the group into fragile individuals—who might then be prone to hesitation. Hesitation created tiny moments of single combat, winnowing the group, which in turn created more hesitation—ferocity pitted against presence of mind, fear trumping logic. In short, it meant attacking like a madman. But such a wanton strategy opened his defense with more holes than Mrs. Wells's natural smile—and any remaining presence of mind in his opponents—which was to say, if they were not inexperienced, stupid, easily rattled farmers— would leave him stuck like a pig. The better aim was to avoid it entirely. He took care to make no noise.

As the corridor curved, he detected a low humming from beyond the inner wall—from the central chamber, whatever that actually was. On the floor in front of him lay a profusion of long boxes, opened and emptied in a great tumbled pile, the same boxes he'd seen on the cart at the canal and in the house of Robert Vandaariff—though these were lined with blue felt rather than orange. The humming grew louder, then steadily louder still, until the very air seemed to vibrate. Chang put his hands over his ears. The discomfort bled horribly into pain. He stumbled forward. The corridor ended at a door, sheathed in metal. He picked his way across the boxes—the great throbbing noise covering the sound of his awkward steps—but he could not concentrate, tripping, knocking boxes aside. He tottered and shut his eyes. He sank to his knees.

It took Cardinal Chang several seconds of brutally reverberating echo in his ears to perceive that the sound had stopped. He sniffed, and felt his face. It was wet. He dug for his handkerchief— his nose was bleeding. He struggled to his feet amidst the littered boxes, shaking away a fog of dizziness, staring at the bright stains on the cloth as he doubled it over and dabbed again at his face. He collected himself, sniffed, stuffed the handkerchief into a side pocket, and stepped carefully to the door. He pressed his ear against it, listening, but it was too thick—which only made him wonder all the more at the true extremity of the throbbing hum, to have so touched him through the massive walls and this heavy door. What had happened to the people *within* the chamber? What was the cause of the noise? He stood for a moment, assessing just where he was in relation to his ostensible aims—to find the true killer of Arthur Trapping and the elusive Isobel Hastings. Chang knew he had pursued a dangerous tangent—perhaps trapped himself there. Then he thought of Angelique, perhaps on the other side of this door, involved he knew not how—but certainly without any protection he could trust. He turned the handle.

The heavy door swung open on silent well-oiled hinges, and Chang entered with all the noise of a ghost—and indeed, as he took in the spectacle before his eyes, the color drained from his face. He had entered a kind of ante-room, divided from a larger, vaulted chamber—whose high walls were lined with gleaming pipes, like a great organ, like a cathedral—which he saw through a large window of thick glass. The pipes ran together down to the floor and gathered under a stage-like platform upon which was a large table. On the table lay Angelique, quite naked, her head covered with an elaborate mask of metal and black rubber, her body a-swarm with black hoses and cables, an infernal, passive vision of St. Isobel's martyrdom. Standing on the platform next to her were several men, their heads covered with great helmets of brass and leather, with thick lenses for their eyes and odd inset boxes over the mouth and ears, all identifiable to Chang from their garments: a small man in grey, a crisp man in elegant black, a slender man who must be Bascombe, and a large man no longer in his fur, shirt-sleeves rolled up, arms covered to his elbows by heavy leather gauntlets. They were all looking in his direction—not at him, but through the window at the delicate procedure taking place before Chang's eyes.

The ante-room was dominated by a wide stone trough of bubbling, steaming liquid, into which fed at least fifty of the slick black hoses, which were draped across nearly every inch of floor space. Suspended by chains above this hissing pool hung a dripping metal slab, obviously just retracted out of the trough. On the opposite side of the trough from Chang was a man in leather gloves, a heavy leather apron, and one of the strange helmets. He was awkwardly leaning forward and in his arms cradled a pulsing rectangular object, brilliantly opaque, the exact shape of a large book, only fabricated from dripping, steaming, gleaming, piercingly indigo blue glass. The glass book was perilously balanced on his open hands and forearms, as if it were too fragile or too dangerous to actually grip. With extreme concentration he had clearly just raised it from the roiling liquid and then taken it off the metal slab. Then the man looked up and saw Chang.

His concentration snapped. His balance shifted, and for an endless sickening moment Chang watched the glass book slide off the slick leather gauntlets. The man lurched, trying to correct the balance, but only sent it skidding uncontrolled in the other direction. He lurched again but it bobbled away from his grasp and dropped onto the edge of the stone trough, where it shattered in a cloud of sharp fragments. Chang saw the figures in the great chamber running toward the window. He saw the man reeling back, his clutching hands bristling with thin daggers of glowing glass. But mainly Chang was overwhelmed by the smell, the same smell he had known near the body of Arthur Trapping, now impossibly more intense. His eyes stung, his throat clenched, his knees sagged. Before him the man was screaming—the muffled shrieks echoed through the helmet. The others were quickly approaching the room. Chang could barely stand. He looked through the window at Angelique on the table, writhing as if the hoses were sucking out her life blood, and stumbled back, his hand over his mouth, his head swimming from the fumes, black spots floating up in front of his eyes. He ran for his life.

He clattered unheedingly through the litter of boxes, sucking in the cleaner air, shouts behind him, and tore his stick apart, readying each piece. He raced around the corridor, his legs pounding, his heart reeling from what he'd just seen, from abandoning Angelique—could he have freed her? Was she there willingly? What had he just *done?*—and charged straight at the guard, who had heard him coming and frantically dug for his pistol. The guard pulled the weapon free just as Chang reached him, swinging his stick at the barrel. The shot was knocked wide and then Chang's right hand was lancing forward. The man twisted desperately away and the blade caught on his right shoulder instead of his throat. The guard bellowed. Chang ripped the blade free and struck him across the face with the stick, knocking the man to his knees. He glanced behind—he could hear people charging through the boxes, and ran up the stairs. He was half-way up when a shot went off below—the guard trying with his left hand. The shot missed but would surely alert the man at the top, who would only have to slam the upper door to trap Chang completely. He pushed forward, his legs protesting—his head still dizzied from the fumes, his thoughts still on the table in the vaulted room, Angelique's thrashing masked face—gasping with effort. Another shot from below, another miss, and Chang had reached the top, charging into the courtyard, already swinging his arms in defense—but seeing no one. He stopped, stumbling, breathing hard, his eyes blind in the darkness. He looked back to the door and located the guard . . . on the ground, face-down and still.

Before he could think—the Doctor?—two black shapes stepped from shadow, one of them slamming the door closed. Chang backed away onto the grass, and then wheeled at the sound of steps behind him. Two more shapes. He adjusted his angle of re-treat away from both pairs, and then heard more steps—he was cut off again. He was surrounded in the dark by six men...all of whom seemed to be wearing black uniforms with silver facings. With a metallic ringing they each drew a saber. There was nothing he could do. Was Angelique dead? He didn't know—he didn't know anything. Chang abruptly sheathed his dagger into the body of his stick, and looked at the soldiers.

"Either you are going to kill me here or escort me to your Major." He pointed at the door. "But *they* will interrupt us any moment."

One of the soldiers stepped aside, making a gap in the circle, and gestured for him to walk that way—toward a large arch, the actual entrance to the courtyard. As Chang stepped forward the soldiers as a group extended their sabers toward him, and the one who had moved demanded, "Your weapon." Chang tossed his stick to him and walked on, half-expecting a blade in his back. Instead, they quickly marched him into the shadow of the archway and toward a black coach. The soldier with his stick sheathed his saber and drew a small pistol, which he held against Chang's neck. Once this was done, the others sheathed their blades as well, and set about their tasks—two climbed up to drive the coach, one opened the coach door and climbed in, turning to help Chang en-ter, two more ran to open the courtyard gates. The trooper with the pistol followed him in and closed the door behind. The three sat on the same side, Chang in the middle, the pistol tight against his ribs. Across and alone on the other side of the coach sat a hard man of middle age, his grey hair cropped short, his face without expression. He rapped his knuckled fist on the roof of the coach and they pulled forward.

"Major Black, how fortunate," said Chang. The Major ignored him, nodding to the man with the pistol, who handed across

Chang's stick. The Major studied it, pulled it apart a few inches, sniffed disapprovingly and shot the pieces back together. He measured Chang with evident disdain, but did not speak. They rode in silence for several minutes, the hard muzzle of the pistol pressed unwaveringly against his side. Chang wondered what time it was—eight o'clock? Nine? Later? Usually he told time by his stomach, but his meals had lately been so arbitrary and sparse as to disrupt that normal sense. He had to assume that they were taking him to an isolated death. He made a point of yawning.

"That's an interesting badge," he said, nodding to the Major. "The wolf Skoll swallowing the sun—not exactly an uplifting image, a portent of Ragnarok—the final battle where the forces of order are doomed to fail, even the gods themselves. Unless you see yourself allied with chaos and evil, of course. Still, curious for a *regiment*. Almost whimsical—"

At a nod from the Major, the trooper on Chang's left drove his elbow deeply into Chang's kidney. Chang's breath caught in his throat, his entire body tensing with pain. He forced himself to smile, his voice choking with effort.

"And Miss Hastings—did you find her? Went to a shocking amount of trouble, didn't you—only to find out that all of your information about her was wrong. You don't have to tell *me*, I know just how you feel—*like a fool*."

Another savage elbow. Chang could taste the bile in his throat. He'd have to be a little more direct if he wanted to avoid vomiting into his own lap. He forced another smile.

"Aren't you even the slightest bit curious about what I saw just now? Your men heard the shots—don't you want to know who was killed? I would expect it to change all sorts of things—balance of power, all that. Excuse me, may I? Handkerchief?"

The Major nodded, and Chang very slowly reached into his outside pocket. His hand was only just there when the man to his left slapped it away and reached into the pocket himself, pulled out the bloody handkerchief and passed it to Chang. Chang

smiled his thanks and dabbed at his mouth. They had been traveling for some minutes. He had no idea in what direction. It was
most probable that they would take him out to the country or
down to the river, but that only meant they could be anywhere in
between. He looked up. The Major was watching him closely.

"So," continued Chang. "Indeed. A struggle—shots—but the
main point of interest being an *odor*—perhaps you have known
it—strange, overpowering—and a noise, an excruciating buzzing
noise, like a great mechanical hive, with the force of a steam engine. I'm sure you know all this. But what they were doing—what
they had done, to that woman . . ." Chang's voice faltered for a moment, his momentum broken by the image of Angelique writhing
beneath the mass of black hose, the men around her in leather
masks—

"I do not care about the *whore*," said Major Black in a thick
Prussian accent, his voice as cold and hard as an iron spike. Chang
looked up at him—already things had become easier—and
coughed thickly into the handkerchief, wiping his mouth, muttering apologies, and as he spoke he casually stuffed the handkerchief
into the *inside* pocket of his coat.

"So sorry—no, of course not, Major—you are concerned
with the *Prince,* and with the *Minister,* the figures of *industry* and
finance—all pieces in the great puzzle, yes? While, I beg your pardon, I—"

"You are no piece at all," the Major sneered.

"How kind of you to say," answered Chang, as he swept his
hand from his pocket, flicking open the razor and laying it against
the throat of the man with the pistol. In the moment of disorien-
tation caused by the touch of cold steel, Chang closed the fingers
of his other hand around the pistol and wrenched the aim away
from him and toward the Major. The men in the coach froze. "If
you move," Chang hissed, "this man dies, and the two of you must
kill an angry man who holds a weapon that is very, *very* useful in
tight spaces. Let *go* of the pistol."

The man desperately looked to Major Black, who nodded, his face furrowed by rage. Chang took the pistol, aimed it carefully at the Major's face, and pushed himself across the coach. He sat next to Black, placed the razor against his neck and then turned the pistol on the two troopers. No one moved. Chang nodded to the trooper nearest the door. "Open it." The trooper leaned forward and did so, the noise of the coach was abruptly louder, menacing, the dark street whipping past them. It was a paved road. They were still in the city—they must have been aiming for the river. Chang threw the pistol out of the coach and reached over for his stick. He knocked on the roof with the stick, and the coach began to slow. He glared at the two troopers and then turned to the Major. "I will tell you this. I have killed one of you already. I will kill all of you if I must. I do not appreciate your ways. Avoid me."

He launched himself through the door and tumbled into an awkward roll on the hard cobblestones. He pulled himself to his feet, stumbling ahead, and stuffed the razor into his coat. As he feared, the two troopers had leapt from the coach after him, along with one from the driver's seat. They had all drawn their sabers. He turned and ran, the bravado of a moment before vanished like any other hopeful bit of theatre.

Somehow, when he had fallen and rolled, his glasses had stayed on. The side pieces wrapped closely around his ears for that very reason, but he was still amazed that they were there. He was running on a block with gas lamps, so he could see *something*, but he had no idea where in the city he was, and so in that sense was running blind—and at top speed. He did not doubt that if they caught him they would cut him down—both that they would be able to do it, and that whatever plan they'd entertained of taking him away in the coach was quite fully abandoned. He rounded a corner and tripped on a broken stone, just managing to avoid sprawling on his face. Instead he careened full into a metal rail fence, grunted with the impact and drove himself forward, along the block. This was a residential street of row houses without coach traffic. He looked behind and saw the troopers gaining ground. He looked ahead and swore. The coach with Major Black had doubled back and was coming toward him on the street. He searched wildly about him and saw an alley looming to his left. He drove his legs to reach it before the coach, which was heading straight for him, the driver lashing his team for speed. Chang was close enough to see the horses rolling their white eyes when he darted into the dark passage, his foot slipping on the filthy brick, grateful that it was too narrow for the coach, which thundered past. For a moment he wondered about stopping, facing the troopers—perhaps one at a time. It was not narrow—or he yet stupidly desperate—enough for that. He ran on.

The alley separated two large houses, without any doors that he could see, or windows lower than the second story. With a sinking feeling he realized that if he were cut off at the other end, it would turn into another trap. His only immediate consolation came from knowing that the soldiers' boots were even less suited to this than his own, and even more prone to slipping on the slimy broken surface. He cleared the alley at a full run, saw no coach, and paused—his momentum carrying him well out into the street, lungs heaving—to grope for his bearings, for any sign or landmark he knew. He was in a part of the city where decent people *lived*—the last place he would know. Then, ahead of him, as sweetly welcome as a child's answered prayer, he saw that the next road began to slope down. The only downward slope in the city went toward the river, which at least told him where he was on the compass. He pushed himself after it—looking back to see the first trooper clearing the alley—for that almost certainly meant pushing himself into fog.

He raced down the street, careening a bit as the slope began to alter his balance. He could hear the troopers clattering after him, their determination positively Germanic. He wondered if Black and the Doctor were in league and if the soldiers were part of Karl-Horst von Maasmärck's retinue. Ragnarok was a Norse legend of destruction—it would have been adopted as a badge by only the harshest of regiments—and he could not immediately associate that with the intemperate insensible Prince. The Doctor he could understand—someone having personal charge of a Royal made a certain sense—but the Major? What interest of the Prince (or the Prince's father?) was served by killing Chang, or by hunting Isobel Hastings? Yet who else could he serve? How else could he be in a foreign country in such force? The first wisps of fog drifted over his feet as he ran. He inhaled the moist air in gulping lungfuls.

The road turned and Chang followed it. Ahead of him he saw a small plaza with a fountain and like a key turning open a lock he knew where he was—Worthing Circle. To the right was the river itself, to the left the Circus Garden, and straight ahead the merchants' district and beyond it the Ministries. There were people here—Worthing Circle was a place of some nefarious business after nightfall—and he veered to the right, for the river and the thicker fog. It was nearly his death. The coach was there in wait. With a whip crack the horses leapt forth, charging directly at him. Chang threw himself to the side, clawing his way clear. He was cut off from the river, and from the merchants—he scrambled to his knees as the coachman wrestled with the horses, trying to make them turn. Chang reached his feet and heard a shot whistle past his head. Black leaned out of the coach window with a smoking pistol. Chang cut across the plaza just ahead of the three troopers, once more right on his heels, and toward the Circus Garden into the heart of the city.

His legs were on fire—he had no idea how far he'd run, but he had to do something or he was going to die. He saw another alley and barreled into it. Once in he stopped and threw himself against the wall, pulling apart his stick. If he could take the first of them by surprise—but before he'd even finished the thought the first trooper charged around the corner, saw Chang, and raised his saber in defense. Chang slashed at his head with the stick, which the man parried, and then lunged with the dagger—but he was too slow and off target. The blade ripped along the man's front, cutting his uniform, but missing its mark. The trooper seized Chang's dagger arm around the wrist. The other troopers were right behind—a matter of seconds before someone ran him through. With a desperate snarl, Chang kicked at the man's knee and felt a horrible snap as it gave. The man shrieked and fell into the legs of the trooper behind. Chang wrenched his arm clear and stumbled back, his heart sinking as the third man hurtled past his struggling comrades, saber extended. Chang continued to retreat. The trooper lunged at him—Chang beat the weapon aside with the stick and stabbed with the dagger, his reach nowhere near the trooper. The trooper lunged again—again Chang beat it aside— and then followed with a sweeping cut at Chang's head. Chang raised the stick—it was all he could do—and saw it splintered to pieces. He dropped the broken fragment and ran.

As Chang careened away through the alley he told himself that in the loss of his stick he had divested himself of one trooper, but a dagger against a saber was no fight at all. Ahead of him he saw the alley's ending, and a knot of people in silhouette. He screamed at them, an inarticulate howl of menace, which had the desirable effect of making them turn and then scatter—but not quickly enough. Chang cannoned into the rearmost figure—a man who, as Chang actually took in the group of people, must have been in negotiation with one of the fleeing women—and seized the back of his collar. He twisted the man behind him and with a brutal thrust sent him directly into the nearest pursuing trooper. The soldier instinctively did his best not to run the fellow through, raising the saber out of the way and clubbing at him with his other arm, but Chang had turned as well, advancing behind his impromptu shield. The moment the bystander was knocked aside Chang's way was clear and he drove his dagger into the trooper's chest. Without looking back he pulled it free and wheeled, running again. He heard the women's screams behind him. Was the third trooper still coming? Chang glanced over his shoulder. He was. Cursing all military discipline, Chang dodged across the road into another narrow alley—the last thing he wanted to see again was the coach.

He'd lost track of his exact location—nearer to the Circus, at least. This alley was cluttered with boxes and barrels, and as he ran he passed more than one doorway. The third trooper was lagging behind, if still determined. Momentarily out of his sight, Chang dashed up the next block in a low crouch until he found what he wanted, a sunken shop front whose entrance was below the street. Chang vaulted the handrail and went to his knees as he landed at the foot of a small set of stairs, dropping his head and doing his best to stifle his heaving breath. He waited. The street was dark and drifting with fog and generally empty—if he had been seen, it was still possible no one would point him out to the soldier. He was sheathed in sweat—he couldn't remember when he'd run as far, or last been in such an idiotic fix. Why had he thrown away the pistol? If it was going to come to murder, why hadn't he shot them all in the coach? He waited. Unable to bear it further, he inched up the steps and peeked into the road. The trooper stood in the street, his saber out, looking up and down the road. He too was unsteady on his feet—Chang could hear the man's ragged breathing and see it clouding in the cool night air—and clearly unaware which direction Chang had fled, taking a few steps one way, craning his head, and then walking back the other. Chang narrowed his eyes, his desperation simmering down closer to cold fury. He quietly transferred the dagger to his left hand, and fished out the razor with his right, flicking it open. The trooper still had his back to him, and stood perhaps fifteen yards away. If he could get up to the street in silence, he was sure that, at a dead run, he would cover half the distance before the man heard . . . another few yards while he turned . . . the final gap as the man raised his blade. The trooper would have one blow, and if Chang could avoid it, it would be over.

And if he didn't avoid it . . . well, it would be over either way— *"in each instant tenderness, and ash,"* to quote Blaine's *Jocasta*. He paused, balancing the outrage of being hunted like an animal through his own streets by a gang of foreign louts against patience and sanity . . . and then shifted his feet on the stairs, preparing to charge (he *had* promised to kill them). Suddenly he threw himself down into cover. A coach clattered near . . . and then stopped next to the trooper. Chang waited, listening. He heard the harsh interrogation from the Major, in German, then silence, and then a moment later the sweet metallic rush of the trooper sheathing his blade. Chang looked up in time to see the trooper hoisting himself onto the driver's bench, and the coach pulling away into the fog. He looked down at his hands and relaxed his grip on his weapons. His fingers ached. His legs ached, and his head was throbbing behind his eyes. He folded the razor into his pocket and tucked the dagger into his belt. He mopped his face with his bloody handkerchief—already the sweat on his neck and back was turning cold. He remembered dully that he had no place to sleep.

Chang crossed the road and entered the next alley, looking purposefully for the proper point of entry. He was between a pair of large buildings he didn't recognize in the dark, but knew this was a district of hotels and offices and shops. He located a first-story window near enough to a stack of barrels and climbed on top of them. The window was in reach. He wedged the dagger under the sill and twisted it, popping the window up, and then opened it the rest of the way with his hands. He stuck the dagger back into his belt and with an embarrassing amount of effort—his entire body wavering in the air as his arms nearly failed him—pulled himself through. He crawled gracelessly onto the floor of a dark room, and pulled the window closed. He groped around him. It was a supply room—shelves stacked with candles, towels, soaps, linen. He managed to find the door and open it.

As Chang walked down the carpeted hallway, paneled with polished wood and aglow with welcoming, warm gaslight, he found his mind chopping the figures of his day into factions. On one side there was Crabbé and the man in fur, who were responsible for the strange burns, so with them he placed Trapping, Mrs. Marchmoor, and Prince Karl-Horst. On the other was Major Black... perhaps with Karl-Horst's Doctor. Scattered between them were far too many others—Vandaariff, Xonck, Aspiche, Rosamonde... and of course, Isobel Hastings. The list always ended with her, the one person about whom he'd never seemed to learn a thing.

The hallway led him into the hushed silence of a lovely vaulted room, decorated with potted palms and walls of plate mirror, with a wide wooden reception desk and a man in a frogged coat behind it. He had broken into a hotel. Chang nodded briskly at the man and reached into his coat for the wallet. Over the day he'd managed to spend nearly everything Aspiche had given him, and this would take the rest of it. He didn't care. He could sleep, have a bath, a proper shave, a meal, and be fresh for the day to come. Tomorrow he could always fetch the saber in the attic and sell it for cash. This made him smile as he reached the desk, dropping the wallet onto the inlaid marble surface.

The desk clerk smiled. "Good evening, Sir."

"I hope it's not too late."

The clerk's eyes flicked to the wallet. "Of course not, Sir. Welcome to the Hotel Boniface."

"Thank you," answered Chang. "I should like a room."

THREE

Surgeon

Doctor Abelard Svenson stood at an open window overlooking the small courtyard of the Macklenburg diplomatic compound, gazing at the thickening fog and the few sickly gaseous lights of the city bright enough to penetrate its fell curtain. He sucked on a hard ginger candy, clacking it against his teeth, aware that a lengthy brood about his current situation was a luxury he could not indulge. With a shove from his tongue he pushed the candy between his left molars and smashed it to sharp pieces, smashed these pieces again, and then swallowed them. He turned from the window and reached for a porcelain cup of tepid black coffee, gulping it, finding a certain pleasure in the mix of sweet ginger syrup coating his mouth and the bitter beverage. Did they drink coffee with ginger in India, he wondered, or Siam? He finished the cup, set it down and dug for a cigarette. He looked over his shoulder at the bed, and the still figure upon it. He sighed, opened his cigarette case, stuck one of the dark, foul Russian cigarettes in his mouth, and took a match from the bureau near the lamp, striking it off of his thumbnail. He lit the cigarette, inhaled, felt the telltale catch in his lungs, shook out the match, and exhaled longingly. He couldn't put it off anymore. He would have to speak to Flaüss.

He crossed the room to the bolted door, skirting the bed, and—sticking the cigarette into his mouth to free both hands to pull the iron bolt clear—glanced back at the pale young man breathing moistly underneath the woolen blankets. Karl-Horst von Maasmärck was twenty-three, though pervasive indulgence and a weak constitution had added ten years to his appearance. His

honey-colored curls receded from his forehead (the thinness especially visible with the hair so clumped together by sweat), his pallid skin sagged below his eyes and around his family's weak mouth
and sunken jaw, and his teeth were already beginning to go.
Svenson stepped over to the insensible man—overgrown boy,
really—and felt the pulse at his jugular, antic despite the lau-
danum, and once more cursed his own failure. The strange looping pattern seared into the Prince's skin around the eyes and across
his temples—not quite a burn, not exactly even raw, more of a
deep discoloration and with luck temporary—mocked Doctor
Svenson's every previous effort to control his willful charge.

   As he looked down, he resisted the impulse to grind the cigarette into the Prince's skin and chided himself for his own mistaken tactics, his foolish trust, his ill-afforded deference. He'd
focused on the Prince himself and paid far too little attention to
those new figures around him—the woman's family, the diplo-
mats, the soldiers, the high-placed hangers-on—never thinking
he'd be tearing the Prince away from them at pistol-point. He
barely even knew who they were—far less what part in their plans
had been laid aside for the easily dazzled Karl-Horst. All that had
been the business of Flaüss, the Envoy—which had either gone
horribly wrong or . . . hadn't. Svenson needed to report to Flaüss on
the Prince's health, but he knew that he must use the interview
with the Envoy to determine whether he was truly without allies
in the diplomatic compound. He noticed his overcoat slung across
the bedpost and folded it over his arm—heavier than it ought to be
from the pistol tucked into the pocket. He looked around the
room—nothing particularly dangerous should the Prince wake up
in his absence. He pulled the bolt on the door and stepped into the
hall. Next to the door stood a soldier in black, carbine at his side,
stiffly at attention. Doctor Svenson locked the door with a large
iron key and returned the key to his jacket pocket. The soldier's attention did not waver as the Doctor walked past and down the
hallway, nor did the Doctor think twice about the guard. He was

used enough to these soldiers and their iron discipline—any question he had would be aimed at their officer, who was unaccountably still absent from the compound.

Svenson reached the end of the hall and stood on the landing, his gaze edging over the rail to the lobby three floors below. From above he could see the black and white checkerboard pattern of the marble floor—an optical illusion of staircases impossibly leading ever upwards and downwards to one another at the same time—with the crystal chandelier hovering above it. For Svenson, who did not like heights, just seeing the chandelier's heavy chain suspended in the air before him gave him a whiff of vertigo. Looking up to the high top of the stairwell, where the chain was anchored above the fourth floor landing—which he could not help but do, like an ass—made him palpably dizzy. He stepped away from the rail and climbed to the third floor, walking close to the wall, his eyes on the floor. He was still staring at his feet as he walked past the guards at the landing and outside the Envoy's door. With a quick grimace he squared his shoulders and knocked. Without waiting for an answer, he went in.

When Svenson had returned from the Institute with the Prince, Flaüss had not been present—nor could anyone say where he'd gone. The Envoy had burst into the Prince's room some forty minutes later—in the midst of the Doctor's squalid efforts to purge his patient of any poison or narcotic—and imperiously demanded what Doctor Svenson thought he was doing. Before he could reply, Flaüss had seen the revolver on the side table and then the marks on Karl-Horst's face and began screaming. Svenson turned to see the Envoy's face was white—with rage or fear he wasn't sure—but the sight had snapped the last of his patience and he'd savagely driven Flaüss from the room. Now, as he entered the office, he was keenly aware that of Conrad Flaüss he actually knew precious little. A provincial aristocrat with pretensions toward the cosmopolitan, schooled for the law, an acquaintance of a royal uncle at university—all the qualifications required to meet the diplomatic needs of the Prince's betrothal visit, and if a permanent embassy were to result from the marriage, as everyone hoped it would, to take over as the Duchy's first full ambassador. To Flaüss—to everyone—Svenson was a family retainer, a nurse-maid, essentially dismissible. Such perceptions generally suited the Doctor as well, creating that much less bother in his day. Now, however, he would be forced to make himself heard.

Flaüss was behind his desk, writing, an aide standing patiently next to him, and looked up as Svenson entered. The Doctor ignored him and sat in one of the plush chairs opposite the desk, plucking a green glass ashtray from a side table as he went past and cradling it on his lap as he smoked. Flaüss stared at him. Svenson stared back and flicked his eyes toward the aide. Flaüss snorted, scrawled his name at the base of the page, blotted it, and shoved it into the aide's hands. "That will be all," he barked. The aide clicked his heels smartly and left the room, casting a discreet glance at the Doctor. The door closed softly behind him. The two men glared at each other. Svenson saw the Envoy gathering himself to speak, and sighed in advance with fatigue.

"Doctor Svenson, I will tell you that I am not . . . *accustomed* . . . to such treatment, such *brutal* treatment, by a member of the mission staff. As the mission *Envoy*—"

"I am not part of the mission staff," said Svenson, cutting him off in an even tone.

Flaüss sputtered. "I beg your pardon?"

"I am not *part* of the mission staff. I am part of the Prince's household. I answer to that house."

"To the Prince?" Flaüss scoffed. "Between us, Doctor, the poor young man—"

"To the Duke."

"I beg your pardon—*I* am the Duke's Envoy. I answer to the Duke."

"Then we have something in common after all," Svenson muttered dryly.

"Are you *insolent*?" Flaüss hissed.

Svenson didn't answer for a moment, in order to increase what powers of intimidation he could muster. The fact was, whatever authority he claimed, he had no strength beyond his own body to back it up—all that rested with Flaüss and Blach. If either were truly against him—and realized his weakness—he was extremely vulnerable. His only real hope was that they were not outright villains, but merely incompetent. He met the Envoy's gaze and tapped his ash into the glass bowl.

"Do you know, Herr Flaüss, why a young man in the prime of his life would need a doctor to accompany him to celebrate his engagement?"

Flaüss snorted. "Of course I know. The Prince is unreliable and indulgent—I speak as one who cares for him deeply—and often unable to see the larger *diplomatic* implications of his actions. I believe it is a common condition among—"

"Where were you this evening?"

The Envoy's mouth snapped shut, then worked for a moment in silence. He could not believe what he had just heard. He forced a wicked, condescending smile. "I beg your pardon—"

"The Prince was in grave danger. You were not here. You were not in any position to protect him."

"Yes, and you will report to *me* concerning Karl-Horst's *medical* condition—his—his face—the strange *burns*—"

"You have not answered my question . . . but you are going to."

Flaüss gaped at him.

"I am here on the direct instructions of his father," continued Svenson. "If we fail further in our duties—and I do include you in this, Herr Flaüss—we will be held most strictly accountable. I have served the Duke directly for some years, and understand what that means. Do you?"

*   *   *

Doctor Svenson was more or less lying. The Prince's father, the Duke, was an obese feather-headed man fixated on military uniforms and hunting. Doctor Svenson had met him twice at court, observing what he could with a general sense of dismay. His instructions truly came from the Duke's Chief Minister, Baron von Hoern, who had become acquainted with the Doctor five years before, when Svenson was an officer-surgeon of the Macklenburg Navy and known primarily—if he was known at all—for treating the effects of frostbite among sailors of the Baltic fleet. A series of murders in port had caused a scandal—a cousin of Karl-Horst had been responsible—and Svenson had shown both acuity in tracing the deeds to their source and then tact in conveying this information to the Minister. Soon after he had been reassigned to von Hoern's household and asked to observe or investigate various circumstances—diseases, pregnancy, murder, abortion—as they might arise at court, always without any reference to his master's interest. To Svenson, for whom the sea was almost wholly associated with sorrow and exile, the opportunity to devote himself to such work—indeed, to the rigorous distractions of patriotism—had become a welcome sort of self-annihilation. His presence in Karl-Horst's party had been attributed to the Duke easily enough, and Svenson had until this day remained in the background, reporting back as he could through cryptic letters stuffed into the diplomatic mail and from subtly insinuating cards sent through the city post, just in case his official letters were tampered with. He had done this before—brief sojourns in Finland, Denmark, and along the Rhine—but was really no kind of spy, merely an educated man likely, because of his position, both to gain access where he ought not and to be underestimated by those he observed. Such was the case here, and the tennis match of pettiness between Flaüss and Blach had livened what otherwise seemed to be trivial child-minding. What troubled him, however, was that in the three weeks since their arrival—and despite regular dispatches to Flaüss from court—Svenson had received no word whatsoever in return. It was as if Baron von Hoern had disappeared.

The idea of marriage had been considered after a continental tour by Lord Vandaariff, where the search for a sympathetic Baltic port had brought him to Macklenburg. His daughter had been a part of the entourage—her first time abroad—and as is so often the case when elders speak business, the children had been thrown together. Svenson had no illusions that any woman smitten to any degree by Karl-Horst retained her innocence—unless she was blindingly stupid or blindingly ugly—but he still could not understand the match. Lydia Vandaariff was certainly pretty, she was extremely wealthy, her father had just been given a title—though his financial empire spanned well beyond the borders of mere nations. Karl-Horst was but one of many such princelings in search of a larger fortune, growing less attractive by the day and never anyone's idea of a wit. The unlikely nature of it all made actual love a more real possibility, he had to admit—and he had dismissed this part of the affair with a shrug, a foolish mistake, for his attention had been set on preventing Karl-Horst from misbehaving. He now saw that his enemies were elsewhere.

In the first week he had indeed tended to the Prince's excessive drinking, his excessive eating, his gambling, his whoring, intervening on occasion but more generally tending to him once he had returned from each night's pursuit of pleasure. When the Prince's time had gradually become less occupied with the brothel and the gaming table—at dinners with Lydia, diplomatic salons with Flaüss and people from the Foreign Ministry, riding with foreign soldiers, shooting with his future father-in-law—Svenson had allowed himself to pass more time with his reading, with music, with his own small jaunts of tourism, content with looking in on

the Prince when he returned in the evenings. He had suddenly realized his folly at the engagement party—could it be only last
night?—when he'd found the Prince alone in Vandaariff's great
garden, kneeling over the disfigured body of Colonel Trapping. At
first he'd no idea what the Prince was doing—Karl-Horst on his
knees usually meant Svenson digging out a moist cloth to wipe
away the vomit. Instead, the Prince had been staring down, quite
transfixed, his eyes strangely placid, even peaceful. Svenson had
pulled him away and back into the house, despite the idiot's
protests. He'd been able to find Flaüss—now he wondered how
coincidentally nearby the Envoy was—gave the Prince over to his
care and rushed back to the body. He found a crowd around it—
Harald Crabbé, the Comte d'Orkancz, Francis Xonck, others he
didn't know, and finally Robert Vandaariff himself arriving with a
crowd of servants. He noticed Svenson and took him aside, questioning him in a low voice, rapidly, about the safety of the Prince,
and his condition. When Svenson informed him that the Prince
was perfectly well, Vandaariff had sighed with evident relief and
wondered if Svenson might be so kind as to inform his daughter—
she had guessed some awkward event had happened, but not its
exact nature—that the Prince was unscathed and, if it were possible, allow her to see him. Svenson of course obliged the great man,
but found Lydia Vandaariff in the company of Arthur Trapping's
wife, Charlotte Xonck, and the woman's older brother, Henry
Xonck, a man whose wealth and influence were surpassed only
by Vandaariff and—perhaps, Svenson was dubious—the aging
Queen. As Svenson stood stammering out some sort of veiled
explanation—an incident in the garden, the Prince's lack of involvement, no clear explanation—both Xonck siblings began
questioning him, openly competing with each other to expose his
obvious avoidance of some truth. Svenson fell by habit into the
pose of a foreigner who only poorly understood their language,
requiring them to repeat as he fruitlessly strove for some story
that might satisfy their strangely suspicious reaction, but this only

increased their irritation. Henry Xonck had just imperiously stabbed Svenson's chest with his forefinger when a modestly dressed woman standing behind them—whom he had assumed to be a companion of the mutely smiling Lydia—leaned forward to whisper into Charlotte Xonck's ear. At once the heiress looked past Svenson's shoulder, her eyes widening—through her feathered mask—with a sudden glare of dislike. Svenson turned to see the Prince himself, escorted by the smiling Francis Xonck, who ignored his siblings and called gaily for Lydia to rejoin her intended.

The Doctor took this moment to quickly bow to his betters and escape, allowing himself one brief glance at the Prince to gauge his level of intoxication, and another for the woman who had whispered in Charlotte Xonck's ear, who he saw was now studying Francis Xonck rather closely. It was only upon walking from their parlor that Svenson realized that he'd been deftly prevented from examining the body. By the time he returned to the garden, the men and the body were gone. All he saw, from a distance, were three of Major Blach's soldiers, spaced several yards apart, walking across the grounds with their sabers drawn.

He'd been unable to interrogate the Prince further, and neither Flaüss nor Blach would answer his questions. They'd heard nothing of Trapping, and indeed openly doubted that such an important figure—or indeed, anyone—had been dead in the garden at all. When he demanded in turn to know why Blach's soldiers had been searching the grounds, the Major merely snapped that he was responding prudently to Svenson's own exaggerated claims of danger, murder, mystery, and sneered that he would hardly waste time with the Doctor's fears again. For his part, Flaüss had dropped the matter completely, saying that even if anything untoward had occurred, it was hardly their affair—out of respect to the Prince's new father-in-law, they must remain disinterested and apart. Svenson had no answer to either (save a silent growing contempt) but wanted very much to know what the Prince had been doing alone with the body in the first place.

But time alone with Karl-Horst had not been possible. Between the Prince's schedule, as arranged by Flaüss, and the Prince's own wish to remain undisturbed, he had managed to keep clear of Svenson all the next morning, and then to leave the compound with the Envoy and Blach while Svenson was tending to the suppurated tooth of one of Blach's soldiers. When they had not returned by nightfall, he had been forced into the city to find them. . . .

He exhaled and looked up at Flaüss, whose hands were tightened into fists above his desk top. "We have spoken of the vanished Colonel Trapping—" he began. Flaüss snorted, but Svenson ignored him and kept on, "of whom you will believe what you want. What you cannot avoid is that tonight your Prince has been attacked. What I am going to tell you is that I have seen the marks on his face before—on the face of that missing man."

"Indeed? You said yourself you did not examine him—"

"I saw his face."

Flaüss was silent. He picked up his pen, then peevishly threw it down. "Even if what you claim is true—in the garden, in the dark, from a distance . . ."

"Where were you, Herr Flaüss?"

"It is none of your affair."

"You were with Robert Vandaariff."

Flaüss smiled primly. "If I was, I could hardly tell you about it. As you imply, there is a delicacy about the whole affair—the need to preserve the reputation of the Prince, of the engagement, of the principals involved. *Lord* Vandaariff has been kind enough to make time to discuss possible *strategies*—"

"Is he paying you?"

"I will not answer insolence—"

"I will no longer suffer idiocy."

Flaüss opened his mouth to reply but said nothing, affronted into silence. Svenson was worried he'd gone too far. Flaüss dug out a handkerchief and mopped his forehead.

"Doctor Svenson—you are a military man, I do forget it, and your way is to be frank. I will overlook your tone this time, for we must indeed *depend* upon one another to protect our Prince. For all your questions, I confess I am most curious to know how *you* came to find the Prince tonight, and how you came to 'rescue' him—and from whom."

Svenson pulled the monocle from his left eye and held it up to the light. He frowned, brought it near his mouth and breathed on it until the surface fogged. He rubbed the moisture off on his sleeve and replaced it, peering at Flaüss with undisguised dislike.

"I'm afraid I must get back to my patient."

Flaüss snapped to his feet behind the desk. Svenson had not yet moved from the chair.

"I have decided," declared the Envoy, "that from now on the Prince will be accompanied by an armed guard at all times."

"An excellent suggestion. Has Blach agreed to this?"

"He agreed it was an excellent suggestion."

Svenson shook his head. "The Prince will never accept it."

"The Prince will have no choice—nor will you, Doctor. Whatever claim to care for the Prince you may have had before this, your failure to prevent this evening's incident has convinced both myself and Major Blach that *he* will from this point be managing the Prince's needs. Any medical matters will be attended to in the company of Major Blach or his men."

Flaüss swallowed and extended his hand. "I will require that you give me the key to the Prince's room. I know you have locked it. As Envoy, I will have it from you."

Svenson stood carefully, replacing the ashtray on the table, not moving his gaze from Flaüss, and walked to the door. Flaüss stood, his hand still open. Svenson opened the door and walked into the hallway. Behind he heard rushing steps and then Flaüss was beside him, his face red, his jaw working.

"This will not do. I have given an order."

"Where is Major Blach?" asked Svenson.

"Major Blach is under my command," answered Flaüss.

"You consistently refuse to answer my questions."

"That is my privilege!"

"You are quite in error," Svenson said gravely and looked at the Envoy. He saw that instead of any fear or reproach, Flaüss was smirking with ill-concealed triumph.

"You have been distracted, Doctor Svenson. Things have changed. So many, many things have changed."

Svenson turned to Flaüss and shifted his grip on his coat, slinging it from his right arm to his left, which had the effect of moving the pocket with the pistol-butt sticking out of it into the Envoy's view. Flaüss's face whitened and he took a step back, sputtering. "W-when M-Major Blach returns—"

"I will be happy to see him," Svenson said.

He was certain that Baron von Hoern was dead.

He walked back to the landing and turned to the stairs, startled to see Major Blach leaning against the wall, just out of sight from the corridor. Svenson stopped.

"You heard? The Envoy would like to see you."

Major Blach shrugged. "It is of no importance."

"You've been told of the Prince's condition?"

"That is of course serious, yet I require your services elsewhere immediately." Without waiting for an answer he walked down the stairs. Svenson followed, intimidated as always by the Major's haughty manner, but also curious as to what might be more important than the Prince's *crise*.

Blach led him across the courtyard to the mess room in the soldiers' barracks. Three of the large white tables had been cleared,

and on each lay a black-uniformed soldier, with another two soldiers standing at each table's head. The first two soldiers were alive;
the third's upper body was covered by a white cloth. Blach indicated the tables and stepped to the side, saying no more. Svenson
draped his coat over a chair and saw that his medical kit had already been fetched and laid out on a metal tray. He glanced at the
first man, grimacing in pain, his left leg probably broken, and absently prepared an injection of morphine. The other man was in
more serious distress, bleeding from his chest, his breath shallow,
his face like wax. Svenson opened the man's uniform coat and
peeled back the bloody shirt beneath. A narrow puncture through
the ribs—perhaps through the lungs, perhaps not. He turned to
Blach.

"How long ago did this happen?"

"Perhaps an hour...perhaps more."

"He may die from the delay," observed Svenson. He turned to
the soldiers. "Bind him to the table." As they did, he went to the
man with the injured leg, pulled up his sleeve, and gave him the
injection. He spoke softly as he pushed on the syringe. "You will
be fine. We will do our best to straighten your leg—but you must
wait until we work on your fellow. This will make you sleep." The
soldier, a boy really, nodded, his face slick with sweat. Svenson
gave him a quick smile and turned back to Blach, speaking as he
peeled off his jacket and rolled up his shirtsleeves. "It's very simple.
If the blade touched his lungs, they're full of blood by now and
he'll be dead in minutes. If it didn't, he may die in any case—from
the blood loss, from rot. I will do my best. Where will I find you?"

"I will remain here," Major Blach answered.

"Very well."

Svenson glanced over to the third table.

"My Lieutenant," said Major Blach. "He has been dead for
some hours."

*   *   *

Svenson stood in the open doorway, smoking a cigarette and looking out into the courtyard. He wiped his hands with a rag. It had taken two hours. The man was still alive—apparently the lungs had been spared—though there was fever. If he lasted the night he would recover. The other man's knee had been broken. While he had done what he could, it was unlikely the man would walk without a limp. Throughout his work, Major Blach had remained silent. Svenson inhaled the last of the cigarette and tossed the butt into the gravel. The two men had been moved to the barracks— they could at least sleep in their own beds. The Major leaned against a table, near the remaining body. Svenson let the smoke out of his lungs and turned back into the room.

For all the savage nature of the Lieutenant's wounds, it was obvious the death had been quick. Svenson looked up at the Major. "I'm not sure what I can tell you that you cannot see yourself. Four punctures—the first, I would say, here: into the ribs from the victim's left side, a stabbing across . . . it would have been painful, but not a mortal blow. The next three, within an inch of each other, driving under the ribs and into the lungs, perhaps even touching the heart—I cannot say without opening the chest. Heavy blows—you can see the force of impact around the wound, the indentation—a knife or dagger driven to the hilt, repeatedly, to kill."

Blach nodded. Svenson waited for him to speak, but the Major remained silent. Svenson sighed and began to unroll and button his sleeves. "Do you wish to tell me how these injuries occurred?"

"I do not," muttered the Major.

"Very well. Will you at least tell me if it had to do with the attack on the Prince?"

"What attack?"

"Prince Karl-Horst was burned about the face. It is entirely possible he was a willing participant, nevertheless, I consider it an attack."

"This is when you escorted him home?"

"Exactly."

"I assumed he was drunk."

"He was drunk, though not, I believe, from alcohol. But what do you mean, you 'assumed'?"

"You were observed, Doctor."

"Indeed."

"We observe many people."

"But apparently not the Prince."

"Was he not with reputable figures of his new acquaintance?"

"Yes, Major, he was. And—I'll say this again if you did not understand it—in such company, indeed, at the behest of such company, he was scarred about the eyes."

"So you have said, Doctor."

"You may see for yourself."

"I look forward to it."

Svenson gathered his medical kit together. He looked up. Major Blach was still watching him. Svenson dropped his catling into the bag with an exasperated sigh. "How many men do you presently have under your command, Major?"

"Twenty men and two officers."

"Now you have eighteen men and one officer. And I assure you that whoever did this—whatever man or gang of men—had nothing to do with observing me, for my business was entirely occupied with preventing an idiot from disgracing himself."

Major Blach did not answer.

Doctor Svenson snapped his bag shut and scooped his coat from the chair. "I can only hope you observed the Envoy as well, Major—he was quite absent through all of this, and refuses to explain himself." He turned on his heels and strode to the door where he turned and called back, "Will you be telling him about the bodies or shall I?"

"We are not finished, Doctor," hissed Blach. He flipped the sheet back over his Lieutenant's face and walked toward Svenson. "I believe we must visit the Prince."

*   *   *

They walked up the stairs to the third floor, where they found Flaüss waiting with two guards. The Envoy and the Major exchanged meaningful looks, but Svenson had no idea what they meant—the men obviously hated each other, but could nevertheless be cooperating for any number of reasons. Flaüss sneered at Svenson and indicated the door.

"Doctor? I believe you have the key."

"Have you tried knocking?" This was from Blach, and Svenson suppressed a smile.

"Of course I have tried," answered Flaüss, unconvincingly, "but I am happy to try again." He turned and banged savagely on the door with the heel of his fist, after a moment calling sweetly, "Your Highness? Prince Karl-Horst? It is Herr Flaüss, here with the Major and Doctor Svenson."

They waited. Flaüss turned to Svenson and nearly spit, "Open it! I insist you open it at once!"

Svenson smiled affably and dug the key from his pocket. He handed it to Flaüss. "You may do it yourself, Herr Envoy."

Flaüss snatched the key and shoved it into the lock. He turned the key and the handle, but the door would not open. He turned the handle again and shoved the door with his shoulder. He turned back to them. "It will not open—something is against it."

Major Blach stepped forward and jostled Flaüss away, placing his hand over the handle and driving his weight against the door. It gave perhaps half an inch. Blach signaled to the two troopers and together all three pushed as one—the door lurched another inch or so, and then slowly ground open enough for them to see that the large bureau had been moved against the door. The three pushed again and the gap widened so a man could fit through. Blach immediately did so, followed by Flaüss, shoving his way past the troopers. With a resigned smile, Svenson followed them through, dragging his medical kit after him.

The Prince was gone. The bureau had been dragged across the room to block the doorway, and the window was open.

"He's escaped! For a second time!" Flaüss whispered. He wheeled upon Svenson. "You helped him! You had the key!"

"Don't be an idiot," muttered Major Blach. "Look at the room. The bureau is solid mahogany—it took the three of us to shift it. It's impossible that the Prince himself moved it alone and impossible for the Doctor to have helped him—the Doctor would have had to leave the room *before* the bureau was blocking the doorway."

Flaüss was silent. Svenson met the gaze of Blach, who was glaring at him. The Major barked out to the men in the hall, "One of you to the gate—find out if the Prince has left the compound, and if he was alone!"

Svenson stepped to the bureau and opened it up, glancing at the contents. "The Prince is wearing his infantry uniform—I do not see it—dark green, a colonel of grenadiers. He fancies it because the badge is of a flaming bomb. I believe it has a sexual significance for him." They stared at him as if he were speaking French. Svenson stepped to the window and leaned out. Below the window, three stories down, was a raked bed of gravel. "Major Blach, if you'll send a trusted man to examine the gravel below this window—it will tell us whether a ladder was used—there will be heavy indentations. Of course, a three-story ladder should have attracted attention. Tell me, Herr Flaüss, does the compound possess such a ladder?"

"How should I know?"

"By asking the *staff,* I expect."

"And if there is no such ladder?" asked Major Blach.

"Then either one was brought—which should have excited notice at the gate—or some other means were used—a grappling hook. Of course"—he stepped back and examined the plaster around the window frame—"I see no indentations, nor any rope remaining by which they may have climbed down."

"Then how *did* they get down?" asked Flaüss. Svenson stepped back to the window, leaning out. There was no balcony, no wall of ivy, no nearby tree—indeed, the room had been chosen for this very reason. He turned and looked upwards—it was but two stories to the roof.

As they climbed the stairwell word came to Blach from the gate— the Prince had not been seen, nor had anyone passed in either direction in the last three hours, since the arrival of the Major. Svenson barely took in the trooper's report, so much was he dreading the inevitable trip to the building's rooftop. He walked on the inside wall, clutching the rail as casually as possible, his guts positively seething. Ahead of them another trooper was unfolding a staircase from the ceiling of the sixth-floor hallway. Above it was a narrow attic and within the attic a hatchway to the roof. Major Blach strode forward—somewhere a pistol had appeared in his hand—and climbed rapidly, disappearing in the darkness above, followed quickly by Flaüss, more nimble than his stout frame would suggest. Svenson swallowed and climbed deliberately after them, one hand gripping each side of the ladder, choking a heave of nausea as the hinges of the ladder bounced with the shifting weight of each footfall. Feeling like a child, he crawled on his hands and knees onto the rough timbers of the attic floor and looked around him. Flaüss was just pulling himself through the narrow hatchway, his body framed against the sickly glow of the city lights within the fog. With a barely suppressed groan, Doctor Svenson forced himself after them.

When he reached the roof, first on his knees and then, swaying, onto his feet, he saw Major Blach crouching near the edge that must be above the Prince's bedroom. The Major turned back and called, "The moss on the stone is worn away in several places—the rubbing of a rope or a rope ladder!" He stood and crossed to Flaüss and Svenson, looking around them as he did. He pointed to the nearby rooftops. "What I don't understand is that none of these seem close enough. I don't deny the Prince was pulled to the rooftop—but this building rises at least a story above any neighbor. Beyond this, it is a full street's width in distance in every direction. Unless they employed a circus, I do not see how anyone might have traversed from this rooftop to escape."

"Perhaps they didn't," suggested the Envoy. "Perhaps they merely re-entered the building from above."

"Impossible. The stair to the attic is bolted from inside."

"Unless someone helped them," offered the Envoy, slightly peevishly, "from inside."

"Indeed," admitted Blach. "In which case, they have still not passed through the gate. My men will search the entire compound at once. Doctor?"

"Mmn?"

"Any *thoughts*?"

Svenson swallowed, and inhaled the cool night air through his nose, trying to relax. He forced his gaze away from the sky and the open spaces around him, down to the black tarred surface of the roof. "Only...what is that?" he asked.

Flaüss followed his pointing finger and stepped to a small white object. He picked it up and brought his find over to the others.

"That is the butt of a cigarette," said Major Blach.

Thirty minutes had passed. They had returned to the Prince's room, where the Major was systematically rooting through each drawer and closet. Flaüss sat in the armchair, brooding, while Svenson stood near the open window, smoking. A complete search of the compound had produced nothing, nor were there any footprints or indentations to be seen in the gravel below the window. Blach had gone back to the rooftop with lanterns, but had found no footprints other than their own—though there were several marks on the side of the building, near where the ropes had worn into the slippery grime along the gutters.

"Perhaps he has merely escaped for an evening of pleasure," offered the Envoy. He looked darkly at Svenson. "Because of your hounding him earlier—he does not trust us—"

"Do not be a fool," snapped Major Blach. "This was planned, with or without the Prince's help—most likely without, if he was insensible as the Doctor describes. At least two men entered the room from above, possibly more—the guard did not hear the bureau being moved, which makes it more likely to be four men—and took the Prince with them. We must assume he has been taken, and must decide how to recover him."

Major Blach slammed the last drawer closed and turned his gaze to Svenson.

"Yes?" the Doctor asked.

"You found him earlier."

"I did."

"So, you will tell me where and how."

"I applaud your eventual concern," replied Svenson, his voice tight with disdain. "Do you think it is the same collection of people? Because if so you know who they are—you both know. Will you challenge them? Will you go to Robert Vandaariff in force? To Deputy Minister Crabbé? To the Comte d'Orkancz? To the Xonck ironworks? Or does one of you already know where he is—so we may end this ridiculous charade?"

Svenson was gratified to see that at this both he and the Major were looking at Flaüss.

"I do not know anything!" the Envoy cried. "If we must ask for the help of these august people you name—if they are *able* to help us—" Doctor Svenson scoffed. Flaüss turned to Major Blach for aid. "The Doctor still has not told us how he located the Prince before. Perhaps he can find him again."

"There is no mystery to it," lied Svenson. "I sought out the brothel. Someone in the brothel was able to assist me. The Prince was right around the corner. Apparently Henry Xonck's generous donations to the Institute provide a certain level of access for his younger brother's friends."

"How did you know the brothel?" asked Flaüss.

"Because I know the Prince at least that well—that is not the point! I have told you who he was with. If anyone knows what has happened, it will be they. I cannot confront these figures. It must be you—Herr Flaüss supported by the Major's men—that is the only way."

Svenson ground his cigarette into the china cup that had held his coffee so long ago. "This gets us nowhere," he told them. He picked up his coat and strode from the room.

With no other thought than that he had not eaten in hours, Svenson walked down the stairs to the great kitchen, which was unoccupied. He dug through the cupboards to find a hard cheese, dry sausage, and a loaf of that morning's bread. He poured himself a glass of pale yellow wine and sat alone at the large work table to think, methodically slicing off a hunk of cheese, a matching thickness of sausage, and piling them onto a piece of bread. After the first bite, realizing the bread was too dry, he got up and found a pot of mustard. He opened it and spooned more than he would normally favor onto the bread and re-stacked the sausage and cheese. He swallowed, and took a sip of wine. A routine established, he ate—the sounds of activity brewing about him in the compound—and tried to decide what to do. The Prince had been taken once, rescued, then taken again—it only followed it was by the same people, for the same reasons. Yet in the front of the Doctor's mind was the cigarette butt.

Flaüss had given it to him and, after the barest glance, he had handed it back and turned to climb off of the roof with what dignity he could muster—but the glance confirmed the idea that had already formed in his mind. The tip of the butt was crimped in a specific way he'd seen the night before—by a woman's lacquered cigarette holder—at the St. Royale Hotel. The woman—he took another sip of wine, slipped the monocle from his eye into his breast pocket and rubbed his face—was shockingly, derangingly lovely. She was also dangerous—obviously so—but in such a complete way as to almost be beside notice, as if one were discussing a particular cobra—a description that might include length or color or markings, but never the possession of deadly venom, which was an *a priori* feature that one could not, he found, take exception to . . . on the contrary. He sighed and pushed his tired mind to focus, to connect that woman at the hotel to her possible presence on the rooftop. He could not make sense of it, but knew that doing so would lead him to the Prince, and began to meticulously recomb his memory.

Much earlier in the day, when he had realized the Prince had not returned, and then that Flaüss and Blach were gone as well, Svenson had let himself into the Prince's room and searched it for any possible clue to the Prince's plans for the evening. In general Karl-Horst was about as cunning as a fairly clever cat or small child. If things were hidden, they were hidden under the mattress or in a shoe, but more likely to be simply tucked into the pocket of the coat he had been wearing and forgotten. Svenson had found embossed books of matches, theatre programs, calling cards, but nothing of any particular, striking nature. He sat on the bed and lit a cigarette, looking around the room, for the moment out of ideas. On the side table next to the bed was a blue glass vase with perhaps ten white lilies stuffed inside, drooping with various degrees of health over the rim. Svenson stared at it. He'd never seen flowers in the Prince's room before, nor were any similar touches of feminine decoration present in the diplomatic compound. He was unaware of any woman's presence in the compound at all, now that he thought of it, nor had Karl-Horst ever shown a preference for flowers or, for that matter, beauty. Perhaps they were a gift from Lydia Vandaariff. Perhaps some shred of affection had actually penetrated Karl-Horst's pageant of appetite.

Svenson frowned and scooted closer to the side table, peering at the vase. He wiped his monocle and looked closer—the glass was somewhat artistic, with a slightly irregular surface and occasional deliberate flaws, whorls, or bubbles. He frowned again—was there something *in* it? He snatched a towel from the Prince's shaving table and laid it on the bed, and then gathered the lilies with both hands and placed them dripping on the towel. He picked up the vase and held it to the light. There *was* something in it, another piece of glass perhaps, deflecting the light passing through, though it itself seemed invisible. Svenson put the vase down and pushed up his sleeve. He reached in, groped for a moment—the thing was quite slippery—and extracted a small rectangle of blue glass, approximately the size of a calling card. He wiped it and his hand on the towel and studied it. Within seconds, as if he had been struck with a hammer, Svenson was on his knees—shaking his head, dizzy, having nearly dropped the glass card in surprise.

He looked again.

It was like entering someone else's dream. After a moment the blue cast of the glass vanished as if he had pierced a veil . . . he was staring into a room—a dark, comfortable room with a great red sofa and hanging chandeliers and luxurious carpets—and then, which was why he had nearly dropped it the first time—the image *moved,* as if he was walking, or standing and turning his gaze about the salon—and he saw *people,* people who were looking right at him. He could hear nothing save the sound of his own breath, but his mind had otherwise fully entered the space of these images—*moving* images—like photographs but not like them also, at once more vivid and less sharp, more fully dimensional and incomprehensibly infused with *sensation,* with the feel of a silken dress, petticoats bunched up around a woman's legs, her satin flesh beneath the petticoats and then of a man stepping between her legs, sensing her smile somehow as his body fumblingly found its position. Her head leaned back over the top of the sofa—for he saw the ceiling and felt her hair hanging around her face and throat—a face that was masked, he realized—and then the sensation in her loins—luscious, exquisite—as, quite clearly—from the liquid sensations shuddering through Svenson's own body—the man was penetrating her. Then the image turned slightly, as the woman's head turned, and just visible against the wall behind her was part of a large wall mirror. For a sharp second, Svenson saw the reflection of the man's face and the back of the room beyond him. The man, perfectly plainly, was Karl-Horst von Maasmärck.

The woman was not Lydia Vandaariff, but someone with brown hair. In the glimpse of the room beyond the Prince, Svenson had been shocked to see other people—spectators?—and something else beyond them—an open door? a window?—but he let it be and with more effort than he expected wrenched his gaze from the card. What was he looking at? He looked down at himself with a spasm of shame—he had become quite aroused. What's more—he forced his mind to think clearly—he had been aware of moments within the interaction that he had not actually seen... the woman touching herself, both for pleasure and to gauge her lubrication, Karl-Horst fumbling with his trousers, and the moment of penetration itself... all of these, he realized, came from the point of view, the *experiential* point of view, of the woman—though the moments themselves had not been seen at all. With a breath of preparation he fixed his eyes again on the glass card, sinking into it as if he was entering a deep pool: first the bare sofa, then the woman pulling up her dress, then the Prince stepping between her legs, the coupling itself, the woman turning her head, the mirror, the reflection, and then, a moment later, the view was again the bare sofa—and then the entire scene was repeated... and then repeated again.

*   *   *

Svenson put down the card. His breath was rapid. What was he holding? It was as if the essence of this woman's feeling had been captured and somehow infused into this tiny window. And who was the woman? Who were the spectators? When had this happened? And who had instructed the Prince on where and how to hide it? He watched it again and found that he was able, with intense concentration, to slow the progress of movement, to dwell in a particular instant, with almost unbearably delicious results. With a firm resolve he pushed himself on to the moment with the mirror, studying the reflection closely. He was able to discern that the figures—perhaps ten men and women—were also masked, but he recognized none of them. He nudged himself onward and saw, in the last instants, an open doorway—someone must have been leaving the room—and through it a window, perhaps distant, with something written on it, in reverse, the letters *E-L-A*. At first, this made him think he was looking out from a tavern—the word "ale" being an advertisement—but the more he thought of the luxury of the room, and the elegance of the party, and the distance between the door and the lettered window the less a tavern or even restaurant seemed likely.

His thinking stalled for a moment and then he suddenly had it. A *hotel*. The St. Royale.

Within five minutes Svenson was in a coach, wheeling toward what was perhaps the most esteemed hotel in the city, in the heart of the Circus Garden, the card and his revolver in separate pockets of his coat. He was no creature of luxury or privilege—he could only adopt the haughty manner of those he knew from the Macklenburg court and hope he found people able to help, either through natural sympathy or by intimidation. His initial intention was merely to locate the Prince and assure himself of the fool's safety. Beyond this, if he could gain any insight into the origin and construction of the glass card, he would be very interested, for it confirmed how yet again Karl-Horst was mixing with figures whose ambitions he did not comprehend. While Svenson had an immediate carnal appreciation for the lurid possibilities of such an invention, he knew the true import was more far-reaching, well beyond his own too deliberate imagination.

He entered the St. Royale's bright lobby and casually glanced at the front windows, locating the letters he had seen reflected. They were to his left, and as he walked toward them he attempted to place the doorway through which the window had been seen. He could not. The wall where it ought to have been was flush and apparently seamless. He crossed to it, leaned against the wall, and took his time digging out a cigarette and lighting it, looking closely but to no avail. Hanging on the wall near him was a large mirror in a heavy gold frame. He stood in front of it, seeing his own frustration. The mirror itself was large, but it did not reach closer than three feet to the floor—it could hardly conceal an entrance. Svenson sighed and looked around him in the lobby— guests walked in and out or sat on the various leather banquettes. Not knowing what else to do, he crossed toward the main desk. As he passed the large stairwell to the upper stories he stepped out of his way to allow two women to more easily descend, nodding to them politely. As he did so his mind suddenly reeled with the fragrance of sandalwood. He looked up in shock, taking in one woman's light brown hair, the delicate nape of her neck as she passed. It was the woman from the glass card—he was sure of it— so strong was the resonance of her perfume, despite the fact that Svenson knew he had never smelled it before, and certainly did not smell it within the card. Nevertheless, the precise interaction of that perfume and this woman's body was something he was as intimately familiar with—he could not say how—as the woman must be herself.

The two women had continued toward the hotel's restaurant.

Doctor Svenson darted after them, catching up just before they reached the entrance, and cleared his throat. They turned. He was taken aback to see the woman with brown hair's face was disfigured by a thin looping burn that wrapped around both of her eyes and onto each temple. She wore an elegant dress of pale blue, her skin was quite fair and otherwise unblemished, her lips were painted red. Her companion was shorter than she, hair a darker brown, face a trifle more round; in her own way equally appealing, yet bearing the same distressing scars. She wore a striped dress of imperial yellow and pale green, with a high lace collar. Under the full beam of their attention, Svenson abruptly began to grope for his words. He had never been married, he had never lived around women at all—it was a sad fact that Doctor Svenson was more comfortable at the side of a corpse than a living female.

"I beg your pardon, ladies—if I might intrude upon a moment of your time?"

They stared at him without speaking. He plunged on. "My name is Abelard Svenson—I am hoping you may assist me. I am a doctor. I am presently searching for a person under my care—a very important person, about whom, you will understand, all inquiries must be discreet."

They persisted in staring. The woman from the card smiled slightly, a brief flicker of interest at the corner of her mouth. Her gaze dropped to his greatcoat, the epaulettes and high collar.

"Are you a soldier?" she asked.

"I am a doctor, as I say, though I am an officer in the Macklenburg Navy—Captain-Surgeon Svenson, if you insist—detailed to special duties for"—his voice lowered—"*diplomatic* reasons."

"Macklenburg?" asked the other woman.

"Indeed. It is a German principality on the Baltic coast."

"You do have an accent," she said, and then giggled. "Is there not such a thing as Macklenburg Pudding?"

"Is there?" asked the Doctor.

"Of course there is," the first woman said. "It has raisins, and cream, and a particular blend of spice—aniseed and cloves—"

"And ground-up hazelnuts," said the other. "Sprinkled on the top."

The Doctor nodded at them, at a loss. "I'm afraid I do not know it."

"I should not worry," said the first woman, indulgently patting his arm. "Doesn't your eye get tired?"

They were looking at his monocle. He smiled quickly and adjusted it. "I suppose it must," he said. "I am so used to the thing, I no longer notice." They were still smiling, though Lord knows he had not been witty or charming—for some reason they had decided to accept him—he did his best to seize the opportunity. He nodded to the restaurant. "I presume you were about to dine. If I might share a glass of wine with you, it would be more than enough time to aid me on my quest."

"A *quest*?" said the woman from the card. "How diverting. I am Mrs. Marchmoor, my companion is Miss Poole."

Svenson offered an arm to each of the ladies and stepped between them—despite himself enjoying the feelings of physical contact, shifting his step slightly so the pistol in his pocket did not grind against Miss Poole. "I am most grateful for your kindness," he said, and led them forward.

Once inside, however, the women guided *him* past several available tables to the far side of the restaurant, where a line of discreet doors concealed private dining rooms. A waiter opened a door for them, the women disengaging themselves from Svenson's arms and entering one after the other. Svenson nodded to the waiter and followed. As the door clicked shut behind him he realized that the room was already occupied. At the far end of a table elegantly laid with linen, china, silver, crystal, and flowers sat—or more accurately presided—a tall woman with black hair and piercing violet

eyes. She wore a small black jacket over a red silk dress, subtly embroidered in yellow thread with Chinese scenes. She looked up at
Svenson with a smile he recognized as neutrally polite but which
nevertheless caused his breath to catch. He met her gaze and nodded respectfully. She took a sip of wine, still gazing at him. The
two others had moved to either side of the table to sit adjacent to
the woman in red. Svenson stood awkwardly at his end—the table
was large enough for at least three people on each side—until Mrs.
Marchmoor leaned forward to whisper into the woman in red's
ear. The woman nodded and smiled at him more broadly. Svenson
felt himself blushing.

"Doctor Svenson, please sit, and avail yourself of a glass of
wine. It is very good, I find. I am Madame Lacquer-Sforza. Mrs.
Marchmoor tells me you are on a *quest*."

Miss Poole passed a bottle of wine on a silver dish to Svenson.
He took the bottle and poured for himself and the other ladies.

"I am very sorry to intrude—as I was about to explain to these
two ladies—"

"It is very strange," wondered Madame Lacquer-Sforza, "that
you should choose to ask them. Was there a reason? Are you *acquainted*?"

The ladies giggled at the thought. Svenson was quick to speak.
"Of course not—you will understand that in asking them for help
I am revealing the desperate nature of my search. In brief—as I have
said—I am in the diplomatic service of the Duchy of Macklenburg,
specifically to my Duke's son and heir, Prince Karl-Horst von
Maasmärck. He is known to have patronized this hotel. I am looking for him. It is perhaps foolish, but if any of you ladies—for I
know the Prince has a great appreciation for such beauty—had perhaps seen him, or heard of his passage, and could direct me toward
his present location, I should be very much obliged."

They smiled at him, sipping their wine. His face was flushed,
he felt hot, and took a drink himself, gulping too much at once

and coughing. He wiped his mouth with a napkin and cleared his throat, feeling like a twelve-year-old.

"Doctor, please, sit down." He'd no idea he was still standing. Madame Lacquer-Sforza smiled at him as he did, stopping halfway to stand again and remove his coat, laying it over the chair to his right. He raised his glass again. "Thank you once more for your kindness. I have no wish to intrude any more than necessary into your evening—"

"Tell me, Doctor," asked Mrs. Marchmoor, "is it often that you lose the Prince? Or is he such a man who needs . . . *minding*? And is such an office fitting for an officer and a surgeon?"

The women chuckled. Svenson waved his hand, drinking more wine to steady himself—his palms were slick, his collar hot against his neck. "No, no, it is an extraordinary circumstance, we have received a particular communication from the Duke himself, and at this moment neither the Mission Envoy nor our military attaché happens to be present—nor, of course, is the Prince. With no other knowledge of his agenda, I have taken it upon myself to search—as the message requires swift reply." He wanted urgently to mop his face but did not. "May I ask if you know of the Prince? He has spoken often of dining at the St. Royale, so you may have seen him—or you may have become acquainted with him yourselves; indeed, he is—if I may be so bold—a man for—excuse me—lovely women."

He took another drink. They did not answer. Miss Poole had leaned over and was whispering into Madame Lacquer-Sforza's ear. She nodded. Miss Poole sat back and took another sip of wine. Mrs. Marchmoor was watching him. He could not help it—as he looked into her eyes he felt a flicker of pleasure, recalling—from his own memory!—the inside of her thighs. He swallowed and cleared his throat. "Mrs. Marchmoor, do *you* know the Prince?"

*   *   *

Before she could answer, the door behind them opened and two men entered. Svenson shot to his feet, turning to face them, though neither spared him a glance. The first was a tall, lean man with a high forehead and close-cropped hair in a red uniform with yellow facing and black boots, the rank of a colonel marked by his epaulettes sewn into his collar. He had handed the waiter his coat and brass helmet and crossed directly to Madame Lacquer-Sforza, taking her hand and bending over to kiss it. He nodded to each of the other women and took a seat next to Mrs. Marchmoor, who was already pouring him a glass of wine. The second man walked to the other side of the table, past Svenson, to sit next to Miss Poole. He took Madame Lacquer-Sforza's hand after the Colonel, but with less self-importance, and sat. He poured his own glass and took a healthy swig without ceremony. His hair was pale but streaked with grey, long and greasy, combed back behind his ears. His coat was fine enough but unkempt—in fact the man's whole appearance gave the impression of a once-cherished article—a sofa, for example—that had been left in the rain and partially ruined. Svenson had seen men like him at his university, and wondered if this man was some kind of scholar, and if so what he was possibly doing among this party.

Madame Lacquer-Sforza spoke. "Colonel Aspiche and Doctor Lorenz, I am pleased to introduce you to Doctor Svenson, from the Duchy of Macklenburg, part of Prince Karl-Horst von Maasmärck's diplomatic party. Doctor Svenson, Colonel Aspiche is the new commander of the 4th regiment of Dragoons, recently made the Prince's Own—it is quite a promotion—and Doctor Lorenz is an august member of the Royal Institute of Science and Exploration."

Svenson nodded to them both and raised his glass. Lorenz took it as another opportunity to drink deeply, finishing his glass and pouring another. Aspiche fixed Svenson with a particularly searching eye. Svenson knew he was looking at Trapping's replacement—he had recognized the uniform at once—and knew the man must feel self-conscious for the circumstances of his promotion—if not, considering the missing body, for other more telling reasons as well. Svenson decided to probe the wound.

"I have had the honor of meeting Colonel Aspiche's unfortunate predecessor, Colonel Trapping, in the company of my Prince—on the very evening the Colonel seems to have vanished. I do hope for the sake of his family—if not a grateful nation as well—that the mystery of his disappearance will soon be solved."

"We are all quite grieved by the loss," muttered Aspiche.

"It must be difficult assuming command in such circumstances."

Aspiche glared at him. "A soldier does what is necessary."

"Doctor Lorenz," interrupted Madame Lacquer-Sforza easily, "I believe you have visited Macklenburg."

"I have," he answered—his voice was sullen and proud, like a once-whipped dog caught between rebellion and fear of another lashing. "It was winter. Cold and dark is all I can say for it."

"What brought you there?" asked Svenson, politely.

"I'm sure I don't remember," answered Lorenz, speaking into his glass.

"They have excellent puddings," giggled Miss Poole, her laugh echoed across the table by Mrs. Marchmoor. Svenson took the moment to study that woman's face. What had seemed at first to be burns struck him now as something else—the skin was not taut like a scar, but instead strangely discolored, as if eaten by a delicate acid perhaps, or scorched by a particularly harsh sunburn, or even a kind of impermanent tattoo—something with diluted henna? But it could not have been intentional—it was quite disfiguring—and he immediately pulled his eyes away, not wishing to stare. He met the gaze of Madame Lacquer-Sforza, who had been watching him.

"Doctor Svenson," she called. "Are you a man who likes games?"

"That would depend entirely on the game, Madame. I am not one for gambling, if that is what you mean."

"Perhaps it is. What of you others—Colonel Aspiche?"

Aspiche looked up, he had not been listening. With shock, Svenson realized that Mrs. Marchmoor's right hand was not visible, but that the angle of her arm placed it squarely in the Colonel's lap. Aspiche cleared his throat and frowned with concentration. Mrs. Marchmoor—and for that matter, Madame Lacquer-Sforza—watched him with a blithely innocent interest.

"Gambling is part of a man's true blood," he announced. "Or at least a soldier's. Nothing can be gained without the willingness to lose—all or part. Even in the greatest victory lives will be spent. At a certain level of *practice,* refusal to gamble becomes one with cowardice." He took a sip of wine, shifted in his seat—pointedly not looking at Mrs. Marchmoor, whose hand had not returned above the table top—and turned to Svenson. "I do not cast aspersions on you, Doctor, for your point of emphasis must be the saving of life—on *preservation.*"

Madame Lacquer-Sforza nodded gravely and turned to the other man. "Doctor Lorenz?"

Lorenz was attempting to see through the table top, staring at the point above Aspiche's lap, as if by concentration he might remove the barrier. Without averting his gaze the savant took another drink—Svenson was impressed by the man's self-absorption—and muttered, "In truth, games are an illusion, for there are only percentages of chance, quite predictable if one has the patience, the mathematics. Indeed there may be risk, for possibility allows for different results, but the probabilities are easily known, and over time the intelligent game player will accrue winnings exactly to the degree that he—or indeed, she"—and here he cast a glance at Madame Lacquer-Sforza—"acts in conjunction with rational knowledge."

He took another drink. As he did, Miss Poole blew into his ear. Doctor Lorenz choked with surprise and spat wine across the table top. The others burst into laughter. Miss Poole picked up a napkin and wiped Lorenz's blushing face. Madame Lacquer-Sforza poured more wine into his glass. Svenson saw that Colonel Aspiche's left hand was no longer visible, and then noted Mrs. Marchmoor shifting slightly in her seat. Svenson swallowed—what was he doing here? Again he met the eyes of Madame Lacquer-Sforza, watching him take in the table with a smile.

"And you, Madame?" he said. "We have not heard your opinion. I assume you raised the topic for a reason."

"Such a German, Doctor—so direct and 'to zee business.'" She took a sip of wine and smiled. "For my part, it is very simple. I never gamble with anything I care for, but will gamble to fierce extremes with everything that I don't. Of course, I am fortunate in that I care for very little, and thus the by far greater part of the world becomes for me infused with a sense of . . . for lack of a better word, *play*. But *serious* play, I do assure you."

Her gaze was fixed on Svenson, her expression placid, amused. He did not understand what was happening in the room. To his left, Colonel Aspiche and Mrs. Marchmoor were openly groping each other beneath the table. To his right, Miss Poole was licking Doctor Lorenz's ear, the Doctor breathing heavily and sucking on his lower lip, both hands clutching his wineglass so hard it threatened to crack. Svenson looked back at Madame Lacquer-Sforza. She was ignoring the others. He realized that they had already been dealt with—they had been dealt with before they'd even arrived. Her attention was on him. He had been allowed to enter for a reason.

"You know me, Madame . . . as you know my Prince."

"Perhaps I do."

"Do you know where he is?"

"I know where he might be."

"Will you tell me?"

"Perhaps. Do you care for him?"

"Such is my duty."

She smiled. "Doctor, I'm afraid I require you to be honest."

Svenson swallowed. Aspiche had his eyes shut, breathing heavily. Miss Poole had two of her fingers in Lorenz's mouth.

"He's an embarrassment," he said rapidly. "I would pay money to thrash him raw."

Madame Lacquer-Sforza beamed. "Much better."

"Madame, I do not know what your intent is—"

"I merely propose an exchange. I am looking for someone—so are you."

"I must find my Prince at once."

"Yes, and if—afterwards—you are in a position to help me, I will take it very kindly."

Svenson's mind rebelled against the entire situation—the others seemed nearly insensible—but could find no immediate reason to refuse. He searched her open violet eyes, found them perfectly impenetrable, and swallowed.

"Who is it you wish to find?"

The air in the Institute laboratory had been pungent with ozone, burning rubber, and a particular odor Svenson did not recognize—a cross between sulfur, sodium, and the iron smell of scorched blood. The Prince had been slumped in a large chair, Crabbé to one side of him, Francis Xonck to the other. Across the room stood the Comte d'Orkancz, wearing a leather apron and leather gauntlets that covered his arms to the elbow, a half-open metal door beyond him—had they just carried Karl-Horst from there? Svenson had brandished the pistol and removed the Prince, who was conscious enough to stand and stumble, but apparently unable to talk or—to Svenson's good fortune—protest. At the base of the stairs he had seen the strange figure in red, who had motioned him on his way. This man had seemed to be intruding as much as Svenson—he had been armed—but there had been no time to spare. The guards had followed to the courtyard, even to the street where he'd been lucky enough to find a coach. It was only back at the compound, in the bright gaslight of the Prince's room—away from the dim corridors and the dark coach—that he'd seen the circular burns. At the time he'd been too occupied with determining the Prince's condition, then with Flaüss's interruption, to work through the connections between the private room at the St. Royale and the Institute laboratory—much less to Trapping's disappearance at the Vandaariff mansion. Now, sitting at the kitchen table, hearing around him the preparations for an expedition into the city, he knew it could no longer wait.

He had said nothing more to Blach or Flaüss—he didn't trust them, and was only happy they were leaving together, as they didn't trust each other either. Obviously Madame Lacquer-Sforza was connected to Mrs. Marchmoor, who had undergone the same process of scarring as the Prince. Then why had Svenson been allowed to break up the procedure? And if Madame Lacquer-Sforza was not in league with the men at the Institute, then what of the blue glass card—depicting a scene clearly taking place at the St. Royale, which must tie her to the plot. Svenson rubbed his eyes, forcing himself back to the immediate point. Which of these two—Crabbé's cabal or Madame Lacquer-Sforza—had the reason or the means to extract the Prince immaculately from the compound rooftop?

He finished the wine in a swallow and pushed his chair from the table. Above him the compound seemed quiet. Without thinking he returned the food to its locker and placed the glass and knife on the counter to be cleaned. He took out another cigarette, lit it with a kitchen match, and threw the match into the stove. Svenson inhaled, then frowned as he picked a bit of tobacco off his tongue. The name she had given him, Isobel Hastings, was unknown to him. He knew nothing of the habits of this city's whores—aside from those met in the process of fetching the incapacitated

Prince—but he didn't think that mattered. If she was choosing to enlist a man like him it must be in addition to others searching who knew the city and its people. This also meant these searchers had failed, and her information was wrong. He pushed the matter aside—it was hardly something she could expect him to waste time on at the moment—no matter what he had bargained.

Svenson walked up into the courtyard, slipping on his coat as he walked, transferring his medical bag from hand to hand as he inserted his arms. He stood in the open air and buttoned it with one hand, looking up. The compound was quiet. They had left without a word to him. He knew he must search on his own, but could not decide where to go. The Prince would not be at the St. Royale—if only because Svenson had openly searched there the night before—nor would he be at the Institute for the same reason. He shook his head, knowing that equally the St. Royale or the Institute might indeed be the perfect place to hide him—both were enormous—precisely *because* they had been searched. Further, if the cabal had taken him, the Prince could be anywhere—between them Crabbé and Xonck must have hundreds of places a man could be housed unseen. Svenson could not search for the Prince himself and hope to find him. He must find one of these people and force them to speak.

He walked to the gate, nodded to the guard and stood in the street, waiting to flag an empty coach, running the options through his mind. He rejected Vandaariff—Blach and Flaüss were already seeing him—as he rejected Madame Lacquer-Sforza. He frankly could not trust himself to confront her with the violence he worried would be necessary. This left Crabbé, Xonck, and the Comte d'Orkancz. He dismissed others on the periphery—the other women, Aspiche, Lorenz, Crabbé's aide. Any attempt with these would take more time, and he had no idea where to find them. The Prince, however, had dined at the homes of Crabbé, the Comte, and Xonck, and Svenson had scrupulously memorized his calendar and thus their addresses. The Doctor sighed and fastened his topmost button around the collar. It was well after midnight, cold, and the road was empty. If he had to walk it would be to the nearest of the three: Harald Crabbé's house at Hadrian Square.

It took him half an hour, walking quickly to keep warm. The fog was thick, the surface of the city cold and moist, but Svenson found it comforting, for this was the weather of his home. When he reached Hadrian Square the house was dark. Svenson climbed the steps and rapped on the door knocker, number 14. He stuck his right hand into his coat pocket, closing his fingers around the revolver. No one answered. He knocked again. Nothing. He walked back to the street and then around the nearest corner. There was an alley providing service access to the square's back entrances, fronted by a barred, locked gate. The lock was undone. Svenson stepped through and crept down the narrow lane.

Crabbé's house was the middle of three. The fog forced Svenson to walk slowly and approach ridiculously close to the buildings before he could tell where one stopped and the other started, much less locate the rear door. There were no lights. Gazing up at the windows, Svenson nearly tripped over an abandoned wheelbarrow, biting back a cry of surprise. He rubbed his knee. Beyond the wheelbarrow was a set of stone steps leading down to a cellar, or perhaps to a kitchen. He looked up—it ought to be Crabbé's house. He gripped the revolver in his pocket and crept down to the door, which was ajar. He silently pulled out the gun and lowered himself to a crouch. He swallowed, and pushed the door open. No one shot him, which he considered a good start to a new career of house-breaking.

The room beyond was dark and silent. Svenson crept in, leaving the door open. He replaced the pistol in his pocket and reached into another for matches. He struck one off his thumb—the flaring match head extremely loud in the quiet night—and quickly looked around him. He stood in a storage room. On the walls were jars and boxes and tins and bales, around his feet were crates, casks, barrels—on the far side of the room was another set of stairs. Svenson blew out the match, dropped it, and padded toward them. He once more removed the revolver from his coat, and climbed the stairs, one painful step at a time. They did not creak. At the top of the stairs was another door, wide open. As his head rose on the steps he looked through it, but saw nothing—the match had destroyed his night vision. He listened, and took a moment to assess what he was doing—how foolish and perilous it seemed. If he could have thought of another path, he would have taken it. As it was, he dearly hoped he would not be forced to shoot any heroic servants, or cause Mrs. Crabbé—was there a Mrs. Crabbé?—to scream. He stepped from the staircase into a hallway, walking forward slowly, debating whether or not to risk another match. He sighed and once more stuffed away the pistol—the last thing he wanted to do was blunder into some porcelain lamp or display of china—and fished out another match.

He heard voices, below him in the storage room.

Moving quickly, Svenson struck the match, shielding it as well as he could with his other hand—which held the medical bag—and strode quietly and directly down the hall to the nearest door and through it. He was in the kitchen, and on the table in front of him was a dead man he did not recognize, covered save for his livid face by a cloth. Svenson spun behind him—footsteps coming up the stairs—and saw on the other side of the kitchen another door. The match was burning his fingers. He dodged around the table and through a swinging doorway. He just saw a quick glimpse of a dining table before he shook out the match. He dropped it, stuck the burned finger into his mouth, stilled the door, and crept to the far side of the table, sinking to the floor. He pulled out the pistol. The footsteps reached the kitchen. He heard the voices of two men, and then the distinct pop of a bottle being uncorked.

*   *   *

"There we are," said the first voice, one that seemed eminently pleased with itself. "I told you he'd have something worthwhile—where are glasses?" In answer there was clinking, more clinking, and then the *dook dook* sounds of wine being poured—a substantial amount of wine. The first man spoke again. "Do you think we can risk a light?"

"The Deputy Minister—" began the second voice.

"Yes, I know—all right—and it's just as well. I don't want to look at this fellow any more than I already have. What a waste of time. When is he supposed to be here?"

"The messenger said he had a prior errand before he could meet us."

The first man sighed. Svenson heard the sound of a match—an orange glow flickering under the door—and then the puffing of a man lighting a cigar.

"Do you want one, Bascombe?" the first man asked. Svenson searched his memory. He'd met or overheard the introductions of so many people in the last weeks—had there been a Bascombe? Perhaps, but he couldn't place him—if he could just *see* the man...

"No, thank you, Sir," replied Bascombe.

"I'm not 'Sir'," the first man laughed. "Leave that for Crabbé, or the Comte, though I daresay you'll be one of them soon enough. How does *that* feel?"

"I'm sure I don't know. It's happening very quickly."

"The best temptations always do, eh?"

Bascombe did not respond, and they were silent for a time, drinking. Svenson could smell the cigar. It was an excellent cigar. Svenson licked his lips. He wanted a cigarette desperately. He did not recognize either of the voices.

"Have you had much experience with corpses?" asked the first voice, with a trace of amusement.

"This is actually my first, in such close quarters," answered the second, with an air that told Svenson the man knew he was being goaded, but must make the best of it. "My father died when I was much younger—"

"And your uncle of course. Did you see *his* body?"

"I did not. I have not yet—I will of course—at the funeral."

"You grow used to it like anything. Ask any doctor, or soldier." Svenson heard more sounds of pouring. "All right, what's after corpses . . . what about women?"

"Beg pardon?"

The man chuckled. "Oh, don't be such a boiled trout—no wonder Crabbé favors you. You're not married?"

"No."

"Engaged?"

"No." The voice hesitated. "There was—but no, never so significant an attachment. As I say, all of these changes have come quickly—"

"Brothels, then, I assume? Or schoolgirls?"

"No, no," Bascombe said, with a professionally patient tone that Svenson recognized as the hallmark of a skilled courtier, "as I say, my own feelings have always, well, always been in service to obligation—"

"My goodness—so it's boys?"

"Mr. Xonck!" snapped the voice, perhaps less appalled than exasperated.

"I am merely asking. Besides, when you've traveled as much as I have, things stop surprising you. In Vienna for example, there is a prison you may visit for a small fee, as one would visit a zoo, you know—but for only a few more silver *pfennigs*—"

"But, Mr. Xonck, surely—I beg your pardon—our present business—"

"Didn't the Process teach you anything?"

Here the younger man paused, taking in that this might be a more serious question than the bantering tone implied.

"Of course," he said, "it was *transforming*—"

"Then have some more wine."

Had this been the right answer? Svenson heard the gurgling bottle as Francis Xonck began to hold forth. "Moral perspective is what we carry around with us—it exists nowhere else, I can promise you. Do you see? There is liberation and responsibility—for what is natural depends on where you are, Bascombe. Moreover, vices are like genitals—most are ugly to behold, and yet we find that our own are dear to us." He sniggered at his own wit, drank deeply, exhaled. "But I suppose you have no vices, do you? Well, once you've changed your hat and become Lord Tarr, sitting on the only deposit of indigo clay within five hundred miles, I daresay you'll find they appear soon enough—I speak from experience. Find yourself some tuppable tea cozy to marry and keep your house and then do what you want elsewhere. My brother, for example . . ."

Bascombe laughed once, somewhat bitterly.

"What is it?" asked Xonck.

"Nothing."

"I do insist."

Bascombe sighed. "It is nothing—merely that, only last week, I was still—as I said, not *significant*—you see, one can only smile at how easy it is to believe—believe so *deeply*—"

"Wait, wait—if you're going to tell a *story*, then we need another bottle. Come on."

Their footsteps moved out of the kitchen, to the hall, and soon Svenson heard them descending the cellar stairs. He didn't feel he could risk slipping past—he had no idea where the wine cellar actually was, or how long they would be. He could try to find the front door—but knew he was in the perfect position to learn more where he was, as long as he wasn't discovered. Suddenly Svenson had it. Bascombe! He was Crabbé's aide—a thin, youngish fellow, never spoke, always paying attention—he was about to be a *Lord*? Chiding himself Svenson realized he was wasting the most immediate source of information of all. He dug out another match and pushed silently through the swinging door. He listened—they were well out of hearing—struck the match and looked down at the dead man on the table.

He was perhaps forty years old, hair thin, clean-shaven, with a sharp pointed nose. His face was covered with red blotches, vivid despite the pallor of death, lips stretched back in a grimace, revealing a mouth half-full of tobacco-stained teeth. Working quickly as the match burned, Svenson pulled back the sheet and could not help but gasp. The man's arms, from the elbows down, were riven with veins of lurid, jagged, gleaming blue, bulging out from the skin, cutting through it. At first glance the veins looked wet, but Svenson was shocked to realize that they were in fact *glass*—and that they ran down through the man's forearms, thickening, seething into and stiffening the flesh around them. He pulled the cloth farther and dropped the match with surprise. The man had no hands. His wrists were completely blue, starred, and broken—as if the hands below them had *shattered*.

The footsteps returned below. Svenson whipped the cloth into place and retreated to the dining room, carefully stilling the swinging door, his mind reeling at what he'd just seen. Within moments he heard the men in the hall and then entering the kitchen.

"Another glass there, Bascombe," called Xonck, and then to a third man, "I'm assuming you will join us—or me, at least— Bascombe doesn't quite share my thirst. Always watching from a distance, aren't you, Roger?"

"If you insist," muttered the new voice. Svenson stopped breathing. It was Major Blach. Svenson slowly slipped his right hand around the butt of the revolver.

"Excellent." Xonck extracted the cork from the new bottle with a pop and poured. He drank, and Svenson could hear him emit little noises of pleasure as he did. "It's very good—isn't it?

Damn—my cigar seems to have gone out." Svenson saw the light of a match flare. While it burned, Xonck chatted on. "Why don't we give him a peek—get the cloth, Bascombe. There you go—in all his glory. Well, Major, what do you say?"

There was no response. After a moment the match went out. Xonck chuckled. "That's more or less what we said too. I think old Crabbé said 'bloody hell!' Except of course it's not *bloody* at all." Xonck cackled. "Find relief where you can, that's what I say."

"What has happened to him?" asked Blach.

"What do you think? He's dead. He was rather valuable, don't you know—rather skilled in the technical mechanics. It's a good thing there's still Lorenz—if there is still Lorenz—because, Major, I'm not quite certain you understand exactly who's responsible for this damned outright *catastrophe*. It is *you*, Major. It is *you* because *you* could not locate one disreputable ruffian who was thus free to disrupt our work at its most delicate moment. Just as *you* could not control the members of your own diplomatic mission—I assume you know the man who took back the Prince, waving a pistol in our faces—which would be laughable if it didn't create problems for everyone *else* to solve!"

"Mr. Xonck—" began Major Blach.

"Shut your foul foreign mouth," snarled Xonck coldly. "I don't want excuses. I want thoughts. Think about your problems. Then tell us what you're going to do about them."

Except for the clink of Xonck's glass, there was silence. Svenson was astonished. He'd never heard Blach spoken to in such a way, nor could he have imagined Blach reacting with anything but rage.

Blach cleared his throat. "To begin—"

"First, Major," and it was Bascombe speaking, not Xonck, "there is the man from your compound, the Prince's Doctor, I believe?"

"Yes," hissed Blach. "He is not a factor. I will go back tonight and have him smothered in his bed—blame it on anything—no one will care—"

"Second," interrupted Bascombe, "the disruptive man in red."

"Chang—he is called Cardinal Chang," said Blach.

"He is Chinese?" asked Bascombe.

"No," snarled Blach—Svenson could hear Xonck snickering. "He has been—he is called that because of scars—apparently—I have not seen them. He escaped from us. He has killed one of my men and seriously injured two more. He is nothing but a vicious criminal without imagination or understanding. I have men posted across his usual haunts as they have been described to us—he will be taken soon, and—"

"Brought to me," said Xonck.

"As you wish."

"Third," continued Bascombe, "the female spy, Isobel Hastings."

"We have not found her. No one has found her."

"She must be somewhere, Major," said Bascombe.

"She is unknown at the brothels I was directed to—"

"Then try a hotel!" cried Xonck. "Try the rooming houses!"

"I do not know the city as you do—"

"Next!" barked Xonck.

"And fourth," continued Bascombe smoothly—Svenson had to admire the man's coolness of manner, "we must arrange for the return of your Prince."

Svenson listened—this would be what he was waiting for—but there was only silence . . . and then Blach's sputtering rage.

"What are you talking about?" he fumed.

"It is quite simple—there is a great deal of work yet to be done. Before the marriage, before anyone may return to Macklenburg—"

"No, no—why are you saying this? You have already taken him—without notifying me! You have taken him hours ago!"

No one spoke. Blach rapidly explained what had happened at the compound—the escape to the roof, the furniture against the door—then how he and Flaüss had just now left complaints and a request for aid with Lord Vandaariff, who had promised to do what he could. "Of course, all the time I assumed he had been taken by you," said Blach, "though I have no idea how it was done."

Once more there was silence.

"We do not have your Prince," said Xonck, in a quiet, calm voice. "All right—fifth, Blach, you will continue in your efforts to find this Chang and this Hastings woman. We will find the Prince. Bascombe will be in touch. Sixth . . . yes, and sixth . . ." He took a moment to toss off the last of his wine. "You can help us get poor Crooner out of Mrs. Crabbé's kitchen. They should have something ready by now at the river. We will take your coach."

Twenty minutes later Svenson stood in the kitchen alone, looking down at the now empty table, smoking a cigarette. He opened his medical kit and rummaged inside for an empty glass jar and pulled out the cork. He lit a match and leaned over the table, looking closely. It took several matches until he found what he wanted, a small flaking of what looked like blue glass. Using a tiny swab he brushed the glass bits into the jar, inserted the cork and stowed it back into his bag. He had no idea what it was, but was certain that a comparison with the Prince's glass card would be useful. He snapped the medical kit shut. He could not return to the compound. He did not know how long he could stay where he was—he should probably be gone already. At least he knew who his enemies were, or some of them—neither Xonck nor Bascombe had mentioned Madame Lacquer-Sforza. Svenson wondered if she could be responsible for taking the Prince. Yet she had been searching for the Hastings woman as well—the different figures overlapped maliciously. Indeed, for these men had mentioned Doctor Lorenz as if he were one of their own, while Svenson had seen with his own eyes the man's attendance to Madame Lacquer-Sforza. Perhaps they were all intent on betraying each other, but up to this point had been in league. Somewhere in the house, a clock chimed three. Svenson picked up his bag and walked out.

The alley gate was now locked, and he climbed over it with the stiffness of a man not used to this kind of exertion at such an hour. The fog was still thick, the street still dark, and Svenson still had no firm destination in mind. He walked away from the compound—generally toward the Circus Garden and the heart of the city—keeping to the shadows and forcing his increasingly tired mind to work. While the Prince was certainly in danger, Svenson doubted it was immediately mortal. At the same time, he'd felt a chill when Xonck had referred to "the Process." Could this be related to the facial burns? It almost sounded like a pagan ritual, like a tribal marking ceremony, or—he thought darkly—like branding one's cattle. The dead man, Crooner, had obviously been involved—there was science behind it, which was why it was taking place at the Institute, and why Lorenz was part of it as well. Who *wasn't* part of it, aside from Svenson himself? The answer came quickly enough: Isobel Hastings and the menacing man in red, this "Chang." He had to find them before Major Blach. They might even know how to locate the Prince.

Svenson kept walking, his boots grinding on the wet cobblestones. His thoughts began to wander, the wet chill of the fog taking him back to his time in Warnemünde, the cold rail of the pier, the snow falling silently into the sea. He remembered, as a boy, walking into the winter forest—wanting to be alone, in despair once again—and sitting in his thick coat under a pine tree, pressing the snow around him into a soft burrow, lying back and looking up into the high branches. He didn't know how long he'd lain there, his mind drifting, perhaps even close to dangerous sleep, when he became aware that he was cold, that the heat from his body had been steadily leeched away by the snow and frosted air. His face was numb. It had happened so gradually, his mind had been elsewhere—he could no longer remember the girl's name—but as he forced his frozen limbs to work, rolling first to his knees and then to a shambling walk, he had a moment of insight, that he had just seen in miniature his own life—and every human life—a process where heat slowly, relentlessly dissipated in the face of unfeeling and beautiful ice.

He stopped and looked around him. The great park entrance of the Circus Garden was just to his right, and to his left the marble pools. He had to make a decision. If he looked for the man in red, Chang, and was lucky enough to locate his haunts, he would in all likelihood only find one of Major Blach's troopers. To look for Isobel Hastings would require knowledge of the city's hotels and rooming houses that he simply didn't possess. The cabal of Crabbé, Xonck, and d'Orkancz did not, by their own words, have the Prince. As much as he dreaded it, as much as his nerves fluttered at the idea, as little as he trusted himself, the best choice that came to mind was Madame Lacquer-Sforza and the St. Royale Hotel. He was only minutes away—perhaps brandishing his doctor's bag would get them to open the door at such an hour.

The windows of the hotel still streamed light, but the street outside was still and empty. Svenson walked to the door. It was locked. Before he could knock on the glass he saw a uniformed clerk walking toward him with a ring of keys, alerted by his pulling on the handle. The man unlocked the door and opened it a few narrow inches.

"May I help you?"

"Yes, excuse me—I realize the hour is late—or early—I am looking for—I am a doctor—it is very necessary that I speak with one of your guests, a Madame Lacquer-Sforza."

"Ah. The Contessa."

"Contessa?"

"That is not possible. You are a doctor?"

"Yes—my name is Svenson—I'm sure she will see me—"

"Doctor Svenson, yes. No, I am afraid it is not possible."

The clerk looked past Svenson to the street and called out with a brisk clicking of his tongue—the sound one makes to move a horse. Svenson wheeled to see whom he was addressing. From the shadows across the street, in answer, stepped four men. Svenson recognized them by their cloaks—they were the guards from the Institute. He turned back to the door—the clerk had pulled it closed and was locking it. Svenson knocked his fist on the glass. The clerk ignored him. Svenson spun to face the men in the street. They stood in a loose semi-circle in the middle of the road, blocking his escape. His hand dug for his coat pocket, feeling for the revolver.

"No need for that, Doctor," hissed a low rasping voice to his right. He looked up to see the broad daunting figure of the Comte d'Orkancz standing in the shadows beyond the window front. He wore a top hat and a heavy fur coat, and held his silver-topped stick in his right hand. He looked at Svenson with a cold appraising eye.

"It may serve you later . . . for the moment there are more pressing matters to discuss, I assure you. I had hoped you might arrive, and you did not disappoint—such *agreement* is a good way to start our conversation. Will you walk with me?"

Without waiting for an answer, the Comte turned and strode into the fog. Svenson glanced at the men, swallowed uncomfortably, and hurried after him.

"Why would you be waiting for me?" he asked, once he had caught up.

"Why would you be calling on the Contessa at such an improper hour?"

Svenson's mouth worked to find a response. He glanced back to see the four men following some yards behind them.

"You need not answer," d'Orkancz whispered. "We each have our mysteries—I do not doubt that your reasons are real. No, when it came to my attention that you were of the Prince's party, I remembered your name—you *are* the author of a valuable pamphlet on the effects of frostbite?"

"I am the author of such a pamphlet—whether or not it has value..."

"A chief point of interest, if I recall, was the ironic similarity between the damage inflicted by certain types of extreme cold, and certain kinds of burns."

"Indeed."

The Comte nodded gravely. "And *that* is why I was waiting for you."

He led Svenson down an elegant side lane, bordered on the east by a walled garden. They stopped at a wooden door, set into an alcove vaulted as if it was part of a church, which d'Orkancz unlocked and led him through. They stepped into the garden, walking across thick, springing turf—behind them Svenson heard the guards enter and close the door. Around him he saw great empty urns and beds, and hanging leafless trees. Above was the fog-shrouded sky. He hurried to keep up with the Comte, who was striding toward a large glowing greenhouse, the smeared windows diffusing the lantern light within. The Comte unlocked a glass-paned door and entered, holding it open for Svenson. Svenson walked through and into a wave of moistly cloying hot air. D'Orkancz shut the door behind, leaving the four guards in the garden. He nodded to a nearby hat stand.

"You will want to take off your coat."

The Comte pulled off his fur as he crossed the greenhouse—which Svenson realized was carpeted—to a large canopied bed, the curtains drawn tight around it. He placed the coat, his hat, and his stick on a small wooden work table and delicately peeked through a gap in the curtains. He stared in for perhaps two minutes, his face impassive. Already Svenson could feel the sweat prickling over his body. He put his medical kit down and peeled off his greatcoat, feeling the weight of the pistol in the pocket, and hung it on the rack. He disliked being apart from the weapon, but he didn't expect he could shoot his way past d'Orkancz and all of the guards in any case. With a glance, d'Orkancz gestured him to the bed. He held the curtain aside as Svenson drew near.

On the bed lay a shivering woman, wrapped in heavy blankets, her eyes closed, her skin pale, her breathing shallow. Svenson glanced at the Comte.

"Is she sleeping?" he whispered.

"I don't believe so. If she were not cold, I should say it is a fever. As she is cold, I cannot say—perhaps you can. Please..." He stepped away from the bed, pulling apart the curtains as he did.

Svenson leaned forward to study the woman's face. Her features struck Svenson as slightly Asiatic. He pulled up her eyelid, felt the pulse in her throat, noted with unease the cobalt cast of her lips and tongue, and with an even greater distress the impressions across her face and throat—similar to the kind of marks a corset (or an octopus) might imprint on a woman's skin. He reached under the blankets for her hand, felt the cold of it, and listened to her pulse there as well. He saw that on the tip of each finger the skin had been worn away. He reached across the bed to find the other hand, where the fingers were identical. Svenson pulled the blankets back to her waist. The woman was nude, and the bluish impressions on her skin ran the length of her torso. He felt a movement at his side. The Comte had brought over the medical kit. Svenson fished out his stethoscope, and listened to the woman's lungs. He turned to the Comte. "Has she been in water?"

"She has not," rasped the Comte.

Svenson frowned, listening to her labored breathing. It sounded exactly like a person half-drowned. He reached back into the bag for a lancet and a thermometer. He would need to know her temperature, and then he was going to need some of her blood.

*   *   *

Some forty minutes later, Svenson had washed his hands and was rubbing his eyes. He looked out to see if the sun was coming up, but the sky was still dark. He yawned, trying to remember when he had last been up through an entire night—when he was more resilient, in any case. The Comte appeared at his side with a white china cup.

"Coffee with brandy," he said, handing the cup to Svenson and walking back to the table to pick up his own. The coffee was hot and black, almost burned, but perfect. Along with the brandy—a rather large amount of brandy for so small a cup—it was exactly what he needed. He took another deep drink, finishing the cup, and set it down.

"Thank you," he said.

The Comte d'Orkancz nodded, then turned his gaze to the bed. "What is your opinion, Doctor? Is it possible she will recover?"

"It would help if I had more information."

"Perhaps. I will tell you that her condition is the result of an accident, that she was not in water—I can only assure you of this, not explain it convincingly—yet water was permeating her person. Nor was this mere water, Doctor, but a liquid of special properties, an energetically *charged* liquid. The woman had laid her person open to this procedure. To my great regret the procedure was interrupted. The direction of the liquid was reversed and she was—how to say this—both depleted and flooded at the same time."

"Is this—I have heard—I have seen, on the Prince—the scarring—the Process—"

"Process?" d'Orkancz snapped in alarm, but then as quickly his voice became calm. "Of course, the Prince . . . you would have spoken to him, he would have been in a state to hold back nothing. It is regrettable."

"You must understand that my interests here are my duty to

protect him, and my duty as a doctor—in good faith—and if *this*"—Svenson gestured to the woman, her pale flesh almost luminous in the lantern glow—"is the danger you have exposed Karl-Horst to—"

"I have not."

"But—"

"You do not know. The woman, if you please, Doctor Svenson."

The sharpness of his tone stopped further protest in Svenson's throat. He wiped the sweat from his face.

"If you've read my pamphlet enough to remember my name you know yourself already. She bears all the evidence of having been rescued after prolonged immersion in freezing water—the winter Baltic, for example. At certain temperatures the bodily functions slow precipitously—this can be both deadly and a preservative. She is alive, she breathes. Whether this has irreparably damaged her mind, I cannot say. Whether she will ever awake from this—this winter sleep—I cannot say either. Yet, I—I must ask about the marks across her body—whatever has been done to her—"

D'Orkancz held up his hand. Svenson stopped talking.

"Is there anything to be done *now*, Doctor—that is the question."

"Keep her warm. Force her to drink warm fluids. I would suggest some kind of massage to encourage circulation—all peripheral—either the damage has been done or it hasn't."

The Comte d'Orkancz was silent. His cup of coffee lay untouched beside him. "One more question, Doctor Svenson, . . . perhaps the most crucial of all."

"Yes?"

"Do you think she's dreaming?"

Svenson was taken aback, for the Comte's tone was not entirely one of sympathy—within the body of his concern ran a vein of iron inquiry. He answered carefully, glancing back to the now-curtained bed.

"There is inconstant movement of the eyes...it might be ascribed to some kind of fugue state...it is not catatonia...she is not aware, but perhaps...within her own mind...perhaps dreams...perhaps delirium...perhaps peace."

The Comte d'Orkancz did not reply, his eyes lost for a moment in thought. He came back to the present, looked up. "And now... what shall I do with you, Doctor Svenson?"

Svenson's eyes flicked over to his coat, hanging on the stand, the pistol buried in the pocket. "I will take my leave—"

"You'll stay where you are, Doctor," he whispered sharply, "until I say otherwise. You have assisted me—I would prefer to reward such cooperation—and yet you stand quite clearly opposed to other interests that I must preserve."

"I must recover my Prince."

The Comte d'Orkancz sighed heavily.

Svenson groped for something to say, but was unsure what to reveal—he could mention Aspiche or Lorenz, or Madame Lacquer-Sforza or Major Blach, he could mention the blue glass card, but would this make him more valuable in the Comte's mind, or more dangerous? Was he more likely to be spared the more ignorantly loyal to the Prince he appeared? He could not see clearly out of the greenhouse due to the glaring lantern light reflecting on the glass—he could not place any of the guards. Even if he were able to reach his pistol and somehow overcome d'Orkancz—by his size an extremely powerful man—how could he elude the others? He didn't know where he was—he was exhausted—he had no safe place to hide—he still knew nothing about the Prince's location.

He looked up at the Comte. "Would you mind if I had a cigarette?"

"I would."

"Ah."

"Your cigarettes are in your coat, are they not?"

"They are—"

"Most likely quite near to the service revolver you brandished earlier this evening. Does it not seem like a great deal has happened since then? I have grappled with death and disruption, with intrigue and retribution—and you have done the same. And you have lost your Prince *again*. We would both be nearly comic, were not these consequences so steeped in blood. Have you ever killed anyone, Doctor?"

"I'm afraid many men have died under my hands..."

"On the table, yes, but that is different—however you may rack yourself with accusation, it is entirely different—as you well know. You do know exactly what I am asking."

"I do. I have."

"When?"

"In the city of Bremen. A man who had—it seemed—corrupted a young niece of the Duke—he was intractable, my instructions...I—I forced him to drink poison, at pistol-point. I am not proud of the incident. Only an idiot would be."

"Did he know what he was drinking?"

"No."

"I'm sure he had his suspicions."

"Perhaps."

Svenson remembered the fellow's red face, the hacking rattle in his throat, his rolling eyes, and then recovering the incriminating letters from his pocket as he lay on the floor, the sharp smell of the man's bile. The memory haunted him. Svenson rubbed his eyes. He was hot—even more hot than he had been—the room was truly stifling. His mouth was so dry. He felt a sudden prickle of adrenaline. He looked at the Comte, then at the empty cup of coffee, then—how long did it take him to turn his head—at the Comte's untouched cup on the table. The table was above him. He had dropped to his knees, realizing dimly that he did not feel the impact. His head swam. The fibers of the carpet pressed into his face. Dark warm water closed over him, and he vanished within it.

*   *   *

He opened his eyes in shadow, goaded by a nagging shapeless urgency, through a warm woolen veil of sleep. He blinked. His eyelids were extremely heavy—impossibly heavy—he closed them. He was jolted awake again, his entire body jarred, and now he took in more of what his senses told him: the rough grain of wood against his skin, the smell of dust and oil, the sound of wheels and hoofbeats. He was in the back of a cart, staring up at a cloth canopy in the near dark. The wagon rattled along—they were traveling across uneven cobbles, the jolts waking him before he otherwise would have. He reached with his right hand and touched the canvas cover, some two feet above him. His mouth and throat were parched. His temples throbbed. He realized with a certain distant pleasure that he was not dead, that for some reason—or so far— the Comte had spared his life. He felt carefully around him, his limbs aching but responsive. Crumpled near his head was his coat—the revolver no longer in the pocket, though he still possessed the glass card. He groped farther, at his arm's length, and flinched as his hand found a booted foot. Svenson swallowed and rolled his eyes. How many corpses—or near-corpses, if he counted the woman and the soldiers—had been thrown Svenson's way this day alone? It would be ridiculous if it were not also sickening. With a grim determination the Doctor felt farther—the body was oppositely laid in the cart, the feet near his head—moving down the boots to the trousers, which had a heavy side seam, braid or frogging—a uniform. He followed the leg until he came to, next to it, a hand. A man's hand, and icy cold.

The cart lurched again and Svenson pushed his exhausted mind to determine in which direction they moved—was his head at the front of the cart or the rear? He couldn't tell—the vehicle was moving so slowly and over such an uneven surface that all he felt were the shakes up and down. He reached above his head and touched a wooden barrier. He felt along the corner, where this piece joined the side of the cart, and found no brackets, no bolts...could it be the rear? If so, it was bolted closed on the outside—to get out he would have to climb over it, perhaps even cutting through the canvas cover—if he had anything to cut it with. He felt for his medical kit, but it was nowhere to be found. With a grimace, he reached again toward the body and groped for the pockets in the man's uniform coat, and then his trousers—all had been emptied. With distaste his fingers found the man's collar, and felt his badge of rank. A colonel. Svenson forced himself to touch the man's face: the heavy neck, the moustache, and then, ever so faintly, the curved ridge of flesh around the eyes. He was next to Arthur Trapping.

Doctor Svenson rolled onto his back, facing up, his eyes squeezed shut, his hand over his mouth. He inhaled through his nose and exhaled, slowly, against his hand. He needed to think. He had been drugged and was en route—undoubtedly for disposal—with a deliberately hidden corpse. He was without weapons or allies, in a foreign country, with no knowledge of where he was—though from the cobblestones he was still in the city at least. He tried to think clearly—his mind was fogged, he was still so very tired—and forced his hands to go through his own pockets: a handkerchief, banknotes, coins, a pencil stub, a folded-over scrap of paper, his monocle. He rolled over toward Trapping and searched the man again, this time more thoroughly. In the jacket, between the layers of fabric over the left breast where it would be covered by dangling medals, he felt something hard. He crawled closer to the body and awkwardly pulled himself up onto his elbows, gripping the seam of Trapping's coat with both hands. He yanked at the fabric and felt it give. Another jolt knocked him off balance. He got a better grip and pulled with all his strength. The seam split open. Svenson inserted a finger into the gap and felt a hard, slick surface. He wedged his thumb into the hole and pulled the object free. He didn't need any light to know it was another glass card. He stuffed it into his coat pocket next to the first. He was suddenly still. The cart had stopped moving.

He felt it jostle as the drivers jumped off, and then heard footsteps on either side of him. He gathered up his coat and shut his eyes—he could at least feign sleep. If the opportunity came to run or knock someone on the head, all the better if they thought him asleep or incapable—though he was far from his best, and even at his best no great fighter. At his feet he heard the sharp metallic clanks of the bolts being shot, and then the back panel was lowered. The canvas cover was flung back and Svenson felt the cooler, damp air of the morning—for the glow through his closed eyelids told him there was light. Before he could fully decide whether or not to open his eyes, he felt a shocking blow in his stomach—a sharp poke from a wooden pole—that doubled him over with gasping pain. His eyes popped open, his mouth strained to take in breath, his hands clutched feebly at his abdomen, the pain lancing the full length of his body. Above he heard the laughter of several men, pitiless and shrill.

With a great effort, to prevent another blow, Doctor Svenson hauled himself up with his arms, rolled to his side and forced his legs underneath him one at a time, so he could kneel. His lank blond hair had fallen into his eyes and he brushed it away stiffly. He pulled his monocle from its pocket and screwed it into position, taking in the scene around him. The cart was stopped in a closed cobbled yard, morning fog clinging to the rooftops around it. The yard was littered with barrels and crates bristling with jagged, rusted pieces of metal. To his other side was an open double doorway, and beyond it a forge. He was at a blacksmith's. Two of the Comte d'Orkancz's ruffians stood at the end of the cart, one with a long pole with a sharp grapple on the end. The other, more practically, held Svenson's own pistol. Svenson looked down at Trapping's body in the light. The grey face was marked with the now-purpled scarring around the eyes. There was no obvious cause of death—no wound, no evidence of trauma, no particular discoloration. Svenson noticed that Trapping's other hand was gloved, and that the tip of the index finger was torn. He leaned down and wrestled the glove off. The tip of the finger was a striking indigo, the skin punctured by some kind of needle or thin blade, the flesh around the incision crusted with a blue-white powder. At a noise from the forge, Svenson looked up to see Francis Xonck and Major Blach walking into the courtyard. He dropped the glove back over the hand.

"At last, at last," called Francis Xonck. "We are ready down at the portage." He smiled at Svenson. "We were, however, only prepared for two. We must innovate. This way—use the barrow." He nodded at a wheelbarrow, and walked over to a wooden wall, which slid to the side on a track at his push. Beyond was a slanted, paved path. Xonck marched down it. Blach fixed Svenson with a glare of hatred and snapped his fingers. From the forge behind him emerged two of his black-coated troopers. Svenson did not recognize them, but he was bad at faces. Major Blach barked at them, "Escort the Doctor!" and followed Xonck. Svenson hobbled off the cart, clutching his coat, and with a trooper on either side walked from the yard. He glanced back once to see the Comte's men lugging Trapping to the barrow.

As they walked, Svenson struggled into his coat, for it was very cold. The path was lined on either side by rough, gapped, plank fencing, and wound between decaying buildings and heaps of refuse. He knew they were walking to the river. The pain in his stomach had eased and his immediate fear was edging into cold, reckless implacability. He called ahead to Major Blach, with as much of a sneer as he could muster.

"Did you find the Prince, Major? Or have you spent the night drinking other men's wine...and licking other men's...boots?"

Blach stopped where he was and turned. Svenson did his best

with a dry mouth and launched a gob of spit in the Major's direction. It traveled only a few feet but still made its point. Major Blach flushed and took a stride toward Svenson. Behind Blach, Francis Xonck called out to him sharply. "Major!" Blach stopped, gave Svenson another murderous look and continued down the path. Xonck looked over the Major's shoulder for a moment, meeting Svenson's gaze, and chuckled. He waited for Blach to reach him, took hold of his arm and shoved him forward, so Xonck was now between them and Major Blach in the lead. Svenson looked back. The Comte's men were bringing down the body, covered by a tarp—one holding the barrow, one in the rear with the pistol. There was no clear way for him to run, should he be foolish enough to try. Instead he called ahead to Blach in an even louder voice.

"Is it an easy thing to betray your country, Major? I am curious—what was your price? Gold? New uniform? Women? Athletic young men? A sheep farm?"

Major Blach wheeled, his hand digging for his pistol. Xonck took hold of his uniform with both hands and with difficulty— Xonck was stronger than he seemed—restrained Blach where he was. Once the Major had stopped his charge, Xonck again turned him around—whispering into his ear—and shoved him forward. When the Major had advanced a few paces, Xonck turned to Svenson, nodding to the troopers. Svenson felt a shove and began again to walk, now with Xonck right ahead of him. Xonck looked back at him with a smile.

"I should have said suckling pigs instead of sheep, but I believe he took your point. I am Francis Xonck."

"Captain-Surgeon Abelard Svenson."

"Rather more than that, I think." Xonck smiled. "You have the distinction of actually impressing the Comte d'Orkancz, which is a rare enough event that there really ought to be a parade." He smiled again and took in the troopers and the men behind them with the wheelbarrow. "Perhaps it is a parade after all."

"I should have preferred more bunting," said Svenson, "and some trumpets."

"Another time, I am sure." Xonck chuckled.

They walked on. Ahead Svenson could see the river. They were actually quite close to it, the fog and the buildings around them having obscured the view.

"Did you locate the Prince?" asked Svenson, as airily as possible.

"Why, did you?" answered Xonck.

"I'm afraid I did not," admitted Svenson. "Though I do know who has taken him."

"Indeed?" Xonck studied him for a moment, his eyes twinkling. "How *satisfying* for you."

"I am not sure you know those responsible. Though I believe you—or your companions—have tried to apprehend them."

Xonck did not reply, but Svenson thought his smile had become that much more fixed on his lips, and disconnected from his searching eyes. Xonck turned his gaze ahead, and saw that they approached the end of the path. "Ah—the splendid waterfront. We are arrived."

The path opened onto a slippery portage way, sloping under the grey surface of the river. To either side was a raised stone pier, where cargo or passengers might more easily be lowered. Tied to the left-hand pier was a flat, featureless barge with one high oar in the rear like a gondola's. In its bow was a latched section that could be let down as a gangplank, as it presently was. In the center of the narrow barge was a closed metal coffin. Another, unsealed, lay on the pier. Svenson realized that once on the water, the ramp could be lowered again and the coffins slipped into the river to sink. If they had tried to push the coffins over the side the entire craft would be dangerously unbalanced. Two more of the Comte's men were in the barge, and they stepped forward to help the others bundle Arthur Trapping into the waiting coffin. As Svenson stood to the side between the troopers, he watched them install the body and secure the lid with a series of clamps and screws. With a small surge of something vaguely like hope he noticed that, under Trapping's body in the wheelbarrow, one of the men had thrown his medical kit. He looked up to see Major Blach on the pier, glaring at him. The Major snarled to Xonck, who had crossed to stand near him.

"What of him?" He nodded toward Svenson. "There are only two coffins."

"What would you suggest?" asked Xonck.

"Send back to the forge—weight him down with scrap metal and chain."

Xonck nodded and turned to the Comte's men who'd brought down the body, "You heard. Metal and chain, quickly." To Svenson's relief they tossed the medical kit on the ground before turning the barrow around and jogging back up the path. Major Blach removed his pistol from his holster and—staring at Svenson—barked at his men. "Help with the loading. I will watch him."

Xonck gestured to Blach's pistol with a smile, and then took in the riverside around them with a wave of his arm. "You will notice how peaceful the morning is, Doctor Svenson. And as a thinking man you will understand how the Major's pistol might shatter that peace and draw unwelcome attention to our efforts. In fact, since such a *thinking* man might also assume a well-placed cry for help might accomplish the same, I am obliged to point out that, were such a cry to occur, preserving this lovely silence would no longer *matter*—which is to say that if you make any noise you will be shot with less hesitation than if you were a foam-spitting cur."

"It is of course kind of you to explain things so nicely," muttered Svenson.

"Kindness costs very little, I find." Xonck smiled.

The troopers crossed to the coffin, but one of them glanced back at the Doctor with an expression of curiosity, if not doubt. Svenson watched as they manhandled the coffin onto the barge.

When they were at the exact moment of balance—two of them knee-deep in water on the sides, one in the barge, one shoving from the rear—he called up to Major Blach.

"Tell me, Major, is Herr Flaüss a traitor like you, or merely incompetent?"

Blach cocked his pistol. Xonck sighed audibly and placed his hand on the Major's arm.

"Really, Doctor, you must desist."

"If I'm going to be murdered, I am at least curious whether I leave my Prince in the hands of two traitors or one."

"But presently he is in no one's hands."

"None of *their* hands."

"Yes yes," snapped Xonck. "As you have already told me. Careful there!"

The men had shoved the coffin too far, to the side of the barge, and the entire craft tilted perilously. One man flung himself onto the barge to balance the weight while the other three dragged the coffin back into position. The Comte's two men carefully took up their places on the barge—one at the rear oar, the other readying shorter paddling oars for each side.

"Why go to the bother of transporting the Colonel here?" asked Svenson. "Why not just sink him in a canal near Harschmort?"

Xonck cast a side glance at the Major. "Call it Germanic thoroughness," he said.

"The Comte examined his body," replied Svenson, suddenly knowing it was true. "In his greenhouse." They didn't know something... or had something to hide—but hidden from someone at Harschmort? Hidden from Vandaariff? Were they not all allies?

"We need to kill him," snarled Blach.

"Not with *that*," answered Xonck, nodding at Blach's pistol.

Svenson knew he should act before the others came back with the wheelbarrow, when there were that many fewer of them. He pointed to his medical kit.

"Mr. Xonck, I see there my own medical kit. I know I am to

die, and I know that you may not shoot me for making too loud a noise. This leaves any number of more hideous options—strangling, stabbing, drowning, all of them slow and painful. If you will allow, I can quite easily prepare an injection for myself that will be swift, silent, and painless—it will perform a service to us all."

"Afraid, are you?" taunted Major Blach.

"Indeed, I admit it freely," answered Svenson, "I am a coward. If I must die—as it seems I must, for the credulous Prince you have abused and kidnapped—then I would prefer oblivion to agony."

Xonck studied him and called to one of the troopers. "Hand me the bag."

The nearest trooper did so. Xonck snapped it open, rummaged inside, and fixed Svenson with a searching, skeptical eye. He snapped the bag shut and threw it back to the trooper. "No needles," he said to Svenson, "and no attempt to throw acid or anything else you may have on hand. You will drink your medicine, and do it quietly. If there is the slightest trouble, I will merely gag you and let the Major do his worst—I assure you no one will hear the difference." He nodded to the trooper. The trooper clicked his heels by instinct and brought the medical kit to Svenson.

"I am grateful to you, I'm sure," he said, snapping the kit open.

"Hurry up," answered Xonck.

Svenson's mind was racing. He had said anything he could think of to try and muddle the loyalty of the two troopers, to cast Blach as a traitor—it hadn't worked. For a moment he wondered at his own loyalty—how far he had come, what desperate straits he had braved—all so beyond his normal character, and for what? He knew then it was not the Prince—a source of constant frustration and disappointment—nor his father, unthinking and proud. Was it for von Hoern? Was it for Corinna? Was it because he must dedicate his life to something, to stay true, no matter what that was, in the face of her loss? Svenson stared into his medical kit, not needing to counterfeit his shaking hands. The fact was, the oblivion of poison *was* a damned sight better than trying some foolhardy escape and failing—as he was bound to do. He had no illusions of the brutal lengths to which Blach would go—especially to quell any doubts in the minds of his men—to render Svenson a gibbering, pleading mess. Such an exit was tempting, and for a brief moment his searching logic was overtaken by an impulsive reverie of his lost past—the high meadows in flower, coffee in an autumn café, the opera box in Paris, Corinna as a girl, her uncle's farm. It was impossible, overwhelming—he could not surrender in such a rush. He plunged his hand into the case, brought out a flask, then deliberately bobbled it out of his grasp so it shattered on the pier. He looked up at Xonck pleadingly.

"No matter—no matter—there are other things to use—let me just find it—a moment, I beg you . . ." He set the kit on the pier and knelt over it, rummaging. He glanced quickly at the trooper to his right. The man carried a saber in a scabbard but no other weapon. Svenson was sane enough to realize that he could not hope to seize the hilt by surprise and draw it cleanly—the angle was all wrong. He was at best likely to have it half-out and be grappling with the trooper when Major Blach shot him cleanly in the back. Xonck was watching him. He selected a flask, looked at it in the light, shook his head, and replaced it, digging for another.

"What was wrong with that one?" called Blach impatiently.

"It was not quick enough," answered Svenson. "Here—this one will do."

He stood, a second glass flask in his hand. The troopers were on either side of him, and together they stood at the corner of one of the piers and the portage. Across from them on the other pier, some five yards away, were Xonck and Blach. Between them was the portage itself and the barge with the two coffins and the Comte's two men.

"What did you select?" called Xonck.

"Arsenic," answered Svenson. "Useful in small doses for psoriasis, tuberculosis, and—most pertinently for princes—syphilis. In larger doses, immediately fatal." He removed the stopper and looked around him, gauging the distances as closely as possible. The men were not yet back from the forge. The men on the barge were watching him with undisguised curiosity. He knew he had no choice. He nodded to Xonck. "I thank you for the courtesy." He turned to Major Blach, and smiled. "Burn in hell."

Doctor Svenson tossed back the contents of the flask in a gulp. He swallowed, choked hideously, his throat constricting, his face turning crimson. He dropped the flask, clutching at his throat, and staggered back into the trooper to his right, pawing for balance. An unearthly rattle rose out of his chest, his mouth worked, his tongue protruded horribly over his lips, his eyes rolled, his knees wobbled—all eyes were upon him. His entire body tensed, as if suspended over a precipice, poised at the very passage into death. In that moment, Svenson became strangely aware of the quiet of the city, that so many people could be so near to them and the only sound the dull lap of the river against the barge and somewhere far away the cry of gulls.

Svenson heaved his weight into the trooper. With a sudden pivot he took hold of the soldier's jacket with both hands and hurled him off the pier toward the barge. The momentum carried the trooper over the gap so he landed with a crash exactly on the side of the barge, causing it to lurch horribly. A sickening moment later, his arms flailing above, his legs thrashing in the water, the coffins slid toward the helpless man. He raised his arms as the first crashed into him, sweeping him viciously from the barge and into the water. Then the second coffin crashed into the first, tipping the entire barge at such a sudden angle that both of the Comte's men were thrown off their feet and into the coffins. Their extra weight tipped the angle even farther, and the shallow barge rolled up and then fully over, all three men and the coffins disappearing below the upended craft.

Svenson ran for the path. The remaining trooper took hold of
Svenson's coat with both hands as he went past. Svenson turned,
grappling with the trooper, furiously trying to wrench himself free.
He could hear the splashes from the water, cries from Blach. The
soldier was younger, stronger—they struggled, twisting each other
in a circle. For a moment the soldier held Svenson in place and
took hold of his throat. In the corner of his eye Svenson saw Blach
raise the pistol. Svenson lurched desperately away, pulling the
trooper into Blach's line of sight. A loud flat crack erupted into his
ear and his face was wet, warm. The trooper fell at his feet—the
side of his head a seething mess. Svenson swept the blood from his
eyes to see Francis Xonck slap Major Blach savagely across the face.
Blach's pistol was smoking.

"You idiot! The noise! You infernal fool!"

Svenson looked down—his feet tangled in the trooper's legs.
He seized the fallen man's saber and swept it clear, causing Xonck
to hastily step back. Svenson turned at the sound of Blach cocking
the pistol.

"If the damage is done," he snarled, "it's no matter to do
more..."

"Major! Major—there is no need," Xonck hissed in a fury.

Svenson could see Blach was going to fire. With a yell he
heaved the saber like an awkward knife—end over end, directly
toward them—and ran. He heard both men cry out and the loud
clang of the blade striking the stone—he'd no idea whether they'd
thrown themselves aside or not. His only thought was to charge up
the path. He ran on—the uneven stones slick from the morning,
his own footsteps obscuring the sound of any pursuit—and was
perhaps half-way to the top when he saw the two men with the
wheelbarrow coming toward him from the top. The barrow was
piled with metal and the men each held one of the handles, balancing it between them. He didn't dare slow his pace, but his heart
sank as they saw him and instantly began to trot forward, each
man with a broad smile breaking over his face. As they picked up

speed scraps of metal bounced out of the pile, clanging on the ground and against the fence. They were perhaps five yards away when they let it go. Svenson flung himself toward the top of the fence to his left, raising his legs. The barrow smashed beneath him, bounced off the wall, and continued recklessly down the slope. With a bestial surge of effort he hauled himself over the fence and dropped into a tangle of boxes and debris.

He had not hurt himself in the fall, though he was on his back and thrashing to rise. On the other side of the fence he could hear the crash of the barrow tipping over and more cries—could it have run into Xonck or Blach? Svenson rolled to his knees as, above him, the fence wobbled back and forth and one of the two barrow men vaulted over it. As the man landed—the drop causing him to double over for just a moment—Svenson snatched a thick wooden board from the mud with both hands and swung. The blow caught the man's near hand—holding a pistol—and hammered it cruelly—Svenson could feel the cracking small bones. The man screamed and the pistol flew across the ground. Svenson swung again, rising up, across the man's face. The man grunted at the impact and crumpled, curled and moaning, at the base of the fence. The fence wobbled again—another man was coming over. Svenson leapt at the pistol—it was his own—and still on his knees turned to the fence above him. The second barrow man was balanced on the fence top, an arm and a leg hooked over, looking down with alarm. Svenson snapped off a shot—missing the man but splintering the wood—and the fellow dropped from sight. A moment later the gleaming length of a saber shot through the fence at the level of Svenson's head, missing him by a matter of inches. He scrabbled away on his back like a crab as the blade scissored back and forth through the slats, probing for him. He could just see the shadows of bodies through the gaps between fence slats and fired again. In reply someone fired back, three shots in rapid succession that tore up the mud around him. Svenson returned fire twice, blindly, and hurled himself away, doing his best to run.

For the first time he saw that the yard was the back of a ruined house, the windows broken and the roof gone, the rear door off its frame and lying broken in the mud. The doorway and the open window frames were lined with faces. Svenson careened toward them even as he tried to take in who they were—children, an older man, women—their skin the color of milky tea, hair black, clothes colorful but worn. He raised the pistol, not at them but toward the sky. "Excuse me—I beg your pardon—please—look out!" He rushed through the door, the bodies around him skittering clear, and glanced back just long enough to see the fence in movement, bodies coming over. He dove ahead into the darkened rooms, leaping cooking pots, pallets, piles of clothing, doing his best not to step on anything or anyone, his senses assailed by the smell of so many persons in such a tangled space, by the open fire, and by pungent spices—he could not even name what they were. Behind him a shot rang out and a splinter of wood whipped into his face. He winced, knew he was bleeding, and nearly ran down a small child—where the hell was the door to the street? He stepped through doorway after doorway—as close as he could come to a dead run—dodging all the occupants—a room of goats?—jumping over an open cooking fire. He heard screams—the other men were in the house—just as he entered what had to be the main hallway, and directly in front of it a ruined set of double doors. He rushed to them, only to find they had been thoroughly nailed shut—of course, the house was condemned. He rushed back, looking for a window to the street. Another shot rang out—he didn't know from where—and he felt a hideous *snip* of air as the bullet traced past his ear. He kicked through a hanging curtain and into someone's occupied bed—a screaming woman, an outraged man—his feet caught up in their sheets but his gaze fixed on another carpet nailed to the wall, hanging down. Svenson threw himself to it and whipped the carpet aside. The window beyond was blessedly clear of glass. He hurdled the frame, tucking his hands around his head, and landed in an awkward sprawl that ended with him facedown on the paving, his pistol bouncing away on the stones.

Svenson thrust himself to his feet—his hands felt raw, his knee bruised, ankle complaining. As he bent to recover the pistol another shot rang out from the window. He turned to see Blach, one hand holding a bloody handkerchief to his face, the other with his smoking pistol, fixing Svenson in his sights. Svenson could not move fast enough. Blach squeezed the trigger, his eyes ablaze with hatred. The hammer landed on an empty chamber. Blach swore viciously and broke open the gun, knocking the empty shells out the window, digging for fresh cartridges. Svenson scooped up his weapon and ran.

He did not know where he was. He kept on until he was winded, doing his best to lose pursuit—dodging from street to street and cutting through what open lots and parks he could find. He finally collapsed in a small churchyard, sitting with his head in his hands on the ancient, cracked cover of a tomb, his chest heaving, his body spent. The light had grown—it was full morning—and the open space between objects struck him as almost shockingly clear. But instead of this making the events of his night seem unreal, Svenson found it was the day he could not trust. The weathered white stone, the worn letters spelling "Thackaray" under his fingers, the leafless branches above—none of these answered the relentless strange world he had entered. For a moment he wondered if he had eaten opium and was in that instant lying stupefied in a Chinaman's den, and all of this a twisting dream. He rubbed his eyes and spat.

Svenson knew that he was no real spy, nor any kind of soldier. He was lost. His ankle throbbed, his hands were scraped, he had not eaten, his throat was raw, and his head felt like a block of rotten cheese from the Comte's drug. He forced himself to remove his boot and palpate his tender ankle—it was not broken, nor probably even seriously sprained, he would simply have to treat it carefully. He scoffed at that unlikely prospect and pulled the revolver from his pocket, breaking it open. There were two cartridges left—he had no others with him. He stuffed it back in his pocket, and realized that the bulk of his money was still at the compound with his box of shells. He'd lost his medical kit, and was for the moment stuck in his uniform and greatcoat that, while a relatively restrained Prussian blue, nevertheless set him apart in a crowd.

His face stung. He brought up a hand to feel dried blood and a small splinter of wood still lodged below his right cheekbone. He delicately pulled it free and pressed a handkerchief to his face. Doctor Svenson realized that he desperately wanted a cigarette. He fished in his coat for his case, extracted one and then snapped a match alight off his thumb. The smoke hit his lungs with an exquisite tug and he exhaled slowly. Taking his time, he worked his way to the butt, concentrating only on his breathing and on each successive plume of smoke sent over the gravestones. He tossed the butt into a puddle and lit another. He didn't want to be light-headed, but the tobacco was restoring some of his resolve. As he replaced the case his hand bumped the glass cards in his pocket. He had forgotten the second card, from Trapping. He looked around him—the churchyard was still quite abandoned and the buildings around it void of any visible activity. Svenson pulled out the card—it looked identical to the one he had taken from the Prince's chamber. Would he be looking into the mind of Arthur Trapping and see some clue about how he had died? He set his burning cigarette down on the tomb next to him and looked into the card.

It took a moment for the blue veil to part, but once it had Svenson found himself amidst a confusing swirl of images, moving rapidly from one to another without any logic he could discern. It was less as if he occupied another's actual experience—as with Mrs. Marchmoor's encounter with the Prince—so much as their free-floating mind, or even perhaps their dreams. He pulled his gaze up from the card and exhaled. He was shaking, it was just as involving, he had been as much outside of himself as before. He tapped the growing cylinder of ash from his cigarette and took a long drag. He set it down again and gathered himself for a second, more focused visit.

The first images were in a fussy, well-appointed interior—a carpeted room of dark wood and glass lamps, delicate Chinoiserie and thickly upholstered furniture—and a woman sitting on a sofa, a young woman only a part of whose body Svenson could see—her bare forearms and her small hands as they clutched the upholstery, and then her shapely calves just emerging from under her dress as she stretched her legs, and then to her charming green ankle boots . . . each glimpse imbued with a particular proprietary hunger from the gaze he was inhabiting.

From here the card jumped abruptly to a rocky scene, a high view into a pit of grey stone—a quarry?—below an only slightly less grey sky. Suddenly Svenson was *in* the pit, the feel of gravel against his knee—kneeling, bending over a seam of colored stone within the rock—a dark stubbled indigo. An arm—his arm, which was young, strong, in a black coat—and a hand in a black leather glove reached forward to touch the seam of blue, digging a finger into it and crumbling out a loose chunk, as if it were a chalky sort of clay.

The next movement began as one of standing up in the quarry, but as his point of vision rose, the scene around him changed, so that when he was fully upright he was in a winter orchard—apple trees, he thought—the base of each trunk packed with straw. His gaze moved to his left and he saw a high stone wall and a weathered hedgerow, and behind them both the peaked rooftop of a country manor.

He turned farther to his left and found himself facing Harald Crabbé, who was smirking, leaning back and looking out the window of a coach—the window beyond it showing a country wood racing past. Crabbé turned to him—to whomever this was—and quite clearly mouthed the words "your decision"...and turned back to the window.

The window now opened onto another room, a curving stone hallway, ending in a metal-banded door. The door swung open and revealed a cavernous chamber, ringed with machinery, a massive man leaning over a table, his broad back obscuring the identity of the woman strapped to it, a woman...Svenson suddenly recognized the room—at the Institute, where he had rescued the Prince.

He looked up from the card. There was more—in the gaps, almost like a window streaming with rain—that he could not clearly see. His cigarette had gone out. He debated lighting another, but knew that he must really decide what to do. He had no idea if they were still searching. If so, they would reach the churchyard eventually. He had to find somewhere he could stay in safety. Or, he countered, he had to seize the bull by the horns. At what point was the Prince beyond aid? Svenson could not in conscience abandon him. He could not go back to the compound—he did not trust Flaüss—and he still had no idea where to find the man in red or Isobel Hastings. If he was not going to simply find a place to hide, the only avenue he had left, however foolish it seemed, was to try once more to confront Madame Lacquer-Sforza. Surely during the busy scramble of morning it would be safe to approach the St. Royale. There were two bullets left in his pistol—more than enough to convince her, if he could just gain entry.

He looked down and saw that he had not replaced his boot, and did so, gingerly pulling it up around his still-throbbing ankle. He stood and took a few steps. Now that the rush of adrenalized fear had faded, he felt the pain more keenly, but he knew he could walk on it—indeed, that he had no choice. All it needed was rest. He would exhaust this last possibility for information and then find some place to sleep—whether he could return safely to Macklenburg he did not know. Svenson sighed heavily and limped from the churchyard, retracing his steps to a narrow alley that ran next to the church. The sun was behind clouds—he had no real idea which direction was which. At the alley's end he looked around him, and then back at the church with its open doors. He entered the dark interior and made his way down the aisle, nodding to the few figures at worship, walking steadily to the base of the bell tower, which must have a staircase. He strode past the puzzled priest with his best scowl of medical authority and snapped a brusque "Good day to you, Father—your bell tower?" He nodded gravely as the man pointed in the direction of a small door. Svenson walked to it and stepped through, inwardly groaning at the number of steps he was going to climb with his injured ankle. He did his best to trot briskly until he was out of the priest's view, and then favored the foot by hopping on the other and holding the rail. He was perhaps seventy galling steps into the climb when he came to a narrow window covered with a wooden shutter. He pushed it open, dislodging an accretion of pigeon droppings and feathers, and smiled. From this height he could see the curving silver loop of the river, the green of Circus Garden, the white stone mass of the Ministries, and the open plaza of St. Isobel's Square. Between them all, its high red-tiled roof spires tipped with black and gold pennants, he found the St. Royale.

He descended as quickly as possible and dropped a coin into the collection box. Once on the street, he traveled through narrow alleys and residential lanes, keeping close to the walls. He passed a block of warehouses, swarming with men loading crates of all shapes onto carts. In the middle of it all was a small canteen, tucked between a storehouse of grain and another of raw fabric, rolling past in colorful bales. Svenson purchased a cup of boiled coffee and three fresh rolls. He tore them apart as he walked, the pith steaming, and drank the coffee as slowly as he could make himself, so as not to burn his mouth. He began to feel a bit more human as he neared the merchants' district near St. Isobel's—so much that he became self-conscious of his gashed face and disheveled greatcoat. He smoothed his hair back and swatted the dust from his coat—it would have to do—and strode ahead with what bluster he could manage. He imagined himself as Major Blach, which was at least entertaining.

Svenson skirted the hotel by a curving path of service alleys behind a row of fashionable restaurants, at this time of day thronged with deliveries of produce and slaughtered fowl. He had been careful, and perhaps lucky, to progress so far unobserved. Any attempt to take him would be swift and unforgiving. At the same time, his enemies were powerful enough to sway any mechanism of law. The slightest infraction—let alone shooting one of the Comte's men in the street—could send him to prison, or straight to the gallows. He stood at the alley's end, facing onto Grossmaere, the broad avenue that, two blocks away, ran past the St. Royale. He first looked in the opposite direction (it was possible that their line of sentries was farther away) but saw no one, or at least saw none of the Comte's men or Blach's troopers. With the involvement of Crabbé—or, heaven forbid, Vandaariff—there could be any number of other minions enlisted to find and kill him.

He looked toward the hotel. Could they be watching from above? The traffic was thick—it was by now well after nine o'clock—and the morning's business in full throng. Svenson took a breath and stepped out, keeping across the street from the hotel, walking close to the walls and behind other pedestrians, his right hand on the revolver in his pocket. He kept his gaze on the hotel, glancing quickly into each shop front or lobby that he passed. At the corner he trotted across and leaned casually against the wall, peering around. The St. Royale was across the avenue. He still saw no one he could place as a sentry. It made no sense. He had already been found here once, trying to see her. Why would they not, even as a contingency, consider he would do the same again? He wondered if the real trap lay inside—perhaps in another private room—where he could be dealt with outside the public view. The possibility made his errand more dangerous, for he would not know until the last moment whether he was safe or not. Still, he'd made his choice. Grimly resolved, Svenson continued down the sidewalk.

He was nearly opposite the hotel when his view became blocked by two delivery carts whose horses had run afoul of each other. The drivers cursed loudly as men jumped from each cart to disentangle the harnesses and carefully back up each team. This caused the coaches behind to stop in turn—with another eruption of curses from each newly inconvenienced driver. Svenson could not help being distracted—his attention on the two carts as they finally worked themselves free and passed by, their drivers each offering one last particularly foul epithet—and so he found himself directly across from the hotel's front entrance when the avenue had cleared. Before him, splendidly arrayed in a violet dress brilliantly shot with silver thread, black gloves, and a delicate black hat, stood Madame Lacquer-Sforza. Next to her, once more in a striped dress—now of blue and white—stood Miss Poole. Svenson immediately shrank away, pressing against the windows of a restaurant. They did not see him. He waited—scanning the street in either direction—ecstatic that he might be able to speak to her without entering the hotel, without being trapped. He swallowed, glanced for an opening in the coach traffic, and stepped forward.

His foot had just left the paved sidewalk for the cobbled street when he froze and then instantly scrambled backwards. From behind the two women had emerged Francis Xonck—now wearing an elegant yellow morning coat and top hat—tugging on a pair of yellow kidskin gloves. With a handsome smile he bent and whispered something that spurred Miss Poole to blush and giggle and Madame Lacquer-Sforza to wryly smile. Xonck extended an arm for each woman and stepped between them as they hooked their arms in his. He nodded toward the street and for a horrified moment Svenson thought he had been seen—he was more or less in plain sight—but saw that Xonck referred to an open coach that was even then drawing to them, blocking Svenson's view. In the coach sat the Comte d'Orkancz, in his fur, his expression dark. The Comte made no effort to speak or acknowledge the others as they entered the coach, Xonck assisting each woman and climbing in last. Madame Lacquer-Sforza sat next to the Comte. She leaned to whisper in his ear. He—grudgingly, but as if he too were unable to resist—smiled. At this Xonck grinned, showing his white teeth, and Miss Poole burst into another fit of giggles. The coach pulled away. Svenson turned and reeled down the street.

She was gone—she was with them. No matter what other webs she might be spinning, Madame Lacquer-Sforza was their ally. If he could have spoken to her alone—but he had no longer any idea where or when or how that might happen. Svenson looked back at the hotel and saw that two of the Comte's men were lounging by the main entrance. He walked steadily away, his face down, seized by the realization of just how close he had come to suicide. At the end of the block he again ducked around the corner and pressed himself against the wall. What could he possibly do? Where could he possibly go? What leverage could he acquire against such a powerful cabal? He looked up and saw across Grossmaere Avenue... was it? It was—the road he had taken so long ago with the Comte, toward the secret garden and the greenhouse. The woman. He could find her—he could take her—he could ransack the greenhouse for information—he might even lay in ambush for the Comte himself. What did he have to lose? He peered back at the hotel entrance—the men were laughing together. Svenson gauged the traffic and darted out, ducking behind one coach and then another, and was across the avenue. He looked back. No one was following. He was clear of them, and moved with a new purpose.

He tried to remember the exact route to the garden. It had been dark and the streets thick with fog, and his attention elsewhere—on the men following and on the Comte's conversation. The streets looked so very different in the day and full of people. Still, he could find it—a turn here, along the next block, across that lane—and then around another corner. He found himself at a broad intersection, feeling as if he had mistaken part of the path, when he saw the entrance to a narrow lane across and farther down the street. Could that be it? He walked rapidly along his side of the street until he could gaze down the lane . . . it was different, but he thought he could see the church-like alcove where the Comte had unlocked the door. Could that be the high wall that lined the garden? Would there be men guarding it? Could he force the lock? Though the alley itself was empty of traffic, he knew all these questions would have to be answered with the crowded avenue only a stone's throw away. Before he crossed the street toward it, he gave one last look around him to make sure he had not been followed.

Svenson froze. Behind him, through the glass double doors of what had to be another hotel, he saw a young woman sitting on a plush settee, her chestnut hair falling in sausage curls over her face, bent seriously over an open journal, scribbling notes, surrounded by books and newspapers. One of her legs was folded under her on the settee, but on the other—her dress riding up just enough to reveal her shapely calf—she wore a darling green ankle boot. Without another thought Doctor Svenson opened the door to the hotel and went in.

FOUR

Boniface

Naturally enough, Miss Temple's first reaction was one of annoyance. She had abandoned her rooms to avoid the mute searching gaze of her maids, silently following her about like a pair of cats, and the far more insistent presence of her Aunt Agathe. She had slept nearly all of the previous day, and when she finally opened her eyes the sky was once again dark. She had bathed and eaten in silence, then slept again. When she woke for the second time in the early morning her aunt had installed herself at the foot of the bed in an armchair dragged by the maids from another room. It had been made clear to Miss Temple the distress she had caused, starting with her unforeseen absence at afternoon tea, and then at dinner, and finally her (characteristically stubborn and reckless) refusal to appear throughout the whole of the evening, to the point that the hotel staff had been alerted—a point of no return, to put it bluntly. This notoriety within the Boniface could only have been inflamed by Miss Temple's own bloody unexplained arrival (only minutes, Agathe insisted, after she herself had fallen asleep from the exhaustion of worry and waiting).

Agathe was the older sister of Miss Temple's father, and had lived in the city all of her life. She had been married once to a man who died young and without money, and Agathe had spent her extended widowhood drawing meagerly upon the fortune of a distant grudging sibling. Her hair was grey and at all times tightly kept beneath a hat or wrap or kerchief, as if exposure to the air might breed disease. Her teeth were whole but discolored where her gums had pulled away, which made them appear rather long and giving the rare smiles she was able to bestow onto her niece an unwholesome predatory aspect.

Miss Temple accepted there had been cause for worry and so she had done all she could to allay the aged woman's fear, even going so far as to answer aloud the delicately pressing question that obviously loomed unvoiced behind her aunt's every euphemistic query—did her niece still possess her virtue? She had assured her aunt that indeed, she had returned intact, and all the more determined to remain so. She did not, however, go into any great detail about where she had been or what she had endured.

The bloody silk underthings and the filthy topcoat had been burnt in the room's coal heater while she'd been asleep—the maids hesitantly bringing them to her aunt's attention when they'd found them littering the floor. Miss Temple herself had refused any suggestion that she see a doctor, a refusal Aunt Agathe had accepted without protest. This acquiescence had surprised Miss Temple, but then she realized her aunt believed that the smaller the circle of knowledge, the smaller the prospect for scandal. They had managed to find a potent salve for the still-raw scoring above her left ear. She would retain a scar, but her hair, once washed and re-curled, hung down to cover it perfectly well, save for a small cherry-red flick the size of a baby's thumbnail that extended, glistening with salve, onto the unblemished skin of her cheekbone. However, as Miss Temple sat in bed eating her breakfast, she found her aunt's investiture in the armchair increasingly odious, watching her every bite like an animal hoping for scraps—in this case hoping for some further explanation, some crumb of surety that her position and pension were not to be obliterated by the foolish, wanton urges of a naïve girl thrown over by her ambitious cad of a sweetheart. The problem was that Agathe said nothing. Not once did she challenge Miss Temple's actions, not once did she trumpet the young lady's reckless irresponsibility or upbraid her for an unlikely escape, which was surely the result of some undeserved divine intervention. All of this Miss Temple could have dealt with, but the silence—the somehow *puling* silence—vexed her extremely. Once the tray had been removed she announced in a voice of unquestionable clarity that, while she again regretted any inconvenience caused, she had become involved in an adventure, she was unharmed and, far from being finished with the matter, had every intention to pursue it most keenly. Her aunt did not answer, but merely cast her disapproving gaze away from Miss Temple and toward the tidy work desk, upon which the large oiled revolver lay like some kind of loathsome stuffed reptile, a gift brought from some strange uncle's journey to Venezuela. Her aunt looked back at Miss Temple. Miss Temple announced that she would also be needing a box of the appropriate cartridges.

Her aunt did not respond. Miss Temple took this as an opportunity to end the discussion—or non-discussion—and left the bed for her dressing room, locking the door behind her. With a sigh of frustration she balled her nightdress over her waist and squatted on the chamber pot. It was still early morning, but there was light enough to see her green boots on the floor where the maids had placed them. She winced with discomfort as she wiped herself and stood, replacing the lid. When she had taken her bath it had been dark, mere candle light. She walked to the mirror and understood why the others had stared so. On her throat, above the collar of her nightdress, were bruises—the exact purpled impressions of fingertips and a thumb. She leaned her face closer to the glass and touched them gingerly: it was a ghost of Spragg's hand. She took a step back and pulled the nightdress over her head. She felt her breath catch, fear dancing along the length of her spine, for it was as if she looked at a different body than her own. There were so many bruises and scratches, the narrow margin of her survival was abruptly, horribly vivid. She ran her fingers over each point of discolored, tender flesh, finally cupping herself where his fingers had most cruelly marked her.

She shut her eyes and sighed heavily, unable to quite expel her unease along with her breath. It was not a feeling Miss Temple could easily tolerate. She reminded herself sternly that she had escaped. The men were dead.

Miss Temple emerged some minutes later in her dressing gown, calling for the maids, and sat at her desk. She pushed up her sleeves—making a firm point not to glance at her aunt, who was staring at her—and picked up the revolver with as much confidence as she could muster. It took her longer than she would have liked—long enough that both maids were now watching as well—but finally she was able to open the cylinder and empty the remaining shells onto the blotter. This done, she quickly wrote a list—again, in the writing taking more time than she would have liked, simply because with each item details emerged that she must make plain. When she was finished she blew on the paper to dry the ink, and turned to the maids. They were two country girls, near enough to her own age that the gaps in respective experience and education became so obvious as to be unbridgeable. To the older, who could read, she handed the folded piece of paper.

"Marie, this is a list of items I will require both from the hotel management and from shops in the city. You will present the management with items one, two, and three, and then from them receive directions as to the shops best suited to satisfy items four and five. I will give you money"—and here Miss Temple reached into the desk drawer and removed a leather notebook with a small pile of crisp banknotes tucked into it. She deliberately peeled off two—then three—notes and handed them to Marie, who bobbed her head as she took them—"and you will make the purchases. Do not forget *receipts*, so I will know exactly how much money has been spent."

Marie nodded gravely, and with some reason, for Miss Temple was habitually watchful with her money and did not allow odd small sums to disappear where others might, or at least not without due acknowledgment of her generosity.

"The first item is a collection of newspapers, the *World,* the *Courier,* the *Herald,* for today, for yesterday, and for the day before. The second item is a map of the local railway lines. The third item is a geographical map, specifically as it relates to the coastal fen country. The fourth item, which you must find, is a box of *these.*" Here she handed Marie one of the bullets from the revolver. "The fifth item, which will most likely take the longest, for you must be extremely exacting, are three sets of undergarments—you know my sizes—in the finest silk: one in white, one in green, and one . . . in black."

With the other maid, Marthe, she retreated into her dressing room to finish her hair, tighten her corset, and apply layers of powder and cream over the bruises on her throat. She emerged, in another green dress, this with a subtle sort of Italian stitchwork across the bodice, and her ankle boots, which Marthe had duly polished, just as a knock on the door brought the first wave of newspapers and maps. The room clerk explained that they had been forced to send out for some of the previous days' editions, but that these should arrive shortly. Miss Temple gave him a coin, and as soon as he was gone placed the pile on the main dining table and began to sort through it. She did not exactly know what she was looking for, only that she was finished with the frustration of not knowing what she had stepped into. She compared the rail map with the topographical atlas, and began to meticulously plot the route from Stropping Station to Orange Canal. Her finger had progressed as far as De Conque when she became particularly aware of Marthe and Agathe staring at her. She briskly asked Marthe to make tea, and merely gazed steadily at her aunt. Far from taking the hint, Aunt Agathe installed herself in another chair and muttered that a cup of tea would suit her very well.

Miss Temple shifted in her chair, blocking her aunt's view with her shoulder, and continued to trace the line to Orange Locks, and from there to the Orange Canal itself. She took a particular pleasure in plotting the progress from station to station, having a visual reference for each one in her memory. The rail map had no further detail about roads or villages, much less particularly great houses, so she pulled the atlas toward her and found the page with the greatest detail of the area. She marveled at the distance she had traveled, and suppressed another shiver at how isolated and in peril she had actually been. The country between the final two stations seemed uninhabited—there were no villages on the map that she could find. She knew the great house had been near the sea, for she remembered the smell of salt in the air, though she well knew that the sea breeze travels far over land as flat as the fen country, so it could have been farther than it seemed. She tried to work out a reasonable radius of possibility, given the time the coach took to reach the house from the station, and looked for any landmark whatsoever on the map. She saw an odd symbol near the canals themselves, which a quick check with the map's legend told her signified "ruin". How old was the map—could a house that size be so new? Miss Temple looked up at her aunt.

"What is 'Harschmort'?"

Aunt Agathe took in a sharp breath, but said nothing. Miss Temple narrowed her eyes. Neither spoke (for in some ways at least the older lady partook of a familial stubbornness) and after a full silent minute Miss Temple slammed the atlas shut and, brusquely rising from the table, strode to her inner room. She returned, to her aunt's great alarm, with the open revolver, reloading the bullets as she went, and making a great effort at slamming the cylinder home. Miss Temple looked up to see the two women gaping at her and sneered—did they think she was going to shoot them?—snatching up a clutch handbag and dropping the revolver into it. She wound the strap around her wrist and then proceeded to gather her pile of papers with both arms. She snapped at Marthe without the least veil over her irritation. "The *door,* Marthe." The servant girl darted to the front door and pulled it open so Miss Temple, her arms full, was free to sail through. "I will be working where I can find *peace,* if not *cooperation.*"

Walking down the thickly carpeted corridor, and then down to the lobby, Miss Temple felt as if she were re-entering the world, and more importantly that she was confronting the events that had overtaken her. As she walked past various maids and porters, she knew that—because it was the morning shift—these were the same that had seen her blood-soaked arrival. Of course they had all spoken of it, and of course they all cast inquiring glances her way as she walked by. Miss Temple's resolve was firm, however, and she knew if anything had changed, it was only that she needed to be even more self-reliant. She knew how fortunate she was to have her independence, and to have a disposition that cared so little for the opinions of others. Let them talk, she thought, as long as they also saw her holding her head high, and as long as she possessed the whip-hand of wealth. At the main desk she nodded at the clerk, Mr. Spanning—the very man who had opened the door upon her bloody return. Society manners were not so different than those among her father's livestock, she knew, or his pack of hounds— and so Miss Temple held Spanning's gaze longer than normal, un- til he obsequiously returned her nod.

She had installed herself on one of the wide plush settees in the empty lobby, a quick, hard glare alerting the staff that she required no assistance, spreading the papers into organized stacks. She be- gan by going back to "Harschmort," jotting down her observa- tions—its status as a ruin, its location. She then turned first to the *Courier,* whose pages would be more likely to follow social affairs. She was determined to learn all she could about the gala evening— first as it was understood by the populace at large, and then, by way of any comments she might find about murdered men in the road or missing women, about its true insidious nature. She read through headlines without any immediate idea of what might be most important: scanning the large black type announcing colonial skirmishes, cunning inventions, international ballooning, society balls, works of charity, scientific expeditions, reforms in the navy, infighting amongst the Ministries—it was clear that she was going to have to *delve*. It had not been ten minutes before she sensed the shadow falling over her work and then heard—had someone come in the main doors?—the vaguely insistent clearing of a throat. She looked up, fully ready to audibly snarl if her Aunt Agathe or Marthe had presumed to follow, but Miss Temple's eyes saw someone quite different.

He was a strange sort of man, tall, crisply rumpled in the way only a neat-minded person can be, wearing a blue greatcoat with pale epaulettes and silver buttons and scuffed black boots. His hair was almost white, parted in the center of his head and plastered back, though his exertions had caused some of it to break free and fall over his eyes, one of which held a monocle on a chain. He had not shaved, and it seemed to her that he was not especially well. She could not tell his age, partly because of his obvious fatigue, but also because of the way his hair, which was long on the top of his head, had been shaved on the back and sides, almost like some medieval lord—though perhaps he was merely German. He was staring at her, his gaze moving from her face down to her boots. She looked down at them, then up at his face. He was having difficulty with his words. There was a sparsity about the fellow she found nearly touching.

"Excuse me," he began. His voice was accented, which caused his phrasing to seem more formal than it actually was. "I—I apologize—I have seen you—I did not realize—but now—somehow—through the window—" He stopped, took a breath, swallowed, and opened his mouth to start again and then snapped it shut. She realized that he was staring at her head—the wound above her cheekbone—and then, with rising discomfort, that his eyes had dropped lower, over her neck. He looked up at her, speaking with surprise.

"You have been injured!"

Miss Temple did not reply. While she had not truly expected her cosmetics could hide the bruises for long, she was not prepared to be so soon discovered, much less confront the spectacle of her mauling, reflected in the man's expression of concern. And yet, who was this man? Could agents of the woman in red have found her so soon? As slowly as she could make her hand do it, she reached for the clutch bag. He saw the movement and put up his hand.

"Please—no—of course. You do not know who I am. I am Captain-Surgeon Abelard Svenson, of the Macklenburg Navy, in diplomatic service to his majesty Prince Karl-Horst von Maasmärck, who at this very moment is missing. I am your ally. It is of the utmost importance that we speak."

As he spoke Miss Temple slowly completed her reach for the bag, bringing it back to her lap. He watched in silence as she inserted her hand, clearly understanding that she took hold of a weapon.

"You said you had . . . seen me?"

"Indeed," he said, and then smiled, chuckling strangely. "I cannot even explain it—for truly, we have never to my knowledge been in each other's presence!"

He glanced behind her, and took a step back—obviously the staff at the desk had taken notice. For Miss Temple this was too much, too quickly—she did not trust it. Her thoughts were spinning back to the terrible evening—Spragg and Farquhar—and who knew how many other minions in service to the woman in red.

"I do not know what you mean," she said, "or indeed, what you *think* you mean, seeing that by your accent you are a foreigner. I assure you that we have never met."

He opened his mouth to speak, then closed it, then opened it again.

"That may be true. Yet, I have seen you—and I am sure you can assist me."

"Why would you possibly think that?"

He leaned toward her and whispered. "Your *shoes*."

To this, Miss Temple had no answer. He smiled and swallowed, glancing back out to the street. "Is there perhaps another place where we might discuss—"

"There is not," she said.

"I am not mad—"

"You do look it, I assure you."

"I have not slept. I have been hunted through the streets—I offer no danger—"

"Prove it," said Miss Temple.

She realized that with her sharp tone there was a part of her that was trying to drive him away. At the same time, another part of her realized that, far from wading through maps and newspapers, she had in his person been presented with the exact advantage she would have wished for in her investigation. She balked because the circumstance was so real, so immediate, and because the man was so obviously stricken with fatigue and distress—qualities from which Miss Temple instinctively withdrew. By continuing these inquiries, what might she herself endure in the future—or endure *again*? No matter how much she might steel herself to it in the abstract, the corporeal evidence shook Miss Temple's resolve.

She looked up at him and spoke quietly. "I should appreciate it if you could . . . in some fashion . . . please."

He nodded, gravely. "Then—permit me." He sat on the end of the settee and reached into his coat pocket. He pulled out two gleaming blue cards, quickly glanced at each and then returned one to the pocket. The other, he held out to her.

"I do not understand what this is. I only know what it shows me. As I say, there is a great deal to talk about and, if my fears are correct, very little time. I have been awake all night—I apologize for my desperate appearance. Please, look into this card—as if you were looking into a pool—take it with both hands or you will surely drop it. I will stand apart. Perhaps it will tell you more than it has told me."

He gave her the card and stepped away from the settee. With shaking hands he took a dark foul-looking cigarette from a silver case and lit it. Miss Temple studied the card. It was heavy, made of a kind of glass she had never seen, brilliant blue that shifted in hue—from indigo to cobalt to even bright aqua—depending on the light passing through. She glanced once more at the strange doctor—he *was* a German, by his accent—and then she looked into the card.

Without his warning she would have certainly dropped it. As it was, she was happy to be sitting down. She had never experienced the like, it was as if she were swimming, so *immersive* were the sensations, so tactile the images. She saw herself—*herself*—in the parlor of the Bascombe house, and knew that her hands were clutching the upholstery because, out of his mother's sight, Roger had just leaned forward to blow softly across her nape. The experience was not unlike seeing herself in the mirror wearing the white mask, for here she somehow appeared through the eyes of another—lustful eyes that viewed her calves and bare arms with hunger, almost as if they were rightful possessions. Then the entire location shifted, somehow seamlessly, as if in a dream . . . she did not recognize the pit or the quarry, but then gasped to see the country house of Roger's uncle, Lord Tarr. Next was the coach and the Deputy Minister—"your decision?"—and finally the eerie curving hallway, the banded metal door, and the terrifying chamber. She looked up and found herself once again in the lobby of the Boniface. She was panting for breath. It was Roger. She knew that all of this had been the experience—in the mind—of Roger Bascombe. Her heart leapt in her chest, surging with anguish that was swiftly followed by rage. Decision? Could that mean what she thought? If it did—and of course it must—it *must*!—Harald Crabbé became in that instant Miss Temple's particular, unpardonable enemy. She turned her flashing eyes to Svenson, who stepped back to the settee.

"How—how does this *work*?" she demanded.

"I don't know."

"Because ... well ... because it is *very* queer."

"Indeed, it is most disquieting—an—ah—unnatural *immediacy*."

"Yes! It is—it is ..." She could not find the words, and then stopped trying and merely blurted, "... *unnatural*."

"Did you recognize anything?" he asked.

She ignored him. "Where did you get this?"

"If I tell you—will you assist me?"

"Possibly."

He studied her face with an expression of concern that Miss Temple had seen in her life before. Her features were pretty enough, her hair fine and her figure, if she were permitted to have an opinion, reasonably appealing, but Miss Temple knew by now and was no longer disquieted by the knowledge that she was only truly remarkable in the way an animal is remarkable, in the way an animal so fully and purely inhabits its *self* without qualm. Doctor Svenson, when faced with her strangely elemental presence, swallowed, then sighed.

"I found it sewn into the jacket of a dead man," he said.

"Not"—she held up the card, her voice suddenly brittle, feeling completely caught out—"not *this* man?"

She was unprepared for the possibility that anything so serious could have happened to Roger. Before she could say more, Svenson was shaking his head.

"I do not know who *this* man is, the—the point of *vantage,* so to speak—"

"It is Roger Bascombe," she said. "He is at the Foreign Ministry."

The Doctor clucked his tongue, clearly annoyed at himself. "Of course—"

"Do you know him?" she inquired tentatively.

"Not as such, but I have seen—or heard—him this very morning. Do you know Francis Xonck?"

"O! He is a terrible rake!" said Miss Temple, feeling foolishly prim as soon as she said it, having so thoughtlessly parroted the gossip of women she despised.

"No doubt," agreed Doctor Svenson. "Yet Francis Xonck and this man—Bascombe—between them were disposing of a body—"

She indicated the card. "The man who had this?"

"No, no, someone else—though they are related, for this man's arms—the blue glass—excuse me, I am getting ahead of myself—"

"How many bodies are involved—to your own knowledge?" she asked, and then, before he could answer, added, "And if you might—if it were possible to—generally—*describe* them?"

"Describe them?"

"I am not merely morbid, I assure you."

"No . . . no, indeed—perhaps you too have merely witnessed— yet I can only hope you have not—in any event, yes—I myself have seen two bodies—there may be others—others in peril, and others I myself may have slain, I do not know. One, as I say, was a man I did not know, an older man, connected to the Royal Institute of Science and Exploration—a fellow I am led to believe of some great learning. The other was a military officer—his disappearance was in the newspaper—Colonel Arthur Trapping. I believe he was poisoned. How the first man—well, the officer was actually the first to die—but how the *other* man, from the Institute, was killed, I cannot begin to understand, but it is part of the mystery of this blue glass—"

"Only those?" asked Miss Temple. "I see."

"Do you know of others?" asked Doctor Svenson.

She decided to confide in him.

"Two men," Miss Temple said. "Two horrible men."

She could not for the moment say more. On impulse she removed a handkerchief from her bag, moistened a corner and leaned forward to dab at a thin line of blood etched across the Doctor's face. He muttered apologies and took the cloth from her, stepping away, and stabbed vigorously at his face. After a moment, he pulled it away and folded it over, offering it back. She motioned for him to keep it, smiling grimly and off-handedly wiping her eye.

"Let me see the other card," said Miss Temple. "You have another in your pocket."

Svenson blanched. "I—I do not think, the time—"

"I do insist." She was determined to learn more about Roger's inner life—who he had seen, the bargains with Crabbé, his true feelings for *her*. Svenson was blathering excuses—did he want some kind of exchange?

"I cannot allow—a lady—please—"

Miss Temple handed him the first card. "The country house belongs to Roger's uncle, Lord Tarr."

"Lord Tarr is his uncle?"

"Of course Lord Tarr is his uncle."

Svenson did not speak. Miss Temple pointedly raised her eyebrows, waiting.

"But Lord Tarr has been murdered," said Svenson.

Miss Temple gasped.

"Francis Xonck spoke of this Bascombe's inheritance," said Svenson, "that he would soon be important and powerful—my thought—when Crabbé says 'decision'—"

"I'm afraid that is quite impossible," snapped Miss Temple.

But even as she spoke, her mind raced. Roger had *not* been his uncle's heir. While Lord Tarr (a gouty difficult man) had no sons, he did have daughters with male children of their own—it had been quite clearly and bitterly explained to her by Roger's mother. Moreover, as if to confirm Roger's peripheral status, on their sole visit to Tarr Manor, its ever-ailing Lord proved disinclined to see Roger, much less make the acquaintance of Roger's provincial fiancée. And now Lord Tarr had been murdered, and Roger somehow acclaimed as his heir to lands and title? She could not trust it for a minute—but what other inheritance could Roger have? She did not think Roger Bascombe a murderer—all the more since having herself recently met several of the species—but she knew he was weak and tractable, despite his broad shoulders and his poise, and she suddenly felt cold . . . the people he had fallen in with, the demonstration he had willingly witnessed in the operating theatre . . . within her vow to ruin him, her utter and complete disdain for all things Bascombe, it was with a tinge of sorrow that Miss Temple felt oddly certain that he was lost. Just as she had wondered, in the operating theatre at Harschmort, if Roger had truly understood with whom or what he had become entangled—and in that wondering felt a pang at being unable to protect him from his own blindness when it came to the powerful and rich—so Miss Temple felt suddenly sure that, one way or another and without it being his intention, these events would be his doom.

She looked up at Svenson. "Give me the other card. Either I am your ally or I am not."

"You have not even told me your name."

"Haven't I?"

"No, you have not," said the Doctor.

Miss Temple pursed her lips, then smiled at him graciously and offered her hand, along with her standard explanation.

"I am Miss Temple, Celestial Temple. My father enjoyed

astronomy—I am fortunate not to be named for one of Jupiter's moons." She hesitated, then exhaled. "Though if we are to be true allies, then—yes—you must call me Celeste. Of course you must—though I am quite unable to call you, what is it—Abelard? You are older, foreign, and it would in any case be ridiculous." She smiled. "There. I am so very pleased to have made your acquaintance. I am sure I have never before met an officer of the Macklenburg Navy, nor a captain-surgeon of any kind."

Doctor Svenson took her hand awkwardly. He bent over to kiss it. She pulled it away, not unkindly.

"You needn't do that. It is not Germany."

"Of course...as you say." Miss Temple saw with some small satisfaction that Doctor Svenson was blushing.

She smiled at him, her gaze pointedly drifting to the pocket that held the second card. He noted this and hesitated, quite awkwardly. She did not see the difficulty—she had already seen the other—she would not be disoriented a second time.

"Perhaps you would prefer to view it in a more private room—"

"I would not."

Svenson sighed and fished out the card. He handed it to her with an evident wave of trepidation. "The man—it is not Bascombe—is my Prince—also a rake. It is the St. Royale Hotel. Perhaps you will know the woman—I know her as Mrs. Marchmoor...or the...ah...spectators. In this glass card—the, ah, vantage of experience—lies with the lady." He stood and turned away from her, making a fuss of finding and lighting another cigarette, refusing to meet her eye. She glanced at the desk clerks, who were still watching with interest, despite being unable to hear the intense conversation, then to Svenson, who she saw had discreetly stepped away and turned to study the leaves of a large potted plant. Her curiosity was thoroughly piqued. She looked into the card.

When she lowered the card some minutes later, Miss Temple's

face was flushed and her breathing rapid. She looked nervously around her, met the idly curious eye of the desk clerk and immediately turned away. She was relieved and somewhat touched to see that Doctor Svenson still had his back to her—for he clearly knew what she had been experiencing, if only by virtue of another woman's body. She could not believe what had just happened— what had *not* happened, despite the intimacy, the utterly persuasive intimacy of the equally disquieting and delicious sensations. She had just—she could not believe—in *public*, for the first time, without warning!—and felt ashamed that she had so insisted, that she had not taken the Doctor's strong hint to withdraw—and so had been—a man she did not know, nor had feelings for—though she had sensed the lady's feelings for him, or for the experience— could those be separated? She shifted in her seat and straightened her dress, feeling to her dismay an undeniable, insistent itching tickle between her legs. If her aunt had at that moment asked again about her virtue, how should she answer? Miss Temple looked down at the glass rectangle in her hands, and marveled at the vast and thoroughly disquieting possibilities residing in such a creation.

She cleared her throat. Doctor Svenson turned at once, his gaze flickering across her, refusing for a moment to meet her eyes. He stepped closer to the settee. She handed him the glass card and smiled up at him quite shyly.

"My goodness…"

He returned it to his pocket, touchingly mortified. "I am desperately sorry—I'm afraid I did not make clear—"

"Do not trouble yourself—please, it is I who should apologize—though in truth I should prefer not to speak of it further."

"Of course—forgive me—it is vulgar of me to go on so."

She did not answer—for she could not answer without prolonging what she herself had just expressed a desire to curtail.

There followed a pause. The Doctor looked at her with an uncomfortable expression. He had no idea what to say next. Miss Temple sighed.

"The lady, whose—as you say, whose *vantage* is conveyed—do you know her?"

"No, no—but did you . . . perhaps . . . recognize anyone?"

"I could not be sure—they were all masked, but I think the lady—"

"Mrs. Marchmoor."

"Yes. I believe I have seen her before. I do not know her name, nor even her face, for I have only seen her so masked."

She saw Doctor Svenson's eyes widen. "At the engagement party?" He paused. "At—at Lord Vandaariff's!"

Miss Temple did not answer at once, for she was thinking. "Indeed, at . . . ah—what is the name of his house?"

"Harschmort."

"That's right—it was once some kind of ruin?"

"So I am told," said Svenson, "a coastal fortification—Norman, perhaps—and then after that, with some expansion—"

Miss Temple recalled the plain, thick, forbidding walls and risked a guess. "A prison?"

"Exactly so—and then Lord Vandaariff's own home, purchased from the Crown and completely re-made at some great expense."

"And the night before last—"

"The engagement party, for the Prince and Miss Vandaariff! But—but—you were there?"

"I confess . . . I was."

He was looking at her with intense curiosity—and she knew that she herself was keenly hungry for more information, particularly after the revelations about Roger and his uncle—and even now, the prospect of another person's narrative of the masked ball was desperately appealing. But Miss Temple also saw the extreme fatigue in the face and frame of her newfound ally, and—especially as he persisted in glancing suspiciously out of the window to the street—thought it by far the wiser course to procure for him a place to rest and recover, so that once they had agreed on a course of action, he would be capable of following it. Also, she had to admit, she wanted more time to go through the newspapers—now she had a better sense of what to look for—so that, once they did fully hash through each other's stories, she could present herself as less a foolish girl. She felt that her own experiences ought not to be undermined by the absence of a handful of place names and perfectly obvious—once one thought of them—hypotheses. She stood up. In an instant, his automatic politeness somehow doglike, Svenson was on his feet.

"Come with me," she said, rapidly collecting her papers and books. "I have been shamefully negligent." She marched across toward the hotel desk, her arms full, looking back at Doctor Svenson, who followed a step behind her, vague protests hovering about his mouth. "Or are you hungry?" she asked.

"No, no," he sputtered, "I—moments ago—in the street—coffee—"

"Excellent. Mr. Spanning?" This was to the sleek man behind the desk, who at once gave Miss Temple his every attention. "This is Doctor Svenson. He will need a room—he has no servants—a sleeping room and a sitting room should suffice. He will want food—some sort of broth, I expect—he is not completely well. And someone to clean his coat and boots. Thank you so much. Charge my account." She turned to face Svenson and spoke over his incoherent protest. "Do not be a fool, Doctor. You need help—there is an end to it. I am sure you will help me in your turn. Ah, Mr. Spanning, thank you so much. Doctor Svenson has no baggage—he will take the key himself."

Mr. Spanning held out the key to Svenson, who took it without a word. Miss Temple heaved her papers onto the counter, quickly signed the chit the clerk had placed in front of her, and then re-gathered her load. With a last crisp smile at Spanning—

openly daring the man to find anything in the transaction to assail propriety or sully her reputation in the slightest—she led the way up the main curving flight of stairs, a small industrious figure, with the lanky Doctor bobbing uncertainly in her wake. They reached the second floor and Miss Temple turned to the right, down a wide, red-carpeted corridor.

"Miss Temple!" whispered Svenson. "Please, this is too much— I cannot accept such charity—we have much to discuss—I am content to find a less expensive room in an unobtrusive lodging house—"

"That would be most inconvenient," answered Miss Temple. "I am certainly not inclined to seek you out in such a place, nor—if your furtive looks are anything to judge—ought you to be wandering the streets until we fully understand our danger, and you have had some sleep. Really, Doctor, it is quite sensible."

Miss Temple was proud of herself. After so many experiences that seemed almost designed to demonstrate the profound degree of Miss Temple's ignorance and incapacity, the exercise of such decisive action was highly satisfying. She was also—though she had only known him for a matter of minutes—pleased with herself for making the choice to accept Doctor Svenson, and to extend what aid she could. It was as if the more she was able to do, the farther she removed herself from the painful isolation of her time at Harschmort.

"Ah," she said, "number 27." She stopped to the side of the door, allowing Svenson to open it. He did so and peered inside, then indicated that she should enter before him. She shook her head. "No, Doctor. You must sleep. I will return to my own rooms, and when you have restored yourself, alert Mr. Spanning and he will send word, and the two of us can properly confer. I assure you I am looking toward that time with great impatience, but until you are fully rested—"

She was interrupted by the sound of a door opening farther down the corridor. Out of habit she glanced toward the sound and then returned her gaze to Svenson . . . and then—her eyes widening in surprise, the words dying on her lips—turned back to the guest who had just stepped into the hallway from his room. The man stood watching her, his eyes shifting quickly between her and Svenson. Miss Temple saw the Doctor's own expression was one of shock, even as she felt him groping in the pocket of his greatcoat. The man in the corridor walked slowly toward them, his footsteps absorbed by the thick carpet. He was tall, his hair black, his deep red coat reaching nearly down to the floor. He wore the same round dark glasses she had seen on the train. His movements were gracefully muscular, like a cat's, exuding ease and menace equally. She knew she should be reaching in her bag for the revolver, but instead calmly placed her hand over the Doctor's, stilling his movement. The man in red stopped perhaps a yard or two away. He looked at her—she could not see his eyes—then looked at the Doctor, and then at the open door between them.

He whispered, conspiratorially. "No blood. No princes. Shall we send for tea?"

The man in red shut the door behind him, his masked, depthless eyes fixed on Miss Temple and the Doctor as they stood in the small sitting room. Each had managed to secure a firm grip on their respective weapons. For a long moment, all three glanced back and forth between each other in silence. Finally, Miss Temple spoke to Doctor Svenson.

"I take it you know this man?"

"We have not spoken . . . perhaps it is better to say that we overlapped. His name—correct me if I am wrong, Sir—is Chang."

The man in red nodded in acknowledgment. "I do not know your name, though the lady . . . it's a pleasure to formally meet the famous Isobel Hastings."

Miss Temple did not answer. Beside her, she could feel Svenson sputtering. He pulled away from her, his eyes goggling.

"Isobel Hastings? But you—you were with Bascombe!"

"I was," said Miss Temple.

"But . . . how did they not know you? I am sure he is looking for you as well!"

"She looks very different in the . . . daylight." Chang chuckled.

Svenson stared at her, taking in the bruises, the red line traced by the bullet.

"I'm a fool. . . ." he whispered. "But . . . how—I beg your pardon—"

"He was on the train," she said to Svenson, her gaze fixed on Chang. "On my return from Harschmort. We did not speak."

"Did we not?" asked Chang. He looked to Svenson. "Did *we* not speak? You and I? I think we did. A man like me. A woman covered in blood—did she tell you that? A man brazening his way into and then away from a pack of enemies with a pistol. I think there was, in each instance . . . recognition."

No one spoke for a moment. Miss Temple took a seat on the small sofa. She looked up at the Doctor and indicated the armchair. He wavered, but then sat in it. They both looked at Chang, who drifted to the remaining chair, across from them both. It was only then that Miss Temple realized that something bright was tucked within his hand—his razor. From the way he moved, she had no doubt that he was far more dangerous with the razor than the two of them with their pistols put together—and if that was the case, then something entirely else was called for. She cleared her throat and very deliberately brought her hand out of her green clutch bag. She then took the bag from her lap and placed it to the side on the sofa. A moment later, Chang abruptly shoved the razor into his pocket. After another few seconds, Svenson removed his hand from his coat pocket.

"Were you in earnest about the tea?" Miss Temple asked. "I should like some very much. It is always best when discussing serious matters to do so around a teapot. Doctor—you are nearest—if you would be so kind as to ring the bell."

*   *   *

They did not speak in the minutes it took for the tea to be ordered
and then arrive, nor again in the time spent pouring, aside from
monosyllabic inquiries about lemon, milk, or sugar. Miss Temple
took a sip from her cup, one hand on the saucer beneath—it was
excellent—and so fortified decided that someone had better take
charge—for the Doctor seemed in danger of falling asleep and the
other man—Chang—was positively wolfish.

"Mr. Chang, you are clearly reticent—I am sure I do not mis-
speak when I say we all have good reason to be suspicious—and
yet you are here. I will tell you that Doctor Svenson and I have
been acquainted not above this hour, and that through a chance
meeting in the lobby of this hotel, exactly as we have met you in its
hallway. I can see that you are a dangerous man—I neither compliment nor criticize, it is merely plain enough—and so understand that if the three of us do come to some profound
disagreement, there may be a violent outcome which will leave at
least one faction, well, probably dead. Would you agree?"

Chang nodded, a smile playing about his lips.

"Excellent. Given this, I see no reason not to be candid—if any
tales are told, it will not disturb the dead, and if we are to join
forces, then we will be stronger for sharing our knowledge. Yes?"

Chang nodded again, and sipped his tea.

"You are very agreeable. I propose then—since I have already
spoken to Doctor Svenson—this is Captain-Surgeon Abelard
Svenson of the Macklenburg Navy"—here the men exchanged an
archly formal nod—"I will briefly narrate my part in this affair. As
the Doctor and I had not reached this level of frankness, I hope it
will be of some interest to him as well. The Doctor has been awake
all night, apparently the object of violent pursuit, and has lost his
Prince—as you so astutely noted in the hall." She smiled. "If
Doctor Svenson is *able* to continue..."

"By all means," Svenson muttered. "The tea has revived me powerfully."

"Mr. Chang?"

"I don't mean to be impertinent," observed Svenson, "but when I overheard men speaking of you—they called you 'Cardinal.'"

"It is what some call me," said Chang. "It derives from the coat."

"And do you know," said Miss Temple, "that Doctor Svenson recognized me by the color of my boots? Already we have so many interests in common."

Chang smiled at her, cocking his head, trying to gauge whether she was serious. Miss Temple chuckled aloud, satisfied to have pushed the razor so far from his thoughts. She took another sip of tea and began.

"My name is not Isobel Hastings, it is Celestial Temple. But no one calls me that—they call me Miss Temple, or—in particularly rare circumstances—they call me Celeste. At this moment, in this city, having met the Doctor and extended to him that privilege, the number has risen to two—the other being my aunt. Some time after my arrival here, from well across the sea, I became engaged to marry Roger Bascombe, a Deputy Under-Secretary in the Foreign Ministry, working primarily for Harald Crabbé." She felt Svenson's reaction to this news, but did not look at him, for it was so much easier to speak of anything delicate or painful to someone she knew not at all—still more to a man like Chang whose eyes she could not see. "Some days ago, after perhaps a week where I did not see him for various but perfectly believable reasons, I received a letter from Roger severing our engagement. I wish to make very plain to you both that I harbor no further feelings—save those of disdain—for Roger Bascombe. However, his brusque and cruel manner prompted me to discover the true cause of his act, for he tendered no explanation. Two days ago I followed him to

Harschmort. I disguised myself and saw many things and many people, none of which I was intended to see. I was captured and questioned and—I will be frank—given over to two men, to be first ravished and then killed. Instead, it was I who killed them—thus, Doctor, my question about *bodies*. On the return journey I made the acquaintance—the nodding acquaintance—of Cardinal Chang. It was during my interrogation that I gave the name Isobel Hastings . . . which seems to have followed me."

The two men were silent. Miss Temple poured more tea for herself, and then for the others, each man leaning forward with his cup.

"I'm sure there are many questions—the details of what and whom I saw—but perhaps it would be better if we continued in the broadest vein of disclosure? Doctor?"

Svenson nodded, drank the whole of his cup and leaned forward to pour another. He took a sip of this, the fresh cup steaming around his mouth, and sat back.

"Would either of you object if I smoked?"

"Not at all," said Miss Temple. "I'm sure it will sharpen your mind."

"I am much obliged," said Svenson, and he took a moment to extract a dark cigarette and set it alight. He exhaled. Miss Temple found herself studying the visible structure of the man's jaw and skull, wondering if he ever ate at all.

"I will be brief. I am part of the diplomatic party of my country's heir, Prince Karl-Horst von Maasmärck, who will marry Lydia Vandaariff. It is a match of international significance, and I am attached to the party in a medical capacity only for the sake of appearance. My prime aim is to protect the Prince—from his own foolishness, and from those around him seeking to take advantage of it—figures of which there has never been short supply. The diplomatic Envoy and the military attaché have both, I believe, betrayed their duty and given the Prince over to a cabal of private interest. I have rescued the Prince from their hands once—after he had been subject, perhaps willingly, to what they called 'the Process'—which leaves a perhaps temporary facial scarring, a burn—"

Miss Temple sat up to speak, and saw Chang do the same. Svenson held up his hand. "I am sure we have all seen evidence of it. My first instance was at the ball at Harschmort, when I briefly viewed the body of Arthur Trapping, but there have since been many others—the Prince, a woman named Mrs. Marchmoor—"

"Margaret Hooke," said Chang.

"Beg pardon?"

"Her true name is Margaret Hooke. She is a whore of the highest *echelon*."

"Ah," said Doctor Svenson, wincing with discomfort at the word being spoken in Miss Temple's hearing. While she was touched by his care, she found the impulse tiresome. If one was engaged in an adventure, an investigation, such delicacy was ridiculous. She smiled at Chang.

"There will be more about her later, for she figures elsewhere in our evidence," Miss Temple told him. "Is this not progress? Doctor, please go on."

"I say the scars may be temporary," continued Svenson, "because this very night I overheard Francis Xonck query Roger Bascombe about his own experience of this 'Process'—though I saw Bascombe's face myself when I was at the Institute—I am getting ahead of myself—and there was no such scarring."

Miss Temple felt a distant pang. "It was before he sent his letter," she said. "The days he claimed to be at work with the Deputy Minister . . . it was happening even then."

"Of course it was," said Chang, not unkindly.

"Of course it was," whispered Miss Temple.

*   *   *

"Harald Crabbé." Svenson nodded. "He is near the heart of it, but there are others with him, a cabal from the Ministry, the military, the Institute, other individuals of power—as I say, the Xonck family, the Comte d'Orkancz, the Contessa Lacquer-Sforza, even perhaps Robert Vandaariff—and somehow my country of Macklenburg is a part of their plan. In the face of indifference from my colleagues, I rescued the Prince from their twisted science at the Institute. It was there I saw Cardinal Chang. At our compound I was forced to attend to several of our soldiers—also, I believe, a result of Cardinal Chang"—again he held up his hand—"I make no judgments, they have since tried to kill *me*. In that time, the Prince was taken in secret from his room, I do not know how—from *above*. I set out alone to find him. In Harald Crabbé's house I heard Francis Xonck and Roger Bascombe discuss philosophy over the strangely disfigured body of an Institute savant—quantities of his blood had been turned to blue glass. They were joined by my own military attaché, Major Blach, who is part of their plans—the only bit of news being Blach's assumption that the cabal had taken the Prince, and Xonck's assurance that they had not. In any case, I escaped, and attempted to find Madame Lacquer-Sforza, but was taken by the Comte d'Orkancz—dragooned to consult on another medical matter, another of their experiments that had gone wrong—and then—it is a long story—given over to be killed, sent to the river bottom with the corpses of this dead scientist and Arthur Trapping. I escaped. I again tried to find Madame Lacquer-Sforza, only to see her with Xonck and d'Orkancz—she is one of them. In my flight from her hotel, I saw Miss Temple through the window—recognizing her from the card—I have not mentioned the cards—" He fumbled the cards onto the small table that held the tea tray. "One from the Prince, one from Trapping. As Miss Temple points out—they are valuable, if mysterious, evidence."

"You did not say where you heard the name Isobel Hastings," observed Chang.

"Didn't I? I'm sorry, from Madame Lacquer-Sforza. She asked

that I help her find one Isobel Hastings in exchange for telling me where the Prince was—at the Institute. That was the curious thing, for she told me where he was, allowing me to take him away quite against the wishes of Crabbé and d'Orkancz. This was why I had thought to find her again—for while someone took the Prince from our rooftop tonight, at least some of these conspirators—Xonck and Crabbé—seemed ignorant of his whereabouts. I had hoped *she* might know."

Miss Temple felt the back of her neck tingle. "Perhaps it would help, Doctor, if you could describe the woman."

"Of course," he began. "A tall woman, black hair, curled about her face and gathered in the back, pale skin, exquisite clothing, elegant to an almost vicious degree, gracious, intelligent, wry, dangerous, and I should say wholly remarkable. She gave her name as Madame Lacquer-Sforza—one of the hotel staff referred to her as Contessa—"

"The St. Royale Hotel?" asked Chang.

"The same."

"Do you know her?" asked Miss Temple.

"Merely as 'Rosamonde' . . . she hired me—that is what people do, hire me to do things. *She* hired me to find Isobel Hastings."

Miss Temple did not speak.

"I assume you know the woman," said Chang.

Miss Temple nodded, her earlier poise slightly shaken; as much as she tried to deny it, the Doctor's description had conjured the woman, and the dread she inspired, freshly into her thoughts.

"I do not know her names," said Miss Temple. "I met her at Harschmort. She was masked. At first she assumed I was one of a party with Mrs. Marchmoor and others—as you say, a group of whores—but then it was she who questioned me . . . and it was she who gave me over to die." As she finished speaking, her voice seemed painfully small. The men were silent.

*   *   *

"What is amusing—genuinely amusing," said Chang, "is that for all they are hunting us, we are not at all what they assume. My own portion of this tale is simple. I am a man for hire. I also followed a man to Harschmort—the man you saw dead, Doctor—Colonel Arthur Trapping. I had been hired to kill him."

He took a sip of tea and watched their reactions over the rim of his cup. Miss Temple did her level best to nod with the same degree of polite detachment as when someone mentioned a secret keenness for growing begonias. She glanced at Svenson, whose face was blank, as if this new fact merely confirmed what he'd already known. Chang smiled, somewhat bitterly, she thought.

"I did *not* kill him. He was killed by someone else—though I did see the scars you mentioned, Doctor. Trapping was a tool of the Xonck family—I do not understand who killed him."

"Did he betray them?" asked Svenson. "Francis Xonck sunk his body in the river."

"Does that mean Xonck killed him, or that he didn't want the body found—that he could not allow it to be found with the facial scars? Or something else? You mentioned the woman—why would she betray the others and allow you to rescue your Prince? I have no idea."

"I was able to examine the Colonel's body briefly, and believe he was poisoned—an injection of some kind, in his finger."

"Could it have been an accident?" asked Chang.

"It could have been anything," answered the Doctor. "I was about to be murdered at the time, and had no mind to reason clearly."

"May I ask who hired you to kill him?" asked Miss Temple.

Chang thought for a moment before answering.

"Obviously it is a professional secret," Miss Temple said. "Yet if you do not wholly trust that person, perhaps—"

"Trapping's adjutant, Colonel Aspiche."

Svenson laughed aloud. "I met him yesterday in the presence of

Madame Lacquer-Sforza at the St. Royale Hotel. By the end of the visit, Mrs. Marchmoor—" He glanced awkwardly at Miss Temple. "Let us say he is their creature."

Chang nodded and sighed. "The entire situation was wrong. The next day there was no body, no news, and Aspiche was useless and withdrawn, because—as you confirm—he was in the midst of being seduced. In short order, it was *I* who met seduction, in the form of this woman, who hired me to find one Isobel Hastings—a prostitute who had murdered her very dear friend."

Miss Temple snorted. They looked at her. She waved Chang on.

"With this description, I searched several brothels—never, for reasons that are now obvious, finding Isobel Hastings, but soon learning that two others—Mrs. Marchmoor and Major Black—"

"*Blach,* actually," said Svenson, providing the proper pronunciation.

"*Blach,* then," muttered Chang. "They were both searching for her as well, and in the Major's case at least, also searching for me. At Harschmort, I had been seen—and I am a figure some people know. When I returned to my own lodgings one of the Major's men tried to kill me. A trip to a third brothel led me to follow a small party—your Prince, Bascombe, Francis Xonck, a large fellow in a fur—"

"The Comte d'Orkancz," said Svenson.

"O!" said Miss Temple. "I have seen him as well!"

"He had taken Margaret Hooke from this same brothel, and was now taking another woman—I followed them to the Institute—saw you enter, Doctor, and followed you down. They are doing strange experiments with great amounts of heat and blue glass . . ." Chang picked up one of the blue cards from the tray. "It is the same glass, but instead of these small cards, here—and with great effort, with vast machinery—they had made a blue glass *book*—unfortunately the man making it was startled—by me—and dropped it. I am sure he is the man you saw on the Deputy Minister's table. In the confusion I escaped, only to meet your

Major and his men. I escaped from them as well, and found my way here . . . quite entirely by chance."

He leaned forward and took up the pot, pouring another round of tea. Miss Temple cradled her fresh cup and allowed it to warm her hands.

"What did you mean when you said we are not what our enemies assume?" she asked Chang.

"I *mean,*" Chang said, "that they believe that we are agents of a larger power—a cabal opposing their interests that has hitherto existed without their knowledge. They are so arrogant as to think that such a body—a mighty union of insidious talents like themselves!—is all that could possibly threaten them. The idea that they have been attacked by the haphazard actions of three isolated individuals—for whom they have contempt? It is the last thing they could believe."

"Only because it does not flatter them," Miss Temple sniffed.

Doctor Svenson was in the other room, asleep. His coat and boots were being cleaned. For a time Miss Temple and Chang had spoken about his experience of the hotel, and the coincidence that had brought all three of them together, but the conversation had fallen into silence. Miss Temple studied the man across from her, trying to make palpable sense of the knowledge that he was a criminal, a killer. What she saw was a certain kind of animal elegance— or, if not elegance, efficiency—and a manner that seemed both brazen and restrained. She knew this was the embodiment of experience, and she found it an attractive quality—wanting it for herself—even as she found the man daunting and disquieting. His features were sharp and his voice was flat and raw, and direct to a point just before insolence. She was intensely curious to know what he thought of her—what he had thought when he saw her on the train, and what he thought now, seeing her normal self—but could not ask him any of these things. She felt he must somehow despise her—despise the hotel room, the tea, the entirety of her life—for if she herself were not born to privilege, she was sure she would carry with her a general hatred for it every day of her life.

Cardinal Chang watched her from his chair. She smiled at him, and reached into her green bag.

"Perhaps you will help me, for I am only now tackling the matter..." She pulled out the revolver and placed it on the table between them. "I have sent out for more ammunition, but have little sense of the weapon itself. If you are knowledgeable about it, I would appreciate any advice you can give me."

Chang leaned forward and took the revolver in his hand, cocking it, and then slowly easing the hammer down. "I am not one for firearms," he said, "but I know enough to load and fire and keep a weapon clean." She nodded with anticipation. He shrugged. "We will need a cloth..."

Over the next half an hour he showed her how to reload, to aim, to break the gun apart, to clean it, to put it back together. When she had done this for herself, to her own satisfaction, she put the pistol back on the table and looked up at him, finally broaching the question she had withheld all that time.

"And what about killing?" she asked.

Chang did not immediately respond.

"I would appreciate your advice," she prompted.

"I thought you were already a killer," observed Chang. He was not smiling at her, which she appreciated.

"Not with this," she said, indicating the revolver.

She realized that he was still trying to decide if she was serious. She waited, a firm expression in her eyes. When Chang spoke, he was watching her very closely.

"Get as close as you can—grind the barrel into the body— there's no reason to shoot unless you mean to kill."

Miss Temple nodded.

"And stay calm. Breathe. You will kill better—and you'll die better too, if it comes to that." She saw that he was smiling. She looked into his black lenses.

"You live with that possibility, don't you?"

"Don't we all?"

She took a deep breath, for all of this was going a bit too quickly. She put the revolver back into her bag. Chang watched her stow it away.

"If you didn't kill them with that, how did you kill them? The two men."

She found she could not easily answer him.

"I—well, one of them—I—it was very dark—I . . ."

"You do not need to tell me," he said quietly.

She took another heavy breath and let it out slowly.

It was after another minute that Miss Temple was able to ask Chang what his plans for the day had been, before seeing them in the corridor. She indicated the papers and maps and explained her own intentions, and then noted that she ought to return to her rooms, if only to allay the worries of her aunt. She also remembered the two glass cards that Doctor Svenson had placed on the table.

"You really should look at them, particularly as you have seen some of their strange glasswork for yourself. The experience is unlike anything else I have known—it is both powerful and diabolical. You'll think I am foolish, but I promise you I know enough to see that in these cards is another kind of opium, and in the books you describe—an *entire* book—well, I cannot imagine it is anything but a splendid—or indeed, horrid—prison."

Chang leaned forward to pick up one of the cards, turning it over in his hand.

"One of them shows the experience—I cannot explain it—of Roger Bascombe. I myself make an appearance. Believe me, it is most disquieting. The other shows the experience of Mrs. Marchmoor—your Margaret Hooke—and is even *more* disquieting. I will say no more, only that it were better to view it in discreet solitude. Of course, to view either, you will really have to remove your spectacles."

Chang looked up at her. He pulled the glasses from his face and folded them into his pocket. She did not react. She had seen similar faces on her plantation, though never sitting across the tea table. She smiled at him politely, then nodded to the card in his hand.

"They really are the most lovely color blue."

Miss Temple left Cardinal Chang with the instruction that he should call for whatever meal the Doctor required upon waking, for which she would sign upon her return. She had her arms full of newspapers and books as she reached her own rooms, and kicked on the door three times instead of shifting her burdens to find her key. After a moment of rustling footsteps, the door was opened by Marthe. Miss Temple entered and dropped the pile of papers on the main table. Her aunt sat where she had left her, sipping a cup of tea. Before she could voice a reproof, Miss Temple spoke to her.

"I must ask you several questions, Aunt Agathe, and I will require your honest replies. You may be able to help me, and I will be very grateful for the assistance." She fixed her aunt with a firm look at the word "grateful" and then turned back to Marthe, to ask for Marie. Marthe pointed to Miss Temple's dressing room. Miss Temple entered to see Marie quickly folding and arranging a row of silk underthings on top of the ironing table. She stepped back as Miss Temple swept in and was silent as her mistress examined her purchases.

Miss Temple was extremely pleased, going even so far as to give Marie a congratulatory smile. Marie then pointed out the box of cartridges that sat by the mirror, and gave Miss Temple the receipts and leftover money. Miss Temple quickly scrutinized the figures and, satisfied, gave Marie an extra two coins for her efforts. Marie bobbed in surprise at the coins and again as Miss Temple

motioned her out of the room. The door shut behind her, Miss
Temple smiled again and turned to her purchases. The silk felt delicious between her fingers. She was happy to see that Marie had
been smart enough to select a green that matched the dress she was
wearing, and her boots. In the mirror, Miss Temple saw her own
beaming face and blushed, looking away. She composed herself,
cleared her throat, and called for her maids.

After the two young women had taken apart her dress and
corset, helped her into the green silk undergarments, and then restored her outer layers, Miss Temple—her entire body tickling
with enjoyment—carried the box of cartridges to the main table.
With all the casual efficiency she could muster, recalling each step
of Chang's instruction, she struck up a conversation with her aunt,
and as she spoke, spun the cylinder, snapped it open, and smoothly
loaded each empty chamber with a shell.

"I have been reading the newspapers, Aunt," she began.

"It seems you have enough of them."

"And do you know what I have learned? I saw the most aston-
ishing announcement about Roger Bascombe's uncle, Lord Tarr."

Aunt Agathe pursed her lips. "You should not be bothering
with—"

"Did you see the announcement?"

"Perhaps."

"Perhaps?"

"There is so much that I do not remember, my dear—"

"That he has been *murdered*, Aunt."

Her aunt did not reply at once. When she did, it was merely to
say, "Ah."

"Ah," echoed Miss Temple.

"He was quite gouty," observed her aunt, "something dire was
bound to happen. I understand it was wolves."

"Apparently not. Apparently the wound was altered to *impli-
cate* wolves."

"People will do anything," muttered Agathe.

She reached to pour more tea. Miss Temple slapped the cylinder back into position and spun it. At the noise, her aunt froze in position, eyes wide in alarm. Miss Temple leaned forward and spoke as deliberately and patiently as she could.

"My dear Aunt, you must accept that the money you need is in my possession, and thus, despite our difference in age, that I am your mistress. These are facts. Your position will not be helped by frustrating me. On the contrary, the more we work in concert, the more I promise your situation will improve. I have no wish to be your enemy, but you must see that your previous sense of what was best—my marriage to Roger Bascombe—is no longer appropriate."

"If you were not so *difficult*—" her aunt burst out, stopping herself just as quickly.

Miss Temple glared at her with unmitigated rage. Aunt Agathe recoiled as if from a snake.

"I am sorry, my dear," whispered the frightened woman, "I merely—"

"I do not care. *I do not care!* I am not asking about Lord Tarr because I *care*! I am asking because—though you do not know it—others have been murdered as well, and Roger Bascombe is in the thick of it—and now he will be the next Lord Tarr! I do not know how Roger Bascombe has become his uncle's heir. But you do, I am sure—and you are going to tell me this minute."

Miss Temple stalked down the corridor toward the stairwell, the clutch bag around her wrist, heavy with the revolver and an extra handful of cartridges. She snorted with annoyance and tossed her head—*difficult*—and cursed her aunt for a small-minded old fool. All the woman thought of was her pension and her propriety, and the number of parties she might be invited to as the relation of a rising Ministry official like Roger. Miss Temple wondered why she should even be surprised—her aunt had only known her for three months, but had been acquainted with the Bascombes for years. How long she must have planned, and how sharp had been her disappointment, Miss Temple sneered. But that her aunt held *her* at fault stung to the quick.

Yet under pressure she had answered her niece's questions, though her answers just added to the mystery. Roger's cousins— the over-fed Pamela and the younger but no less porcine Berenice—both had infant sons of their own, each of whom should have assumed Lord Tarr's title and lands before Roger. Yet both had signed a paper to waive their children's claims, to abdicate, and clear the way for Roger's inheritance and ennoblement. Miss Temple did not understand how Roger had managed this, for he was not especially wealthy, and she knew each woman well enough to be sure that no small sum would have satisfied either. The cash had been supplied by others, by Crabbé or his cohorts, that was obvious enough. But what was so important about Roger, and how did his advancement possibly relate to the various other plots and murders she had stumbled into? Further—though she told herself the question was merely academic—as Roger took up the rightful property of his cousins, what was he giving up of himself, and for what grand purpose?

In short order she had also learned—for her aunt followed the city's gossip with an evangelical fervor—the owner of Harschmort, the occasion of the masked ball, the reputations of Prince Karl-Horst and his bride (wretched and unsullied, respectively), and what she could about the various other names she had heard: Xonck, Lacquer-Sforza, d'Orkancz, Crabbé, Trapping, and Aspiche. The latter two her aunt did not know—though she was acquainted with the tragedy of Trapping's disappearance. Crabbé she knew by way of the Bascombes, but even that family concentrated their attention on the Chief Minister, and not his respected deputy—he was a figure in the government, but hardly public. As the Xonck family's fame was by way of business, it was signifi-

cantly less interesting to her aunt—though she had *heard* of
them—who was generally attracted to titles (indeed, Robert
Vandaariff's elevation within Agathe's mind to the rank of a Man
who Mattered had only occurred upon his becoming a Lord,
though Miss Temple understood that at a certain point such a man
must be made a Lord, lest the government appear peripheral to
him). Francis Xonck was of course a figure of scandal, though no
one knew exactly why—there were whispers about deviant tastes
from abroad newly appeared—but his elder siblings were merely
substantial. The Comte d'Orkancz her aunt only knew as a patron
of the opera—apparently he was born in some dire Balkan enclave,
raised in Paris, and inherited family titles and wealth after a particularly devastating series of house fires cleared the way. Beyond this,
Agathe could merely say he was a man of serious refinement,
learned and severe, who could have been at a university if those
university people were not so very dreadful. The final name, which
Miss Temple had put to her aunt with a quaver in her otherwise
sure interrogation, met with a hapless shrug. The Contessa Lacquer-
Sforza was of course *known,* but nothing seemed to be known
about her. She had arrived in the city the previous autumn—
Agathe smiled, and observed that it must have been very near to
when Miss Temple herself had arrived. Agathe had never seen the
lady, but she was said to rival Princess Clarissa or Lydia Vandaariff
for beauty. She smiled and sweetly asked her niece if *she* had seen
the Contessa, and if that were indeed the case. Miss Temple merely
snapped that of course not, she had seen none of these people—
she saw no one in society unless during her excursions with
Roger—and certainly none of these figures from the very cream of
the continent. She snorted that the Roger Bascombe *she* had
known was hardly the type to mix with such company. Her aunt,
with a rueful shake of her head, admitted this was true.

*   *   *

Miss Temple stopped on the landing between the third and second floors and, after looking around to see that she was not observed, sat on the stairs. She felt the need to order her thoughts
before rejoining her new comrades—she needed to order her
thoughts *about* her new comrades—and before advancing further
into her adventure. The sticking point, to her great dismay, remained Roger, neck deep in whatever was taking place. The man
was a fool, she knew that now without question—but she felt she
was constantly brought up against her former feelings as she strove
to move forward without them. Why could she not simply carve
them from her thoughts, from her heart? For moments she was
sure she had, and that the ache she felt, the pressure in her chest
and at the catch of her throat, was not love for Roger, but in fact
its absence, as the removal of anything substantial must leave behind it open space—a hole in her heart, so to speak, around which
her thoughts were, temporarily at least, forced to navigate. But
then without warning she would find herself worrying at how
Roger had placed his entire life so thoughtlessly at risk, and craving just one minute of sharp speech to wake him to his folly. Miss
Temple sighed heavily and had for some reason a vivid memory of
the plantation's sugar works, the great copper pots and the spiraled
coils that converted the raw cane into rum. She knew that Roger
had allied himself with people who sanctioned murder—her own
murder—and she feared, as cane was by rough science and fire reduced to rum, that this must inevitably lead to a mortal confrontation between Roger and herself. She felt the weight of the
revolver in her clutch bag. She thought of Chang and Svenson—
did they have any similar torment of feeling? They both seemed so
sure—especially Chang, who was a type of man she had never before known. Then she realized that this was not true, that she had
known other men with such open capacity for brutal action—in
fact, her father was just such a man—but there the brutality had
always been clothed in the guise of business and of ownership.
With Chang, the truth of the work was worn openly. She strug-

gled to find this refreshing—she told herself it was exactly that—but could not repress a shudder. Doctor Svenson seemed to her less formidable and more stricken by common fears and hesitancies, but then, so was she—and Miss Temple knew no one in her world would have granted her the capacity to survive what she already had. She trusted in the Doctor's resilience then, as she trusted in her own. Besides, she smiled to think it, many otherwise capable men were not at their best around a fetching woman.

She was at least confident that armed with her aunt's gossip she would be able to follow the conversation. So much of her comrades' accounts referred to a city she did not know—to brothels and institutes and diplomatic compounds—a mix of lower depths and exclusive heights quite apart from her middling experience. She wanted to feel that she brought to their partnership an equal third, and wanted that third to be something other than money to provide a room or a meal. If they were to continue in league against this—what was the Doctor's word?—*cabal,* then she must continue to expand her capacities. What she had done so far seemed a mix of actual investigation and mere tagging along, where even the killing of Spragg and Farquhar struck her as unlikely happenstance. The figures arrayed against her were beyond imagination, her few allies equally so—what did she possess besides her change purse? It was a moment when she could easily spiral into self-doubt and fear, assurance melting like a carnival ice. She imagined herself alone in a train compartment with a man like the Comte d'Orkancz—what could she possibly do? Miss Temple looked around her at the Boniface's stairwell wallpaper, painted with an intricate pattern of flowers and leaves, and bit her lip hard enough to draw blood. She wiped her eyes and sniffed. What she would *do* is to press the barrel of her revolver against his body and pull the trigger as many times as it took to bring his foul carcass to the floor. And then she would find the Contessa Lacquer-Sforza and thrash the woman until her arm was too tired to hold a whip.

And then...Roger. She sighed. From Roger Bascombe she would merely walk away.

She stood and made her way down to the second floor, but paused at the final step, hearing voices in the corridor. She peered around the corner to see three men in black uniforms and another man in a dark brown cloak standing directly outside the door to room 27. The men muttered to each other (Miss Temple was a foe of muttering in general and always resented not hearing what other people said, even if it was not strictly her business) and then as a group marched away from her, to the main stairs at the far end of the hall. She crept into the corridor, moving as quickly as she could to the door. She gasped to see it was ajar—the men must have been inside—and with great trepidation pushed the door open. The sitting room was empty. What papers she had left behind had been scattered across the room, but she saw no token of Chang or Svenson, nor of any particular struggle. She crossed quickly to the bedchamber, but it too was empty. The bedclothes were pulled apart, and the window was open, but she saw no sign of either man. Miss Temple peered out of the window. The room was directly above the rear alley, with a sheer drop of some thirty feet to the paving. She tightened her grip on the clutch bag and made her way back to the corridor. Both Chang and Svenson had been chased by soldiers—but which had drawn them here? She frowned with thought—it could not have been Chang, for as far as anyone knew, Chang was not in room 27. She raced to the door she had seen him leave—number 34—to find it also open. The room was empty. The window was locked. She returned to the hall, more agitated—somehow the soldiers had known of Svenson's room and of Chang's. With a sudden bolt of horror she thought of her own, and her aunt.

*   *   *

Miss Temple charged up the stairs, feverishly digging the revolver from her bag. She rounded the landing, cocking the pistol and taking a breath. She strode into the corridor and saw no one. Were they already inside? Or about to arrive any moment? This door was shut. Miss Temple banged on it with the heel of her fist. There was no sound from beyond the door. She knocked again. Still there was no answer, and her mind was assailed by images of her aunt and her maids slaughtered, the room running with blood. Miss Temple dug her key from her bag and, using her left hand, which made it awkward, unlocked the door. She shoved it open and threw herself to the side. Silence. She peeked around the corner. The entryway was empty. She held the revolver with both hands and walked slowly through the doorway. The outer parlor was empty as well, with no signs of disturbance. She turned to the inner parlor door, which was closed. It was never closed. She crept toward it, looked about her and reached her left hand toward the knob. She slowly turned it and, hearing the click of the bolt, thrust it open. She shrieked—a small shriek, she later hoped—for before her, his revolver extended to Miss Temple's face, stood Doctor Svenson in his stockinged feet. Sitting next to him, trembling and white with terror, was her aunt. Behind them sat the two maids, frozen with fright. A sudden prickling caused Miss Temple to wheel. Behind her, a long double-edged knife in his hand, stood Cardinal Chang, having just stepped out from the maids' room. He smiled at her grimly.

"Very good, Miss Temple. Would you have shot me before I'd cut your throat? I do not know, which is the profoundest of compliments."

She swallowed, unable quite yet to lower the pistol.

"The front door, I'd suggest," called Doctor Svenson from behind her.

Chang nodded. "Indeed." He turned and walked to the door, glancing quickly into the hall before stepping back and closing it, turning the lock. "And perhaps a chair..." he said to no one in particular, and selected one of the inner parlor chairs to wedge beneath the knob. This done, he turned to them and smiled coolly. "We have made the acquaintance of your aunt."

"We were extremely worried when you were not here," said Svenson. He had pocketed his pistol, and was looking uncomfortable to be standing among the openly terrified women.

"I used the other stairs," said Miss Temple. She saw both men were watching her closely and followed their gaze to her hands. She forced herself to slowly release the hammer of the revolver, and to exhale. "There are soldiers—"

"Yes," said Chang. "We were able to escape."

"But how—they were on one staircase and you did not pass me on the other. And how did you know which room was mine?"

"The chit you signed for the tea," said Svenson. "It noted your room—we did not leave it for them to find, do not worry. As for the escape—"

"Doctor Svenson is a sailor." Chang smiled. "He can climb."

"I can climb when I am pushed," said Svenson, shaking his head.

"But—I looked out the window," cried Miss Temple, "there was nothing to climb but brick!"

"There was a metal pipe," said Svenson.

"But that was tiny!"

She saw that the Doctor's face had paled as they spoke. He swallowed awkwardly and wiped his brow.

"Exactly." Chang smiled. "He is a clambering marvel."

Miss Temple caught the gaze of her aunt, still trembling in her chair, and she was flooded with guilt for so endangering the woman. She looked up at the others, her voice sharp with urgency.

"It does not matter. They will know from the desk—from that vile Mr. Spanning, whose pomaded hair I shall set aflame. The Doctor's room is paid for by me. They will be here any moment."

"How many men did you see?" asked Chang.

"Four. Three soldiers and another, in a brown cloak."

"The Comte's man," said Svenson.

"We are three," said Chang. "They'll want to take us quietly, not force a pitched battle."

"There may be others in the lobby," warned Svenson.

"Even if there are, we can beat them."

"At what cost?" asked the Doctor.

Chang shrugged.

Miss Temple looked around her, at the comfort and security that had been her life at the Hotel Boniface, and knew that it was over. She turned to her maids. "Marthe, you will prepare a traveling bag—light enough for me to carry, with the barest essentials— the flowered carpet bag will do." The girl did not move. Miss Temple shouted at her. "At once! Do you think this is any time to shirk? Marie, you will prepare traveling bags for my aunt and for the two of you. You will be spending time at the seaside. Go!"

The maids leapt to their work. Her aunt looked up at her.

"Celeste—my dear—the seaside?"

"You must move to safety—and I apologize, I am so very, very sorry to have placed you in such danger." Miss Temple sniffed and gestured toward her own room. "I will see what ready money I have, of course you will have enough for travel, and a note to draw upon—you must take both maids—"

Agathe's gaze went, rather wide-eyed, from Miss Temple over to the figures of Chang and Svenson, neither of whom seemed anywhere near respectable enough for her niece to be alone with. "But—you cannot—you are a well-bred young lady—the scandal—you must come with me!"

"It is impossible—"

"You will not have a maid—that is impossible!" The aged lady huffed at the men, chiding them. "And the seaside will be so cold—"

"That is the exact point, my Aunt. You must go to a place no one would expect. You must tell no one—you must tell no one."

Her aunt was silent as the maids bustled around them, studying her niece with dismay—though whether at the present

predicament or at what her niece had become, Miss Temple was
not sure. She was particularly aware that Svenson and Chang were
watching the entire exchange.

"And what of you?" whispered her aunt.

"I cannot say," she answered. "I do not know."

At least twenty minutes had passed, and Miss Temple—idly tracing her fingers back and forth across one of the Doctor's blue glass
cards—saw Chang at the main door, peering out into the hall. He
stepped back, caught her eye, and shrugged. Marthe had brought
the carpet bag for her to inspect. Miss Temple sent her to help
Marie, tucked the blue card into her own clutch bag—without
looking at the Doctor, who having given it to her again to examine
had not perhaps agreed it was hers to *keep*—and carried the carpet
bag over to an armchair, where she sat. Her attention elsewhere,
she glanced through what the maid had chosen and tied the bag
shut without finishing. Miss Temple sighed. Her aunt sat at the
table, watching her. Chang stood by the door. Svenson leaned
against the table near her aunt, his attempts to help pack having
been rebuffed by the maids.

"If these men have not come," said her aunt, "then perhaps
they are not coming at all. Perhaps there is no need to go anywhere. If they do not know Celeste—"

"Whether they know your niece is not the issue," said Svenson
gently. "They know who I am, at least, and also Chang. As they
know we have been here, they will be watching the hotel. It will be
a mere matter of time before they connect your niece to us—"

"They already have," said Chang, from the doorway.

"Then once they *act* on it," continued Svenson, "as your niece
has said—you yourself are in danger."

"But," her aunt persisted, "if they are not here yet—"

"It is a blessing," said Miss Temple. "It means we may all get
away unseen."

"That will be difficult," said Chang.

Miss Temple sighed. It would be very difficult. Each entrance would be watched from the street. The only question, and their only hope, was in what those men were watching *for*—and surely it was not two maids and an old woman.

"You had best accomplish it, Sir—and neatly!" sniffed Aunt Agathe, as if Chang were a workman whose expression of doubt was a prelude to an increase in his fee.

Miss Temple exhaled and stood.

"We must assume that the clerk who pointed the way to the Doctor's room has been paid to inform on us further. We must distract him while my aunt and the maids depart. The men in the street will not be looking for them, or at least not without some signal. Once you do leave," she said to her aunt, "you must go directly in a coach to the railway station, and from there to the shore, the southern shore—to Cape Rouge, there must be many inns—and I will send a letter to you, to the post office, once we are secure."

"What of yourself?" asked Agathe.

"Oh, we shall shift ourselves easily enough," she said, forcing a smile. "And this business will soon be over." She looked over to Svenson and Chang for confirmation, but neither man's expression would have convinced a credulous child. She called sharply for the maids to finish and gather their coats.

Miss Temple knew that she herself must go to Mr. Spanning, for the others would more profitably assist with the luggage—as well as best remaining concealed. She looked back to see them making their way to the rear stairs, Chang and Svenson each with an end of her aunt's clothes trunk, the maids on either side of Agathe, one hand on their own small bags, the other steadying the aged lady. Miss Temple herself made for the main staircase carrying a large satchel and the green purse, wearing as carefree an expression as she could produce and nodding cheerfully at the other guests she passed. At the second floor her path opened onto a large gallery above the splendid lobby and then to the great curve of the main stairs. She glanced over the railing and saw no black-coated soldiery, but directly outside the doors were two men in brown cloaks. She continued down the wide steps and saw Mr. Spanning behind his counter, his gaze snapping up to hers as she descended into view. She smiled brilliantly at him. Spanning's eyes darted about the lobby as she neared, and so before he could make any signal she gaily called to him.

"Mr. Spanning!"

"Miss Temple?" he answered warily, his normally sleek manner caught between distrust and pride in his own cunning.

She crossed to the desk—from the corners of her eyes seeing that no one lurked under the stairs—while watching the front door in the mirror behind Spanning's desk. The cloaked men had seen her, but were not coming in. Quite apart from her habit, Miss Temple stood on her toes and leaned her elbows playfully on the counter.

"I'm sure you know why I have come." She smiled.

"Do I?" replied Spanning, forcing an obsequious grin that did not suit him.

"O yes." She batted her eyes.

"I'm sure I do not..."

"Perhaps you have been so set upon by business that it has slipped your mind..." She looked around the vacant lobby. "Though it does not appear so. Tell me, Mr. Spanning, *have* you been so set upon with pressing duties?" She was still smiling, but a hint of steel had crept into her otherwise honeyed tone.

"As you know, Miss Temple, my *normal* duties are very—"

"Yes, yes, but you haven't had to bother with anyone *else*?"

Spanning cleared his throat with suspicion. "May I ask—"

"Do you know," continued Miss Temple, "I have always meant to inquire as to your brand of pomade, for I have always found your hair to be so very...*managed*. And slick—managed *and* slick. I have wanted to impart such grooming to any number of other men in the city, but have not known what to recommend—and always forget to ask!"

"It is Bronson's, Miss."

"*Bronson's*. Excellent." She leaned in with a suddenly serious expression. "Do you never worry about fire?"

"Fire?"

"Leaning too close to a candle? I should think—you know—*whoosh*!" She chuckled. "Ah, it is so pleasant to laugh. But I *am* in earnest, Mr. Spanning. And I do require an answer—no matter how you strive to charm me!"

"I assure you, Miss Temple—"

"Of what, Mr. Spanning? Of what do you—this day—*assure* me?"

She was no longer smiling, but looking directly into the man's eyes. He did not reply. She brought the green bag onto the counter top, allowing its weight to land with a *thump*. Its contents were not usual for a lady's purse. Spanning saw her deftly angle the bag in his direction and take hold of it through the fabric—her manner still casual but unaccountably menacing.

"How precisely may I help you?" he asked meekly.

"I will be traveling," she said. "As will my aunt, but to another destination. I wish to retain my rooms. I assume my note of credit will answer any worries?"

"Of course. You will be returning..."

"At some point."

"I see."

"Good. Do you know, earlier, that this hotel seemed absolutely full of foreign soldiers?"

"Did it?"

"Apparently they were directed to the second floor." She looked around them and then dropped her voice to a whisper. Despite himself Spanning leaned closer to hear. "Do you know, Mr.

Spanning...do you know the *sound* a person makes...when they're *thrashed*...to such an *extreme*...they can no longer even cry out...with pain?"

Mr. Spanning flinched, blinking his eyes. Miss Temple leaned even closer and whispered, "Because I do."

Spanning swallowed. Miss Temple stood up straight and smiled. "I believe you have the Doctor's boots and his coat?"

She climbed back up the main staircase to the second floor and then dashed down the hallway to the rear stairs, her green bag in one hand, the boots in the other, and the Doctor's coat over her left arm. The satchel, thickly packed with unnecessary clothing, had been left in Spanning's care with the request for him to hold it until she was ready to leave, which she announced would most likely be after luncheon—thus making a point to inform Spanning (and the soldiers) that she (and by extension, via the boots, Svenson and Chang) could be found in her rooms for the next few hours. Once out of sight from the lobby, Miss Temple picked up her dress as best she could and briskly climbed. With luck the others had used her distraction to get her aunt and the maids out the service entrance. The porters would take the luggage and find a coach, allowing Svenson and Chang to remain hidden indoors. But were the soldiers marching into the lobby even then, men who moved much faster than she? She reached the fourth floor and stopped to listen. She heard no bootsteps and resumed her trotting pace upwards. At the eighth floor she stopped again, flushed with exertion and panting. She had never been to this topmost floor and had no idea where to find what Chang assured her was there. She walked along the corridor, past what looked like doors to normal rooms, until she rounded a corner and faced the end of the hall. She looked back the other way and saw an identical dead end. Hot and out of breath from her climb, Miss Temple worried about what next might follow her up the stairs. She whispered—or rather hissed—to the air around her with frustration. *"Pssssst!"*

She wheeled abruptly at a wooden squeak. A section of the red-flocked wallpaper swung forward on hinges she had not seen, revealing Doctor Svenson, and behind him, on a narrow staircase steep enough to be more like a ladder, Chang, silhouetted in an open doorway to the roof. Despite the distress of a moment before, she could not suppress her admiration at the cunningly concealed doorway.

"My goodness," she exclaimed, "whoever made that is as clever as five monkeys put together!"

"Your aunt is safely away," said Svenson, stepping into the hall to collect his things.

"I am relieved to hear it," replied Miss Temple. The Doctor struggled into his coat, which—after being brushed and steamed—did restore some of his military crispness. "I could not see this door at all," she continued, admiring the inset hinges. "I don't know how anyone should find it—"

"Are they following?" hissed Chang from inside the passage.

"Not that I have seen," Miss Temple whispered in return. "I could not see them in the lobby—O!" She turned sharply at Doctor Svenson's hand clutching her shoulder.

"I beg your pardon!" he said, bracing himself as he tried to put on his right boot. He could not do it with one hand and was reduced to trying with two while awkwardly hopping.

"We should hurry," called Chang.

"Half a moment," whispered Svenson—the first boot was nearly on. Miss Temple waited. His task remained difficult. She tried to find encouraging conversation.

"I have never been on a rooftop before, or not one so high. I'm sure we'll have quite a view—up with the birds!"

Somehow it seemed the wrong thing to say. Svenson looked up at her, his face more pale, and started in on the second boot.

"Are you perfectly well, Doctor? I know you did not find but a few hours' rest—"

"Go on ahead," he said, essaying a casual tone that did not persuade. The second boot was on half-way. He stumbled, stepping upon it, the excess flopping around like an odd fish attached to the base of his leg. "I shall follow—I assure you—"

"Doctor!" hissed Chang. "It will be fine. The roof is wide, and the climb will be nothing like the pipe!"

"The pipe?" asked Miss Temple.

"Ah—well—that—" said Doctor Svenson.

"I thought you managed it splendidly."

From the passage Chang scoffed.

"I have a difficulty with height. An excruciating difficulty—"

"I have the same with root vegetables." Miss Temple smiled. "We shall help one another—come!" She anxiously looked past his shoulder down the hallway, relieved to see it still empty, and took his arm. He thrust his foot down into the boot—fully in but for a last uncooperative inch. They stepped through the door.

"Pull it tight," whispered Chang, who had continued on above them. "It is better they not notice we have forced the lock."

The sky above was grey and so low as to seem palpably near, the sun well behind a thick bank of winter cloud. The air was cool and moist, and if there were only more wind Miss Temple might have told herself she was on the sea. She inhaled with pleasure. She looked down to see with a certain small wonder that under her feet was a crusty layer of tarred paper and copper sheathing—so this was walking on a roof! Behind her Doctor Svenson had knelt, concentrating closely on his left boot, eyes fixed to the ground. Chang secured the door with bits of broken wood, wedging them into the frame to prevent it from opening easily. He stepped away and wiped his hand on his coat. She saw that his other hand held her carpet bag—she had completely forgotten it, and reached to take it from him. He shook his head and nodded toward a nearby building.

"I believe we can go this way—north," he said.

"If we must," muttered Svenson. He stood, still keeping his eyes low. Miss Temple saw it was time for her to act.

"Excuse me," she said, "but before we travel further together, I believe—I am convinced—that we need to speak."

Chang frowned at her. "They may be coming—"

"Yes, though I do not think they are. I think they are waiting for us in the street, or waiting for Mr. Spanning to make sure the guests in the rooms near to mine will not be disturbed by any screams. I am confident we have at least some few minutes."

The two men looked at each other. She could sense the doubt in the glance that went between them. She pointedly cleared her throat, bringing their eyes back to her.

"To the great distress of my only available relative, I have been thrust into the company of two men at the very border—if that—of respectability. This morning we were strangers. In this instant all three of us are without sanctuary. What I want—in fact demand—is that we make quite clear what we each hope to achieve in this matter, what masters we serve—in short, what is our *agreement*."

She waited for their reaction. The two men were silent.

"I do not find the request excessive," said Miss Temple.

Svenson nodded at her, looked to Chang and muttered, groping in his pocket. "Excuse me—a cigarette—it will distract from the altitude, this sea of vacant space—" He looked back at Miss Temple. "You are correct. It is most sensible. We do not know each other—chance has thrown us together."

"Can we not do this later?" asked Chang, his tone clinging to the merest edge of civility.

"When would that be?" answered Miss Temple. "Do we even know where we are going next? Have we decided how best to act? Who to pursue? Of course we haven't, because we have each made assumptions from our very different experiences."

Chang exhaled, vexed. After a moment, he nodded sharply, as if to invite her to begin. Miss Temple did so.

"I have been attacked and now uprooted. I have been misled, threatened, and lied to. I wish for justice . . . which means the *thorough* settling of each person involved." She took a breath. "Doctor?"

Svenson took the moment to actually light his cigarette, return the case to his coat pocket, and exhale. He nodded to her.

"I must recover my Prince—no matter this conspiracy, it remains my duty to *disentangle* him. I have no doubt that this entails a kind of war—but I have little choice. Cardinal?"

Chang paused, as if he found this a pointless, formal exercise, but then spoke quietly and quickly. "If this business is not answered I have no work, no place to live, and no good reputation. For these all being set at hazard, I will have revenge—I must, as I say, to preserve my name. Does that satisfy you?"

"It does."

"These figures are intertwined, and deadly," said Chang. "Are we to follow them all—to an end?"

"I would insist upon it, actually," said Miss Temple.

Doctor Svenson spoke. "I too. No matter what happens with Karl-Horst, the work must be finished. This conspiracy—this cabal—I cannot say *what* drives its members, but I know together they are like rot around a wound, like a cancer. If not removed in its entirety, what remains will only grow back, more virulent and vicious than ever. Not one of us or any that we care for shall be safe."

"Then it's agreed," said Chang.

He smiled wryly and put his hand out. Doctor Svenson stuck his cigarette into his mouth and, his hand free, took hold of Chang's. Miss Temple placed her small hand over theirs. She had no idea what this would portend—it was intrigue after all—but she did not think she had ever been happier in her life. As she had agreed to something exceedingly serious, she did her best not to giggle, but she could not prevent herself from beaming.

"Excellent!" announced Miss Temple. "I am happy to have it so directly spoken. And now, the other question—as I have said—is how to proceed. Do we find another place of refuge? Do we go on the attack—and if so, where? The St. Royale? The Ministry? Harschmort?"

"My first thought would be to move from the rooftop," said Chang.

"Yes, yes, but we can talk while we go—no one will overhear us."

"Then this way—stay with us, Doctor—to the north. The hotel is connected to the next building—I believe there is no gap at all."

"Gap?" asked Svenson.

"To jump across," said Chang.

Svenson did not reply.

"Surely," said Miss Temple, "we should look down to the street—to see the men arrayed around the Boniface."

Chang sighed, acquiescing, and looked to Svenson, who waved them toward the edge of the building. "I shall proceed to the next roof—so as not to detain you . . ." He walked slowly in that direction, looking down at his boots. Miss Temple marched to the edge and carefully looked down. The view was exquisite. Below her the avenue was laid out like a doll's house full of tiny creatures. She looked over to see Chang had joined her, kneeling in the cover of the copper moldings. "Do you see anyone?" she whispered. He pointed to the end of the street: behind a grocer's cart were two men in black, quite out of sight from the Boniface but able to view its entrance with ease. With growing excitement Miss Temple looked the other way and smiled, tugging Chang's coat. "The iron fence—at the corner!" Another two figures lurked behind it, just visible to them above but concealed from the street by the fence's veil of ivy.

"They are watching at each corner," Chang said. "Four men in uniform—already more than you saw in the hotel. Now they think we are trapped, they may bring every man at their command. They will be in your rooms even now. We must go."

They found Svenson advanced across the rooftops of two very fine town houses, connected to each other and the Boniface. He gestured vaguely to the far edge. "The drop is significant," he said, "and the distance across farther than any of us can leap. To the front of the building is the avenue, which is even wider, and to the rear is an alley, narrower, but still more than we can manage."

"I should quite like to see in any case," said Miss Temple, and walked smilingly to the rear edge. The town house roof was at least two stories taller than the building across the street, whatever it was—she could not tell, its few windows small and blackened by smoke. She looked down and felt a giddy pleasure. The Doctor was right, she could not imagine any person breasting it. She saw Chang crouched at the far edge looking down—more soldier-counting, she assumed.

Miss Temple returned to the Doctor, who she saw was having a hard time of it. In truth this was a comfort, for compared to the menacing capacity of Chang, her own feelings of ignorance and weakness were lessened by Svenson's obvious distress.

"We saw several pairs of soldiers watching the front of the hotel," she said to him. "More than were inside—Chang thinks they are *gathering*."

Svenson nodded. He was digging out another cigarette.

"You consume those at quite a rate, don't you?" she said affably. "We shall have to find you more."

"That will be difficult," he said, smiling. "They are from Riga, from a man I know in a Macklenburg shop—I cannot get them otherwise *there*, and doubt anyone could find them *here*. I have a cedar box of them in my room at the compound—for all the good it does me."

Miss Temple narrowed her eyes. "Without them . . . will you become peevish and ill?"

"I will not," said Svenson. "What is more, the effects of tobacco are entirely beneficial to me—a restorative that both soothes and awakens."

"It is the chewing and spitting of tobacco I dislike," said Miss Temple. "Such usage is common where I come from, and fully abhorrent. Besides, tobacco of any kind stains the teeth most awfully." She noticed the Doctor's teeth were stained the color of new-cut oak.

"Where are you from?" asked Svenson, pressing his lips together self-consciously.

"An island," Miss Temple answered simply. "Where it is *warmer,* and one may eat fresh fruit on a regular basis. Ah, here is Chang."

"I can see soldiers in the main streets," he said, walking up to them, "but not at the alley. There is a chance we can go through this rooftop"—here he pointed to an undoubtedly locked door that led into the town house—"and out to the alley. I do not, however, see how we can hope to leave the alley itself, for each end of it will lead us to them."

"Then we are trapped," said Svenson.

"We can hide downstairs," said Chang.

They turned to Miss Temple for her opinion—which in itself was gratifying—but before she could answer, there was the sound of trumpets, echoing to the rooftops.

She turned to the sound, its clear call seemingly answered by a crisp low rumbling. "Horses," she said, "a great many of them!" All three, Miss Temple steadying the Doctor's arm, crept carefully to look over the main avenue. Below them, filling the street, was a parade of mounted soldiers in bright red tunics and shining brass helmets, each draped with a black horse's tail.

"Are they coming for us?" she cried.

"I do not know," said Chang. She saw him share a look with Svenson, and wished they would not do this so often, or at least so openly.

"The 4th Dragoons," said the Doctor, and he pointed to an important-looking figure whose epaulettes dripped with gold fringe. "Colonel Aspiche."

Miss Temple watched the man ride by, officers to either side, lines of troopers in front and behind—a stern figure, gaze unwavering, his finely groomed horse immaculately controlled. She tried to count his men but they moved too quickly—at least a hundred, perhaps more than twice that. Then there was a gap between the lines of horsemen, and Miss Temple squeezed Doctor Svenson's arm. "Carts!"

It was a train of some ten carts each driven by uniformed soldiers.

"The carts are empty," said Svenson.

Chang nodded toward the Boniface. "They are going past the hotel. This has nothing to do with us."

It was true. Miss Temple saw the red mass of uniforms continuing past the hotel and then winding toward Grossmaere.

"What is in that direction?" she asked. "The St. Royale is the other way."

Doctor Svenson leaned forward. "It is the Institute. They are going to the Institute with *empty* carts—the glass machinery—the—the—what did you say, both of you—the *boxes*—"

"Boxes in carts were delivered to Harschmort," said Chang. "Boxes were all over their Institute laboratory."

"The boxes at Harschmort were lined with orange felt, and had numbers painted on them," said Miss Temple.

"At the Institute . . . the linings were not orange," said Chang. "They were blue."

"I would bet my eyes they are collecting more," said Svenson. "Or relocating their workplace, after the death at the Institute."

Below them the trumpets sounded again—Colonel Aspiche was not one for a demure passage. Svenson tried to speak over them but the words were lost to Miss Temple. He tried again, leaning closer to them, pointing down. "Major Blach's men have entered the hotel." Miss Temple saw that he was right—a stream of black figures, just visible along the edges of the red horsemen, scurrying toward the Boniface like rats for an open culvert. "If I might suggest," the Doctor said, "it seems an excellent time to attempt to leave through the alley."

As they made their way down a luxuriously carpeted stairway, Miss Temple wondered that anyone thought themselves immune to housebreaking or burglary at all. It had taken Chang but a moment to effect their entry into a dwelling whose owners she was sure prided themselves on inviolable security. They were fortunate not to find anyone at home on the upper stories (for the servants who lived in those rooms were at work), and were able to creep quietly past the floors where they heard footsteps or clinking crockery or even in one case an especially repellent huffing. Miss Temple knew that the ground floor and the rear entrance itself would be the most likely places for a confrontation—these *would* be occupied by servants, if no one else—and so as they stepped free of the staircase she made a point to thrust herself in front of Chang and Svenson despite their looks of surprise. She knew full well that she could offer an appearance that was unthreatening but nevertheless imperious, where each of them would invite the outrage sparked by any interloping man. From the corner of her eye she saw a young housemaid stacking jars who out of instinct bobbed into a curtsey at her passing. Miss Temple acknowledged the girl with a nod and strode on into the kitchen, which held at least three servants hard at work. She smiled at them crisply.

"Good afternoon. My name is Miss Hastings—I require your rear door." She did not pause for their reply. "I expect it is this way? I am obliged to you. What a well-kept room—the teapots are especially fine—" Within moments she was beyond them and down a short flight of stairs to the door itself. She stepped aside for Chang to open it, for behind him and over the Doctor's shoulder she saw the crowd of curious faces that had followed. "Have you seen the parade of cavalry?" she called. "It is the Prince's Own 4th Dragoons—my goodness, they are splendid! Such trumpets, and so many fine animals—remarkable. Good day!" She followed the Doctor through the door and exhaled with relief as Chang closed it behind them.

The sound of hoofbeats was fainter—the parade was already passing by. As they ran toward the alley's end, Miss Temple noted with alarm that Chang had drawn his long double-edged knife and Svenson his revolver. Miss Temple groped at her green bag, but needed one hand to hold up her dress to run and could not successfully open it with the other. If she was a cursing sort of girl she would have been cursing then, for the obvious urgency with which her companions treated the situation had caught her unawares. They were at the street. Svenson took hold of her arm as they walked rapidly away from the Boniface. Chang loped a pace or two behind, his eyes searching for enemies. There were no cries, no shots. They reached the next street and Svenson wheeled her around the corner. They pressed themselves against the wall and waited for Chang to follow a moment later. He shrugged, and the three of them continued away as quickly as they could. It seemed incredible to be free so easily, and Miss Temple could not help but smile at their success.

Before either of the men could set a path, Miss Temple picked up her pace so that they would be forced to follow her. They rounded the corner into the next broad avenue—Regent's Gate—where ahead of them, Miss Temple spotted a familiar awning. She steered them toward it. She'd had an idea.

"Where are you going?" asked Chang, brusquely.

"We must strategize," answered Miss Temple. "We cannot do it in the street. We cannot do it in a café—the three of us would be much talked of—"

"Perhaps a private room—" suggested Svenson.

"Then we would be even *more* talked of," interrupted Miss Temple. "But there is a place where no one will comment on our strange little band."

"What place?" asked Chang with suspicion.

She smiled at her cleverness. "It is an art gallery."

The artist presently exhibited was a Mr. Veilandt—a painter from somewhere near Vienna—whose work Roger had taken her to see as a way of showing favor to a visiting group of Austrian bankers. Miss Temple had been alone among the party to pay the art itself any attention—in her case, a negative interest, for she found the paintings unsettling and presumptuous. Everyone else had ignored them in favor of drinking schnapps and discussing markets and tariffs, as Roger had assured her they would. Reasoning that the gallery would not mind another such visit of ill-attention, she pulled Svenson and Chang into the outer lobby to speak to the attending gallery agent. She explained in a low tone that she had been part of the Austrian party and here brought a representative of the Macklenburg court, in search of wedding presents for his Prince—a figure of *taste*—surely the man had heard of the impending match? He nodded importantly that he had. The man's gaze drifted to Chang and Miss Temple noted with some tact that her second companion was also an *artist,* much impressed with Mr. Veilandt's reputation as a *provocateur.* The agent nodded in sympathy and ushered them into the main viewing room, delicately slipping a brochure with printed prices and titles into the hands of Doctor Svenson.

The paintings were as she remembered them: large, lurid oils depicting in an almost obscenely deliberate manner incidents of doubt and temptation from the lives of saints, each chosen for its thoroughly unwholesome spectacle. Indeed, without the establishing context within each composition of the single figure with a halo, the collection of canvases created a pure pageant of decadence. While Miss Temple perceived how the artist used the veil of the sacred to indulge his taste for the depraved, she was not sure whether, on a level deeper than cynical cleverness, the paintings were not more truthful than was ever intended. Indeed, when she had first seen them, among the throng of self-important financiers, her dismay had been not with the profligate and blasphemous carnality but, on the contrary, the precarious isolation, the barely persuasive presence, of virtue. Miss Temple led her companions down the length of the gallery, away from the agent.

"Good Lord," whispered Doctor Svenson. He peered at the small card to the side of a largely orange canvas whose figures seemed to slither from the surface fully fleshed into the air around them. *"St. Rowena and the Viking Raiders,"* he read, and turned up to the face that could perhaps charitably be said to be glowing with religious fervor. "Good *Lord.*"

Chang was silent, but equally transfixed, his expression unreadable behind the smoked-glass lenses. Miss Temple spoke in a low tone, so as not to attract the agent.

"So . . . now that we may speak without concern . . ."

"The Blissful Fortitude of St. Jasper," read the Doctor, glancing up at a canvas on the other wall. "Are those *pig snouts*?"

She cleared her throat. They turned to her, slightly abashed.

"Good Lord, Miss Temple," said Svenson, "these paintings do not take you aback?"

"In fact they do, yet I have already seen them. I had thought, since we have already shared the blue cards, we could weather their challenge."

"Yes—yes, I see," said Svenson, at once even more obviously awkward. "The gallery is certainly empty. And convenient."

Chang did not offer any opinion on the place or the paintings of Mr. Veilandt, but merely smiled—once more rather wolfishly, it seemed.

"My own idea..." began Miss Temple. "You *did* look at the glass cards, Cardinal?"

"I did." The man was positively *leering*.

"Well, in the one with Roger Bascombe—and myself—" She stopped and frowned, gathering her thoughts—there were too many at wing inside her brain. "What I am trying to decide is where we ought to next direct our efforts, and most importantly whether it is best for us to remain together or if the work is more effectively accomplished in different directions."

"You mentioned the *card*?" prompted Chang.

"Because it showed the country house of Roger's uncle, Lord Tarr, and some kind of quarry—"

"Wait, wait," Svenson broke in. "Francis Xonck, speaking of Bascombe's inheritance... he referred to a substance called 'indigo clay'—have you heard of it?"

She shook her head. Chang shrugged.

"Neither had I," continued Svenson. "But he suggested that Bascombe would soon be the owner of a large deposit of the same. It has to be the quarry, which has to be on his uncle's land."

"*His* land," corrected Chang.

Svenson nodded. "And my thought is that it may be vital to making their glass!"

"Thus why Tarr was killed," said Chang. "And why Bascombe was chosen. They seduce him to their cause, and then this indigo clay is under their control."

Miss Temple saw the ease of it—a few words from Crabbé about the usefulness of a title to an ambitious man, the flattering company of a woman like the Contessa or even—she sighed with disappointment—Mrs. Marchmoor and cigars and brandy with a flattering rake like Francis Xonck. She wondered if Roger had any real idea of the value of this indigo clay, or if his allegiance was being purchased as cheaply as that of an Indian savage, with these people's equivalent of beads and feathers. Then she remembered that he too had borne the purple scars. Did he even retain his own unfettered mind, or had this *Process* transmuted him into their slave?

"He *is* a pawn after all...," she whispered.

"I'd wager every preening member of this cabal sees every other as a pawn." Chang chuckled. "I would not single out poor Bascombe."

"No," said Miss Temple. "I'm sure you're correct. I'm sure he's only like them all."

She shrugged away the glimmer of sympathy. "But the question remains—should we direct our efforts to Tarr Manor?"

"There is another possibility," said Doctor Svenson. "I've been distracted. Not three minutes from here is the walled garden where the Comte d'Orkancz brought me to look at the injured woman—it was my destination when I saw you in the window."

"What woman?" asked Chang.

Svenson exhaled heavily and shook his head. "Another unfortunate caught up in the Comte's experiments, and another mystery. She bore all the features of drowning in frozen water, though the damage had apparently been inflicted by some machine—I assume it has to do with the glass, or the boxes—I could not say if she survived the night. But the location—a greenhouse, to keep her warm—must be a stronghold of the Comte, and it is very near. He sought me to treat her—"

"Sought you?" asked Miss Temple.

"He claimed to have seen a pamphlet I wrote, years ago, on the afflictions of Baltic seamen—"

"He is indeed widely read."

"It is ridiculous, I agree—"

"I do not doubt it, but *why*?" Miss Temple frowned, her

thoughts quickening. "But wait . . . if the pamphlet is so old, then it means the Comte must have had cause, even then, to be mindful of such injuries!"

Svenson nodded. "Yes! Would this mean the Comte is the chief architect of these *experiments*?"

"At Harschmort it was quite clearly he who managed the boxes and the strange mechanical masks. It only follows he is master of the science itself . . ." She shivered at the memory of the large man's callous manipulation of the somnolent women.

"What did the woman look like?" interrupted Chang. "At this greenhouse?"

"Look like?" said Svenson, his train of thought jarred. "Ah—well—there were disfiguring marks across her body—she was young, beautiful—yes, and perhaps Asiatic. Do you know who she is?"

"Of course not," said Chang.

"We can see if she is still there—"

"So that is another possibility," said Miss Temple, attempting to keep the conversation clear. "I can also think of several destinations in search of particular people—back to Harschmort, to the St. Royale for the Contessa—"

"Crabbé's house on Hadrian Square," said Svenson.

They turned to Chang. He was silent, lost in thought. Abruptly he looked up, and shook his head. "Following an individual merely gives us a prisoner—at best, that is. It means interrogation, threats—it is awkward. True, we may find the Prince—we may find anything—but most likely we will catch Harald Crabbé at dinner with his wife and end up having to cut both their throats."

"I have not made Mrs. Crabbé's acquaintance," said Miss Temple. "I should prefer any mayhem be directly applied to those who we know have harmed us." She knew that Chang had raised the idea of murdering the woman just to frighten them, and she *was* frightened—a test, as she realized the paintings were a way for her to test the two of them. As they stood speaking, she saw that placing herself with two men amidst a room full of undulating flesh was actually a declaration of a certain capacity and knowledge that she did not in fact possess. It had not been her initial intention, but it made her feel more their equal.

"So you are not content to simply kill everyone." Chang smiled.

"I am not," replied Miss Temple. "In all this I have wanted to know *why*—from the first moment I decided to follow Roger."

"Do you suppose we should separate?" asked Svenson. "Some to visit the greenhouse—which may involve the throat-cutting you describe, if it is full of the Comte's men—and one to visit Tarr Manor?"

"What of your Prince?" asked Miss Temple.

Svenson rubbed his eyes. "I do not know. Even *they* did not know."

"Who did not?" asked Chang. "Specifically."

"Xonck, Bascombe, Major Blach, the Comte..."

"Did they rule out the Contessa?"

"No. Nor Lord Vandaariff. So...perhaps the Prince is in a room at the St. Royale, or at Harschmort—perhaps, if we *were* able to find him, it would accentuate the divisions between them, and who can say—thus provoke some rash action or at least reveal more of their true aims."

Chang nodded. He turned to Miss Temple and spoke quite seriously. "What is your opinion about dividing our efforts? About pursuing one of these choices alone?"

Before she could answer—as she knew she must answer—Miss Temple felt the whole of her mind relocated to the jolting coach with Spragg, the hot smell of his sweating, bristled neck, the suffocating weight of his body, the imperious force of his hands, the crush of fear that had taken such implacable hold over her body.

She blinked the thought away and found herself again facing the woman in red, her piercing violet eyes sharper than any knife, her dismissive, lordly insolence of expression, her dark chuckling laugh that seemed to flay the nerves from Miss Temple's spine. She blinked again. She looked around her at the paintings, and at the two men who had become her allies—because she had chosen them, as she had chosen to place her very self at hazard. She knew they would do whatever she said.

"I do not mind at all." Miss Temple smiled. "If I should have the chance to shoot one of these fellows by myself, then all the better, I say."

"Just a moment..." said Doctor Svenson. He was looking past her at the far wall and walked over to it, wiping his monocle on the lapel of his greatcoat. He stood in front of a small canvas—perhaps the smallest on display—and peered at the identifying card, then back at the painting with close attention. "Both of you need to come here."

Miss Temple crossed to the painting and abruptly gasped with surprise. How could she have not remembered this from before? The canvas—clearly cut from a larger work—showed an ethereal woman reclining on what one first assumed to be a sofa or divan, but which on further study was clearly an angled table—there even seemed to be straps (or was this merely the artist's conception of a Biblical garment?) securing her arms. Above the woman's head floated a golden halo, but on her face, around her eyes, were the same purpled looping scars they had all witnessed in the flesh.

Svenson consulted his brochure. "*Annunciation Fragment*... it is... a moment—" He flipped the page. "The painting is five years old. And it is the newest piece in the collection. Excuse me."

He left them and approached the agent, who sat making notes in a ledger at his desk. Miss Temple returned to the painting. She could not deny that it was unsettlingly lovely, and she noticed with horror that the woman's pale robe was bordered at the neck with a line of green circles. "The robes in Harschmort," she whispered to Chang, "the women under the Comte's power—they wore the same!"

The Doctor returned, shaking his head. "It's most bizarre," he hissed. "The artist—Mr. Oskar Veilandt—was apparently a mystic, deranged, a dabbler in alchemy and dark science."

"Excellent," said Chang. "Perhaps he's the one to tie these threads together—"

"He can lead us to the others!" Miss Temple whispered excitedly.

"My exact thought." The Doctor nodded. "But I am told that Mr. Veilandt has been dead for these five years."

All three were silent. Five years? How could that be possible? What did it mean?

"The lines on her face," said Chang. "They are definitely the same..."

"Yes," agreed Svenson, "which only tells us that the plot itself—the Process—is at least that old as well. We will need to know more—where the artist lived, where he died, who holds custody of his work—indeed, who has sponsored this very exhibition—"

Miss Temple extended her finger to point at the small card with the work's title, for next to it was a small blot of red ink. "Even more, Doctor, we will need to know who has *bought* this painting!"

The gallery agent, a Mr. Shanck, was happy to oblige them with information (after the Doctor had thoroughly inquired as to prices and delivery procedures for several of the larger paintings, in between mutters about wall space in the Macklenburg Palace), but unfortunately what Mr. Shanck knew was little: Veilandt himself was a mystery, school in Vienna, sojourns in Italy and Constantinople, *atelier* in Montmartre. The paintings had come from a dealer in Paris, where he understood Veilandt had died. He glanced toward the opulent compositions and tendered that he did not doubt it was due to consumption or absinthe or some other such destructive mania. The present owner wished to remain anonymous—in Mr. Shanck's view because of the *oeuvre*'s scandalous nature—and Shanck's only dealings were with his opposite number at a gallery in the Boulevard St. Germain. Mr. Shanck clearly relished the patina of intrigue around the collection, as he relished sharing his privileged information with those he deemed discerning. His expression faltered into suspicion however when Miss Temple, in a fully casual manner, wondered who had purchased the "odd little painting," and if he might have any others like it for purchase. She quite fancied it, and would love another for her home. In fact, he outright blanched.

"I...I assumed—you mentioned the wedding—the Prince—"

Miss Temple nodded in agreement, dispelling none of the man's sudden fear.

"Exactly. Thus my interest in buying one for myself."

"But none are available for purchase at all! They never were!"

"That seems no way to run a gallery," she said, "and besides, *one* has been sold—"

"Why—why else would you come?" he said, more to himself than to her, his voice fading as he spoke.

"To see the paintings, Mr. Shanck—as I told you—"

"It was not even *bought*," he sputtered, waving at the small canvas. "It was given, *for* the wedding. It is a gift for Lydia Vandaariff. The entire exhibition has been arranged for no other reason than to reunite each canvas with the others in a single collection! Anyone acquainted with the gallery—anyone suitable to be *informed*—surely, the union of the artist's themes...religion...morality... appetite...mysticism...you must be aware...the forces at work—the *dangerous*..."

Mr. Shanck looked at them and swallowed nervously. "If you did not know *that*—how did you—who did you—"

Miss Temple saw the man's rising distress and found she was
instinctively smiling at him, shaking her head—it was all a misunderstanding—but before she could actually speak, Chang stepped
forward, immediately menacing and sharp, and took up a fistful of
Mr. Shanck's cravat, pulling him awkwardly over his desk. Shanck
bleated in futile protest.

"I know nothing," he cried. "People use the gallery to meet—I
am paid to allow it—I say nothing—I will say nothing about any
of you—I swear it—"

"Mr. Shanck—" began Miss Temple, but Chang cut her off,
tightening his grip on the man with a snarl.

"The paintings have been gathered together you say—by
whom?"

Shanck sputtered, utterly outraged and afraid—though not, it
seemed to her, of them. "By—*ah!*—by her *father*!"

Once released, the man broke away and fled across the gallery into
a room Miss Temple believed actually held brooms. She sighed
with frustration. Still, it gave them a moment to speak.

"We must leave at once," she said. There were noises from beyond the distant doorway. She reached out an arm and prevented
Chang from investigating. "We did not yet decide—"

Chang cut her off. "This greenhouse. It may be dangerous
enough that numbers will help our entry. It is also nearby."

Miss Temple bristled with irritation at Chang's peremptory
manner, but then perceived a flicker of emotion cross his face.
Though she could not, with his eyes so hidden, guess what feelings
were at work, the very fact of their presence piqued her interest.
Chang seemed to her then like a kind of finely bred horse whose
strengths were at the mercy of any number of infinitesimal tem-
pests at work in the blood—a character that required a very particular sort of managing.

"I agree," replied Svenson.

"Excellent," said Miss Temple. She noted with alarm a growing clamor from amongst the brooms. "But I suggest we leave."

"Wait...," called Doctor Svenson, and he dashed away from them toward Veilandt's *Annunciation*. With a quick glance after Mr. Shanck's closet, the Doctor snatched it from the wall.

"He's not going to *steal* it?" whispered Miss Temple.

He was not. Instead, the Doctor flipped the picture over to look at the back side of the canvas, the deliberate nodding of his face confirming that he'd found something there to see. A moment later the painting was returned to the wall and the Doctor running toward them.

"What was it?" asked Chang.

"Writing," exclaimed Svenson, ushering them toward the street. "I wondered if there might be any indication of the larger work, or—seeing as the man was an alchemist—some kind of mystical formula."

"And was there?" asked Miss Temple.

He nodded, groping for a scrap of paper and a pencil stub from his coat pocket. "Indeed—I will note them down, though the symbols mean nothing to me— but also, I cannot say what they portend, but there were words, in large block letters—"

"What words?" asked Chang.

" '*And so they shall be consumed,*' " Svenson replied.

Miss Temple said nothing, recalling vividly the blackboard at Harschmort, for there was no time. They were on the avenue, the Doctor taking her arm as he led the way toward the greenhouse.

"In blood?" asked Chang.

"No," answered Doctor Svenson. "In *blue*."

"The entrance to the lane that I know is directly opposite the Boniface," said Svenson, speaking low as they walked. "To reach the garden gate safely, we will have to walk some distance around the hotel and come at it from the opposite side."

"And even then," observed Chang, "you say it may be guarded."

"It was before. But of course, the Comte was there—without him, the guards may be gone. The problem is, I entered through the garden, that is, the back way—and it was dark and foggy, and I have no real idea whether there is a house connected to it—still less if the house is presently occupied."

Chang sighed. "If we must circle around it will be longer to walk, yet—"

"Nonsense," said Miss Temple. The men looked at her. She really would need to take a firmer hand. "We will hire a coach," she explained, and realized that neither of her companions even thought of hiring a coach as a normal part of their day. It was obvious that between the three of them were different sorts of strength, and different brands of fragility. As a woman, Miss Temple perceived how each of her companions felt sure about where *she* might fail, but lacked a similar sense of their own vulnerabilities. It was, she accepted, her own responsibility, and so she directed their attention down the avenue.

"There is one now—if one of you would *wave* to the man?"

Thus conveyed, each one pressing themselves into their seat and away from the windows, they were on the other side of the lane within minutes. Chang gave Miss Temple a nod to indicate he saw no soldiers. They climbed out and she sent the coach on its way. The trio entered the empty, narrow, cobbled lane, which Miss Temple saw was called Plum Court. The gate stood in the middle of the lane—as they neared it the sounds of the adjoining avenues faded before the deepening shadow, for the buildings around them blocked out whatever light did not fall from directly above, which from this clouded sky was very feeble. Miss Temple wondered how any kind of garden could thrive in such a dull and airless place. The entrance was a strange church-like arch set into the wall

THE GLASS BOOKS OF THE DREAM EATERS 301

around a thick wooden door. The arch itself was decorated with subtle figures carved into the wood, a strange pattern of sea monsters, mermaids, and shipwrecked sailors who were smiling even as they drowned.

Miss Temple turned her gaze to the end of the lane and saw, in the brighter light of the avenue, as if it were a framed colored picture, the front of the Boniface. Standing at the door was Mr. Spanning, with a soldier to either side. Miss Temple tapped Chang on the shoulder and pointed. He stepped quickly to the doorway, set down Miss Temple's flowered bag and dug in his pocket for a heavy ring of many keys. He rapidly sorted through them, and muttered out of the side of his mouth, "Let me know if they see us . . . and you might step closer to the wall."

Miss Temple and the Doctor did press themselves against the wall, each of them readying their pistols. Miss Temple felt more than a little anxious—she had never fired any weapon in her life, and here she was, playing the highwayman. Chang inserted a key and turned. It did not work. He tried another, and another, and another, each time patiently flipping through the ring for a new one.

"If there is anyone on the other side of the door," whispered Svenson, "they will hear!"

"They already have," Chang whispered in reply, and Miss Temple noticed that he had casually insinuated himself—and they behind him—to the side of the door, clear of any shots that might be fired through it. He tried another key, and another, and another. He stood back and sighed, then looked up at the wall. It was perhaps ten feet tall, but the sheer face was broken around the door by the ornamental arch. Chang pocketed his keys and turned to Svenson.

"Doctor, your hands please . . ."

Miss Temple watched with some alarm and a certain animal appreciation as Chang placed his boot in the knitted hands of Doctor Svenson, and then launched himself at the overhanging archway. With the barest grip he slithered up to where he could wedge his knee onto the shingles, shift his weight, and then reach as high as the edge of the wall itself. Within moments, and by what Miss Temple felt to be a striking display of physical capacity, Chang had swung a leg over the wall. He looked down with what seemed to be a professional lack of expression, and dropped from her sight. There was silence. Svenson readied his revolver. Then the lock was turning, the door open, and Chang beckoning them to enter.

"We have been anticipated," he said, and reached out to take the bag from her.

Under its pall of shadow, the garden was a dreary place, the beds withered, the patches of lawn brown, the limbs of the delicate ornamental trees hanging limp and bare. Miss Temple walked between stone urns taller than her head, their edges draped with the dead fallen stalks of last summer's flowers. The garden bordered the rear of a large house that had once, she saw, been painted white, though it was now nearly black from a layered patina of soot. Its windows and rear door had been nailed shut with planks, effectively sealing it off from the garden. Before her, Miss Temple saw the greenhouse, a once-splendid dome of grey-green glass, streaked with moss and grime. The door hung open, dark as the gap of a missing tooth. As they walked toward it, she saw that Doctor Svenson was studying the garden beds and muttering under his breath.

"What do you see, Doctor?" she asked.

"I beg your pardon—I was simply noting the Comte's choice of plants. It is the garden of a dark-hearted herbalist." He pointed to various withered stalks that to Miss Temple looked all the same. "Here is black hellebore, here is belladonna...foxglove...mandrake...castor beans...bloodroot..."

"My goodness," said Miss Temple, not knowing the plants

Svenson was listing, but willing to approve of his recitation. "One would think the Comte was an apothecary!"

"To be sure, Miss Temple, these are all, in their way, poisons." Svenson looked up and drew her eye to the door, where Chang had entered without them. "But perhaps there is time to study the flower beds later . . ."

The light in the greenhouse bore a greenish cast, as if one were entering an aquarium. Miss Temple walked across thick Turkish carpets to where Chang stood next to a large canopied bed. The curtains had been pulled from the posts and the bedding stripped away. She looked down at the mattress with rising revulsion. The thick padding was stained with the deep ruddy color of dried blood, but also, near the head, marked with strange vivid spatters of both deep indigo blue and an acid-tinged orange. Taking her rather aback, Doctor Svenson climbed onto the bed and bent over the different stains, sniffing. For Miss Temple, such intimacy with another person's bodily discharges—a person she did not even know—extended well beyond her present sphere of duty. She turned away and allowed her eyes to roam elsewhere in the room.

While it seemed like the Comte had vacated the greenhouse and taken with him anything that might have explained his use of it, Miss Temple could still see how the circular room had held different areas of activity. At the door was a small work table. Nearby were basins and pipes where water was pumped in, and next to the basins a squat coal stove topped by a wide flat iron plate for cooking either food or, more probably, alchemical compounds and elixirs. Past these was a long wooden table, nailed to the floor and fitted, she noted with a fearful shiver, with leather straps. She glanced back at the bed. Doctor Svenson was still bent over the mattress, and Chang was looking underneath it. She walked to the table. The surface was scored with burns and stains, as was—she noted when her foot snagged in an open tear—the carpet. In fact, the carpet was absolutely ruined with burns and stains along a small pathway running from the stove to the table, and then again from the stove to the basins, and then, finishing the triangle, from the basins to the table directly. She stepped to the stove, which was cold. Out of curiosity, she knelt in front of it and pried open the hatch. It was full of ash. She looked about her for some tongs, found them, and reached in, her tongue poking from her mouth in concentration as she sifted through the ashes. After a moment she stood up, wiped her hands, and turned quite happily to her companions, holding out a scrap of midnight blue fabric.

"Something here, gentlemen. Unless I am mistaken it is *shantung* silk—is it possible this was the woman's dress?"

Chang crossed to her and took the piece of burnt cloth. He studied it a moment without speaking and handed it back. He called to Svenson, his voice a trifle brusque.

"What can *you* tell us, Doctor?"

Miss Temple did not think the Doctor noticed Chang's tone, nor the distressed tapping of his fingertips against his thigh, for Svenson's reply was unhurried, as if his mind was still occupied with solving this newest puzzle. "It is unclear to me...for, you see, the bloodstains *here*...which do, to my experience with the varied colors of drying blood, seem to be relatively recent..."

He pointed to the center of the mattress, and Miss Temple found herself prodding Chang to join her nearer to the bed.

"It seems a lot of blood, Doctor," she said. "Does it not?"

"Perhaps, but not if—if you will permit the indelicacy—if the blood is the result of a *natural*—ah, monthly—process. You will see the stain *is* in the center of the bed—where one would expect the pelvis—"

"What about childbirth?" she asked. "Was the woman pregnant?"

"She was not. There are of course other explanations—it could be another injury, there could be violence, or even some kind of poison—"

"Could she have been raped?" asked Chang.

Svenson did not immediately reply, his eyes flitting to Miss Temple. She bore no expression, and merely raised her eyebrows in encouragement of his answer. He turned back to Chang.

"Obviously, yes—but the quantity of blood is prodigious. Such an assault would have had to be especially catastrophic, possibly mortal. I cannot say more. When I examined the woman, she was not so injured. Of course, that is no guarantee—"

"What of the other stains? The blue and the orange?" asked Miss Temple, still aware of Chang's restless tapping.

"I cannot say. The blue . . . well, firstly, the *smell* is consistent with a strange odor I have smelt both in the Institute and on the body in Crabbé's kitchen—mechanical, chemical. I can only hazard it is part of their glass-making. Perhaps it is a narcotic, or perhaps . . . I do not know, a preservative, a fixative—as it fixes memories into glass, perhaps there is some way in which d'Orkancz hoped to fix the woman into life. I am certain he sought to preserve her," he added, looking up into Chang's stern face. "As for the orange, well, it's very queer. Orange—or an essence of orange peel—is sometimes used as an insecticide—there is an acidity that destroys the carapace. Such is the smell of this stain—a bitter concentrate derived by steam."

"But, Doctor," asked Miss Temple, "do not the stains themselves suggest that the fluid has come—been expelled—*from* the woman? They are sprayed—spattered—"

"Yes, they are—very astute!"

"Do you suggest she was *infested*?"

"No, I suggest nothing—but I do wonder about the effects of such a solvent with regard to the possible properties of the blue fluid, the glass, within the human body. Perhaps it was the Comte's idea of a remedy."

"If it melts an insect's shell, it might melt the glass in her lungs?"

"Exactly—though, of course, we are ignorant of the exact

ingredients of the glass, so I cannot say if it might have proven effective."

They said nothing for a moment, staring at the bed and the traces of the body that had lain there.

"If it worked," said Miss Temple, "I do not know why he has burnt her dress."

"No." Svenson nodded, sadly.

"No," snapped Chang. He turned from them and walked out to the garden.

Miss Temple looked to Doctor Svenson, who was still on the bed, his expression one of concern and confusion, as if they both knew something was not right. He began to climb off—awkwardly, his coat and boots cumbersome and his lank hair falling over his face. Miss Temple was quicker to the door, snatching up her flowered bag where Chang had left it—it was shockingly heavy, Marthe was an idiot to think she could carry the thing for any distance—and lurching into the garden. Chang stood in the middle of the lifeless lawn, staring up at the boarded windows of the house—windows that in their willful impenetrability struck Miss Temple as a mirror of Chang's glasses. She flung down the bag and approached him. He did not turn. She stopped, perhaps a yard from his side. She glanced back to see Doctor Svenson standing in the greenhouse doorway, watching.

"Cardinal Chang?" she asked. He did not answer. Miss Temple did not know if there was anything so tiresome as a person ignoring a perfectly polite, indeed sympathetic, question. She took a breath, exhaled slowly, and gently spoke again. "Do you know the woman?"

Chang turned to her, his voice quite cold. "Her name is Angelique. You would not know her. She is—she *was*—a whore."

"I see," said Miss Temple.

"Do you?" snapped Chang.

Miss Temple ignored the challenge and again held up the scrap of burnt silk. "And you recognize this as hers?"

"She wore such a dress yesterday evening, in the company of the Comte—he took her to the Institute." Chang turned to call over her shoulder to Svenson. "She was with him there, with his machines—she is obviously the woman you saw—and she is obviously dead."

"Is she?" asked Miss Temple.

Chang snorted. "You said it yourself—he has burnt the dress—"

"I did," she agreed, "but it really makes little sense. I do not see any freshly turned earth here in this garden, do you?"

Chang looked at her suspiciously, and then glanced around him. Before he could answer her, Svenson called out from the doorway, "I don't."

"Nor did—forgive the indelicacy—I find any *bones* in the stove. And I do believe that if one were to burn such a thing as a body—for I have seen the bodies of animals in such a fire—that at least some bones would remain. Doctor?"

"I would expect so, yes— the femur alone—"

"So my question, Cardinal Chang," continued Miss Temple, "is why—if she is dead and he is abandoning this garden—does he not bury or burn her remains right here? It truly is the sensible thing—and yet I do not see that he's done it."

"Then why burn the dress?" asked Chang.

"I've no idea. Perhaps because it was ruined—the bloodstains the Doctor described. Perhaps it was *contaminated*." She turned to Svenson. "Was she wearing the dress when *you* saw her, Doctor?"

Svenson cleared his throat. "I saw no such dress," he said.

"So we do not know," announced Miss Temple, returning to Chang. "You may hate the Comte d'Orkancz, but you may also yet hope to find this woman alive—and who can say, even recovered."

*   *   *

Chang did not reply, but she sensed something change in his body, a palpable shifting in his bones to accommodate some small admission of hope. Miss Temple allowed herself a moment of satisfaction, but instead of that pleasure she found herself quite unexpectedly beset by a painful welling of sadness, of isolation, as if she had taken for granted a certain solidarity with Chang, that they were alike in being alone, only to learn that this was not true. The fact of his feelings—that he *had* feelings, much less that they were of such fervor, and for this particular sort of woman—threw her into distress. She did not desire to be the object of such a man's emotions—of course she didn't—but she was nevertheless unprepared to face the depth of her loneliness so abruptly—nor by way of consoling someone else—which seemed especially unjust and was hardly Miss Temple's *forte* to begin with. She could not help it. She was pierced by solitude, and found herself suddenly sniffing. Mortified, she forced her eyes brightly open and tried to smile, making her voice as brisk and amiable as she could.

"It seems that we have each lost someone. You this woman, Angelique, the Doctor his Prince, and my own . . . my cruel and foolish Roger. While there is the difference that the two of you have some hope—and indeed the desire—to recover the one you have lost . . . for me I am content to assist how I can, and to achieve my share of understanding . . . and revenge."

Her voice broke, and she sniffed, angry with her weakness but powerless to fight it. Was this her life? Again she felt the gagging absence in her heart—how could she have been such a fool as to allow Roger Bascombe to fill it? How could she have allowed such feelings to begin with—when they had only left her with this unanswerable ache? How could she be still beset by them, still want to be somehow simply misunderstood by him and taken by the hand—her own weakness was unbearable. For the first time in her twenty-five years Miss Temple did not know where she was going to sleep. She saw Doctor Svenson stepping toward her and forced a smile, waving him away.

"Your aunt," he began, "surely, Miss Temple, her concern for you—"

"*Pffft!*" scoffed Miss Temple, unable to bear his sympathy. She walked to her bag and hefted it with one hand, doing her best to conceal the weight but stumbling as she made her way to the garden gate. "I will wait in the street," she called over her shoulder, not wanting them to see the emotion on her face. "When you are finished, I'm sure there is much for us to do . . ."

She dropped the bag and leaned against the wall, her hands over her eyes, her shoulders now heaving with sobs. Only moments ago she had been so proud to find the scrap of silk in the stove and now—and why? Because Chang had feelings for some whore?— the full weight of all she had suffered and sacrificed and stuffed aside had reappeared to rest on her small frame and tender heart. How did anyone bear this isolation, this desolated hope? In the midst of this tempest, Miss Temple, for her mind was restless and quick, did not forget the sharp fear inspired by her enemies, nor did she refrain from berating herself for the girlish indulgence of crying in the first place. She dug for a handkerchief in her green bag, her hand searching for it around the revolver, another sign of what she had become—what she had embraced with, if she was honest, typically ridiculous results. She blew her nose. She *was* difficult, she knew. She did not make friends. She was brisk and demanding, unsparing and indulgent. She sniffed, bitterly resenting this sort of introspection, despising the need for it nearly as much as she despised introspection itself. In that moment she did not know which she wanted more, to curl up in the sun room of her island house, or to shoot one of these blue-glass villains in the heart . . . yet were either of these the answer to her present state?

She sniffed loudly. Neither Chang, for all his hidden moods, nor Svenson, for all his fussy hesitance, were standing in the open street in tears. How could she face them as any kind of equal?

Again, and relentlessly, she asked herself what she thought she was doing. She'd told Chang that she was willing to pursue her investigations alone, though in her heart she had not believed it. Now she knew that this was exactly what she must do—for at the moment *doing* seemed crucial—if she was ever going to scour this awful sense of being *subject* from her body. She looked back at the garden door—neither man had appeared. She snatched up the bag with both hands and walked back the way they had come, away from the Boniface. With each step she felt as if she were in a ship leaving its port to cross an unknown ocean—and the farther down Plum Court she went, the more determined she became.

At the avenue, she hailed a coach. She looked back. Her heart caught in her throat. Chang and Svenson stood in the garden doorway. Svenson called to her. Chang was running. She climbed into the coach and threw the bag to the floor.

"Drive on," she called. The coach pulled away and with an almost brutal swiftness she was beyond the lane and any vision of her two companions. The driver looked back at her, his face an unspoken inquiry for their destination.

"The St. Royale Hotel," said Miss Temple.

FIVE

Ministry

By the time Chang reached the end of the lane, the coach was out of sight and he could not tell in which direction it had vanished. He spat with frustration, his chest heaving with the wasted effort. He looked back to see Svenson catch up, the Doctor's face a mask of concern.

"She is gone?" he asked.

Chang nodded and spat again. He had no idea what had transpired in the girl's head, nor where the irresponsible impulses had carried her.

"We should follow—" began Svenson.

"How?" snapped Chang. "Where is she going? Is she abandoning her efforts? Is she attacking our enemies on her own? Which one? And when, between being taken and being killed, will she tell them all they need know to find us?"

Chang was furious, but in truth he was just as angry at himself. His display of bad temper with regard to Angelique had touched off the foolishness—and what was the point? Angelique had no feelings for him. If she were alive and he could find her, it would help his standing with Madelaine Kraft. That was the end of it, the only end. He turned to Svenson, speaking quickly.

"How much money do you have?"

"I—I don't know—enough for a day or two—to eat, find a room—"

"Purchase a train ticket?"

"Depending on how far the journey—"

"Here, then." Chang thrust his hand into his coat pocket and pulled out the leather wallet. It held only two small banknotes, change from his night at the Boniface, but he had a handful of gold coins in his trouser pocket to fall back on. He handed one of the notes to Doctor Svenson with a bitter smile. "I don't know what will befall us—and the change purse of our partnership has just walked away. How are you for ammunition?"

As if to reinforce his reply, Svenson hefted the revolver from his pocket. "I was able to reload from Miss Temple's supply—the weapons share a caliber—"

"That's a service .44."

"It is."

"As was hers?"

"Yes, though her weapon *was* deceptively small—"

"Has she ever fired it, do you know?"

"I do not think so."

The two men stood for a moment between thoughts. Chang attempted to shrug off his feelings of remorse and recrimination. How had he not realized the gun was so powerful—he'd helped her clean it, for God's sake. He wondered what he'd been thinking— but in truth knew exactly what had distracted him: the surprise at seeing her again in such different apparel than on the train, the curves of her throat marked by bruises instead of bloodstains, her small nimble fingers working to disassemble the black oiled metal parts of the revolver. He shook his head. The kick from such a weapon would knock her arm up back over her head—unless she pressed the barrel into her target's body, she would never hit a thing. She had no idea what she was doing, in any of this.

"It is senseless to consider what's done," the Doctor said. "Do we go after her?"

"If she is taken, she is dead."

"Then we must part to cover more ground. It really is unfortunate—it seems but a moment ago we were each running for our lives in isolation. I will miss someone to help me scale what water pipes I must." He smiled and extended his hand. Chang took it.

"You will scale them by yourself—I am sure."

Svenson smiled with a pinched expression, as if he appreciated Chang's encouragement but remained unpersuaded. "Where do we each go?" he asked. "And where shall we meet again?"

"Where would *she* go?" Chang asked. "Do you think she is running to her aunt? That would be easier for us all..."

"I do not think so," said Svenson. "On the contrary, whatever distress she has felt, I believe it has spurred her to direct action."

Chang frowned, thinking. What had she said to him in the garden, her face, the smile belied by her grey eyes.

"Then it has to be this Bascombe idiot."

Svenson sighed. "The poor girl."

Chang spat again. "Will she shoot him in the head or blubber at his feet—that's the question."

"I disagree," said Svenson quietly. "She is brave and resourceful. What do we know about anyone—very little. But we know Miss Temple has surprised any number of powerful people into thinking she was a deadly assassin-courtesan. Without her we both could have been taken in the hotel. If we can find her, I will wager you that she will save each of us in our turn before this is finished."

Chang did not answer, then smiled.

"What is your Macklenburg currency—gold shillings?"

Svenson nodded.

"Then I will happily wager you ten gold shillings that Miss Temple will not preserve our lives. Of course, it's a fool's bet—for if we are not so preserved, then neither shall we be in any position to profit."

"Nevertheless," said Svenson, "I accept the wager." They shook hands again. Svenson cleared his throat. "Now... this Bascombe—"

"There's the country house—Tarr Manor. He could well be there. Or he could be at the Ministry, or with Crabbé." Chang looked quickly up and down the avenue—they really ought not to be standing so long in the street so near to the Boniface. "The trip to Tarr Manor—"

"Where is it?"

"To the north, perhaps half a day by rail—we can find out easily enough at Stropping—we may even catch her at the station. But the trip will take time. The other possibilities—his home, the Ministry, Crabbé—these are in the city, and one of us can easily move from one to another as necessary."

Svenson nodded. "So, one to the country, one to stay here—do you have a preference? I am an outsider in either instance."

Chang smiled. "So am I, Doctor." He gestured to his red coat and his glasses. "I am not one for country gentry, nor for the drawing rooms of respectable townsfolk..."

"It is still your city—you are its animal, if you will forgive me. I will go to the country, where they may be more persuaded by a uniform and tales of the Macklenburg Palace."

Chang turned to flag another coach. "You should hurry—as I say, you may find her at Stropping. The path to the Ministry takes me the other way. We will part here."

They shook hands for a third time, smiling at it. Svenson climbed into the coach. Without another word Chang began to walk quickly in the opposite direction. Over his shoulder he heard Svenson's voice and turned.

"Where do we meet?" called the Doctor.

Chang called back, shouting through his hands. "Tomorrow noon! The clock at Stropping!"

Svenson nodded and waved before sitting back down in the coach. Chang doubted that either of them would be there.

As soon as he could, Chang left the avenue for a winding trail of alleys and narrow lanes. He had not decided where he ought to go first. More than anything he wanted to orient himself to his task in his normal manner and not rush headlong into circumstances he didn't understand—even though this was exactly what Celeste was doing. Celeste? He wondered how he used that name in his thoughts, but not to her face, nor when speaking to Doctor

Svenson, when it was always "Miss Temple." It hardly mattered—it was undoubtedly because she was behaving like a child. With this thought, Chang resolved that if he were to try and enter the offices of the Foreign Ministry, or the house of Harald Crabbé, he needed to be better prepared. He increased his pace to a loping trot. He could not brave the Raton Marine, for it would certainly be watched—he had to believe Aspiche was now one with this Cabal. He would have very much liked to reach the Library. There were so many questions to answer—about indigo clay, about the Comte and the Contessa, about Bascombe and Crabbé, about the foreign travels of Francis Xonck, about Oskar Veilandt, even, he admitted, about Miss Celestial Temple. But the Library was where Rosamonde had found him, and they would certainly be waiting. Instead, his thinking more practical and dark, he made his way to Fabrizi's.

The man was an Italian ex-mercenary and weapons master who catered to a clientele drawn from all across the city and whose only shared characteristic was an elegant bloody purpose. Chang entered the shop, glancing to either side at the glass display cases with his usual surge of covetous pleasure. He was relieved to see Fabrizi himself behind the counter, a crisp suit covered by a green flannel apron.

"*Dottore,*" said Chang, with a nod of greeting.

"*Cardinale,*" answered Fabrizi, his tone serious and respectful.

Chang pulled out his dagger and placed it before the man. "I have had a misadventure with the rest of your splendid cane," he said. "I would like you to repair it, if possible. In the meantime, I would request the use of a suitable replacement. I will of course pay for all services in advance." He took the remaining banknote from the wallet and laid it on the counter. Fabrizi ignored it, instead picking up the dagger and studying the condition of the blade. He returned the blade to the counter, looked at the banknote with mild surprise, as if it had appeared there independently, and quietly folded it into the pocket of his apron. He nodded to one of the glass cases. "You may select your replacement. I will have this ready in three days."

"I am much obliged," said Chang. He walked to the case, Fabrizi following him behind the counter. "Is there one you would suggest?"

"All are superb," said the Italian. "For a man like you, I recommend the heavier wood—the cane may be used alone, yes? This one is teak...this one Malaysian ironwood."

He handed the ironwood to Chang, who held it with immediate satisfaction, the hilt curved like a black-powder pistol grip in his hand. He pulled out the blade—a bit longer than he was used to—and hefted the stick. It was lovely, and Chang smiled like a man holding a new baby.

"As always," he whispered, "the work is exquisite."

It was after three o'clock. Without the Library to tell him where Bascombe lived, the easiest thing would be to follow the man from the Ministry. Besides, if Celeste were truly intent on finding him quickly, she would certainly go to the Ministry herself, doing her best to meet him—kill him?—in his office. If he was not there... well, Chang would answer that when it became necessary. He weighed the coins in his pocket, decided against a coach, and began to jog toward the maze of white buildings. It took him perhaps fifteen minutes to reach St. Isobel's Square, and another five to walk—taking the time to ease his breathing and his countenance—to the front entrance. He made his way under the great white archway, through a sea of coaches and the throng of serious-faced people pursuing government business, and into a graveled courtyard, with different lanes—paved with slate and lined with ornamental shrubbery—leading off to different Ministries. It was as if he stood at the center of a wheel, with each spoke leading to its own discrete world of bureaucracy. The Foreign Ministry was directly before him, and so he walked straight ahead, boots crunching on the gravel and then echoing off the slate, to another smaller archway opening into a marble lobby and a wooden desk where a man in a black suit was flanked by red-coated soldiers. With some alarm, Chang noticed that they were troopers from the 4th Dragoons, but by the time he had realized this, they had seen him. He stopped, ready to run or to fight, but none of the soldiers stirred from their stiff postures of attention. Between them, the man in the suit looked up at Chang with an inquiring sniff.

"Yes?"

"Mr. Roger Bascombe," said Chang.

The man's gaze took in Chang's apparel and demeanor. "And...who shall I announce?"

"Miss Celeste Temple," said Chang.

"Excuse me—Miss Temple, you say?" The man was well enough trained in dealing with foreign manners not to sneer.

"I bring word from her," said Chang. "I am confident he will want to hear it. If Mr. Bascombe is unavailable, I am willing to speak to Deputy Minister Crabbé."

"I see, you are...*willing*...to speak to the Deputy Minister. Just a moment." The man jotted a few lines onto a piece of paper and stuffed it into a leather tube, which he fed into a brass opening in the desk, where it was sucked from sight with an audible hiss. Chang was reminded of the Old Palace, and found it somehow comforting that the highest levels of government shared the latest means of communication with a brothel. He waited. Several other visitors arrived and were either allowed to pass through or became the subject of another such message sent through the leather tubes. Chang glanced at the others waiting—a dark-skinned man in a white uniform and a hat with peacock feathers, a pale Russian with a long beard and a blue uniform of boiled wool with a line of medals and a sash, and two elderly men in run-down black tailcoats, as if they had been continuously attending the same ball for the last twenty years. He was not surprised to see all four of them staring at him in return. He casually looked around to make sure the exit behind was still clear, and to note the hallways and staircases on the other side of the desk, the better to anticipate any danger that might arrive. The troopers remained still.

It was five more minutes before an answering tube thumped into its receptacle near the desk. The clerk unfolded the paper, made a note in the ledger next to him, and handed the paper to one of the troopers. He then called to Chang.

"You're to go up. This man will show you the way. I will need your name, and your signature...here." He indicated a second ledger on the desk top, and held out a pen. Chang took it and wrote, and handed it back.

"The name is Chang," he said.

"Just 'Chang'?" the man asked.

"For the moment, I'm afraid so." He leaned forward with a whisper. "But I am hoping to win at the races...and then I shall purchase another."

The soldier led Chang along a wide corridor and up an austere staircase of polished black granite with a wrought-iron rail. They moved among other men in dark suits walking up and down, all clutching thickly packed satchels of paper, none of whom paid Chang the slightest attention. At the first landing the soldier led the way across a marble corridor to another staircase blocked off with an iron chain. He unlatched the chain, stepped back for Chang to pass, and replaced it behind them. On this staircase there was no other traffic, and the farther they climbed the more Chang felt he was entering a labyrinth he might never escape from. He looked at the red-coated trooper ahead of him and wondered if it would be better to simply slip a knife between the man's ribs here, where they were alone, and then take his chances. As it was, he could only hope that he was indeed being taken to Bascombe— or Crabbé—and not into some isolated place of entrapment. He had mentioned Miss Temple's name on a whim, to provoke a response—as well as to see if she had been there before him. That he had gained entry without any particular reaction left him mystified. It could mean that she was there, or that she wasn't—or that they merely wanted to find her, which he already knew. He had to assume that the people who had allowed him in did not ultimately plan for him to leave. Still, the impulse to kill the soldier was mere nervousness. All that would come soon enough.

They climbed past three landings but never a door or window. At the landing of the next floor, however, the soldier took a long brass key from his coat, glanced once at Chang, and stepped to a heavy wooden door. He inserted the key and turned it several times in the lock, the machinery echoing sharply within the stairwell, before pulling it open. He stepped aside and indicated that Chang should go in. Chang did so, his attention neatly divided between the instinctive suspicion about the man at his back and the room he was entering—a short marbled corridor with another door on the opposite side, some five yards away. Chang looked back to the soldier, who nodded him on toward the far door. When Chang did not move the soldier suddenly slammed the door shut. Before Chang could leap for the knob he heard the key being turned. The thing would not budge. He was locked in. He berated himself for a credulous fool and strode to the far door, fully expecting it to be locked as well, but the brass knob turned with a well-oiled *snick*.

He looked into a wide office with a deep green carpet, and a low ceiling made less oppressive by a domed skylight of creamy glass rising over the center of the room. The walls were lined with bookshelves stuffed with hundreds of massive numbered volumes— official documents no doubt, collected through the years and from around the world. The wide space of the room was divided between two great pieces of furniture—a long meeting table to Chang's left and an expansive desk to his right—that, like oaken planets, cast their nets of gravity across an array of lesser satellites—

end tables, ashtrays, and map-stands. The desk was unoccupied, but at the table, looking up from an array of papers spread around him, sat Roger Bascombe.

"Ah," he said, and awkwardly stood.

Chang glanced around the office more carefully and saw a communication door—closed—in the wall behind Bascombe, and what might well be another hidden entrance set into the bookcases behind the desk. He pushed the main door closed behind him, turned to Bascombe and tapped the tip of his stick lightly on the carpet.

"Good afternoon," Chang said.

"Indeed, it is," Bascombe replied. "The days grow warmer."

Chang frowned. This was hardly the confrontation he had expected. "I believe I was announced," he said.

"Yes. Actually, Miss Celeste Temple was announced. And then your name of course, in turn." Bascombe gestured to the wall where Chang could see the sending and receiving apparatus for the message tubes. Bascombe gestured again toward the end of the table. "Please . . . will you sit?"

"I would prefer to stand," said Chang.

"As you wish. I prefer a seat, if it is all the same to you . . ."

Bascombe sat back at the table, and took a moment to rearrange the papers in front of him. "So . . . ," he began, "you are acquainted with Miss Temple?"

"Apparently," said Chang.

"Yes, apparently." Bascombe nodded. "She is—well—she is herself. I have no cause to speak of her beyond those terms."

It seemed to Chang that Bascombe was choosing his words very carefully, almost as if he were afraid of being caught out somehow . . . or being overheard.

"What terms exactly?" asked Chang.

"The terms she has set down by her own choices," answered Bascombe. "As you have done."

"And you?"

"Of course—no one is immune to the consequences of their own actions. Are you sure you will not sit?"

Chang ignored the question. He stared intently at the slim, well-dressed man at the table, trying to discern where in all the competing spheres of his enemies he might fit in. He could not help seeing Bascombe as he thought a woman must—his respectability, his refinement, his odd assumption of both rank and deference—and not any woman, but Miss Temple in particular. This man had been the object of her love—almost certainly was still, women being what they were. Looking at him, Chang had to admit that Bascombe possessed any number of attractive qualities, and was thus equally quite certain that he disliked the young man intensely, and so he smiled.

"Ambition ... it does strange things to a fellow, would you not agree?"

Bascombe's gaze measured him with all the dry, serious purpose of an undertaker. "How so?"

"I mean to say ... it often seems that until a man is given what he assumes he wants ... he has no real idea of the cost."

"And why would you say that?"

"Why would I indeed?" Chang smiled. "Such an opinion would have to be derived from actual achievement. So how *could* I possibly know?" When Bascombe did not immediately respond, Chang gestured with his stick to the large desk. "Where are your confederates? Where is Mr. Crabbé? Why are you meeting me alone—don't you know who I am? Haven't you spoken to poor Major Blach? Aren't you just the slightest bit worried?"

"I am not," replied Bascombe, with an easy self-assurance that made Chang want to bloody his nose. "You have been *allowed* into this office for the specific purpose of being presented with a proposition. As I assume you are no idiot, as I assure you *I* am no idiot, I am in no danger until that proposition has been made."

"And what proposition is that?"

*   *   *

But instead of answering, Bascombe stared at him, running his gaze over Chang's person and costume, very much as if he were an odd kind of livestock or someone from a circus. Chang had the presence of mind to realize that the gesture was deliberate and designed to anger—though he did not understand why Bascombe would take the risk, being so obviously vulnerable. The entire situation was strange—for all that Bascombe spoke of plans and propositions, Chang knew his appearance at the Ministry must be a surprise. Bascombe was delaying him at personal risk so something else could happen—the arrival of reinforcements? But *that* made no sense, for the soldiers could have stopped him at any time on the way up. Instead, what they had accomplished was to divert Chang from the entrance. Was this all a performance—was Bascombe somehow demonstrating his loyalty, or was it possible that Bascombe played a double game? Or was the delay not to bring anyone *to* the room, but to get someone away *from* it?

In a swift movement Chang raised his stick and strode to Bascombe. Before the man could half-rise from his chair the end landed viciously against his ear. Bascombe slumped down with a cry, holding the side of his head. Chang took the opportunity to press the stick roughly across his neck. Bascombe choked, his face abruptly reddening. Chang leaned forward and spoke slowly.

"Where is she?"

Bascombe did not immediately answer. Chang shoved the stick sharply into his windpipe.

"Where is she?"

"Who?" Bascombe's voice was a rasp.

"Where is she?"

"I don't think he knows who you mean."

Chang whirled around and with a smooth motion pulled apart his stick. Behind the desk, leaning indolently against the bookcases, stood Francis Xonck, in a mustard yellow morning coat, his red hair meticulously curled, an unlit cheroot in his hand. Chang took a careful step toward him, risking a quick glance back to Bascombe, who was still laboring to breathe.

"Good afternoon," said Chang.

"Good afternoon. I hope you haven't hurt him."

"Why? Does he belong to you?"

Xonck smiled. "That's very clever. But you know, I'm clever too, and I must congratulate you—the mystery about the 'she' you so desperately seek is positively diverting. Is it Rosamonde? Is it little Miss Temple—or should I say Hastings? Or even better, the Comte's unfortunate, slant-eyed trollop? Either way, the idea that you're actually looking for any of them is richly amusing. Because you're so *manly*, don't you know, and at the same time such a *buffoon*. Excuse me."

He pulled a small box of matches from his waistcoat and lit the cheroot, looking over the glowing tip at Chang as he puffed. His eyes shifted to Bascombe. "Will you survive, Roger?" He smiled at Bascombe's reply—a hacking cough—and tossed the spent match onto the desk top.

Chang took another step closer to Xonck, who seemed as uncaring in his manner as Bascombe had been moments before, but oddly gay where Bascombe had been watchful. "Shall I ask you?" he hissed.

"You would do better to listen," Xonck replied dryly. "Or, in lieu of that, to think. The way behind you is locked, as is the door behind me. If you were able to make your way through the door behind Bascombe—which you won't—I promise you will be quickly lost within a dense maze of corridors with absolutely no chance of evading or surviving the very large number of soldiers even now assembling to kill you. You would die, Mr. Chang, in such a way as to serve no one—a dog run down by a coach in the dark." He frowned and picked a scrap of tobacco off his lower lip and flicked it away, then returned his eyes to Chang.

"And you would suggest I serve *you*?" asked Chang.

"Serve yourself," croaked Bascombe, from the table.

"He rallies!" laughed Xonck. "But you know, he is right. Serve yourself. Be reasonable."

"We're wasting time—" muttered Chang, moving for Xonck. Xonck did not move, but spoke very quickly and sharply.

"That is foolish. It will kill you. Stop and think."

Against his better judgment, Chang did. He was nearly within reach of the man, if he lunged with the long part of the stick. But he didn't lunge, partly because he saw that Xonck wasn't frightened . . . not in the slightest.

"Whatever reason brought you here," Xonck said, "your *search*—you must postpone. You were allowed up for the sole reason, as Mr. Bascombe has said, to make you a proposition. There is plenty of time to fight, or to die—there is always time for that—but there is no more time to find whichever woman you hoped would be here."

Chang wanted very much to leap over the desk and stab him, but his instincts—which he knew to trust—told him that Xonck was not like Bascombe, and that any attack on him needed to be as carefully considered as one on a cobra. Xonck did not seem to be armed, but he could easily have a small pistol—or for that matter a vial of acid. At the same time, Chang did not know what to make of the man's warning about escaping into the Ministry. While it might be true, it was in Xonck's every interest to lie. But why *had* they let him ascend without any soldiers to take him in hand? He had too many questions, but Chang knew that nothing revealed more about a man than his estimation of what your price might be. He stepped away from Xonck and sneered.

"What proposition?"

Xonck smiled, but it was Bascombe who spoke, clearly and coolly despite the hoarseness of his voice, as if he were describing the necessary steps in the working of a machine.

"I cannot give you details. I do not seek to convince, but to offer opportunity. Those who have accepted our invitation have and will continue to benefit accordingly. Those who have not are no longer our concern. You are acquainted with Miss Temple. She may have spoken of our former engagement. I cannot—for it is impossible to say how I was then, for that would be to say how I was a child. So much has changed—so much has become clear— that I can only speak of what I have become. It's true I thought myself to be in love. In love because I could not see past the ways in which I was subject, for I believed, in my servitude, that this love would release me. What view of the world had I convinced myself I understood so well? It was the useless attachment to an-other, to *rescue*, which existed in place of my own action. What I believed were solely consequences of that attachment—money, stature, respectability, pleasure—I now see merely as elements of my own unlimited capacity. Do you understand?"

Chang shrugged. The words were eloquently spoken, but somehow abstractly, like a speech learned by heart to demonstrate rhetoric . . . and yet, through it all, had Bascombe's eyes been as steady? Had they betrayed some other tension? As if responding to Chang's thought, Bascombe then leaned forward, more intently.

"It is natural that different individuals pursue different goals, but it is equally clear that these goals are intertwined, that a bene-fit to one will be a benefit to others. Serve yourself. You are a man of capacity—and even, it seems possible, of some intelligence. What you have achieved against our allies only certifies your value. There are no grievances, only interests in competition. Refuse that competition, join us, and be enriched with clarity. Whatever you want—wherever you direct your action—you will find reward."

"I have no uncle with a title," observed Chang. He wished Xonck was not there—it was impossible to read Bascombe's true intention apart from his master's presence.

"Neither does Roger, anymore." Xonck chuckled.

"Exactly," said Bascombe, with all the evident emotion of the wooden chair he sat in.

"I'm afraid I don't actually understand your proposition," said Chang.

Xonck sneered. "Don't be coy."

"You have desire," said Bascombe. "Ambition. Frustration. Bitterness. What will you do—struggle against them until one of your adventures goes wrong and you die bleeding in the street? Will you trust your life to the whims of a"—his voice stumbled just slightly—"a provincial *girl*? To the secret interests of a German spy? You have met the Contessa. She has spoken for you. It is at her urging you are here. Our hand is out. Take it. The Process will transform you, as it has transformed us all."

The offer was enormously condescending. Chang looked to Xonck, whose face wore a mild, fixed smile of no particular meaning.

"And if I refuse this proposition?"

"You won't," said Bascombe. "You would be a fool."

Chang noticed a smear of blood on Bascombe's ear, but whatever pain he had caused made no impression on the man's self-assurance, nor on the sharpness of his gaze, the meaning of which Chang could not discern. Chang glanced back to Xonck, who rolled the cheroot between his fingers and exhaled a jet of smoke toward the ceiling. The question was how best to learn more, to find Angelique, or Celeste—even, he had to admit, confront Rosamonde. But had he only come here to deliver himself into their hands so effortlessly?

About the Ministry at least, Xonck had been telling the truth. They walked down a twisting narrow hallway in the dark—Bascombe in the front with a lantern, Xonck behind. The rooms they passed— the flickering light giving Chang brief, flaring glimpses before they fell back into shadow—had been constructed without any logic he could see. Some were crammed with boxes, with maps, with tables and chairs, day beds, desks, while others—both large and small— were empty, or contained but a single chair. The only point of unity was the complete absence of windows, indeed of any light at all.

With his poor eyesight, Chang soon lost any sense of direction as Bascombe led him this way and that, up short sets of stairs and then down odd curving ramps. They had allowed him to keep his stick, but he was deeper in their power with each step he took.

"This Process of yours," he said, ostensibly to Bascombe though hoping for a reply from Xonck. "Do you really think it will alter my desire to ruin you both?"

Bascombe stopped, and turned to face him, his gaze flicking briefly to Xonck before he spoke.

"Once you have experienced it yourself, you will be ashamed of your doubts and mockery, as well as the purposeless life you have so far pursued."

"Purposeless?"

"Pathetically so. Are you ready?"

"I suppose I am."

Chang heard a slight rustle from the darkness behind him. He was sure Xonck held a weapon.

"Keep walking," muttered Xonck.

"You swayed Colonel Aspiche to your cause, didn't you? The 4th Dragoons are a fine regiment—so helpful to the Foreign Ministry. Good of him to step into the breach." He clucked his tongue and called back to Xonck. "You're not wearing black. Trapping *was* your brother-in-law."

"And I am devastated, I do assure you."

"Then why did he have to die?"

He received no answer. Chang would have to do better than this to provoke them. They walked on in shuffling silence, the lantern light catching on what seemed to be chandeliers in the air above them. Their passageway had opened into some much larger room. Xonck called ahead to Bascombe.

"Roger, put the lantern on the floor."

Bascombe turned, looked at Xonck as if he didn't fully comprehend, and then placed the lantern on the wooden floor, well out of Chang's reach.

"Thank you. Now go ahead—you can find your way. Give word to prepare the machines."

"Are you quite sure?"

"I am."

Bascombe glanced once, rather searchingly, at Chang, who took the opportunity to sneer, and then disappeared into the dark. Chang heard his footsteps well after the man had passed from the light, but soon the room was silent once more. Xonck took a few steps into the shadow and returned with two wooden chairs. He placed them on the floor and kicked one over to Chang, who stopped its momentum with his foot. Xonck sat, and after a moment Chang followed his example.

"I thought it worthwhile to attempt a frank discussion. After all, in half an hour's time you will either be my ally or you will be dead—there seems little point in mincing words."

"Is it that simple?" asked Chang.

"It is."

"I don't believe you. I don't mean my decision to submit or die—that *is* simple—but your own reasons . . . your desire to speak without Bascombe . . . not simple in the slightest."

Xonck studied him, but did not speak. Chang decided to take a chance, and do exactly what Xonck asked—speak frankly.

"There are two levels to your *enterprise*. There are those who have undergone this Process, like Margaret Hooke . . . and then there are those—like you, or the Contessa—who remain free. And in competition, despite your *rhetoric*."

"Competition for what?"

"I do not know," Chang admitted. "The stakes are different for each of you—I imagine that's the problem. It always is."

Xonck chuckled. "But my colleagues and I are in complete agreement."

Chang scoffed. He was aware that he could not see Xonck's

right hand, that the man held it casually to the side of his chair behind his crossed leg.

"Why should that surprise you?" Xonck asked. Chang scoffed again.

"Then why was Tarr's death so poorly managed? Why was Trapping killed? What of the dead painter, Oskar Veilandt? Why did the Contessa allow the Prince to be rescued? Where is the Prince now?"

"A lot of questions," Xonck observed dryly.

"I'm sorry if they bore you. But if I were you, and *I* didn't have those answers—"

"As I explained, either you'll be dead—"

"Don't you think it's amusing? You're trying to decide whether to kill me before I join you—so I won't tell your colleagues about your independent plans. And I'm trying to decide whether to kill you—or to try and learn more about your Process."

"Except I don't have any independent plans."

"But the Contessa does," said Chang. "And you know it. The others *don't.*"

"We're going to disappoint Bascombe if you don't show up. He's a keen one for *order.*" Xonck stood, his right hand still behind his body. "Leave the lantern."

Chang rose with him, his stick held loosely in his left hand. "Have you met the young woman, Miss Temple? She was Bascombe's fiancée."

"So I understand. Quite a shock to poor Roger, I'm sure—quite a good thing his mind is so *stable.* So much fuss for nothing."

"Fuss?"

"The search for Isobel Hastings," Xonck scoffed, "mysterious killer whore."

Xonck's eyes were full of intelligence and cunning, and his body possessed the easy, lithe athleticism of a hunting wolf—but running through it all, like a vein of rot through a tree, was the arrogance of money. Chang knew enough to see the man was dangerous, perhaps even his better if it came to a fight—one never knew—but all of this was still atop a foundation of privilege, an unearned superiority imposed by force, fear, disdain, by purchased experience and unexamined arrogance. Chang found it odd that his estimation of Xonck was crystallized by the man's dismissal of Celeste—not because she wasn't in part a silly rich girl, but because she was that and still managed to survive, and—more important than anything—accept that the ordeal had changed her. Chang did not believe Francis Xonck ever changed—in fact change was the exact quality he held himself above.

"I take it you haven't made her acquaintance then," Chang said.

Xonck shrugged and nodded at the door in the shadows behind Chang. "I will bear the loss. If you would . . ."

"No."

"No?"

"No. I've found what I meant to. I'll be going."

Xonck swung his hand forward and aimed a shining silver-plated pistol at Chang's chest. "To hell?"

"At some point, certainly. Why invite me to join you—your *Process*? Whose idea was that?"

"Bascombe told you. Hers."

"I'm flattered."

"You needn't be." Xonck stared at him, the lines of his face deeply etched in the flickering lantern light. His sharp nose and pointed chin looked positively devilish. Chang knew it was a matter of moments—either Xonck would shoot him or drive him along to Bascombe. He was confident that his guesses about the fissures within the Cabal were correct, and that Xonck was smart enough to see them too. Was Xonck arrogant enough to think they didn't matter, that he was immune? Of course he was. Then why had he wanted to talk? To see if Chang was still working for Rosamonde? And if he thought Chang was . . . did that mean he would kill him, or try to satisfy the Contessa and let him escape— thus the need to get rid of Bascombe . . .

Chang shook his head ruefully, as if he had been caught out. "She did say you were the smartest of them all, even smarter than d'Orkancz."

For a moment Xonck didn't respond. Then he said, "I don't believe you."

"She hired me to find Isobel Hastings. I did. Before I could contact her, I was waylaid by that idiot German Major—"

"I don't believe you."

"Ask her yourself." He suddenly dropped his voice, hissing with annoyance. "Is that Bascombe coming back?"

Chang turned behind him as if he'd heard footsteps, so naturally that Xonck would have been inhuman not to look, even for a moment. In that moment Chang, whose hand was on the back of the wooden chair, swept it up with all his strength and hurled it at Xonck. The pistol went off once, splintering the wood, and then once more, but by that time Xonck was flinching against the chair's impact and the shot went high. The chair hit his shoulder with a solid cracking sound, causing him to swear and stumble back against the possibility that Chang would rush him with his stick. The chair rebounded away and, his face a mask of fury, Xonck brought the pistol back to bear. His third shot coincided exactly with a scream of surprise. Chang had scooped up the oil lantern and flung it at him, the contents soaking Xonck's extended arm. When he fired, the spark from the gun set his arm ablaze. The shot missed Chang by a good yard. His last image of Xonck, screaming with rage, was the man's desperate attempt to rip off his morning coat, his fingers—the pistol dropped—roiling with flame and clutching in agony against the sizzling rush of the fire that swallowed his entire arm. Xonck thrashed like a madman. Chang dove forward into the darkness.

Within moments he was blind. He slowed to deliberate steps, hands held out to prevent walking into walls or furniture. He needed to put distance between himself and Xonck, but he needed to do it quietly. His hand found a wall to his left and he moved along it in what seemed to be another direction—had he entered a corridor? He paused to listen. He could no longer hear Xonck... could the man have put out the fire so quickly? Could he be dead? Chang didn't think so. His one comfort was that Xonck was now forced to shoot with his left hand. He crept along, pawing at a curtain in front of him until he found an opening. Behind it—he nearly twisted his ankle missing the first step—was an extremely narrow staircase—he could easily touch the walls on either side. He silently made his way down. At the landing, some twenty steps below, he heard noises above him. It had to be Bascombe. There would be lights, a search. He groped ahead of himself for the far wall, found a door, then the knob. It was locked. Chang very carefully dug in his pockets for his ring of keys and, clutching them hard to stop them jingling into one another, tried the lock. It opened with the second key, and he stepped through, easing the door closed behind him.

The new room, whatever it was, was still pitch black. Chang wondered how long before these corridors were full of soldiers. He felt his way forward, his hands finding a stack of wooden crates, and then a dusty bookcase. He worked his way past it, and to his great relief felt a pane of glass, a window undoubtedly painted black. Chang pulled the dagger from his cane and smartly rapped the butt into the glass, punching it clear. Light poured into the room, transforming it from formless dark to an unthreatening vestibule full of dusty unused furniture. He peered out through the broken pane. The window overlooked one of the wheel-spoke pathways, and was—he craned his neck—at least two floors below the roof. To his dismay he saw the outer wall was sheer, with no ledges or molding or pipes to cling to, going up or down. There was no exit this way.

Chang wheeled around at a sudden draft of cool air behind him—as if the door had been opened. The breeze came from a metal vent in the floor, the cool air—which with a sense of smell might well have made him nauseous—flowing out to the open window. Chang knelt at the vent. He could hear voices. He sighed with frustration—he could not make out the words for the echoing effect of the vent. The opening was wide enough for a man to crawl through. He felt inside and was gratified to find it was not moist. Keeping as quiet as possible, he pried apart the housing until it was wide enough for him to get at the hole. It was pitch black. He set his stick inside and wormed his way after it. There was just room for him to move on his hands and knees. He crawled forward as quietly as he could.

He'd gone perhaps five yards when the vent split three ways, to either side and angling upwards. He listened carefully. The voices were coming from above—from the floor he'd just escaped. He peered up, and saw a dim light. He climbed upwards, pressing his legs against both sides to keep himself from sliding back. As he rose, the vent leveled off again—where the light bled in. He kept climbing, finding it more and more difficult, for the surface of the vent was covered with a fine powder that prevented him from getting any solid purchase. Was it soot? He couldn't see in the dark—he cursed the fact that he was probably filthy—and kept struggling to reach the light. He reached up, his fingers finding a ledge and just beyond it, a metal grate over the opening. He laced his fingers over the grating and pulled his body up until he could see out the hole, but the only view was a slate-covered floor and a tattered dark curtain. He listened . . . and heard a voice he did not recognize.

"He is a protégé of my uncle's. Of course, I do not approve of my uncle, so this is not the highest recommendation. Is he quite secured? Excellent. You will understand that I am not—given these recent events—inclined toward the risks of *politesse.*"

A woman chuckled politely in response. Chang frowned. The voice spoke with an accent quite like the Doctor's, but with an

indolent drawl that announced its words one at a time without regard to conversational sense or momentum, so draining them of
any possible wit.

"Excuse the interruption, but perhaps I should assist—"

"You will not."

"Highness." The word was followed by the clicking of heels.
The second voice was also German.

The first voice went on, and obviously not to the second voice,
but to the woman. "What people do not understand—who have
not known it—is the great burden of obligation."

"Responsibility," she agreed. "Only a few of us can bear it well.
Tea?"

"*Danke.* Is he able to breathe?"

It was a question from curiosity, not from concern, and it was
answered—to Chang's ears—with a swift meaty impact followed
by a violent expulsion of coughing discomfort.

"He should not expire before the Process re-makes him," continued the voice rather pedantically. "He will know what it means
to be faithful, yes? Is there a lemon?"

The voices were still some distance away, perhaps across the
room, he could not tell. He reached out and tentatively exerted
pressure on the grated covering. It gave, but not enough to come
loose. He pushed again, steadily and with more force.

"Who is this man they have with them?" asked the first voice.

"The criminal," answered the second man.

"Criminal? Why should we be joined by such a fellow?"

"I would not agree that we should—"

"Different walks of life bear different cares, Highness," said the
woman smoothly, cutting into the second man's words. "Truly
when we have nothing more to learn, we have stopped living."

"Of course," the voice agreed eagerly. "And by this logic you're
very much alive, Major—for you have obviously very much to
learn about sensible thinking!"

Chang's brain took in the fact that the second voice must be

Major Blach and the first voice—though his manner contradicted the sense-drugged dissipation as described by Svenson—Karl-Horst von Maasmärck, but these were hardly the crux of his attention. The woman was Rosamonde, Contessa Lacquer-Sforza. What she was doing here he could not say. He was too much stirred at the knowledge she was speaking of *him*.

"The Major is angry, Highness, for this man has caused him much discomfort. But yet, that is exactly why Mr. Bascombe, at my suggestion, has importuned him to join our efforts."

"But will he? Will he see the sense of it?" The Prince slurped his tea.

"We can only hope he is as wise a man as you."

The Prince chuckled indulgently at this *ridiculous* suggestion. Chang pressed again against the grate. He knew it was foolish, but he very much wanted to see her, and to see—for he recognized the particular sounds—who was being kicked on the floor. He could feel the grate giving way, but had no idea what sound it would make when it pulled free. Then the room's door was kicked open with a bang, the commotion of a man violently swearing, and another calling for aid. He heard Bascombe shouting for help and the room was an uproar—Xonck's vitriolic profanity, Rosamonde sharply issuing commands for water, towels, scissors, the Prince and Blach bawling contradictory orders to whoever else was present. Chang slipped backwards from the grate, for the commotion had driven his enemies into view.

The cries had faded to fierce muttering as Xonck was attended to. Bascombe attempted to explain what had happened in the office, and then that he had gone ahead.

"Why did you do that?" snapped Rosamonde.

"I—Mr. Xonck asked that—"

"I told you. I told you and you did not pay attention."

But her words were not addressed to Bascombe.

"I *did* pay attention," Xonck hissed. "You were wrong. He would not have submitted."

"He would have submitted to *me*."

"Then next time you can get him yourself . . . and pay the consequences," Xonck replied malevolently.

They stared at each other and Chang saw the others watching with various degrees of discomfort. Bascombe looked positively stricken, the Prince—the scars still visible on his face—looked curious, as if not sure he should be concerned, while Blach viewed them all with a poorly masked disapproval. On the floor behind them, trussed and gagged, was a short stocky man in a suit. Chang did not know him. Kneeling to the other side of Xonck was another man, balding with heavy glasses, wrapping the burned arm with gauze.

Xonck sat on a wooden table, his legs between dangling leather straps. Around them on the floor were several of the long boxes. Covering one wall were large maps stuck with colored pins. Hanging over the table from a long chain was a chandelier. Chang looked up. The ceiling was very high, and the room itself was round— they were in one of the building's corner cupolas. Just under the ceiling beams was a row of small round windows. He knew from his view on the street that these were just above the rooftop, but he saw no way to reach them. He returned his gaze to the maps. With a start he realized that they were of northern Germany. The Duchy of Macklenburg.

Xonck rolled off of the table with a snarl and strode for the door. His face was drawn and he was biting his lip against what must have been excruciating pain.

"Where are you going?" Bascombe asked.

"To save my bloody hand!" he cried. "To find a surgeon! To prevent myself from *killing one of you!*"

"You see what I mean, Highness," Rosamonde said lightly to the Prince. "Responsibility is like courage. You never know you possess it until the test. At which point, of course, it is too late—you succeed or fail."

Xonck stopped in the doorway, doing his best not to whimper—Chang had just seen the livid blistering flesh of his arm before they'd wrapped it—while he spoke. "Indeed . . . *Highness*," he snarled dangerously, as if his very words were smoking vitriol. "Abdicating *responsibility* can be mortal—one is scarcely in more peril than when trusting those who promise all. Was not Satan the most beautiful of angels?" Xonck staggered away.

Bascombe appealed to the Contessa. "Madame—"

She nodded tolerantly. "Make sure he doesn't hurt anyone." Bascombe hurried out.

"Now we are alone," said the Prince, in a satisfied tone that was meant to be charming. The Contessa smiled, looking around the room at the other men.

"Only a Prince thinks of himself 'alone' with a woman when there are merely no other women in the room."

"Does that make Francis Xonck a woman—as he's just left us?" laughed Major Blach. He laughed like a crow.

The Prince laughed with him. Chang felt a twinge of empathy for Xonck, and was tempted to simply step out and attack them—as long as he killed Blach first, the others would be no trouble. Then Rosamonde was speaking again, and he found her voice still fixed him where he was.

"I would suggest we place Herr Flaüss on the table."

"Excellent idea," agreed the Prince. "Blach—and you there—"

"That is Mr. Gray, from the Institute," said Rosamonde patiently, as if she had said this before.

"Excellent—pick him up—"

"He is very heavy, Highness . . . ," muttered Blach, his face red with exertion. Chang smiled to see Blach and the older Mr. Gray futilely struggling with the awkward, kicking mass of Herr Flaüss, who was doing his best to avoid the table altogether.

"Highness?" asked the Contessa Lacquer-Sforza.

"I suppose I must—it is ridiculous—stop struggling, Flaüss, or indeed it will go the worse for you—this is all for your benefit, and you will thank me later!"

The Prince shoved Gray to the side and took the writhing man's legs. The effort was not much more successful, but with much grunting they got him aboard. Chang was pleased to see Rosamonde smiling at them, if discreetly.

"There!" gasped Karl-Horst. He gestured vaguely to Gray and returned to his seat and his tea. "Tie him down—prepare the—ah—apparatus—"

"Should we question him?" asked Blach.

"For what?" replied the Prince.

"His allies in Macklenburg. His allies here. The whereabouts of Doctor Svenson—"

"Why bother? Once he has undergone the Process he will tell us of his own accord—indeed, he will be one of our number."

"You have not undergone the Process yourself, Major?" asked the Contessa in a neutral tone of polite interest.

"Not as of yet, Madame."

"He will," declared the Prince. "I insist upon it—all of my advisors will be required to partake of its . . . *clarity*. You do not know, Blach—you do not *know*." He slurped his tea. "This is of course why you have failed to find Svenson, and failed with this—this—*criminal*. It is only by the grace of the Contessa's wisdom that you were not relied on to effect changes in Macklenburg!"

Blach did not answer, but less than deftly tried to change the subject, nodding to the door. "Do we need Bascombe to continue?"

"Mr. Gray can manage, I am sure," said the Contessa. "But perhaps you will help him with the boxes?"

Chang watched with fascination as the long boxes were opened

and the green felt packing pulled onto the floor. While Blach secured Flaüss to the table—without the slightest scruple for tightening the straps—the elderly Mr. Gray removed what looked to be
an oversized pair of eyeglasses, the lenses impossibly thick and
rimmed with black rubber, the whole apparatus—for indeed, it
was part of a machine—run through with trailing lengths of
bright copper wire. Gray strapped the glasses over the struggling
man's face—again, viciously tight—and then stepped back to the
box. He removed a length of rubber-sheathed cable with a large
metal clamp at either end, attaching one end to the copper wire
and then kneeling for the box with the other. He attached it
there—Chang could not see exactly to what—and then, with
some effort, turned some kind of switch or nozzle. Chang heard a
pressurized hiss. Gray stood, looking to Rosamonde.

"I suggest we all step away from the table," she said.

Blue light began to radiate from inside the box, growing in
brightness. Flaüss arched his back against his bonds, snorting
breath through his nose. The wires began to hiss. Chang realized
that this was his moment. He shoved the grate forward and to the
side, slithering quickly into the room. He felt a pang for Flaüss—
especially if he was indeed an ally of Svenson, though Svenson had
mentioned no ally—but this was the best distraction he was likely
to find, as all four of them were watching the man's exertions as if
it were a public hanging. Chang gathered his stick, stood, took
three quick steps and swung his fist as hard as he could against the
base of Blach's head. Blach staggered forward with the force of the
blow before his knees buckled and he crumpled to the floor.
Chang turned to the Prince, whose face was a gibbering mask of
surprise, and backhanded him savagely across the jaw, so hard the
man sprawled over his chair and into the tea table. Chang spun to
Gray, who'd been on the other side of Blach, and stabbed the blunt
end of his stick into the man's soft belly. Gray—an old man, but
Chang was not one for taking chances—doubled up with a groan
and sat down hard on the floor, his face purpling. Chang wheeled

toward Rosamonde and pulled his stick apart, ready to answer whatever weapon she had drawn. She had no weapon. She was smiling at him.

Around them the ringing wires rose to a howl. Flaüss was vibrating on the table hideously, foam seeping around the gag in his mouth. Chang pointed to the box. "Stop it! Turn it off!"

Rosamonde shouted back, her words slow and deliberate. "If you stop now it will kill him."

Chang glanced at Flaüss with horror, and then turned quickly to the other men. Blach was quite still, and he wondered if the blow had broken his neck. The Prince was on his hands and knees, feeling his jaw. Gray remained sitting. Chang looked back at Rosamonde. The noise was deafening, the light flaring around them brilliantly blue, as if they were suspended in the brightest, clearest summer sky. It was pointless to speak. She shrugged, smiling still.

He had no real idea how long they stood there, minutes at least, looking into each other's eyes. He did force himself to check the men on the floor, and once snapped the stick into Karl-Horst's hand as the Prince attempted to palm a knife from the scattered tea tray. The roaring Process made it all seem as if it occurred in silence, for he could not hear any of the normal sounds of reality— the tinkling of the knife on the stone floor, the Prince's profanity, the groans of Mr. Gray. He returned to Rosamonde, knowing she was the only danger in the room, knowing that to look into her eyes as he was doing was to cast the whole of his life up for judgment where it must be found desolate, wanting, and mean. Steam rose up from Flaüss's face. Chang tried to think of Svenson and Celeste. They were both probably dead, or on their way to ruin. He could do nothing for them. He knew he was alone.

With a sharp cracking sound the Process was complete, the light suddenly fading and sound reduced to echo. Chang's ears rang. He blinked. Flaüss lay still, his chest heaving—he was alive at least.

"Cardinal Chang." Rosamonde's voice sounded unsettlingly small in the shadow of such a din, as if he wasn't hearing correctly.

"Madame."

"It seemed as if I would not see you. I hope I am not forward to say that was a disappointment."

"I was not able to accompany Mr. Xonck."

"No. But you are here—I'm sure through some very cunning means."

Chang glanced quickly to the Prince and Gray, who were not moving.

"Do not trouble yourself," she said. "I am intent that we should have a conversation."

"I am curious whether Major Blach is dead. A moment..." Chang knelt at the body and pressed two fingers into the man's neck. The pulse was there. He stood again, and restored the dagger to the stick. "Perhaps next time."

She nodded politely, as if she understood how that could be a good thing, then gestured to the older man. "If you will permit— as long as we are interrupted—perhaps Mr. Gray can attend to Herr Flaüss? Just to make sure he has not injured himself— sometimes, the exertions—it is a violent transformation."

Chang nodded to Gray, who rose to his feet unsteadily and moved to the table.

"May we sit?" asked Rosamonde.

"I must ask that you... behave," replied Chang.

She laughed, a genuine burst of amusement he was sure. "O Cardinal, I would never dream of anything else... here—" She stepped to the two chairs she'd shared with the Prince—who was still on his hands and knees. She sat where she had, and Chang picked up the Prince's upended chair and extended his stick toward Karl-Horst. The Prince, taking the hint, scuttled away like a sullen crab.

"If you will give Cardinal Chang and me a moment to discuss our situation, Highness?"

"Of course, Contessa—as you desire," he muttered, with all the dignity possible when one is crouched like a dog.

Chang sat, pushing his coat to the side, and looked to the table. Gray had removed the restraints and was detaching the mask of glass and wire, peeling it away from what looked to be a pink gelatinous residue that had collected where the mask touched the skin. Chang was suddenly curious to see the fresh scarring firsthand, but before the mask was pulled completely free Rosamonde spoke, drawing his attention away from the spectacle.

"It seems a long time since the Library, does it not?" she began. "And yet it was—what—but little more than a day ago?"

"A very full day."

"Indeed. And did you do what I asked you?" She shook her head with a mocking gravity.

"What was that?"

"Why, find Isobel Hastings, of course."

"That I did."

"And bring her to me?"

"That I did not."

"What a disappointment. Is she so beautiful?" She laughed, as if she could not keep the pretense of it being a serious question. "Seriously, Cardinal—what is it that prevents you?"

"Now? I do not know where she is."

"Ah ... but if you did?"

He had not remembered the color of her eyes correctly, like petals of the palest purple iris flower. She wore a silk jacket of the precise same color. Dangling from her ears were beads of Venetian amber, fitted with silver. Her exquisite throat was bare.

"I still could not."

"Is she so remarkable? Bascombe did not think so—but then, I would not ask a man like Bascombe for the truth about a woman. He is too ... well, 'practical' is a kind word."

"I agree."

"So will you not describe her?"

"I believe you have met her yourself, Rosamonde. I believe you consigned her to rape and murder."

"Did I?" Her eyes widened somewhat coyly.

"So she says."

"Then I'm sure I must have."

"So perhaps *you* should describe her."

"But you see, Cardinal, that is exactly the trouble. For—and perhaps this is obvious—in my own interaction with the lady I judged her to be an insignificant insolent chit of no value whatsoever. Is there any more tea?"

"The pot is on the floor," Chang said. He glanced to the table. Gray was still bent over Flaüss.

"Dommage," Rosamonde smiled. "You have not answered me."

"Perhaps I'm unsure of the question."

"I would think it evident. Why have you insisted on choosing her over me?"

If it was possible her smile became even more engaging, adding a tinge of sensuality to her lips, teasingly revealed as the first hint of explicit temptations to follow.

"I did not know it *was* my choice."

"Really, Cardinal, . . . you will disappoint me."

It was an odd conversation to have in the midst of toppled bodies, crouching princelings, and the trappings of scientific brutality—all in a secret room in the maze of the Foreign Ministry. He wondered what time it was. He wondered if Celeste was in another room nearby. This woman was the most dangerous of anyone in the Cabal. Why was he behaving like her suitor?

"Perhaps it had to do with your associates trying to kill me," he replied.

She dismissed this with a wave. "But *did* they kill you?"

"Did you kill Miss Temple?"

"*Touché.*" She studied him. "Is it merely that? That she survived?"

"Perhaps it is. What else am I, but survival?"

"A provocative question—I shall inscribe it in my diary, I assure you."

"Xonck knows, by the way," he said, desperate to shift the conversation.

"Knows what?"

"That there are diverging interests."

"It's very charming of you to get ahead of yourself like this, but—and please do not take this as in any way a criticism—you were best to concentrate on mayhem and rooftops. What Mr. Xonck knows is my affair. Ah, Herr Flaüss, I see you are with us."

Chang turned to see the man on his feet next to the table, Gray at his side, his face livid with looping burns, the skin around them drawn and slick, his collar moist with sweat and drool. His eyes were disturbingly, utterly, vacant.

"I do admire you, Cardinal," said Rosamonde.

He turned to her. "I'm flattered."

"Are you?" She smiled. "I admire very few people, you know... and tell even fewer."

"Then why are you telling me?"

"I do not know." Her voice dropped to a provocatively intimate whisper. "Perhaps what has happened to your eyes. I can glimpse the scars, and I can only imagine how terrible they are without your glasses. I expect they would repulse me, and yet at the same time I have imagined myself running my tongue across them with pleasure." She gazed at him closely, then seemed to restore her composure. "But there it is, you see, now I am ahead of my own self. I do apologize. Mr. Gray?"

She turned to Gray, who had walked Flaüss quite near to them. Chang was sickened by the man's dead eyes, as if he were an example of ambulatory taxidermy. He turned away with discomfort, wishing he had been able to intervene more quickly—what had happened to Flaüss was somehow worse than if he had been killed. A rattling choking snapped Chang's gaze back—Gray's hands were around Flaüss's neck from behind, throttling him. Chang half-rose from his chair, turning to Rosamonde. Hadn't they done enough?

"What is he—"

The words died on his lips. Both of Flaüss's hands had shot forward and wrapped around Chang's windpipe, squeezing horribly. He pulled at Flaüss's arms, tried to pry apart his grip. It was like steel, the man's face still expressionless, the fingers digging into his neck. Chang could not breathe. He drove his knee into Flaüss's stomach, but there was still no reaction. The vise of his hands tightened. Black spots swam before Chang's eyes. He wrenched apart his stick. Gray's face was staring at him, over Flaüss's shoulder, Gray's hands were still squeezing Flaüss . . . Flaüss was reacting to Gray! Chang drove the dagger into Gray's forearm. The old man screamed and flung himself away, blood pouring from his wound. Released, Flaüss immediately relaxed, his hands still in place around Chang's neck but loosened. Chang thrashed free of his grip, sucking in air. He did not understand what had happened. He turned to Rosamonde. There was something in her gloved hand. She blew on it. A puff of blue smoke burst into Chang's face.

The sensation was instantaneous. His throat clenched and then felt bitterly cold, as if he was swallowing ice. The bitter feeling flowed into his lungs and up through his head, wherever he had breathed in the powder. His stick and dagger fell from his hands. He could not speak. He could not move.

"Do not be alarmed," said Rosamonde. "You are not dead." She looked past Chang to the Prince, still on the floor. "Highness, if you would assist Mr. Gray with his bleeding?" She turned her violet gaze back to Chang. "What you are, Cardinal Chang, . . . is my own." She reached out to take hold of Karl-Horst's arm, stopping

him on his way to Gray. "Actually, why doesn't the Cardinal help
Mr. Gray? I'm sure he has more experience staunching wounds
than the Crown Prince of Macklenburg."

He helped them with everything, his body answering her commands without question, his mind watching from within, as if
from a terrible distance, through a frost-covered window. First he
effectively bound Gray's wound, then lifted Blach onto the table so
Gray could examine his head. How long had this taken? Bascombe
returned with several red-coated Dragoons and spoke to the
Contessa. Bascombe nodded and whispered earnestly in the Prince's
ear. He then called to the others—the Dragoons lifted Blach, Gray
took Flaüss by the arm—and led them all from the circular room.
Chang was alone with Rosamonde. She crossed to the door and
locked it. She returned to him and pulled up a chair. He could not
move. Her face bore an expression he had never seen, as if deliberately purged of the barest trace of kindness.

"You will find that you can hear me, and that you can respond
in a rudimentary way—the powder in your lungs makes it impossible to speak. The effects will fade—unless I desire them to be
permanent. For now I will be satisfied with a yes or no answer—a
simple nod will suffice. I had hoped to sway you with conversation, or barring that give you over to the Process, but now there is
no time and no one to properly assist—and I should be very annoyed to lose all of your information in a mishap."

It was as if she was asking someone else. He felt himself nod in
agreement, that he understood. Resistance was impossible—he
could barely follow her words, and by the time he made sense of
them his body had already answered.

"You have been with the Temple girl, and the Prince's Doctor."
Chang nodded.

"Do you know where they are now?"
He shook his head.

"Are they coming here?"

He shook his head.

"Do you have plans to meet them?"

Chang nodded. Rosamonde sighed.

"Well, I'm not going to spend all my time guessing where... you spoke to Xonck. He is suspicious—of me in particular?"

Chang nodded.

"Did Bascombe hear you speak?"

Chang shook his head. She smiled.

"Then there is ample time... it is true that Francis Xonck carries some of his older brother's great power, but only a very little, for he is so rebellious and rakish that there is no intimacy of friendship between them, and little prospect of inheritance. But of course *I* am a friend to Francis no matter what—so he truly has nowhere else to go. So, enough of that—imagine, *you* trying to scare *me*—what about what *you* know, from your *investigations*... do you know who killed Colonel Trapping?"

Chang shook his head.

"Do you know why we have chosen Macklenburg?"

Chang shook his head.

"Do you know of Oskar Veilandt?"

Chang nodded.

"Really? Good for you. Do you know of the blue glass?"

Chang nodded.

"Ah... not so good—for your survival, I mean. What have you seen... wait, were you at the Institute?"

Chang nodded.

"Breaking in—that was you, when that idiot dropped the book—or did you perhaps *cause* him to drop the book?"

Chang nodded.

"Incredible—you're an unstoppable force. He's dead, you know—and then of course what happened to the Comte's girl because of it—but I don't suppose that would bother you?"

In the prison of his mind Chang was wrenched by the

confirmation that his actions had doomed Angelique. He nodded. Rosamonde cocked her head.

"Really? Not for the man. Wait—wait, the girl...she was from the brothel—I did not think you so chivalrous—but wait, could you *know* her?"

Chang nodded. Rosamonde laughed.

"It is the coincidence of a novel for ladies. Let me guess...did you love her terribly?"

Chang nodded. Rosamonde laughed even louder.

"Oh, that is priceless! Dear, dear Cardinal Chang...I believe you have just given me the nugget of information I require to make friends again with Mr. Xonck—an unintended prize." She attempted to compose her face but was still grinning. "Have you seen any glass other than the broken book?"

Chang nodded.

"I *am* sorry, for your sake. Was it—yes of course, the Prince had one of the Comte's novelty cards, didn't he? Has there ever been a man who likes more to watch himself? Did the Doctor find it?"

Chang nodded.

"So the Doctor and Miss Temple know of the blue glass as well?"

Chang nodded.

"And they know of the Process—never mind, of course they do—she saw it for herself, and the Doctor examined the Prince... do you know the significance of Lydia Vandaariff's marriage?"

Chang shook his head.

"Have you been to Tarr Manor?"

Chang shook his head. Her eyes narrowed.

"Miss Temple has been there, I expect, with Roger...but so long ago it would not signify. All right. One last question for the moment...am I the most exquisite woman you've ever known?"

Chang nodded. She smiled. Then, slowly, like a sunset slipping over the horizon, her smile faded and she sighed. "It is a sweet thought to end on, perhaps for both of us. The end itself is regrettable. You are an exotic dish for me . . . quite raw . . . and I would have preferred to linger over you. I am sorry." She reached into the tiny pocket of her fitted silk jacket and came up with another dose of fine blue powder on the tip of her gloved finger. "Think of it as a way to join your lost love . . ."

She blew the powder into his face. Chang's mouth was closed but he could feel it enter through his nose. His head felt as if it was freezing then and there, his blood stiffening, splitting the veins within his skull. He was in agony but could not move. His ears echoed with an audible crack. His eyes swam. He was staring at the floor tiles. He had fallen. He was blind. He was dead.

The chandelier was formed of three concentric large iron rings, each ring set with forged-metal sockets to hold candles . . . in all three rings perhaps a hundred sockets. Chang looked up to the high ceiling above him and saw perhaps eight of them still lit. How much time had passed? He had no idea. He could barely think. He rolled over to be sick and found that he had already done so, perhaps many times. The discharge was blue and—even to him—stinking. He rolled in the other direction. He felt as if someone had cut off his head and packed it in ice and straw.

It was his nose that had saved him, he was sure. The damage inside, the scars, the blockages—somehow the powder, or enough of the powder to kill, had not fully penetrated. He wiped his face—blue smears of mucus ran from his mouth and each nostril. She had intended to kill him with an overdose but his scarred passages had prevented the fatal concentration from taking effect, absorbing the vile chemicals more slowly and allowing him the time to survive. How long had it taken? He looked up at the round windows. It was after nightfall. The room was cold, with wax spattered on the floor in a sloppy ring where it had dripped to the floor. He tried to sit up. He could not. He curled up away from the vomit and shut his eyes.

*　　*　　*

He woke feeling distinctly better, if still only slightly more spry than a slaughtered pig on a hook. He rolled to his knees, working his tongue in his mouth with revulsion. He dug for a handkerchief and wiped his face. There did not seem to be any water in the room. Chang stood, shutting his eyes. The darkness weaved about him, but he did not fall. He saw the teapot, on its side on the floor. He picked it up and shook it gently—the dregs were still there sloshing. Taking care not to cut himself on the broken spout, he poured the bitter tea into his mouth, worked it around and then spat it on the floor. He took another sip and swallowed, then set the broken pot on the tea tray. With no small feeling of wonder, he saw his stick underneath the table. He understood that leaving it was a gesture of contempt—mainly so his body would be found with a weapon. As weak and sick as he felt, Chang was more than willing to make them regret it.

The room had a lantern and, after some minutes of search, matches to light it. The door opened into darkness as before, but now Chang was able to navigate clearly, if not with any knowledge of where he should go. He wandered for some minutes, finding no other person, nor hearing any noise, through various storage rooms, meeting rooms, and hallways. He did not see any of the rooms he remembered passing through with Bascombe and Xonck, and instead simply forged ahead, alternating left and right turns in an attempt to keep a straight line. This eventually brought him to a dead end: a large door without lock or knob. It would not budge. It was either sealed or barred from the other side. Chang shut his eyes. He felt sick again, his weakened body overtaxed by the walking. In frustration, he pounded on the door.

A muffled voice answered him from the other side. "Mr. Bascombe?"

Instead of calling out, Chang pounded again on the door. He heard the bar being shifted. He did not know what to prepare

for—whether he should fling the lantern, ready his stick, or re-
treat. He was without the energy for any of them. The door was
pulled back. Chang was faced with a red-coated Dragoon private.

He took in Chang. "You're not Mr. Bascombe."

"Bascombe's gone," said Chang. "Hours ago—you didn't see
him?"

"I've just been on watch since six." The trooper frowned.
"Who are you?"

"My name is Chang. I was part of Bascombe's party. I became
sick. Would you..." Chang shut his eyes for a moment and
strained to finish the sentence. "Would you have some water?"

The trooper relieved Chang of the lantern and took his arm,
leading him to a small guardroom. This, like the hallway, was fitted
with gaslight fixtures and had a warm, hazy glow to it. Chang could
see that they were near a large staircase—perhaps the main access
for this floor, as opposed to Bascombe's secret lair where he had
been taken. He was too tired to think. He sat on a simple wooden
chair and was given a metal mug of tea with milk. The trooper, who
offered that his name was Reeves, put a metal plate of bread and
cheese on Chang's lap, and nodded that he should eat something.

The hot tea stung his throat as it went down, but he could feel
it restoring him all the same. He pulled off a hunk of the white loaf
with his teeth and forced himself to chew, if only to stabilize his
stomach. After the first few bites however he realized how hungry
he was and began to steadily devour everything the man had given
him. Reeves refilled his mug and sat back with one of his own.

"I am much obliged to you," said Chang.

"Not at all." Reeves smiled. "You looked like death, if you don't
mind me saying. Now you just look like hell." He laughed.

Chang smiled and drank more tea. He could feel the rawness of
his throat and the roof of his mouth, where the powder had
burned him. Each breath came with a twinge of pain, as if he'd
broken his ribs. He could only speculate about the true state of his
lungs.

"So you said they all left?" asked Reeves.

Chang nodded. "There was an accident with a lantern. One of the other men, Francis Xonck—do you know him?" Reeves shook his head. "He spilled oil on his arm and it caught fire. Mr. Bascombe went with him for a surgeon. I was left, and unaccountably became ill. I thought he might return, but find I have been asleep, with no idea of the time."

"Near nine o'clock," said Reeves. He eyed the door a bit nervously. "I need to finish rounds—"

Chang put out his hand. "Do not let me disturb you. I will leave—just point me the way. The last thing I would want is to be more of a bother—"

"No bother to help a friend of Mr. Bascombe." Reeves smiled. They stood, and Chang awkwardly put his mug and plate on the sideboard.

He looked up to see a man in the doorway, a polished brass helmet under his arm and a saber at his side. Reeves snapped to attention. The man stepped in. The rank of captain was in gold on the collar and the epaulettes of his red uniform.

"Reeves . . . ," he said, keeping his gaze on Chang.

"Mr. Chang, Sir. An associate of Mr. Bascombe's."

The Captain did not reply.

"He was inside, Sir. When I was on my rounds, I heard him knocking on the door—"

"Which door?"

"Door five, Sir, Mr. Bascombe's area. Mr. Chang's been sick—"

"Yes. All right, off with you. You're overdue to relieve Hicks."

"Sir!"

The Captain stepped fully into the room and motioned for Chang to sit. Behind them, Reeves snatched up his helmet and dashed from the room, pausing at the door to nod to Chang behind the Captain's back. His hurried steps clattered down the hallway, and then down the stairs. The Captain filled a mug with tea and sat. Only then did Chang sit with him.

" 'Chang', you say?"

Chang nodded. "It's what I am called."

"Smythe, Captain, 4th Dragoons. Reeves says you were unwell?"

"I was. He was most kind."

"Here." Smythe had reached into his coat and removed a small flask. He unscrewed the cap and handed it to Chang. "Plum brandy," he said, smiling. "I have a sweet tooth."

Chang took a sip, feeling reckless and very much wanting a drink. He felt a sharp spasm of pain in his throat, but the brandy seemed to burn through the blue dust's residue. He returned the flask.

"I am obliged."

"You're one of Bascombe's men?" asked the Captain.

"I would not go so far. I was calling upon him at his request. Another man of the party had an accident involving lantern oil—"

"Yes, Francis Xonck." Captain Smythe nodded. "I hear he was quite badly burned."

"It does not surprise me. As I told your man, I became ill waiting for their return. I must have slept, perhaps there was fever . . . it was some hours ago—and I woke to find myself alone. I expected Bascombe to return. Our business was hardly finished."

"Undoubtedly the trials of Mr. Xonck demanded his attention."

"Undoubtedly," said Chang. "He is an . . . important figure."

He took the liberty of pouring more tea for himself. Smythe did not seem to notice. Instead, he stood and crossed to the door, pulled it shut, and turned the key. He smiled somewhat ruefully at Chang.

"One can never be too careful in a government building."

"The 4th Dragoons are newly posted to the Foreign Ministry," observed Chang. "I believe it was in the newspaper. Or was it to the Palace?"

Smythe drifted back to his chair and studied Chang for a moment before answering. He took a sip of tea and leaned back, cradling the mug in both hands. "I believe you are acquainted with our Colonel."

"Why would you say that?"

Smythe was silent. Chang sighed—there was always a cost to idiocy.

"You saw me yesterday morning," he said. "At the dockside, with Aspiche."

Smythe nodded.

"It was a stupid place to meet."

"Will you tell me the reason for it?"

"Perhaps..." Chang shrugged. He could sense Captain Smythe's suspicion and defensiveness, but decided to test him further. "If you tell me something first."

Smythe's mouth tightened. "What is that?"

Chang smiled. "Were you with Aspiche and Trapping in Africa?"

Smythe frowned—it was not the question he expected. He nodded.

"I ask," Chang went on, "because Colonel Aspiche made much of the moral and professional differences between Trapping and himself. I have no illusions about the character of Colonel Trapping. But—if you will forgive me—the insistence on our meeting place was just one example, in our dealings together, of Aspiche's thoughtless *arrogance*."

Chang wondered if he'd gone too far—one never knew how to read loyalty, especially with an experienced soldier. Smythe studied him closely before speaking.

"Many officers have purchased their commissions—to serve with men who are not soldiers save by money paid is not unusual." Chang was aware that Smythe was picking his words with exceptional caution. "The Adjutant-Colonel was not one of those... but..."

"He is no longer the man he once was?" suggested Chang.

Smythe studied him for a moment, measuring him with a hard professional acuity that was not entirely comfortable. After a moment he sighed heavily, as if he had come to a decision he did not like but could not for some reason avoid.

"Are you acquainted with opium eating?" he asked.

It was all Chang could do not to smile, instead offering a disinterested, knowing nod. Smythe went on.

"Then you will know the pattern whereby the first taste can corrupt, can drive a man to sacrifice every other part of his life for a narcotic dream. So it is with Noland Aspiche, save the opium is the example of Arthur Trapping's position and success. I am not his enemy. I have served him with loyalty and respect. Yet his envy for this man's undeserved advancement is consuming—or has consumed—all that was dutiful and fair in his character."

"He *does* now command the regiment."

Smythe nodded in brusque agreement. His face hardened. "I've said enough. What was your meeting?"

"I am a man who *does* things," said Chang. "Adjutant-Colonel Aspiche engaged me to find Arthur Trapping, who had disappeared."

"Why?"

"Not for love, if that's what you mean. Trapping represented powerful men, and their power—their interest—was why the regiment had been transferred from the colonies to the Palace. Now he was gone. Aspiche wanted to take command, but was worried about the other forces at work."

Smythe winced with disgust. Chang was happy with his decision to withhold the whole truth.

"I see. Did you find him?"

Chang hesitated, and then shrugged—the Captain seemed plain enough. "I did. He is dead, murdered. I do not know how, or by whom. The body has been sunk in the river."

Smythe was taken aback. "But why?" he asked.

"I truly don't know."

"Is that why you were here—reporting this to Bascombe?"

"Not . . . exactly."

Smythe stiffened with wariness. Chang raised his hand.

"Do not be alarmed—or rather, be alarmed, but not by me. I came here to speak to Bascombe—what is your impression of the man?"

Smythe shrugged. "He is a Ministry official. No fool—and without the superior airs of many here. Why?"

"No reason—his is a minor role, for my errand truly lay with Xonck, and with the Contessa Lacquer-Sforza, because *they* were in league with Colonel Trapping—Xonck especially—and for reasons I do not understand, one of them—I don't know which, nor, perhaps, do they—arranged for him to die. You know as well as I that Aspiche is now in their pocket. Your operations today, taking the boxes of machinery from the Royal Institute—"

"To Harschmort, yes."

"Exactly," said Chang, not missing a beat but elated at what Smythe had revealed. "Robert Vandaariff is part of their plan, likely its architect, along with the Crown Prince of Macklenburg—"

Smythe held up his hand to stop him. He dug out his flask, unscrewed it with a frown and took a deep drink. He held it to Chang, who did not refuse. The swig of brandy set off another fire in his throat, but in some determined self-punishing way he was sure it was for the better. He returned the flask.

"All of this . . . ." Smythe spoke almost too low to hear. "So much has felt wrong—and yet, promotions, decorations, the Palace, the Ministries—so we can spend our time escorting carts, or socialites stupid enough to set themselves on fire—"

"Whom do you serve at the Palace?" asked Chang. "Here it is Bascombe and Crabbé—but even they must receive some approval from above."

Smythe was not listening. He was lost in thought. He looked up, his face marked by a fatigue that Chang had not previously seen. "The Palace? A nest of impotent Dukes posing around an unloved, fading hag." Smythe shook his head. "You should go. The guard will be changing, and the Colonel may be with them—he often meets with the Deputy Minister late in the evening. They are making plans, but none of the other officers know what they are. Most, as you can imagine, are as full of arrogance as Aspiche. We should hurry—they may have been given your name. I take that your story of being ill was a fabrication?"

Chang stood with him. "Not at all. But it was the result of being poisoned—and having the dreadful manners to survive."

Smythe allowed himself a quick smile. "What has come of the world when a man won't obey his betters and simply die when they ask him?"

Smythe led him quickly down the stairs to the second floor, and then through several winding corridors to the balcony above the rear entrance. "It is relieved later than the front, and my men will still be here," he explained. He studied Chang closely, glancing over his clothing and ending at his impenetrable eyes. "I fear that you are a scoundrel—or so I would normally find you—but strange times make for strange meetings. I believe you are telling the truth. If we can help each other...well, we're that much less alone."

Chang extended his hand. "I'm sure I *am* a scoundrel, Captain. And yet I am these people's enemy. I am much obliged for your kindness. I hope some time to return it." Smythe shook his hand and nodded to the gate.

"It is half-past nine. You must go."

They walked down the stairs. On a whim, Chang whispered to him. "We are not alone, Captain. You may meet a German doctor,

Svenson, of the Prince's party. Or a young woman, Miss Celeste
Temple. We are together in this—mention my name and they will
trust you. I promise they are more formidable than they appear."

They were at the gate. Captain Smythe gave him a curt nod—
anything more would have been noticed by the troopers—and
Chang walked out into the street.

He made his way to St. Isobel's Square and sat at the fountain,
where he could easily see anyone approaching him from any direction. The moon was a scant pale glow behind the murky clouds.
The fog had risen from the river and crawled toward him across
the bricks, its moist air tickling his raw throat and lungs. With a
nagging dismay he wondered how badly he'd been injured. He had
known consumptives, hacking their life away into bloody rags—
was this the first stage of such a misery? He felt another twinge as
he inhaled, as if he had glass in his lungs, cutting into the flesh
with the movement of each breath. He hawked up a gob of thick
fluid from his throat and spat on the paving. It seemed darker than
normal, but he could not tell if it was more of the blue discharge or
if it was blood.

The boxes were sent to Harschmort. Because there was more
room? More privacy? Both were true, but a further thought arose
to him—the canals. Harschmort was the perfect location to send
the boxes away to sea . . . to Macklenburg. He berated himself for
not studying the maps in the cupola room when he'd had the
chance. He could have at least described them to Svenson—now
he only had the barest sense of where they had placed a few colored
pins. He sighed—a lost opportunity. He let it go.

The time he'd been insensible had spoiled his hope to find Miss
Temple, for wherever she might have reasonably gone, it was doubtful she would still be there—no matter what had happened. The obvious possibility was Bascombe's house, but he resisted it, as much as
thrashing Bascombe might have pleased him, no matter what the

man's true loyalties. For the first time he questioned whether Celeste might not have the same resistance—was it possible that Bascombe hadn't been her destination? She had left them churning with emotion, after speaking of what she had lost. If that didn't mean Bascombe, then who could it mean? If he took her at her word—which he realized he never had—Bascombe was no longer anchored to her heart. Who else had so punctured her happiness?

Chang cursed himself for a fool and walked as quickly as he could to the St. Royale Hotel.

He ignored the front and instead went directly to the rear alley, where white-jacketed men from the night kitchen were dragging out metal bins heaped with the evening's scraps and refuse. He strode to the nearest, gestured to the growing collection of bins and snapped at him. "Who told you to leave these here? Where is your manager?"

The man looked up at him without comprehension—clearly they *always* put the bins there—but stuttered when faced with Chang's harsh, strange demeanor. "M-Mr. Albert?"

"Yes! Yes—where is Mr. Albert? I will need to speak to him at once!"

The man pointed inside. By this time the others were watching. Chang turned to them. "Very well. Stay here. We'll see about this."

He stalked inside along a service corridor, taking the first turn he could find away from the kitchen and Mr. Albert. This led him, as he had hoped, to the laundry and storage rooms. He hurried on until he found what he wanted: a uniformed porter loafing with a mug of beer. Chang stepped in—amidst mops and buckets and sponges—and shut the door behind him. The porter gulped with surprise, backing up instinctively into a clattering array of broomhandles. Chang reached out and took him by the collar, speaking quickly and low.

"Listen to me. I am in haste. I must get a message—in person, discreetly—to the rooms of the Contessa di Lacquer-Sforza. You

know her?" The man nodded. "Good. Take me there now, by the
rear stairs. We cannot be seen. It is to preserve the lady's reputation—she must have my news." He reached into his pocket and
pulled out a silver coin. The man saw it, nodded, and then in one
movement Chang pocketed the coin and pulled the man out of
the room. He'd get it once they were there.

It was on the third floor, in the rear, which made sense to a suspicious mind like Chang's—too high to climb to or jump from,
and away from the crowds on the avenue. The porter knocked on
the door. There was no answer. He knocked again. There was no
answer. Chang pulled him away from the door, and gave him the
coin. He took out a second piece of silver. "We have not met," he
said, and flipped the coin into the porter's hand, doubling his fee.
The porter nodded, and backed away. After a few steps—Chang
staring at him fiercely—he turned and ran from sight. Chang took
out his ring of keys. The bolt snapped clear and he turned the
knob. He was in.

The suite was everything that Celeste's suite at the Boniface
had not been—exuding the excess that defined the St. Royale,
from the carpets to the crystal, the monstrously over-carved furniture, the profusion of flowers, the luxurious draperies, the
painfully delicate pattern of the wallpaper, to the truly expansive
size of the suite itself. Chang shut the door behind him and stood
in the main parlor. The suite seemed empty of life. The gaslight
had been lowered, but the dim glow was enough for him to see. He
smiled wryly at another difference. Clothes—admittedly, laces and
silks—were strewn haphazardly over the arms of the chairs and sofas, even on the floor. It was impossible for him to imagine such a
thing under the tight scrutiny of Aunt Agathe, but here, the occupant's decadent experience extended a casual disregard for so naïve
a sense of order. He stepped to a lovingly fashioned writing desk
cluttered with empty bottles and took its equally elegant wooden
chair back to the front door, wedging it under the handle. He did
not want to be interrupted as he searched.

He turned up the gaslight and returned to the main parlor. There were open doorways to either side and a closed door at the far end. He quickly glanced to each side—maids' rooms and second parlor, equally strewn with clothing and in the case of the parlor, glasses and plates. He stepped to the closed door, and pushed it open. It was dark. He fumbled for the gaslight sconce and illuminated another elegant sitting room, this with a handsome pair of chaise longues and a mirror-topped tray full of bottles. Chang stopped where he stood, a twinge of dread at his heart. Under one chaise was a tumbled pair of green ankle boots.

His gaze swept the room for any other signs. The drinks tray held four glasses, some half-empty and smeared with lipstick, and there were two more glasses on the floor beneath the other chaise. High on the wall across from him was a large mirror in a heavy frame pointing to his doorway at a looming angle. Chang looked into it with distaste—he disliked seeing himself at any time—but his eye was caught by something else in the reflection—on the wall next to him, a small painting that could only have been executed by the hand of Oskar Veilandt. He reached up and took it from the wall, and flipped it over to examine the rear of the canvas. In what he assumed was the artist's own hand, in blue paint, he read "*Annunciation Fragment, 3/13,*" and then beneath it a series of symbols—like a mathematical formula incorporating Greek letters—which were in turn followed by the words, *"And so they shall be Reborn."*

He turned the canvas to the painted image and found himself astonished by its bluntly lurid nature. Perhaps it was the contrast between the image and its luxurious gold frame, the subsequent isolation—the *fragmentary* nature, its *containment*—of the subject matter that made the whole seem such a transgression, but Chang could not turn his eyes away. It was not so much pornographic—indeed it was not precisely explicit—as it was, somehow, palpably

monstrous. He could not even say why, but the stark tremor of revulsion was as undeniable and as simultaneous as the stirring in his
groin. This portion of the painting did not seem to be adjacent to
the one they had seen in the gallery, of the woman's—the very idea
of thinking of her as "Mary" was appalling—rapturous scarred
face. This section showed her naked pelvis from the side, her
splendid thighs wrapped around the hips of a figure in blue who
had quite obviously mounted her. On a second glance however,
Chang saw the hands of the blue figure clutching the woman's
hips . . . the hands were blue as well, and decorated with many
rings, as the wrists glittered with many bracelets of different
metals—gold, silver, copper, iron—the man was not wearing a
blue garment, *the blue was his skin*. Perhaps he was an angel—
blasphemy enough—but the work's unnatural quality was compounded by the perfectly realized corporeality of the bodies, the
sensual immediacy of the weight of the woman's haunches in the
man's grip, the twisting angle of their conjoinment, fixed for a moment, but directly evocative of the writhing exquisite union that
would continue—in the mind of the viewer if nowhere else.

Chang swallowed and clumsily replaced the painting on its hook.
He glanced at it again, mortified at his reaction, compelled and
disturbed anew at the long nails at the tip of each blue finger and
the tenderly rendered impressions they made in the woman's flesh.
He turned away to the chaise and collected the green boots from
beneath it. They had to belong to Celeste. It was rare enough that
Chang felt any obligation to another soul that to have formed such
a bond—to so unlikely a person—and then find it so swiftly broken gnawed terribly at his conscience. The poignance of the empty
boots—the very idea that her feet could be so small, could fit
within such a space and yet enable her willful marching, was suddenly unbearable. He sighed quite bitterly, stricken with regret,
and dropped them back on the chaise. The room had one door,

which was ajar. He forced himself to push it with the tip of his stick. It opened silently.

This was clearly Rosamonde's bedroom. The bed itself was massive, with high mahogany pillars at each corner and a heavy purple damask curtain drawn across each side. The floor was littered with clothing, mainly underthings, but also here and there pieces of a dress, or a jacket, or even shoes. He recognized none of them as belonging to Celeste, but knew that he wouldn't in any case. The very idea of Celeste's underthings forced his mind to a place it had not formerly been, which seemed somehow—now that he feared she was dead—transgressive. Perhaps it was just the residual impact of Veilandt's painting, but Chang found his thoughts—indeed, he wondered, his heart—punctured by the idea of his hands around her slim ribcage...sliding down to her hips, hips unencumbered by a corset or petticoats, the unquestionably creamy texture of her skin. He shook his head. What was he thinking? For all he knew, he was about to part the purple curtains and find her corpse. He forced himself grimly back to the task, to the room and away from his insistent fantasies. Chang took a deliberately deep breath—his chest seizing in pain—and stepped to the bed. He pulled the curtain aside.

The bedclothes were heavy and tangled, kicked into careless heaps, but Chang could see a woman's pale arm extending from beneath them. He looked to the pillows piled over the woman's head and pulled the topmost away. It revealed a mass of dark brown hair. He pulled away another and saw the woman's face, her eyes closed, her lips delicately parted, the skin around her eyes displaying the nearly vanished looping scars. It was Margaret Hooke—Mrs. Marchmoor. Chang realized that she was naked at about the same moment she opened her eyes. Her gaze flickered as she saw him above her, but her face betrayed no lapse in composure. She yawned and lazily rubbed the sleep from her left eye. She sat up, the sheets slipping to her waist before she absently pulled them up to cover herself.

"My goodness," she said, yawning again. "What is the time?"

"It must be near eleven," answered Chang.

"I must have slept for *hours*. That is very bad of me, I'm sure." She looked up at him, her eyes dancing with coy pleasure. "You're the Cardinal, aren't you? I was told you were dead."

Chang nodded. At least she had the manners not to sound disappointed.

"I am looking for Miss Temple," he said. "She was here."

"She *was*..." answered the woman somewhat dully, her attention elsewhere. "Is there no one else you can ask?"

He resisted the impulse to slap her. "You're alone, Margaret. Unless you'd prefer that I take you to Mrs. Kraft—I'm sure she's worried sick over your disappearance."

"No thank you." She looked at him as if she was seeing him clearly for the first time. "You're unpleasant." She spoke as if it were a surprise.

Chang reached out and took hold of her jaw, wrenching her eyes to face his. "I haven't *started* to be unpleasant. What have you done with her?"

She smiled at him, fear fretting at the edges of her expression. "What makes you think she didn't do it to herself?"

"Where is she?"

"I don't know—I was so sleepy—I am always so sleepy...afterwards...but some people find they want something to eat. Did you ask in the kitchens?"

Chang didn't reply to her vulgar implication—he knew she was lying to provoke him, to buy time, but her words were nevertheless a spur to lurid thoughts flickering impulsively across his inner eye...the image of this woman's mouth flinching with surprise at her own pleasure—and then with disturbing ease that face became Celeste's, her lips curled in a desperate mixture of anguish and delight. Chang was startled and stepped away from Mrs.

Marchmoor, releasing his grip. She threw back the covers and stood, walking toward a pile of discarded clothes on the floor. She was tall and more graceful than he would have thought. Quite deliberately she turned her back to him and bent over at the waist for a robe—rather like a dancer—exposing herself lewdly in the process. As she stood—glancing back to confirm Chang's appreciation with a smile—he noticed a lattice-work of thin white scars across her back, whip marks. She slipped into her robe—pale silk with a great red Chinese dragon across the back—and tied the sash with a practiced gesture, as if her hands were marking the well-known end, or the start, of some arcane ritual.

"I see your face is healing," said Chang.

"My face is of no consequence," she answered, nudging her foot through the pile of clothes, finding a single slipper as she spoke and stuffing her foot into it. "The change takes place within, and is sublime."

Chang scoffed. "I only see you've left the service of one brothel for another."

Her eyes became sharp—he had offended her, he saw with great satisfaction.

"You have no idea," she said, affecting a lightness he knew was false.

"I've just watched another undergo your hideous Process—quite against his wishes—and I can tell you now, if you've done that to Miss Temple—"

She laughed—contemptuously. "It is no *punishment*. It is a *gift*—and the very notion—the very ridiculous notion that—*that* person—your precious Miss Inconsequent—"

Chang felt a moment of profound relief, a reprieve from a fear he hadn't realized was with him—that Celeste would become one of them . . . almost as if he would rather she were dead. But Mrs. Marchmoor was still speaking. ". . . cannot appreciate the capacity, the reserves of power . . ." It was a quality of pride, he knew, especially in those who in their lives have been subject and then

elevated—years of withheld speech turned their mouths into arrogant floodgates, and her quick turn from coy seductress to haughty
lady made Chang sneer. She saw the sneer. It inflamed her.

"You think I do not know what you are. Or who *she* is—"

"I know you hunted us both through the brothels—without
skill or success."

"Without success?" She laughed. "You are here, aren't you?"

"As was Miss Temple. Where is she now?"

She laughed again. "You truly do not *understand*—"

Chang stepped forward quickly, took a handful of the front of
her robe and threw the woman bodily onto the bed, her white legs
kicking free as she fell. He stood over her, giving her a moment to
shake the hair from her face and look up into his depthless eyes.

"No, Margaret," he hissed. "*You* do not understand. You have
been a whore. Giving up your body is no longer cause for delicacy,
thus you will understand, given *my* profession . . . well, just imagine what no longer causes *me* to hesitate. And I am hunting *you*,
Margaret. This day I have set Francis Xonck on fire, I have de-
feated the Prince's Major, and I have survived the trickery of your
Contessa. She will not trick me again—do you understand? In
these things—and I know these things—there are rarely second
chances. Your people have had their chance to kill me—the only
one of you that could—and I survived. I am here to find—
quickly—whether you are of the slightest—*the slightest*—use to
me whatsoever. If you are not, then I assure you I don't have the
slightest qualm in exterminating you as if you were just one more
rat in a filthy *infestation* that I am—believe me—going to destroy."

He pulled his stick apart as dramatically as he could—hoping
the speech hadn't been too much—and allowed his voice to become more conversationally reasonable.

"Now, as I have asked . . . Margaret . . . where is Miss Temple
now?"

*   *   *

It was then that Chang first took in the severity of the Process. The woman was not stupid, she was alone, she possessed reason and experience, and yet, even though her eyes had widened in terror when he had taken out his blade, she began to rant at him, as if the words themselves were weapons to drive him away.

"You're a fool! She is gone—you'll never find her, she is beyond rescue—she will be beyond your comprehension! You live like a child—you are all children—the world was never yours, and it never will be! I have been consumed and reborn! I have surrendered and been renewed! You cannot harm me—you cannot change anything—you are a worm in the mud—get away from me! Get out of this room—cut your own throat in the gutter!"

She was screaming and Chang was suddenly furious—the deep disdain in her voice pricking his composure like a venomous fang. He dropped his stick and with his left hand took hold of her kicking ankle and yanked her body sharply toward him. She sat up, screaming still, her face quite mad now, not even bothering to fend him off with her arms, spittle flying from her lips. The dagger was in his right hand. Instead of stabbing her, he forced himself to drive a punch into her jaw, his fist bolstered by the cane-hilt. Her head snapped back—his fingers were jarred cruelly—but she did not fall. Her words became more disjointed, there were tears at the corners of her eyes, her hair was ragged.

"—worth nothing! Ignorant and abandoned—alone in rooms—pathetic rooms of pathetic bodies—kennels—the rutting of dogs—"

He dropped the dagger and struck her again. She sprawled across the bed with a grunt, her head hanging over the other side, silent. Chang shook his hand, wincing, and sheathed the dagger. His fury was gone. Her contempt for him was so clearly one with her contempt for herself—he remembered Mrs. Kraft saying Margaret Hooke had been the daughter of a mill owner—that he let it pass. He wondered if anyone else in the hotel had heard, and hoped that such screams—judging perhaps by the profusion of empty bottles—were not unusual in the rooms of Rosamonde, Contessa Lacquer-Sforza. He looked down at Margaret Hooke's body—the gapping robe showed the softness of her belly and the open tangle of her legs, somehow strangely poignant. She was a handsome woman. Her ribs rose and fell with each still-ragged breath. She was an animal like anyone else. He thought of the scars on her back, so different perhaps from the scars on her face—both testament to her submission to the desires of others more powerful, yet each also the mark of some inarticulate groping on her part, for peace of mind. Her vitriolic eruption told Chang she had not found it yet, but merely imprisoned her discontent beneath layers of control. It was perhaps more poignant than anything. He straightened her robe, allowing himself a moment to run his hand along her hips, and made his way unseen from the hotel.

As he walked in the darkened streets, Chang ran over the words of Mrs. Marchmoor in his mind . . . "beyond rescue" . . . which either meant that something had already happened to Celeste, or was so certain to happen that he would be unable to alter it. Her arrogance made him think the latter. He felt the clumping weight of Celeste's ankle boots in each side pocket of his coat. It was likely, he felt, that they had taken her to some concentration of power—perhaps to convert her with the Process, perhaps to merely kill her—but if that were so, why not already do it? With a sickening thought, his mind went to Angelique and the glass book. Would they dare to repeat that ritual with Celeste? Their attempt with Angelique had been spoiled by his interruption—but what would be a successful outcome? He had no doubt that it was somehow even more monstrous.

The first question was where they would take her. It would be either Harschmort—where they had taken the boxes—or Tarr Manor—which Rosamonde had asked him about. Both places would offer solitude and space, without any outside interference. He assumed Svenson had reached the Manor, and so perhaps he ought to go to Harschmort . . . but if such forces were in fact in play, could he rely on the Doctor to effect a rescue? He had an image of that earnest man, an inert Celeste over one shoulder, trying to walk while firing the pistol at a pursuing gang of Dragoons... utterly doomed. He had to know where they had taken her. A wrong guess could destroy them all. He would have to risk a visit to the Library.

Like most great buildings, the Library was of a size to be without adjacent rooftops that might have removed the problem altogether. The high front double doors and the rear staff entrance both had regular postings of guards inside, even during the night. From a vantage point of forty yards away, Chang could also see the black Macklenburg troopers slouching in the shadow of the columns that lined the front steps. He assumed they were at the rear as well—presenting him with guards within and without. Neither mattered. Chang jogged to a squat stone structure perhaps fifty yards away from the main edifice. The door had a crude wooden bolt, but a minute of concerted effort with the dagger—sliding it through the gap, digging into the bolt, pushing it a fraction of an inch to the side, again and again—had the door open. He stepped in and closed it behind him. In the dim light from the one barred window he saw a stack of lanterns, selected one and checked the oil, and then carefully struck a match. He turned the wick low, allowing just enough of a glow to find the hatch in the floor. He set the lamp down and with all his strength pulled on the handle. The heavy metal hatch creaked on its hinges, but swung open. He picked up the lantern again and stared into the pit below. For the second time in the day he thanked fate for his damaged nose. He descended into the sewers.

He had done it before during a protracted disagreement with a client unwilling to pay. The man had sent agents into the Library and Chang had been forced to use this most loathsome bolt-hole. He was still dripping sewage when he kicked in the client's window later that evening—resolving the disagreement at razor's edge—but that had been in late spring. Chang hoped it was close enough to winter and the water levels still low so he could pass without getting soaked in filth. The hatch led to a slimy set of stone steps, without any kind of rail. He walked down, stick in one hand and lantern in the other, until he reached the sewage tunnel itself. The fetid stream had shrunk since his last visit and he was relieved to see a slippery yard of stone to the side where he could walk. He bent his shoulders beneath the overhang and stepped very carefully.

It was very dark, and the lantern wick sputtered and sparked in the foul air. He was under the street, and then soon enough—counting his steps—under the Library itself. It was another twenty paces to another set of stairs and another hatch. He climbed up, heaved on the hatch with his shoulder, and entered the lowest Library basement—three floors below the lobby. He scraped his boots as best he could and shut the hatch behind him.

Keeping the lamp wick low, Chang made his way up to the main floor and darted across the corridor into the stacks. The building itself he knew intimately—indeed, like a blind man. There were three floors of hidden book stacks for each spacious floor of the Library that was open to the public. The stack aisles were crammed, dusty, and narrow, stuffed with seldom used books that could nevertheless never be disposed of. The walls—and floors and ceilings—were no more than iron scaffolding, and during the day one could look up through the gaps, as if through a strange sort of kaleidoscope, to the very top of the building, some twelve levels above. Chang climbed quickly up six narrow flights of stairs to what was the third floor of the Library proper, pushed open the door with his shoulder—it always stuck—and entered the vaulted map room, where he had so recently been hired by Rosamonde.

Now Chang turned up the wick, knowing there was no chance the guards would see—the map room was well away from the main staircase where light might be glimpsed from below. He set the lantern on one of the great wooden cases and searched for a particular volume on the curator's desk—the massive *Codex of Royal Surveyor's Maps,* and the easiest source for a detailed view of Harschmort and Tarr Manor. He did not, however, know where each of them was exactly located—or not precisely enough to guess the map that would contain them. He braced himself for the small print of the *Codex* and found his way to the index of place names, squinting painfully. It took him several minutes to find each, with grid references to the main master map in the front of the *Codex.* By locating them on the grid-marked master map that unfolded awkwardly from the front of the *Codex,* he would then have the citation numbers for the detailed surveyor maps, of which there were hundreds and hundreds in the Library's collection. It was another matter of minutes, closely poring over the master map, and he was off to the surveyor maps, kept in a high bureau of wide, thin drawers. Again, with his face inches from their identifying numbers, he located the two maps in question and pulled them from the bureau. He dragged the maps—each of them easily six feet square—over to one of the wide reading tables and collected the lantern. He rubbed his eyes and began the next step of his search.

The map of Tarr Manor—and Lord Tarr's quite expansive grounds—showed it to be in the county of Floodmaere. It was easy enough to find the quarry, some five miles from the main house, where the Lord's estate claimed a low range of craggy hills. The manor house itself was large but not abnormally so, and the immediate grounds did not strike any particularly suspicious chord: orchards, pasture, stables. The land seemed generally wild, without notable cultivation or building. The map did show a number of small outlying structures at the quarry itself, but were they large enough to contain the Comte's experiments?

The map of Harschmort was similarly inconclusive. The house was larger, certainly, and there were the nearby canals, but the surrounding land was fen and flat pasture. He had been in the house itself—it was not especially high. He was looking for any place where they might replicate the great sunken building at the Institute, which had been set well into the earth, but in these places must mean some kind of high tower. He could see no such location on either map. Chang sighed and rubbed his eyes. He was running out of time. He returned his attention to the map of Harschmort, for that had been where Aspiche's Dragoons had taken the Cabal's boxes, looking for anything he might have missed. He could not see the far edge of the map, and rotated it on the table to bring it closer to the light. In his haste, his fingers tore at the lower corner. He swore with annoyance and glanced at the damage. There was something there, something written. He peered closer. It was a citation to another map, a second map of the same area. Why another map? He noted the number in his head and crossed back to the *Codex,* searching quickly for the reference. He did not immediately make sense of it. The second map was part of a survey of buildings. Chang rushed to the bureau, hurriedly dug for it and spread it onto the table. He had forgotten. For his great house, Robert Vandaariff had purchased and re-made a prison.

It was only a moment before he found the clue he sought. The present house was a ring of buildings around an open center occupied by a substantial formal garden in the French geometrical style. In the prison map, this center was dominated by a circular structure that—Chang's mind raced to take it in—descended many floors, a panopticon of prison cells arranged around a central observation tower, all of it sunk under the earth. He looked again at the map of Vandaariff's Harschmort . . . there was no visible trace of it at all. Chang knew in an instant that it was still there, underground. He thought of the Institute chamber, the mass of pipes running down the walls to the table where Angelique had lain. The prison panopticon could be easily re-made for the same purpose. There could be nothing like it at Tarr Manor—the expense would be well beyond the income of such a middling estate. He left the maps where they were and strode back to the stacks with the lantern. For all he knew Celeste was in that table's embrace at Harschmort even then.

By the time he descended into Stropping it was after midnight. If anything, the spectacle of the place was even more infernal than he remembered (for Chang disliked leaving the city and so the station was invariably colored by annoyance and resentment)—the shrieking whistles, the fountains of steam, the glowering angels to either side of the awful clock, and below them all a desperate handful of driven souls, even at this hour, isolated under the vast iron canopy. Chang raced toward the large board that detailed the trains and their platforms and destinations, forcing his eyes to focus as he ran. He was half-way across the floor when the blurred letters congealed into a shape he could read—platform 12, leaving at 12:23 for Orange Canal. The ticket counter was closed—he would pay the conductor—and he dashed for the platform. The train was there, steam rising from the stack of its red engine.

As he came nearer he noted with a stab of wariness a line of finely dressed figures—men and women—boarding at the rear car. He slowed to a walk. Could it be another ball? After midnight? They would not be arriving at Harschmort until nearly two o'clock in the morning. He loitered until the last of the line had boarded—he recognized none of them—and approached the rear carriage himself, unseen. Perhaps twenty people had entered. He looked up at the clock—it was 12:18—and allowed another minute for them to clear the rear car before he climbed the steps and entered. The conductor was not there. Had he escorted the others forward? Chang took a few steps farther in and looked around. No one was in the rear-most compartments. He turned back to the door and froze. Advancing toward the train across the marble floor of Stropping Station was the unmistakable form of Mrs. Marchmoor, in a dress of dramatic black and yellow, and marching behind her a group of some fifteen red-coated Dragoons, their officer at her side. Chang spun on his heels and dashed forward into the car.

The compartments were empty. At the far end of the corridor Chang pulled open the door and closed it behind him, moving steadily ahead. This car seemed to be empty as well. It wasn't surprising for so late an hour, especially since the people boarding seemed to make up a single large party. They would undoubtedly be seated together—and Chang had little doubt that Mrs. Marchmoor would be joining them, once she had established to her satisfaction he was not to be found. He reached the end of the second car and plunged on into the third. He looked back with a start, for through the glass doors and down the length of two corridors, he could see the reddish shapes of the Dragoons. They were aboard. Chang broke into a run. These compartments were equally empty—he was barely bothering to look into them as he passed. He reached the end of the third car and stopped dead. This door was different. It opened onto a small open platform with a handrail of chain on either side. Beyond it, just a short step away, was another car, different from the others, painted black with gold fittings, with a forbidding doorway of black-painted steel. Chang reached out for the handle. The door was locked. He turned to see red coats at the far end of the corridor. He was trapped.

With a lurch the train began to move. Chang looked to his right and saw the ground of the station drop away. Without another thought he vaulted the chain and landed heavily in a crouch on the gravel; the wind was knocked from his lungs with a wickedly sharp wrench. He forced himself up. The train was still picking up speed. He stumbled after it, driving his body to move, fighting the sensation that he had just inhaled a box full of needles. He broke into a tormented run, legs pumping, catching up to the platform where he had jumped and then racing to reach the front of the black car. Ahead the track disappeared into a tunnel. He looked up at the black car's windows, dark, covered by curtains— or was it paint? Or steel? His lungs were in agony. He could see the gap at the front of the car, but even if he reached it, had he the strength to pull himself up? The vision of dropping under the train's wheels flashed hideously into his mind—legs sheared off in an instant, the gouts of blood, his last glimpse of life the filthy soot-covered slag of a Stropping railway track. He pushed himself harder. The whistle sounded. They were nearing the tunnel. With a surge of relief he saw a ladder bolted to the far end of the car. Chang leapt for it and caught hold, legs swinging near the rails, and clawed his way madly up hand over hand—somehow not dropping his stick—until he could hook a knee into the lowest rung. He panted desperately, his lungs and throat on fire. The train swept into the tunnel and he was swallowed by the dark.

Chang held on for his life, working both legs through the rungs to take the burden from his arms. His chest heaved. He hawked and spat repeatedly into the darkness, away from the train, the taste of blood in his mouth. His head was swimming and he felt danger-ously close to a faint. He tightened his grip on the iron rungs and took deep, agonizing breaths. With a sickening thought he realized that if anyone had seen him, he was utterly unable to defend him-self. He cursed Rosamonde and her blue powder. His lungs were being ground up like sausage-meat. He spat again and squeezed his eyes shut against the pain.

He waited until the end of the tunnel, which was at least fifteen minutes. No one emerged from the car. The train raced through the city to the northeast, past desolate yards and crumbling brick houses, to the wood and tar-paper hovels that lined the tracks at the city's edge. The hidden moon still gave Chang enough light to see another platform with a chain rail connecting the black car to the next, which had no door at all, only another ladder rising to its

upper edge. With a slowness that revealed how spent he had become, he understood. This was the coal wagon, and ahead of it the
engine. He worked his legs free and, wedging his foot tightly,
reached across the empty space toward the coal wagon's ladder. His
arm was perhaps three inches short. If he threw himself, he was almost sure to make it, and it was another sign of his fatigue that he
even thought twice. But he couldn't stay where he was, and he
trusted himself to leap over the chain rail even less. He stretched
out his arm and one leg, glancing once at the gravel track rattling
past beneath him, the rail ties a flickering blur. He turned his gaze
solely to the ladder, took a breath and jumped . . . and landed perfectly, his heart pounding. He looked over at the metal door from
this better angle. It seemed exactly like its counterpart on the opposite side: heavy, steel, windowless—as welcoming as the front of
any bank safe. Chang turned his gaze to the top of the ladder and
began to climb.

The coal wagon had been recently filled, so the drop from the
top of the ladder into the bed of coal was perhaps two feet—just
enough to conceal Chang from anyone on the platform between
cars. More than this, the level of coal was higher in the center,
where it had been poured into the wagon, creating a hillock between Chang and the engineers and stokers on the other side. He
lay on his back, looking up into the midnight fog as the train raced
through it, the sound of the wheels and the steam loud in his ears,
but so constant as to become soothing. He rolled over and spat
onto the wall of the wagon. From the taste in his mouth there was
no question, this was blood. He felt a thin primal vibration of fear
running up his spine, recalling the terrible year when he'd first felt
the crop across his eyes—damned to a poorhouse sickroom, and
lucky to survive the fever, his every thought trapped in the fearful
space between the person he remembered himself being and the
person he was terrified to become—weak, dependent, con-
temptible. If anything, once he'd left the sickroom and attempted
to reclaim his life, the reality had been worse than his fear—after

the first day he had abandoned everything for a new existence fueled by bitterness and rage and the desperation of the destitute. As for the young nobleman who had struck him...Chang hadn't known who he was at the time—the blow had come in the common room of a university drinking hall in the midst of a larger, tangled disagreement between gangs of students—and still didn't. The glimpse had been very, very brief—a sharp jaw, a rictus of vicious glee, mad green eyes. For all he knew—or hoped—the man had succumbed to syphilis years ago . . . he had left that kind of impression.

In the coal wagon however, it was all starting again. If his lungs were ruined, then so was his livelihood. He could wheeze through his work at the Library, but actually settling the business—which he both enjoyed and found a source of self-defining pride—would be beyond him. He thought of his impromptu adventures over the past days and knew that he never would have escaped the soldier in his room—or from the Institute, or the Major, or Xonck, or survived Rosamonde . . . none of them with his body in such a state. He had re-made himself by an assertion of will, learning to survive, learning his business (when and who and to what degree to trust, when and how and who to kill or merely thrash) and most importantly where to safely locate, in a life of apportioned areas—work and peace, action and oblivion—some semblance of human contact. Whether it was chatting about horses with Nicholas the barman between drinks at the Raton Marine, or allowing himself the painful leisure to approach Angelique (the clacking rush of the train brought to mind her native tongue—he'd said that someone speaking Chinese sounded like an articulate cat, and she'd smiled, because he knew she liked cats), the space for all of these interactions depended on his place in the world, on his ability to take care of himself. What if this was gone? He shut his eyes, and exhaled. He thought of dying in his sleep, choking on the blood in his chest and being found whenever the stokers reached this far into the coal for fuel. When would that be—days? His body would go to a pauper's grave, or simply into the river. His mind drifted to Doctor Svenson, and he saw him stumbling away from pursuit—limping, as Chang realized dimly the Doctor had done throughout their time together, though he had not mentioned it—out of shells, dropping the pistol . . . he would die. Chang would die. The stability of Chang's thoughts drifted, and without him noticing, as if in a dream, his sympathy for the Doctor's plight caused his gaze to transpose itself into the struggle—he saw his own hands throw down the pistol and fumble for and draw apart his stick (somewhere in the back of his mind he wondered that the Doctor would have such a weapon) and flail at the many men who followed him through the fog (or was it falling snow—he must have lost his glasses)—sabers everywhere, surrounded by soldiers in black and in red . . . swinging helplessly, his weapons knocked away . . . the blades flashing toward him like starving bright fish darting up from the depths of the sea, their hideous punctures in his chest—or was he merely breathing?—and then behind him, from far away yet insistently in his ear, the whispered voice of a woman, her moist, warm breath. Angelique? No . . . it was Rosamonde. She was telling him that he was dead. Of course he was . . . there was no other explanation.

When Chang opened his eyes the train was no longer moving. He could hear the desultory hiss of the engine in repose, like a muttering, tamed dragon, but nothing else. He sat up, blinking, and dug out a handkerchief to wipe his face. His breath was easier, but there was a dark crust at each corner of his mouth and around both nostrils. It did not exactly look like dried blood—he couldn't be certain in the dark—but rather like blood that had been crystallized, as if seeped into sugar, or ground glass. He peered over the lip of the coal wagon. The train was at a station. He could see no one on the platform. The black car was still closed—or re-closed, he had no idea if it had been vacated or not. The station house itself was dark. As the train did not seem about to move on, he reasoned they had to be at the end of the line, at Orange Canal. Chang laboriously swung his leg over the side of the wagon and climbed down, tucking the stick under his arm. His joints were stiff, and he looked up at the sky, trying to judge by the moon how long he'd been asleep. Two hours? Four? He dropped onto the gravel and brushed himself off as best he could—he knew the back of his coat was blackened with coal dust. There would be no chance to brazen his way past servants looking like this, but it made no difference. The situation was beyond disguise.

As so often happens, the return trip to Harschmort seemed much shorter than his flight away from it. Small landmarks—a dune, a break in the road, the stump of a tree—appeared one after the other with almost dutiful dispatch, and it was a very brief half an hour before Chang found himself standing on a hillock of knee-high grass, gazing across a flat fennish pasture at the brightly lit, forbidding walls of Robert Vandaariff's mansion. As he advanced he weighed different avenues of approach, based on the parts of the house he knew. The gardens in the rear were bordered by a number of glass doors which would offer easy entry, but the garden was above the hidden chamber—the inverse tower—and might be closely watched. The front of the house was sure to be well-occupied, and the main wings only had windows high off the ground, as per the original prison. This left the side wing, where he'd smashed through a lower window to escape, which also seemed to be where much of the secret activity had been found before—Trapping's body, at any rate. Should he try there? He had to assume Mrs. Marchmoor had warned them of his possible arrival, despite not finding him on the train. They would expect him, to be sure.

The fog broke apart at a rise in the wind, laying the ground before him more open to the moonlight. Chang stopped, a pricking of suspicion at the back of his neck. He was mid-way across the pasture, and could suddenly see that in front of him the grass had been flattened in narrow trails. People had been here recently. He stepped slowly forward, his eyes noting where these trails might cross his path. He stopped again and sank to one knee. He extended his stick ahead of him and pushed aside the grass. Just visible in the sandy dirt was a length of iron chain. Chang dug the stick under it and lifted, pulling the chain free of the sand. It was only two feet long, with one end bolted to a metal spike driven deep into the earth. The other end, he noted with a weary kind of dread, was attached to a metal bear trap—or in this case, man trap, the vicious circle of iron teeth stretched apart and ready to shatter his leg. He looked up at the house, then behind him. He had no idea where else they had placed these—he didn't even know if this was their beginning or his progress so far just luck. The road was well away—and getting to it didn't offer any safer route than going forward. He would have to take a chance.

Not wanting it broken, he wormed the tip of his stick under the rim of the trap's teeth and edged it within reach of the small sensitive plate. He rapped with the tip on the plate and the trap went off with vicious speed, snapping savagely through the air. Even though he expected it, Chang was still startled and chilled— the trap's action was just shockingly brutal. He screamed, cupping his hand around his mouth to propel the sound toward the house. He screamed again, desperately, pleadingly, allowing it to trail off in a moan. Chang smiled. He felt better for the release of tension, like an engine venting built-up steam. He waited. He screamed a third time, still more abjectly, and was rewarded by a new chink of light in the nearest wall, an opened doorway and then an exiting line of men carrying torches. Keeping low, Chang scuttled back whence he had come, aiming for a part of the pasture where the grass was high. He threw himself down and waited for his breath to settle. He could hear the men, and very slowly raised his head enough to watch them approach. There were four men, each with a torch. With a sudden thought he pulled off his glasses, not want-ing the lenses to reflect the torchlight. The men came nearer, and he noted with satisfaction the very deliberate path they walked, one after another, marking it clearly in the grass. They reached the sprung trap, perhaps twenty yards from where he watched, and it quite visibly dawned on them that they saw no writhing man in the grass, nor heard any further screaming. They looked around with suspicion.

Chang smiled again. The coal dust absorbed the light and made him nearly invisible. The men were speaking low to each other. He couldn't hear them. It didn't matter. Three were Dragoons, in brass helmets that caught the torchlight, but the one in front was from the household, his head bare, his coat flapping about his knees. The soldiers had torches in one hand and sabers in the other. The man held a torch and a carbine. He planted the torch in the sandy ground and inspected the trap, looking for blood. The man stood up, collected his torch, and quite deliber-ately scanned the pasture around him. Chang slowly lowered him-self—there was no point botching it now—and waited, following the man's thoughts as clearly as if he saw into his mind. The man knew he was being watched, but had no idea from where. Chang was abstractly sympathetic, but whoever's idea the traps actually were, this was obviously the man who had set them. While Chang was a killer, he did not admire those whose traffic was agony. He made a point of fixing the man's face—a wide jaw with grizzled side whiskers and a balding pate—in his mind. Perhaps they would meet indoors.

After another minute, when it became clear that they were not willing to blunder around searching amongst the unsprung traps, they retreated to the house. Chang let them go, and then very cau-tiously followed in the safe pathway of their steps, crouching low. At the edge of the grass and the end of his cover, he waited—for all he knew they were watching from a darkened window. He was facing the same side wing, but could not place the window he'd broken through only two nights before. It had already been reglazed. Chang smiled wickedly, and felt around him for a stone. With Mrs. Marchmoor having arrived before him, the only way he was going to get inside was by creating a bit of fuss.

He rolled to one knee and threw—it was a lovely, smooth stone, and sailed very well—as hard as he could at the window to the right of the doorway where the men had emerged, which shattered with a gratifying crash. Chang ran toward the house, vaulting a border of flower beds, to the left of the door, reaching the wall as he heard cries within and saw answering light flooding out from the broken window. The door opened. He pressed himself flat. An arm appeared holding a torch, and just after it the man with the grizzled whiskers. The torch was between his face and Chang, and the man's attention—naturally—was toward the broken window, in the other direction.

Chang snatched the torch from his astonished grasp and kicked him soundly in the ribs. The man went down with a grunt. Behind, through the door, Chang saw a crowd of Dragoons. He thrust the torch in their faces, driving them back until the handle of the door was in reach. Before they could react he threw the torch into the room, against what he hoped was drapery. He slammed the door shut, turned to the grizzled man, who was rising, and slashed the stick against his head. The man cried out, with shock at the impropriety as much as pain, and raised his arms to block another blow. This allowed Chang to kick him again in the ribs, and shoulder him aside, knocking him off balance and down with another squawk of outrage. Chang bolted past him along the wall. With luck the Dragoons would prevent the house from catching fire before giving chase.

He rounded the corner and kept running. Harschmort was a kind of nearly closed horseshoe, and he was on the far right end. In the center was the garden, and he quickly raced for the depths of its ornamental trees and hedges, putting as much distance as he could between himself and any pursuers. During the day, he was sure the garden gave the impression of being rigid and arid, nature subdued to the strictures of geometry. Now, in his headlong rush to escape, it seemed to Chang a murky labyrinth fabricated solely to provoke collision, as benches, fountains, hedges, and pedestals loomed abruptly up at him through the fog and the night. But if he could elude pursuit here they would be forced to re-group and look for him *everywhere*, which would mean fewer enemies in any single place—it would give him a chance. He stopped in the shadow of boxed shrubbery, pain rising damnably in his lungs like an unde-terred creditor. There were bootsteps somewhere behind. He drove himself forward, keeping low, making a point to tread on the grass paths instead of the gravel. It occurred to him that he was even then moving across the great submerged chamber. Could there be any entrance left through the garden? He had no leisure to look—in any case the fog was too thick—and continued to creep across the garden to the opposite wing. That was where he had first met Trapping, where the great ballroom was. If tonight's events were in-deed of a more secretive nature, perhaps it would be unoccupied.

The bootsteps were growing unpleasantly closer. Chang lis-tened carefully, waiting, trying to determine how many men there were. Fighting two or three Dragoons with sabers in the open air was suicidal, even without his lungs seething blood. He padded rapidly along a waist-high hedge, bent double, and then across a gravel lane into another ornamental thicket. The few steps on the gravel would draw them like a pack of hounds, and Chang imme-diately changed direction, angling toward the house and the near-est of the glass garden doors. He reached the cover of another low hedge and listened to the boots converge behind him, gratified that they had not thought to send men around the borders of the garden to trap him from the sides. It was just as he congratulated himself that Chang heard the unmistakable rattle of a scabbard-belt, somewhere *ahead* of him. He swore silently and drew apart his stick—had he been seen? He didn't think so. He took a bead on the man's location . . . near a short conical pine tree . . . Chang crept toward it, quiet as a corpse. He inched around the tree and the back of a red coat came into view.

Whether it was his rasping breath or the smell of the blue crystals that signaled his presence, or merely his own fatigue, Chang knew as soon as his arms shot out for the man that there would be a struggle. His left hand clamped over the Dragoon's mouth and stifled any scream, but his right arm didn't cleanly clear the man's shoulder and so his blade was not at once in position. The man thrashed, his brass helmet falling onto the grass and his saber waving for some kind of purchase. In the next moment Chang pulled him off balance and dug the edge of the dagger into the man's throat . . . but in that same moment he also saw that the man whose life he held in his hands was Reeves.

What did it matter? The 4th Dragoons were his enemies, paid lackeys of the corrupt and wicked. Did he care whether Reeves was merely duped into their service? Chang recalled the man's kindness in the Ministry and knew the answer, just as he knew any alliance with Smythe would crumble to nothing if he started killing Dragoons. All this went through Chang's mind—along with an estimate of where the other Dragoons might be and how much noise he was making—in the time it took to place his mouth next to Reeves's ear.

"Reeves," he whispered, "do not move. Do not speak. I am not your enemy." Reeves stopped struggling. Chang knew there were perhaps seconds before they were found. "It is Chang," he hissed. "You have been lied to. A woman is in the house. They are going to kill her. I am telling you the truth."

He released his hold and stepped away. Reeves turned, his face pale and his hand drifting up to his throat. Chang whispered urgently.

"Is Captain Smythe at Harschmort?"

Their attention was drawn by a sharp noise. Reeves wheeled. Over his shoulder Chang saw the grizzled bald man with the carbine step from the shadow of the hedges, along with a knot of Dragoons. They were well away—some twenty yards distant.

"You there!" the man shouted. "Stand clear!"

The man whipped the carbine to his shoulder and took aim. Reeves turned to Chang, his face a mask of confusion, just as the shot of the carbine echoed across the garden. Reeves arched his body with a hideous spastic clench and jackknifed into Chang, his face twisting with pain. Chang looked up to see the man with the carbine eject the shell and advance another into the chamber. He slammed the bolt home and raised the weapon. Chang dropped Reeves—whose legs kicked feebly, as if their action might yet undo the damage of the bullet—and dove behind the tree.

The next shot carried past him into the night. Chang ran, tearing his way into the hedges, trying to reach the house. He had no illusion it would be any safer, but there would at least be less room for shooting. A third shot rang out, whistling near him and then a fourth, sent he didn't know where... had he slipped them for a moment? He heard the man's voice, barking to the soldiers. He reached the far edge of the garden and stopped, gasping. Between where he crouched and the nearest glass door was an open band of grass perhaps five yards across. He would be entirely visible for the time it took to gain the door and—somehow—force it open. It was a fool's risk. He'd be shot where he stood. He glanced behind him—he could feel the Dragoons getting closer. There had to be another way.

But Chang's mind was blank. He was spent with pain, with fatigue, and with the sudden murder of Reeves. He looked at the glass doors, tensing himself—ridiculously—for a reckless, suicidal dash. They were waiting for him to show himself. Above the glass doors the wall rose two stories of sheer granite before there was an elegant bay window set out over the garden. There was no way to reach it. He imagined the view from that window was delightful. Perhaps it was Lydia Vandaariff's own room. Perhaps it was covered with pillows and silk. She was a lovely young woman, he remembered from his visit to Harschmort. He wondered idly if she was a virgin, and felt a ripple of disgust at the subsequent image of Karl-Horst climbing aboard and crowing like a peacock. The thought brought him instantly, horribly, back to Angelique, the ever-piercing distance between them and his failure to preserve her. He shut his eyes as the final words of DuVine's *Christina* rose to his scattered mind:

What is the pull of a planet to the gravity of care?
What the flow of time to her unfathomable heart?

Chang shrugged off his despair—he was drifting again—and found himself staring at the window. Something was wrong with the reflection. Because of the odd angle of the glass he could see part of the garden behind him . . . and the scraps of fog billowing in the wind. He frowned. There was no wind in the garden that he could feel, or not to cause such billowing. He turned behind him, trying to place the reflected ground. Hope rose in his heart. The wind was coming from *below*.

Chang crept quietly along the edge of the garden, on the bordering band of grass, until he could see the wisps of fog shifting, and stepped in to find a row of four large stone urns, each as tall as himself. Three were topped by the withered stalks of seasonal flowers. The fourth was empty and quite obviously the source of a steady exhalation of warm air. He placed his hands on the rim and went on his toes to peer inside. The hot air was foul and set off the raw flesh in his mouth and lungs. He winced and stepped back—his hands now covered in a pale crust of crystalline powder left by the chemical exhaust. Chang kneeled and pulled out his handkerchief. He tied it tightly across his face, stood again, and took a last glance around the garden. He saw no one—they were still waiting for him to run for the house. Tucking the stick under his arm he hoisted himself up and threw a leg over the lip of the urn. He looked down into it. Just below his boot was a wooden lattice-work across the urn, also covered with chemical accretions, in place to prevent the leaves and twigs from the garden that were trapped against it—and now dusted an icy blue—from blowing into the pipe. Chang leaned down and kicked once, very hard, on the lattice. His foot went through with an audible crack. He kicked again, knocking in the entire thing. Behind him there were sounds from the Dragoons—he had been heard, they were converging on the sound. He dropped completely inside, disappearing from their view, pulling apart the last bits of the lattice with his arms. He slid to the base of the urn, pressing against each side of it with his legs to stop himself from sliding down into the dark hole. He had no idea how far it went, if it was a sheer drop, or if it led into a furnace, but he knew it was better than being shot in the back. He lowered himself into the pipe—the steel sides warm to the touch—until he hung by his hands from the bottom edge of the urn.

Chang let go.

SIX

Quarry

As he stepped from the coach outside the yawning entrance to Stropping Station, Doctor Svenson's attention was elsewhere. During his ride from Plum Court he had allowed his thoughts to drift, spurred by the poignant quality of Miss Temple's reckless pursuit of lost love, to the sorrows and vagaries of his own existence. As he descended the crowded staircase his eyes mechanically scanned the crowds for a diminutive figure with chestnut sausage curls and a green dress, but his mind was awash with a particular astringent quality of Scandinavian reproach he had inherited from a disapproving father. What had he made of his life? What more than unnoticed service to an unworthy Duke and his even less worthy offspring? He was thirty-eight years old. He sighed and stepped onto the main station floor. As always, his regrets were focused on Corinna.

Svenson tried to recall when he had last been to the farm. Three winters? It seemed the only season he could bear to visit. Any other time, when there was life or color in the trees, it reminded him too painfully of her. He had been at sea and returned to find her dead from an epidemic of "blood fever" that had swept the valley. She'd been ill for a month before, but no one had written. He would have left his ship. He would have come and told her everything. Had she known how he felt? He knew she had—but what had been in her heart? She was his cousin. She had never married. He had kissed her once. She'd stared up at him and then broken away...there wasn't a day he did not find a moment to torment himself...not a day for the past seven years. On his last

THE GLASS BOOKS OF THE DREAM EATERS 389

visit there were new tenants (some disagreement with his uncle had driven Corinna's brother off the land and into town) and though they greeted Svenson politely and offered him room when he explained his relation to the family, he found himself devastated by the fact that the people living in her house no longer knew— had no memory of, no celebration in their hearts for—who was buried in the orchard. A profound sense of abandonment took hold of him and he had not, even in the depths of this present business, been able to shake himself free. His home—no matter where he had been—had lain with her, both living and in the ground. He had ridden back to the Palace the next day.

He had since traveled to Venice, to Berne, to Paris, all in the service of Baron von Hoern. He had performed well—well enough to merit further tasks instead of being sent back to a freezing ship—and even saved lives. None of it mattered. His thoughts were full of her.

He sighed again, heavily, and realized that he had no earthly clue where to find Tarr Manor. He walked to the ticket counter and joined one of the lines. The station buzzed with activity like a wasps' nest kicked by a malicious child. The faces around him were marked with impatience, worry, and fatigue, people unified in their desperate rushing to make whichever train they sought, relentlessly flowing in awkward clumps back and forth, like the noisome circulatory system of a great distended creature of myth. He saw no trace of Miss Temple, and the place was so thronged that his only real hope was to find the train she sought and search there. In the time it took to light and smoke the first third of another cigarette, he reached the front of the line. He leaned forward to the clerk and explained he needed to reach Tarr Manor. Without pause the man scribbled a ticket and shot it toward him through the hole in the glass and announced the price. Svenson dug out his money and pushed it through the hole, one coin at a time as he counted. He picked up the ticket, which was marked "Flood-maere, 3:02," and leaned forward again.

"And at which stop do I get off?" he asked.

The clerk looked at him with undisguised contempt. "Tarr *Village*," he replied.

Svenson decided he could wait to ask the conductor how long the journey would be, and walked onto the station floor, looking around for the proper platform. It was at the other end of the great terminal hall. He looked up at the hideous clock and judged he did not need to run. His ankle was behaving itself, and he had no desire to aggravate it without reason. He made a point to look in the various stalls as he passed—food, books, newspapers, drink—but in none of them saw the slightest sign of Miss Temple. By the time he got to the train itself, it was clear that Floodmaere was not the most illustrious of destinations. There were only two cars attached to a coal wagon and an engine that had certainly seen better days. Svenson looked around once more for any woman in green—for a glimpse of green anywhere—but saw no one. He flicked away his cigarette butt and entered the rear of the train, resigned that his was a fool's errand and that she would be located by Chang. He caught himself. Why the flicker of jealousy, of—he had to admit—peevish possessiveness? Because he'd met her before Chang? But he hadn't—they'd seen each other on the train...he shook his head. She was so young...and Chang—an absolute rogue—practically feral—not that he or Chang presented any kind of match—not that he even could consider—or in conscience desire...it really was too ridiculous.

A greying, unshaven conductor, his face looking as if it had been stippled with paste, snatched Svenson's ticket and brusquely indicated he should walk forward. Svenson did so, reasoning that he could speak to the man later about arrival times, return trips, and other passengers. It would be better to find her himself without drawing attention, if possible. He walked down the aisle of the first car peering into each compartment as he passed. They were empty, save for the rear-most, which held the many members of a family of gypsies, and at least one crate of indeterminate fowl.

He entered the second and last car, which was more crowded, with each compartment occupied, but none by Miss Temple. He stood at the end of the corridor and sighed. It seemed a futile errand—should he get off the train? He went back to the conductor, who watched him approach with a reptilian expression of cold dislike. Svenson screwed in his monocle and smiled politely.

"Excuse me. I am taking this train to Tarr Village, and had hoped to meet an acquaintance. Is it possible they could have taken an earlier train?"

"Of course it's possible," the conductor spat.

"I am not clear. What I mean to ask is when was the last train, the previous train, which my acquaintance might have taken?"

"2:52," he spat again.

"That is but ten minutes before this one."

"I see you're a professor of mathematics."

Svenson smiled patiently. "So another train stopping at Tarr Village left as recently as that?"

"As I have said, yes. Was there anything else?"

Svenson ignored him, weighing his choices. It was possible, if her coach had made good time, that Miss Temple could have caught the 2:52. If that were so, then he needed to follow her on this train, with hope to catch her at the Tarr Village station. But if she hadn't come here at all—if she were still in town—he should go to Roger Bascombe's house, or to the Ministry, to do what he could to help Chang. The conductor watched his indecision with evident pleasure.

"Sir?"

"Yes, thank you. I shall require information about my return tomorrow—"

"Best to get that from the station master himself, I usually find."

"The Tarr Village station master?"

"Exactly so."

"Then that is excellent. Thank you."

Svenson wheeled and strode down the corridor toward the second car, the conductor audibly snorting behind him. He was hardly confident in his choice, but if there was even a chance she'd come this way, he needed to follow. He could ask for her at the station—they would have to notice her—and if she had not appeared, take the next train directly back. At most it would be only a few hours' delay. And at the worst, he would still find Chang at Stropping the next morning—if he was lucky, with Miss Temple on his arm.

He glanced into the first compartment and saw it held a man and a woman, sitting next to each other on one side. As the opposite row of seats was empty, he pulled the door open, nodded to them, and installed himself by the window. He slipped the monocle into his pocket and rubbed his eyes. He had not slept above two hours. His heavy mood was now compounded by the likely pointless nature of his journey, and a vague gloomy disapproval of the reckless danger Miss Temple had thrown herself—indeed, all of them—into without any larger plan or understanding. He wondered when their descriptions would be given to the constabulary. Was this Cabal so confident as to involve the power of the law? He scoffed—for all practical purposes they *were* the law...Crabbé had a regiment at his call, Blach had his troopers...Svenson could only hope that a train to the country would take him free of their immediate influence. The whistle blew and the train began to move.

It took perhaps a minute to clear the station and enter a tunnel. Once they emerged into a narrow trough of soot-stained brick buildings, Svenson availed himself of the opportunity to examine his traveling companions. The woman was young, perhaps even younger than Miss Temple, her hair the color of pale beer, stuffed under a blue silk bonnet. Her skin was white and her cheeks pink—she could have been from Macklenburg—and her slightly plump fingers held a black volume tightly in her lap. He smiled at her. Instead of returning the smile, she whipped her eyes to the man, who in turn gazed at Doctor Svenson with a glaring suspicion. He was also fair—Svenson wondered if they could be siblings—and had the antic, rawboned look of an underfed horse. His arms were long and his hands large, gripping his knees. He wore a brown striped suit and a cream-colored cravat. On the seat next to him he had placed a tall brown beaver hat. Svenson could not help noticing, as the man studied him openly, that the fellow's complexion was poor and there were circles under his eyes—most probably from self-abuse.

As someone who was generally tolerant and at least conversationally kind, it took Doctor Svenson a moment to realize that the pair stared at him with unfeigned hatred. He glanced again at their faces and was confident that he had never before made their acquaintance... could it be merely that his presence interrupted their privacy? Perhaps the fellow had planned to propose? Or perhaps an explanation more *louche*... in Venice he'd once bought a battered volume of lurid stories celebrating the physical pleasures associated with different modes of transport—trains, ships, horse-carts, horseback, dirigibles—and despite his fatigue he was just recalling the particular details of a caravan of camels (something about the unique rhythm of that animal's gait...) when the young woman across from him snapped open her book and began to read aloud.

"In the time of redeeming the righteous shall be even as lanterns in the night, for by their light will be told the faithless from the true. Look well into the hearts of those around you and traffic only with the holy, for the cities of the world are realms of living sin, and shall suffer in reclamation the scouring of the Lord.

Corrupted vessels shall be smashed. The unclean house will be burned. The tainted beasts will be put to slaughter. Only the blessed, who have already opened themselves to purifying flame, shall survive. It is they who shall re-make the world a Paradise."

She closed the book and, once more holding it tightly with both hands, looked at the Doctor with narrowed disapproving eyes. Her voice, which held all the charm of broken crockery, made it that much easier for him to now see the signs of rigid stupidity in her features, where before he had been willing to assume a neutral bovine placidity. Her companion was gripping his knees even more tightly, as if to release them would be cause for damnation. Svenson sighed—he really could not help himself—but in this mood he could not be fully answerable.

"What a *gratifying* homily," he began. "Yet... when you say *Paradise*"—the woman's mouth pursed with shock that he could presume to answer—"would that refer back to the conditions of life *before* the Fall, when shame was unknown and the course of desire without stain? That *would* be exquisite. It has always seemed a cunning part of God's wisdom that he offers to each of us who are saved the innocence and joy of beasts rutting in the road—or, who knows, in a train car. The point, of course, being the *purity* of experience. I thank the Lord each minute of the day. I could not agree with you *more*."

He reached in his pocket for another cigarette. They did not answer, though he noted with some satisfaction their eyes had widened with discomfort. He replaced his monocle and nodded. "I *do* beg your pardon..." and made his way to the corridor.

Once there Svenson found a match and lit his cigarette, breathing deeply and attempting to gather his scattered mind after this ridiculous interruption. The train was racing north, the trackside lined with hovels and debris and tattered stunted trees. He could see clustered figures around cooking fires, and ragged children running, followed by excited dogs. Moments later these were gone and the train shot through a luxuriant royal park, then past a small square of white stone monuments that reminded him of France. He exhaled, blowing smoke against the glass, and noted the differences between traveling by land and by sea—the relative density and variety of spectacle one saw on the land versus the sparse nature of even the richest seascape. It was an irony, he noted, that the relative plenty of the land absolved him of thought—he was content to watch it flow by—whereas the sameness of the sea drove him inward. Life on land—though he welcomed it, in some northern sort of self-criticism—struck him as somehow lazy and distracted from the higher goals of ethical scrutiny, of philosophical contemplation that the sea enforced upon a man. The couple in the compartment—apes, really—were a perfect example of land-bound self-satisfaction. His mind drifted painfully to Corinna, and her life in the country—though she had read so voraciously that it seemed to him she carried an ocean in her mind—for they had spoken of this very thing . . . she had always promised to visit him and sail . . . Doctor Svenson pushed his thoughts elsewhere, to Miss Temple. He reflected that her own experience of the sea, on an island and on her passage over, must inform the part of her character he found most remarkable.

He forced himself to walk down the corridor, glancing again into the compartments—perhaps there was a more hospitable place for him to sit. The other passengers certainly represented a variety—merchants and their wives, a party of students, laborers, and several better-dressed men and women that Svenson did not recognize, but could not help (for such was the world of Lacquer-Sforza, Xonck, and d'Orkancz) but view with great suspicion. What was more, it seemed that in every compartment there were couples of men and women—sometimes more than one—but never another single traveler, except possibly in one compartment, which held a single man and woman, sitting on opposite sides and apparently not speaking to each other. Svenson crushed his cigarette on the corridor floor and entered their compartment, nodding as each looked up at the sound.

Both were in the window seats of their respective row, so Doctor Svenson installed himself on the man's side, nearest the door. Upon sitting he was at once markedly aware of his fatigue. He removed his monocle, rubbed his eyes with a forefinger and thumb, and replaced it, blinking like a dazed lizard. The man and woman were looking at him discreetly, not with the hostility of the couple in the first compartment, but rather with the mild civilized rebuke of suspicion that is natural when one's relative solitude on public transport has been disturbed by a stranger. Svenson smiled deferentially and asked, by way of a conversational olive branch, if they were familiar with the Floodmaere line.

"Specifically," he added, "if you might know the distance to Tarr Village, and the number of stops in between."

"You are bound for Tarr Village?" asked the man. He was perhaps thirty and wore a crisp suit of indifferent quality, as if he were clerk to a lawyer of middling importance. His black hair was parted in the center and plastered flat to either side, the rigid grooves from his comb revealing furrows of pale flaking scalp contrasting with the flushed pink of his face. Was it hot in the compartment? Svenson did not think so. He turned to the woman, a lady of perhaps his own age, her brown hair braided into a tight bun behind her head. Her dress was simple but well-made—governess to some high-placed brats?—and she wore her age with a handsome frankness Svenson found immediately compelling. Where were his thoughts? First Corinna, then Miss Temple, the rutting dogs of Paradise, now he was ogling every woman he saw—and the Doctor chided himself for, even within that moment, examining the tightly bound swell of her bosom. And then in that same instant, he looked at the woman and felt a vague prick of recognition. Had he met her before? He cleared his throat and answered briskly.

"Indeed, though I have never been before."

"What draws you there, Mr. . . . ?" The woman smiled politely. Svenson returned the smile with pleasure—he'd no idea where he might have seen her, perhaps in the street, perhaps even just then in the station—and opened his mouth to reply. In that very moment, when he felt it was just possible for his heavy mood to shift, his eyes took in the black leather volume she held in her lap. He glanced at the man. He had one as well, poking out from the side pocket of his coat. Was this a train of Puritans?

"Blach—Captain Blach. You will know from my accent that I am not from this land, but indeed, the Duchy of Macklenburg. You may have read of the Macklenburg Crown Prince's engagement to Miss Lydia Vandaariff—I am attached to Prince Karl-Horst's party."

The man nodded in understanding—the woman did not seem to Svenson to react at all, her face maintaining its friendly cast while her mind seemed to work behind it. What could *that* mean? What might either of them know? Doctor Svenson decided to investigate. He leaned forward conspiratorially and dropped his voice.

"And what draws me are dire events . . . dire events in the world—I'm sure I have no need to elaborate. The cities of the world . . . well, they are realms of living sin. Who indeed shall be redeemed?"

"Who indeed?" echoed the woman quietly, with a certain deliberate care.

"I was traveling with a woman," Svenson went on. "I was prevented—perhaps I should say no more about her—from meeting this lady. I believe she may have been forced to take an earlier train. In the process, I was deprived of my"—he nodded to the book in the woman's lap—"that is, my *guide*."

Was this too thick? Doctor Svenson felt ridiculous, but was met by the man shifting his position to face him fully, leaning forward in earnest concern.

"Prevented how? And by whom?"

This type of intrigue—play-acting and lies—was still awkward for Doctor Svenson. Even in his work for Baron von Hoern, he preferred discretion and leverage and tact over any outright dissembling. Yet, faced with the man's open desire for more information, he had—as a doctor—enough experience with conjuring credible authority when he felt helpless and ignorant (how many doomed men had asked him if they were going to die? To how many had he lied?) to frame his immediate hesitation—trying to think of *something*—as the troubled moment of choice where he *decided* to trust them with his tale. He glanced at the corridor and then leaned forward in his turn, as if to imply that perhaps their compartment alone was safe, and spoke just above a whisper.

"You must know that several men have died, and perhaps a woman. A league has been organized, working in the shadows, led by a strange man in red, a half-blind Chinaman, deadly with a blade. The Prince was attacked at the Royal Institute, the powerful work there disrupted...the glass...do you know...have you seen...the blue glass?"

They shook their heads. Svenson's heart sank. Had he completely misjudged them?

"You do know of Lord Tarr...that he—"

The man nodded vigorously. "Has been redeemed, yes."

"Exactly." Svenson nodded, more confident again—but was the man insane? "There will be a new Lord Tarr within days. The nephew. He is a friend of the Prince...a friend to us all—"

"Who prevented you from meeting your lady?" the woman asked, somewhat insistently. The nagging sense he had seen her persisted...something about the slight tilt of her head when she asked a question.

"Agents of the Chinaman," Svenson answered, feeling an idiot even as he said the words. "We were forced to take separate coaches. I pray she is safe. These men have no decency. We were—as you well know—to travel together—as arranged..."

"To Tarr Village?" asked the man.

"Exactly."

"Could any of these agents have boarded the train?" the woman asked.

"I do not believe so. I did not see them—I believe I was the last to board."

"That is good at least." She sighed with a certain small relief, but did not relax her shoulders, nor her cautious gaze.

"How should we know these agents?" asked the man.

"That is just the thing—they have no uniform, save duplicity and cunning. They have penetrated even to the Prince's party and turned one of our number to their cause—Doctor Svenson, the Prince's own physician!"

The man inhaled through his teeth, a disapproving hiss.

"I am telling you," Svenson went on, "but I fear no one else should know—it may be all is fine, and I should hesitate to agitate—or, that is, make public—"

"Of course not," she agreed.

"Not even to . . . ?" the man began.

"Who?" asked Svenson.

The man shook his head. "No, you are right. We have been invited—we are guests, after all, guests to a *banquet*." With this he smiled again, shaking off the Doctor's tale of dread. His hand went to the book in his pocket and patted it absently, as if it were a sleeping puppy. "You look very tired, you know, Captain Blach," he said kindly. "There will be time enough to find your friend. Tarr Village is at least another hour and a half away. Why not rest? We will all need our strength for the *climb*."

Svenson wondered what he meant—the quarry? The hills? Could it mean the manor house? Svenson could not say, and he was exhausted. He needed to sleep. Was he safe with them? The woman interrupted his thoughts.

"What is your lady's name, Captain?"

"Beg pardon?"

"Your friend. You did not say her name."

Svenson caught a worried glance from the man to the woman, though her face remained open and friendly. Something was wrong.

"Her name?"

"You did not say what it was."

"No, you didn't," confirmed the man, somewhat after the fact and a touch more insistent for it, as if he'd been caught out.

"Ah. But you see... I do not know it. I only know her clothes—a green dress with green shoes. We were to meet and travel together. Why... did you know each other's name before this journey?"

She did not immediately answer. When the man answered for her, he knew he had guessed correctly. "We do not know each other's names even now, Captain, as we were indeed instructed."

"Now you really should rest," the woman said, genuinely smiling for perhaps the first time. "I promise we will wake you."

Within his dream, a part of Doctor Svenson's mind was aware that he'd not had a regular stretch of sleep in at least two days, and so expected turbulent visions. This sliver of rational distance might contradict but did not alter the successive waves of vivid engagement thrust upon him. He knew the visions were fed by his feelings of loss and isolation—more than anything by his helplessness in the face of Corinna's death and then his own chronic reticence and cowardice in life—and then all of this regret swirling together with a world of cruelly unquenched desire for other women. Was it merely that, so exhausted, even in sleep, his guard was so much lowered? Or was it, could he admit, that his feelings of guilt provoked in turn a secret pleasure in the act of dreaming with such erotic fervor in an open train compartment? What he knew was the deep warm embrace of sleep, twisting effortlessly in his mind into the embrace of pale soft arms and sweet caressing fingers. He felt as if his body were refracted in a jewel, seeing—and feeling—multiple instances of himself in hopelessly delicious circumstances...Mrs. Marchmoor stroking him under a table...Miss Poole with her tongue in his ear ... his nose buried in Rosamonde's hair, inhaling her perfume...on his hands and knees on the bed, licking each circular indentation on the luscious flesh of the bedridden Angelique...his hands—O shamefully!—cupping Miss Temple's buttocks beneath her dress...his eyes closed, nursing tenderly, hungrily, at the bared breast of the brown-haired governess, who had moved to sit next to him, to ease his torment, offering herself to his lips...the incomparably soft sweet pillow of flesh...her other hand stroking his hair...whispering to him gently...shaking his shoulder.

He snapped awake. She was sitting next to him. She was shaking his arm. He sat up, painfully aware of his arousal, thankful for his greatcoat, his hair in his eyes. The man was gone.

"We are near Tarr Village, Captain," she said, smiling. "I am sorry to wake you."

"No, no—thank you—of course—"

"You were sleeping very soundly—I'm afraid I had to shake your arm."

"I am sorry—"

"There is no reason to be sorry. You must have been tired."

He noticed that the top button of her dress was now undone. He felt a smear of drool on his lip and wiped it with his sleeve. What had happened? He nodded at where the man had been.

"Your companion—"

"He has gone to the front of the train. I am about to join him, but wanted to make sure you were awake. You were...in your dream, you were speaking."

"Was I? I do not recall—I seldom recall any dream—"

"You said 'Corinna'."

"Did I?"

"You did. Who is she?"

Doctor Svenson forced a puzzled frown and shook his head. "I've no idea. Honestly—it's most strange." She looked down at him, her open expression, along with the insistent pressure in his trousers, inspiring him to speak further. "You have not told me your name."

"No." She hesitated for just a moment. "It is Elöise."

"You're a governess, for the children of some Lord."

She laughed. "Not a Lord. And not a governess either. Perhaps more a *confidante,* and for my salary a tutor, in French, Latin, music, and mathematics."

"I see."

"I do not begin to know how you could have guessed. Perhaps it is your military training—I know that officers must learn to read their men like books!" She smiled. "But I do not mind my pupils all the day. They have another lady for that—*she* is their proper governess, and enjoys children much more than I."

Svenson had no reply, for the moment happy enough to look into her eyes. She smiled at him and then stood. He struggled to stand with her, but she put a hand on his shoulder to dissuade him. "I must get to the front of the train before we arrive. But perhaps we shall see each other in the Village."

"I should like that," he said.

"So should I. I do hope you find your lady friend."

In that moment Doctor Svenson knew where he had seen her, and why he could not place her face, for this Elöise had worn a mask—leaning forward to whisper into the ear of Charlotte Trapping at Harschmort, the night Colonel Trapping had been killed.

Then she was gone, and the compartment door latched shut behind her. Svenson sat up and rubbed his face, and then, with self-conscious reproach, adjusted his trousers. He stood, shrugging his coat more comfortably onto his shoulders, the weight of the pistol in the pocket, and exhaled. He worked to reconcile the instinctive warmth he felt toward the woman with the knowledge that she had been amongst his enemies at Harschmort, and was now here on the train, unquestionably in the service of them still. He did not want to believe that Elöise was aware of the dark forces at work and yet how could it be otherwise? They all had a black book, and responded easily to his spun story...and it was *she* who had worked to make sure of him, asking questions...and yet...he thought of her role in his dream with simultaneous spasms of sympathy and discomfort. With another breath he pushed her from his mind entirely. Whatever the purpose of the other passengers' pilgrimage to Tarr Village, Doctor Svenson's only goal was to find Miss Temple before any further mischance. If the station agent had not seen her, then he would return at once—wherever she was, she would need his help.

He stepped to the window, looking out on the passing landscape of county Floodmaere: low scrubby woods clinging to worn rolling hills, with here and there between them a stretch of meadow and, breaking through like damaged teeth, crags of reddish stone. Doctor Svenson had seen such stone before, in the hills near his home, and knew it meant iron ore. He recalled the taste of it in the winter snow-melt, ruddying the water as it flowed down the valley. No wonder there was mining here. He was amused to notice the clear sky—he'd spent so many days in the clouds and fog that he could not remember when he'd last seen it so open— smiling that it must be nearing five o'clock, for the sun was already going down, as if he were journeying to a blue sky merely to be denied it. At least—as opposed to earlier in the day—he could laugh at the irony. Beneath his feet, the train's momentum shifted, and he felt it slow. They were arriving. He dug out another cigarette— how many did he have left?—and stuck it in his mouth, lit it and shook out the match, dreading a return journey without tobacco. The train came to a stop. He'd have to find some other brand in the village.

*   *   *

By the time he stepped onto the platform, the party of couples was well ahead of him, walking toward the station house. As near as he could figure—save perhaps for the gypsies—the train had emptied. He did not see Elöise or the clerk she was apparently paired with, though he did spy the hateful couple from his first compartment. The young blond woman turned back, saw him, and tugged on the arm of her companion, who turned as well. They quickened their pace, her plump bottom moving in a way that Svenson might have normally—surreptitiously—enjoyed but now made him only want to thrash it. He let them all go ahead, through the wooden archway of the station and out into the Village proper, while he stepped into the small station house. There were perhaps three waiting benches, all empty, and a cold metal stove. He walked over to the ticket counter, but found the window shuttered. He knocked on it and called out. There was no answer. At the end of the counter was a door. He knocked on it as well, again received no answer, and then tried the handle, which was locked. If Miss Temple had been here, which he doubted, she was not here now.

On the wall was a blackboard with a painted grid of train departures and arrivals. The next return train was, he was exasperated to read, at eight o'clock the next morning. Svenson sighed with annoyance. He would be wasting hours and hours of time—who knew where she was, and what help he might have offered to Chang had he stayed with him. He looked around the room, as if by remaining there he might find some reprieve, but Doctor Svenson had to accept that his only real recourse was to walk into the Village and find a room for the night. Perhaps he should catch up to Elöise and her mysterious party, all with their black books. Were they Bibles? He had no idea what else they could be, especially with the hectoring specter of redemption and sin, but who could take such a thing seriously? He felt sure the answer was more insidious and complicated... or did he merely prefer to associate Elöise with villains rather than with fanatics?

He walked from the station onto the road. By now, the others were gone from his view. The road was lined on either side with an overgrown tangle of black briar, the hard thorns casting wicked shadows onto the road. Shadows? There was a rising moon, and Svenson looked up at it with pleasure. Above the briars, in the distance, he could see the thatched rooftops of Tarr Village. He walked toward them with a brisk purpose, and it was only another minute before the road opened up onto a small square with a common green in the center and a cobbled lane running around it. On the far side was a church with a white steeple, but—happily—the building nearest to him announced itself by a hanging wooden sign, painted with a picture of a crow wearing a silver crown. Svenson stopped at the door, one foot on the step, and looked around the square. There were lights here and there in the buildings he could see, but no people in the street, nor any sound in the air. If there had been visible sentries, Tarr Village would have reminded him of nothing more than a military camp after nightfall. He went into the tavern.

As a foreigner, Doctor Svenson knew he was no knowledgeable judge, but the King Crow struck him as a decidedly odd village pub, adding—with the excessively orderly nature of the town itself and the apocalyptic halo of the party from the train—to his growing suspicion that Tarr Village might in fact be one of those *communities,* purposely organized around religious or moral principles (but what was the doctrine, and who its charismatic—or stern—leader?). For one, the King Crow did not smell like a tavern at all, of beer and smoke and the sour pungence of sweat and human grease. Indeed, the air was all soap and vinegar and wax, and the main room scrubbed and sparse as the bare, clean insides of a ship, with the walls whitewashed and a fire in its modest hearth. For another, the only two occupants were wearing crisp black suits with high white shirt collars and black traveling cloaks. Each man stood near the fire with a glass of red wine, not even, or no longer, speaking to each other, but obviously waiting for some word, or someone. Both turned swiftly at his entrance.

One cleared his throat and spoke. "Excuse me. Are you just arrived...on the 3:02 train?"

Svenson nodded politely, his face impassive. "I am."

They were examining him, or waiting for him to speak...so, he did not.

"That is a Macklenburg uniform coat, if I am not mistaken?" asked the other man.

"It is."

One whispered into the other's ear. The listener nodded. They continued to look at him, as if they could not come to a decision. Svenson turned his gaze to the bar, behind which a porcine fellow in a spotless white shirt stood silently.

"I require a room for the night," Svenson told him. "Do you have any?"

The man looked at his two customers—whether to receive instruction or to simply see if they needed anything before he left, Svenson could not say—and then walked out around the bar, wiping his hands. He continued past Svenson, muttering, "This way..."

Svenson looked once more to the two men by the fire, and turned to follow the innkeeper's heavy steps up the stairs.

The room was simple, the price fair. After a moment of looking at it—a narrow bed, a stand with a basin, a hard chair, a mirror— Svenson said it would do well and asked where he might find some food. Once more, the man muttered, "This way..." and led him back down to the fire. The other two were still there—it could only have been two minutes—and continued to watch him as he removed his greatcoat and sat at the small table his host indicated before disappearing through a door behind the bar, into what

Svenson assumed was the kitchen. That there was no discussion of what the food might be did not trouble him. He was used to traveling in the country and doing with what he could find. But when had he last eaten—tea at the Boniface with Miss Temple and Chang? And before that? His bread and sausage the night before... two sparse meals in as many days. It was no way to manage an adventure.

The two men were still studying him, now with the barest pretense of manners.

"Was there something you wanted to say?" he asked.

They shuffled and muttered and cleared their throats to no great purpose. It was his turn to stare at them, so he did. Beyond the room he could hear gratifying noises of pots and crockery. Fortified by the mere prospect of a meal, Svenson spoke again.

"I take it you are here to meet a traveler from the 3:02 train from Stropping Station. I also take it that you do not know the traveler you are meeting. Thus, I take your habit of studying my person as if I were a zoo animal to be not so much a personal affront as an admission of your own foolish predicament. Or—you must tell me, please—am I in error? Is there an offense that, as gentlemen"—he lowered his voice meaningfully—"we need to settle out-of-doors?"

Svenson was not normally given to such arrogant posturing, but he felt sure that the two were not men of violence—that indeed, they were educated and accustomed to clean cuffs and uncalloused hands... rather like himself, actually. Perhaps Chang was rubbing off on him. After a moment the one who had spoken first, who was taller and with a sharper nose, held up his open palm.

"We are sorry to have disturbed you—it was never our intent. It is merely that such a uniform—and accent—is understandably rare around these parts—"

"You are *from* these parts?" asked Svenson. "I would find that a surprise. I would think it much more likely that you came today on the train—on the 2:52 train, though I suppose you could have come earlier. The person you now seek was supposed to travel with you, but did not appear. You then hoped he would appear on the next train. That you at all entertained the possibility it might be me confirms, as I say, that you have never met this person. One cannot help wondering if the purpose of the meeting is entirely savory."

At this, the door to the kitchen banged open and their host appeared carrying a wooden platter with both hands, loaded with several plates—roasted meat, thick bread, steaming boiled potatoes, a pot of gravy, and a plate of buttered mashed turnips. He laid it down on Svenson's table, his hand then drifting half-heartedly toward the bar.

"Drink..." he muttered.

"A mug of beer, if you will."

"He does not have beer," announced the second man, whose hair was receding and brushed hopefully forward in the old Imperial fashion.

"Wine then," said Svenson. The innkeeper nodded and stepped behind the bar. Doctor Svenson returned to the two men. He breathed in the smells of the food before him, feeling the intensity of his hunger. "You have not answered my... hypothesis," he said.

The two men exchanged one quick look, set their wineglasses on the hearth, and strode abruptly from the King Crow without another word.

The clock in the entryway of the King Crow chimed seven. Doctor Svenson lit the first of his remaining cigarettes, inhaled deeply, and then slowly blew smoke across the remains of his meal. He swirled the contents and tossed off the last of his second glass of wine—a meaty, country claret—then set down his glass and stood. The innkeeper was behind the bar, reading a book. Svenson shrugged on his greatcoat and called to the man.

"I should like to take a walk across the green. Will there be any difficulty getting back inside? When do you retire?"

"Doors are not locked in Tarr Village," the man replied, and went back to his book. Svenson saw he was to get no further communication, and walked to the front door.

Outside, the night was clear and cool, with bright moonlight casting a pale, silvered sheen over the grassy common, as if it had just rained. Across the square, he could see light through the windows of the church. No other building seemed to be so occupied, again as if an order had been given to extinguish all candles by a particular hour. In possible confirmation, the light vanished behind him in the windows of the King Crow, its proprietor closing down for the night. It could not be much past seven! When did these villagers wake—before dawn? Perhaps the puritanical nature of the train party was not so out of place after all—perhaps his recent time in the sin-filled city (he could hardly deny it was so) had overly influenced his skeptical views. Svenson set off across the grass toward the church, to see if he could discover what kept these particular people awake.

In the center of the common was a very large, old oak tree, and Svenson made a point of walking beneath it and looking up at the moon through its enormous, tangled network of leafless branches, just to torment himself with the subsequent whiff of vertigo. As he turned down to his boots to steady himself, he heard across the square the unmistakable sound of a horse-drawn coach rattling into Tarr Village. It was small and efficient, drawn by two black horses and driven by a well-wrapped coachman who reined the horses directly in front of the King Crow. Svenson knew instantly this was the party, arriving late, who was to meet the two men. The coachman went to the door, knocked, waited, knocked again much more loudly, and several minutes later—receiving no response—returned to the coach. Svenson could not but admire the pugnacious reticence on the part of the innkeeper. After another word with his master, the coachman climbed back into place. With a sharp whistle and a snap of the reins the coach pulled forward along the square and then disappeared into the heart of the village.

Soon it had passed beyond Svenson's hearing, and in the re-gathering of the night's quiet it was as if the coach had never been.

In construction, the church in Tarr Village was quite plain: white-painted wood with a boxy steeple in the rear more like a watchtower than a pinnacle rising to heaven. The front of the church was more of a mystery. The double doors were closed, but they were also, he realized as he neared them, bolted shut with a heavy chain wound through each handle and held fast with a blockish padlock. Svenson ambled onto the cobbled lane and looked up at the doorway. He saw no one, and walked quietly up the three stone steps and put his ear to the door. Something . . . a sound that, the more he took it in, set his nerves on edge . . . a low, undulating sort of buzz. Was it chanting? A queer, dyspeptic drone from a pipe organ? He stepped back again, got no other clue from anything he could see. The church was bordered by an open lot, so he walked quietly through untended grass that rose above his ankles and, with the evening dew, wetted his boots. A row of tall windows ran along the side of the church. The glass bore the knotted surface of elaborate leaded detail, without any particular colors to make plain the illustration. It made him wonder if the images were merely decoration—a geometrical pattern, say—as in a mosque, where any depiction of a man or woman, much less the Prophet, would be a blasphemy. Looking up, all he could see was a dim glow from within—there was *some* kind of light, but nothing more than a modest lantern or small collection of candles. Suddenly, Svenson saw a blue flash like a bolt of azure lightning snap out of the windows. Just as instantly it was gone. There was no accompanying sound, and no sound of reaction from within . . . had he truly seen it? He had. He raced to the back of the church, for another door, rounded the corner—

"Captain Blach!"

It was the man from the train, Elöise's ostensible partner, the lawyer's clerk. He stood in the open rear door of the church, in one hand a lit cigarette and in the other—incongruously—a heavy cast iron wrench, for use on only the most unwieldy of machines. Before Svenson could speak, the man stuck the cigarette between his lips and offered the Doctor his hand.

"You arrived after all—I was worried you would not. Did you ever find your lady friend?"

"I'm afraid I did not—"

"Not to worry—I'm sure she went ahead to the house with the others."

"The light." Svenson gestured behind him to the windows. "A blue flash, just moments ago—"

"Yes!" The man's eyes lit up. "Isn't it splendid? You really are just in time!"

He took another drag on his cigarette, dropped it to the stone porch and ground it beneath his shoe. Svenson's gaze went to the wrench—it was perhaps as long as the man's forearm. The man noticed his look and chuckled, hefting the hunk of iron as if it were a prize. "They are letting us help with the works, you see—it really is just as engaging as I hoped! Come, everyone will be delighted to see you!"

He turned and went into the church, holding the door open for Svenson to follow. The blue flash made him think of d'Orkancz and the Institute. He'd given this man a false name— but any member of the Cabal, if present, would know him instantly. Further—his mind raced, gesturing for the man to go first, and closing the door behind them—were the women at Tarr Manor? What other house could be meant? If that was so, there was no hiding the connection of this group—the black books, the Puritan brimstone—with Bascombe and his Cabal. But—he must decide, he must do something (even then the man was leading him into a dressing vestibule hung with church robes). Lord Tarr had been killed to gain control of the quarry and the deposits of indigo clay. What did that have to do with this religious nonsense? And what religious ceremony involved that size of . . . wrench?

The man abruptly stopped, one hand on Doctor Svenson's chest, the other—with the wrench, which could not but look foolish—held over his mouth to indicate silence. He nodded ahead of them at an open door, and then stepped quietly ahead until they could see into the next room. Svenson followed, apprehensive and curious in equal measure, craning his head over the man's shoulder.

They were to the side of the altar, looking past it into the nave of the church, where the pews had been pushed away and stacked against either side wall. In the center of the open floor was an impromptu table made of stacked wooden boxes... boxes like those Chang described from the Institute, or that Colonel Aspiche's men had taken away in carts that morning. Atop the table was a... machine—an interlocking conglomeration of metal parts sticking out of a central casket not unlike a visored medieval helmet, and trailing bright twists of copper wire that ran into an open box on the floor (which Svenson could not see into). The air was sharp with that same mechanical smell—ozone, cordite, burnt rubber, oil—that he'd known on the bodies of Trapping and Angelique and the man in Crabbé's kitchen, only now so intense that his nostrils wrinkled in protest, even from this far away. Around the machine, in a circle, was a collection of men—the same mix of classes and types he'd seen on the train, including the tall horse-ish fellow from his first compartment. Most had taken off their coats and rolled up their sleeves, some held tools, some oily rags, some merely rested their hands on their hips with satisfaction, and all of them gazed lovingly at the machine between them. At the circle's head was another man, in an unkempt but elegantly cut black coat, his streaked hair pushed back behind his ears, his sharp face dominated by a pair of dark goggles, and his hands magnified— like a giant's—by a pair of padded leather gauntlets that went up to his elbows. It was Doctor Lorenz.

*   *   *

Svenson stepped away from the door. His companion felt him move and turned with a look of concern. Svenson held up his hand and began to silently gag, motioning that there was some trouble with his breathing, with his throat—he took another step back and waved the man forward, as if this would only take a moment, he would be right with him. Instead of going ahead, the man stepped after him—forcing Svenson to gag still more theatrically—and then to the Doctor's dismay turned to the room, as if to call for help. Svenson took hold of the man's arm and tugged him along back toward the rear door of the church. They reached the far side of the dressing room before Svenson allowed himself to audibly cough and gag.

"Captain Blach, are you all right? Are you unwell? I'm sure Doctor Lorenz—"

Svenson charged through the rear door and bent over on the paved portico, hands on his knees, sucking in great gasps of air. The man followed him outside, clucking with concern. Svenson could not go in. Lorenz would know him. And now, whatever else happened, this man was sure to mention him—perhaps he had already?—in such a way that would leave little mystery to those who already marked him as an enemy. He felt a comforting hand on his back and tilted up his head.

"I hope we are not disturbing them," Svenson rasped.

"O no," the man answered. "I'm sure they did not even know we were there—"

As he had hoped, the man instinctively turned his head toward the door as he spoke. Svenson stood up swiftly, the butt of the pistol in his right hand, and brought it down hard behind the man's ear. The man grunted with surprise and staggered into the doorframe. Svenson hesitated—he did not want to hit him again. He was no judge on giving blows to the head, though he knew well enough they could kill. The man groaned and tried to stand, wobbling. Svenson cursed and struck him once more, feeling the sickening thud of impact through his entire arm. The man went down in a heap. Svenson quickly stowed the pistol and dragged him into the church. He listened—he heard nothing from within—and quietly snatched several of the robes from the inner room. He spread these over the body, leaving him in a sitting position behind the propped-open door, so he was quite hidden to any casual eye. Doctor Svenson felt the back of the man's head. It was swollen, pulpy, but he did not think there was a fracture—though he could hardly tell for sure, leaning over the fellow in the dark. The man was alive—he told himself perhaps that was enough, though it did not ease his guilt. Svenson picked up the wrench. He then rolled his eyes at his own forgetfulness and knelt again, digging through the layers of robe, and came up with the man's black book. He stuffed this into his greatcoat and crept again to the inner doorway. The buzzing sound had returned.

The machine vibrated on the table top with an escalating whine that seemed—by the reactions of the men around it—to indicate that it was nearing the successful achievement of whatever process it performed. Lorenz held a pocket watch in his hand, his other hand raised, with the men around him alertly poised for his signal. To Svenson, it looked like nothing more than a group of overgrown boys waiting for their schoolmaster's permission to start a scrimmage. The machine kicked, shaking the boxes beneath it with a dangerous rattle. Was it going to explode? Lorenz had not moved. The men were still clustered close around. At once the scientist dropped his arm and the men leapt to the machine, holding it firmly in place. The restraint seemed to drive the machine's energy inward, and Svenson could detect first thin plumes of smoke and then a rising glow. He saw that the men had all screwed their eyes shut and faced away from the machine and, realizing what this meant just before it happened, Svenson spun from the door, his back to the wall, eyes shut. A bright blue flash erupted from the other room that he could feel through his eyelids, seeing a floating after-flash in the air without even having opened them. He placed a hand over his mouth and nose—the smell was intolerable. He could hear the men in the other room choking and laughing in equal measure, congratulating themselves. He rolled his head back to the door, risking a peek.

Lorenz bent over the machine. He'd pulled back a metal plate on a hinge, like the cover of a stove, and was reaching inside with his heavily gloved hand, into a bright blue light that washed all color from his already pallid face. The attention of the men was fixed on Lorenz's hand as it penetrated the open chamber and then returned with a ball of pulsing blue (stone? glass?) in his palm. He held it up for them all to see and the men erupted with a ragged, exuberant cheer. The faces of the men were flushed and crazed. The chemical smell had Svenson feeling light-headed already, he could just imagine what it was doing to all of them. Lorenz flipped back his cloak. Slung across his chest he bore a heavy leather bandolier, from which hung many capped metal flasks, like the powder charges of an old musketeer. He carefully unscrewed one of the flasks and then squeezed—as if it was glowing, malleable clay— the ball in his hand into the narrow flask opening. When it was completely in, he replaced the cap and with a small flourish flipped his cloak back into place.

Doctor Lorenz looked up at the men around him and asked, with an even-toned curiosity, "Where is Mr. Coates?"

Svenson wheeled from sight, his back against the wall. In two long silent strides he was through the dressing room and then, now running, out of the church entirely. He crossed the empty lot and ducked behind the next building, back to the cobbled road and across it onto the common. He did not stop until he had reached the trunk of the oak tree, running low and as quietly as he could, where he knelt and finally looked back, his heart pounding. There were men standing in the grassy lot, and one who had walked as far as the front of the church, looking across its steps and onto the common. Svenson ducked back. Had they seen him running?

With any luck, their discovery of the unfortunate Coates slowed any pursuit long enough for him to make his way. Of course, given the high spirits of the group, it could just as well fire them up for immediate vengeance. Would Coates revive? What could he tell them? Svenson dared not risk running across the open ground to the King Crow. He glanced above him. Any other man might cleverly climb the tree and rest undetected. Svenson shuddered. He was not Cardinal Chang.

The man in front of the church gave another long look to the grassy common and then retreated back to the rear door, collecting the men in the lot on his way. Svenson heard the rear door close. Now was the time for him to dash to cover, but he remained behind his tree, watching. It was another fifteen minutes of gnawing cold before the door opened again, and a line of men emerged, carrying the boxes between them. Last of all came Lorenz, no longer with the gauntlets and goggles, holding his cloak closely about him. The line vanished from Svenson's view, along the same road the coach had followed earlier. He could only assume it went to Tarr Manor.

Svenson gave them another two minutes before leaving the oak tree and walking back to the church. He had no idea what he thought to find, but anything was better than another ignorant walk in the dark. Coates was no longer in the corner where he placed him—hopefully he'd been able to walk away upon being revived—and Svenson picked his way through the dressing room into the darkened church. Moonlight still poured in through the windows, but without the machine's blue glow the room had a different feel, more mournful and abandoned—though the pews had been hastily restored to their places. Svenson glanced over to the altar, which had acquired a peculiar shadow beneath it. He looked at the windows but did not see what could be blocking the light—some kind of smudge or deposit on the glass—soot from the machine? He crossed to the altar itself and saw his mistake. The shadow was a pool. Svenson pulled back the white cloth and saw, beneath it, the crumpled figure of Mr. Coates, whose throat had been quite cleanly cut.

Svenson bit his lip. He dropped the cloth and turned, reaching into his pocket for the service revolver. He checked the cartridges and the hammer, spun the chamber, and stuffed it away. He looked around him with a rising urge to kick over the pews and forced himself to breathe evenly. He could do nothing for Coates except remember him as affable and attentive. He walked out of the church and made for the road.

Because the line of men carried the boxes of machinery, Svenson half-thought he might overtake them—or at least come within sight—on the way, but he had walked a mile on the country road, briar hedges to his left and barren winter fields to his right, without doing so. At the mile marker the road forked, and he stood under the moonlight trying to decide. There was no delineating sign, and each road seemed equally traveled. Looking ahead, the left fork sloped up a gentle rise, which made him recall Coates's reference to a climb. With nothing else to go on, Svenson turned his steps that way.

At the top, he saw that the road dipped and then continued to rise in a gentle winding path around an escalating series of scrubbish hills. As he crested each new height, the Doctor saw his destination more clearly, and by the time he faced it directly—still without trace of the men—he could see an estate house of such size that it must be Tarr Manor: orchards in the surrounding fields, a tall windbreak of leafless poplars, and fronted by an old-fashioned stone fence and high iron gate. The out-buildings were few and small, and the house itself, though nothing compared to a monstrosity like Harschmort, was a great, crenellated cube bristling with gables and pipes and brickwork, more than half smothered in ivy whose leaves looked to Svenson, under the insidious moonlight, like the scales of a reptile's skin.

The ground-floor windows of the house were blazing with light. With a prick to his curiosity, the Doctor saw that the only other so lit was a gable window in the highest attic, which made, as he counted the windows, four completely dark stories in between. He approached the gate with caution—being shot for trespassing would be a particularly stupid way to die—and found it chained. He called out to the small guard's hut on the other side of the wall, but received no answer. He looked up—the gate was very high— and shuddered at the prospect of climbing. He preferred to find another, less egregious point of entry, and remembered from Bascombe's blue glass card an image near an orchard, of a crumbled wall that, could he find it, would be simple to scramble over. He set off around the side, tramping through the high, dry grass drifting—from the wind, he supposed—up against the stone— like sand.

Svenson tried to form a plan of action, a task at which he never felt particularly skilled. He enjoyed studying evidence and drawing conclusions, even confronting those he had managed to entrap with facts, but all of this activity—running through houses, climbing drainage pipes, rooftops, *shooting,* being shot *at* . . . it was not his *métier*. He knew his approach to Tarr Manor ought to be an order of battle—he tried to imagine Chang's choices, but this didn't help at all: it only spelled out the degree to which he found Chang utterly mysterious. Svenson's trouble was contingency. He was searching for several things at once, and depending on what he found, all of his goals would shift. He hoped to find Miss Temple, though he did not think he would. He hoped to find the women from the train, which was also to say that he wanted to know if Elöise was corrupt as he feared, or perhaps a duped innocent like Coates. He hoped to find some information about Bascombe and the previous Lord Tarr. He hoped to find the true nature of the work at the quarry. He hoped to find the truth behind Lorenz and his machinery, and what it had to do with these men from the city. He hoped to find who was in the coach and thus more about the two men who had journeyed from the city themselves to meet it. But all these goals were a jumble in his head, and all he could think to do was to enter the house and skulk about with as much secrecy as possible—and what, his stern skeptical logic demanded, would he do if he found someone from the Cabal who could name him directly, aside from Lorenz? What if he were to be brought before the Contessa, or the Comte d'Orkancz? He stopped and sighed heavily, a dry pinch in his throat. He had no idea what he would do at all.

When he found the crumbled gap in the wall, Svenson peered over it first to make sure the path was safe. He was much closer to the house here—it seemed that there were only a few small fruit trees and fallow garden beds between him and the nearest windows. He recalled the newspaper report of Lord Tarr's death—had he not been discovered in his garden? Svenson heaved his body up and over the wall, scraping his hands just a little, and dropped onto grass. The nearest windows were actually dark; perhaps this was the old Lord's study, which no one was presently using (did that mean Bascombe was not in residence?). Svenson padded quietly across, stepping on the grass to avoid boot prints in the earthen beds. He reached the windows; the inner two were actually a pair of French doors—from the wall he had not seen the stairs that rose from the garden to meet them. Svenson leaned forward and adjusted his monocle. One of the doors was broken, a whole pane of glass missing near the handle. He looked on the steps below him and found no glass—of course, it would have been cleaned up—but then turned again to the missing pane. Around the wooden frame small flicks of wood had broken away. If he read the signs correctly, the blow had come from within, punching the glass outward. Even if Svenson credited that it was an animal that slew the old Lord (which he did not)—and why should an animal break open the door in such a way to reach through to the lock?—he would expect the assailant to come from outside. If he were already on the inside, why break the door at all? Could perhaps Lord Tarr have broken it himself, in his hurry to escape? But that only made sense if the door had been locked from the *outside* . . . if Lord Tarr had been confined to his room . . .

The door was locked now, from the inside, and Svenson reached in carefully and opened it. He stepped into the darkened room and closed the glass door behind him. In the moonlight he could see a desk and long walls completely fitted with bookshelves. He fumbled a match from his pocket, struck it on his nail and located a candle in an old copper holder on a side bookshelf. With this much light, he carefully went through each drawer of the desk, but at the end all he knew was that Lord Tarr had a keen interest in medicine, and next to none in his estate. For the single ledger—completely written in what Svenson assumed was his overseer's hand—detailing Lord Tarr's business, there were many, many notebooks and banded stacks of receipts from different physicians. Svenson had seen this enough before to realize that the Lord's own ebbing health had been itself a pursuit of pleasure beyond any particular restorative or cure—indeed, the man seemed to record the failures with as much satisfaction in his journal. This was a neat volume Svenson had found in the top drawer, under another larger ledger of receipts for potions and procedures. He flipped through it idly, just ready to put it down when his eye caught a reference to "Doctor Lorenz: Mineral Treatment. Ineffective!" He turned the page and found two more entries, identical save for a growing number of exclamation points, the last also describing Lord Tarr's bilious reaction and the subsequent forceful voiding of many chambers in his body. This was the final page in the journal, but Svenson saw a small ridge of paper between this and the journal's back cover . . . there had been another page, several, but someone had carefully cut them out with a razor. He frowned with frustration. The entries were undated—the egotism of the patient assumed no need to record what he already knew—so Svenson had no idea how long this had been going on. No matter. He dropped the journal back in the drawer and slid it shut. The Cabal had made its attempt to swing Lord Tarr to their party long before they settled on Bascombe's succession . . . and murder.

Svenson knelt at the keyhole and looked unhelpfully onto a bare wall some three or four feet away. He sighed, stood, and very, very slowly turned the knob, feeling the latch release with a far-too-audible *click*. He did not move, ready to shoot the bolt and run back for the garden. Apparently, no one had heard. He took a breath and just as slowly eased the door open, his eye against the growing gap. He desperately wanted a cigarette. The hallway was empty. He opened the door enough to poke his head and look in the other direction. The hall itself was dim, illuminated only from lighted rooms at either end. He could not see what those rooms were, nor could he hear. Svenson's nerves were fraying. He forced himself to step into the hallway and close the door—he didn't want anyone to come across it ajar and start investigating—even though he was afraid of getting lost in the house and not recognizing it again when he was trying to escape. He steeled himself—he did not need to escape. *He* was the predator. The people in the house should be afraid of *him*. Svenson stuck his hand into the pocket of his greatcoat and took hold of his revolver. It was foolish for a weapon to reassure him—either he had courage or he didn't, he chided himself, anyone can carry a gun—but he nevertheless felt better able to walk to the end of the hallway and peer around the corner.

He whipped his head back and brought his hand up over his face. The smell—that sharp sulfurous mechanical smell—assaulted his nostrils and his throat as if he had inhaled the fumes of an iron works. He wiped his nose and eyes with his handkerchief and looked again, the handkerchief held over his face. It was a large room, a reception parlor, ringed with elegant old-fashioned sitting chairs and sofas, all with wide seats to accommodate

women with bustles or hoops. Around the chairs were small end
tables, the tops of each punctuated with half-empty tea cups and
small plates bearing crusts and demurely unfinished slices of cake.
Doctor Svenson made a quick count and came up with a total of
eleven cups—enough to supply the women from the train? But
where were they now—and who was their host? He crept across
the parlor and peeked out the opposite doorway—directly into a
small ante-room that housed a dauntingly steep staircase and, beyond it, an archway to another parlor. Peeking in from this archway at that exact instant was a short, well-fed woman dressed in
black. As one they both recoiled in surprise, the woman with a
squeak, Svenson with his open mouth inaudibly groping for an explanation. She held up a hand to him and swallowed, using her
other to fan her reddening face.

"I do beg your pardon," she managed. "I thought they—you—
had all gone! I would have never—I was merely looking for the
cake. If any is left. To put away. To bring to the kitchen. The cook
will have retired—and it is a very large house. There may very well
be rats. Do you see?"

"I am terribly sorry to surprise you," replied Doctor Svenson,
his voice tender with concern.

"I thought you all had gone," she repeated, her own voice reedy
and wheezing.

"Of course," he assured her. "It's most understandable."

She cast an apprehensive glance up the staircase before looking
back to Svenson. "You're one of the Germans, aren't you?"

Svenson nodded and—because he thought it would appeal to
her—clicked his heels. The woman giggled, and immediately covered her mouth with a pudgy pink hand. He studied her face, which
reminded him of nothing more than a smirking child's. Her hair
was elaborately arranged but without any particular style. In fact—
he realized he was desperately slow at this kind of observation—it
was a rather ambitious wig. The black dress meant mourning, and
it occurred to him that her eyes were the same color as Bascombe's,

and that her eyes and her mouth bore his same elliptical shape . . . could she be his sister? His cousin?

"May I ask you something, Madame?"

She nodded. Svenson stepped aside and with his hand indicated the parlor behind him. "Do you apprehend the *smell*?"

She giggled again, this time with a wild uncertain gleam at work in her vaguely porcine eyes. She was nervous, even frightened, by the question. Before she could leave, he spoke again.

"I merely mean, I did not expect them to be . . . working . . . *here*. I assumed it would be elsewhere. I speak for us all when I hope it does not too much *infuse* your upholstery. May I ask if you spoke to any of the women?"

She shook her head.

"But you saw them."

She nodded.

"And you *are* the present Lady of the house."

She nodded.

"Can you—I am merely making sure of *their* work, you understand—tell me what you saw? Here, please, come in and take advantage of a chair. And perhaps there is some cake left after all . . ."

She installed herself on a settee with striped upholstery and pulled a plate of untouched cake slices onto her lap. With impulsive relish the woman crammed the whole of a slice into her mouth, giggled with her mouth full, swallowed with practiced determination, picked up another slice—as if having it in her hand was a comfort. She spoke in a rush.

"Well, you know, it is the sort of thing that seems, well, it seems awful, just *awful*—but then so many things seem that way at first, so many things that are good for one, or actually—eventually— delicious—" She realized what she had just said, and to whom, and erupted in another shrill laugh, stifled only by another bite of cake. She choked it down, her full bosom heaving with the effort beneath the bodice of her dress. "And they did seem happy—these women—alarmingly so, I must say. If it wasn't so frightening I would have been envious. Perhaps I still am envious—but of course I have no reason to be. Roger says it will do wonders for the family—all of this—which perhaps I shouldn't tell you, but I do believe he is right. My boy is a child—he can do nothing for his family for years—and Roger has promised, aside from every other generosity, that Edgar will inherit from him, that Roger—who has no children, but even if he did—he had a fiancée, but doesn't any longer—not that *that* matters—she was a wicked girl, I always said, never mind her money—he's quite eligible—and most impressively connected—he will pass it all back when the time comes. Fair is fair! And do you know—it is nearly certain—we shall be invited to the Palace! I cannot say it should have happened with Edgar on his own!"

Doctor Svenson nodded encouragingly.

"Well, Mr. Bascombe's work is very important."

She nodded vigorously. "I know it!"

"Though it must—I can only imagine, of course—surely some would find it a touch . . . unsettling . . . to have such *intrusions* into their house."

She did not answer, but smiled at him stiffly.

"May I also inquire—the recent loss of your father—"

"What of that? There is no sense—no decent sense to dwell on—on—on—*tragedy*!"

She persisted in smiling, though once more her eyes were wild.

"Were you with him in the house?"

"No one was with him."

"No one?"

"If there'd been anyone with him, they'd have been killed by wolves as well!"

"Wolves?"

"What's worse is that the creature's not been found. It could happen again!"

Svenson nodded gravely. "I should stay indoors."

"I do!"

He stood, gesturing to the ante-room with the staircase. "The others . . . are they . . . upstairs?"

She nodded, then shrugged, and finished the second slice.

"You've been very helpful. I shall inform Roger when I see him . . . and Minister Crabbé."

The woman giggled again, blowing crumbs.

Svenson walked up the stairs, realizing that he was searching for Elöise. He knew Miss Temple was not here. In all likelihood, Elöise did not want to be found—that is, she was his enemy. Was he such a sentimental fool? He looked back down the stairs and saw the Bascombe woman cramming another piece of cake into her mouth, tears streaming down her face. She met his gaze, cried out with dismay and dashed awkwardly from sight like a silk-wrapped scuttling dog. Svenson thought about stopping to find her for perhaps one second and then continued up the stairs. His hand drifted again to his revolver. His other hand absently bounced against the black book in his other pocket. Was he an idiot? He'd forgotten completely about it—the lack of light to read, probably—but it was the surest thing to explain what Elöise—and everyone else—was doing there.

He reached a dark landing and remembered that this and the following floors were completely dark from outside. Tarr Manor was an old house, subsisting solely on lanterns and candles, which meant there was always a near sideboard with a drawer of tallow stubs for contingencies. The Doctor stumped down the hallway until he found the very thing, and snapped a match to the candle. Now for some place to read. Svenson glanced at the labyrinthine passages and doorways and decided to stay where he was. Even taking this long went against a nagging fear that something might be happening to the women even now. He remembered

Angelique. What if Lorenz, who clearly lacked the Comte d'Orkancz's esthetic scruples, was upstairs even then, unscrewing one of his glass-packed metal flasks?

Svenson controlled his thoughts—he was working himself up to no purpose. Two minutes. He would give the book that much.

It was all the task required. On the first page was the quotation he'd had read to him on the train. And on the second page, and the next, and throughout the entirety of the book, printed again and again in small script, one great continuous flow of the identical passage. He looked on the inside and back covers, to see if Coates had written anything... and saw that he had, a series of numbers, jotted in pencil and then ineffectively erased. Svenson held the candle close, and turned to the first of the pages listed, 97... it seemed like any other page, with no special sign or significance that he could see. An idea gnawed at him... he looked at the first word at the top of the page—could these add up to a message? Some kind of basic code? Svenson took a pencil stub from his pocket and began to jot notes on the inner flap of the book. The first word of page 97 was "the"... he looked at the next number in Coates's list, page 132... the first word was "already"... Svenson quickly flipped the pages.

He frowned. "The already remake realms vessels into..." did not seem like anything sensible. Perhaps it was itself a code—he tried to puzzle it out: "already" meant the past... so "already remake" might mean their progress so far... but why bother with "the" at the beginning? Weren't coded messages supposed to be economical? Svenson sighed, looking at the book with as much insight as if it were a Hungarian newspaper, but feeling just within reach of the solution... he tried the last words of each page, but this gave him "of Lord will their night only". It sounded like a dire prediction of some kind, but wasn't right...

The letters! He looked at the list of first words—if he only took the first letters he got... "T-A-R-R-V-I"...he anxiously looked for the next page—the first word was "look"—it meant Tarr Village! He kept going and got as far as "Tarr Vill" when the next page, page 30, began with a blank line...as did the next, page 2. It came in an instant—3:02!—it was the time of the train! It was the matter of another minute before Svenson had nearly the whole of it done—there was only the last number, whose page started with the letter *p*...which gave him a last word of "bravep"...which could not be correct. He double-checked Coates's numbering, and noticed that this last number was underlined. Could it mean something different? He chuckled and had it—it indicated the whole word! He jotted it down and looked at what he'd written:

Tarr Vill. 3:02. Who offers sin shall brave Paradise

Doctor Svenson snapped the book closed and picked up the candle. These people—in ignorance of one another—had been invited to come, to submit "sin" in exchange for "Paradise." He knew enough to shudder at what this Paradise might actually be. Did any of them know with whom they trafficked? Had Coates? He walked back to the stairs, wondering *why*—why these people? Karl-Horst, Lord Tarr, Bascombe, Trapping—suborning *them* made mercenary sense, they were perfect well-placed tools. He thought of the stupid woman on the train and he thought of Elöise. He thought of Coates under the altar, and knew exactly how little these people were worth to those who had seduced them. At the base of the stairs Doctor Svenson took the pistol out of his coat and blew out his candle. He climbed into the darkness.

He heard nothing until he stepped onto the fourth floor. Above were the gabled attics, where he'd seen the light. His steps climbing were as light as he could make them, but anyone listening would have heard the creaks and groans of the old wood well in advance of his arrival. As he ascended the steps he also met a thicker concentration of the mechanical smell—perversely, as if he were in the thinning alpine air, his breath more shallow and his head dizzied. He stopped and put his handkerchief over his nose and mouth, sweeping across the shadowed landing with the pistol.

The silence was broken by a footstep above him in the attic. Svenson cocked the pistol and searched for the way up, nearly tripping on it: a ladder, flat on the floor. Whoever it was above him, they'd been marooned.

Svenson eased back the hammer and stuffed the pistol into his pocket. He picked up the ladder and looked above him for the hatch, only noticing it—the thing was quite flush with the ceiling—because of the bolt that held it shut. There was a wooden lip to rest the ladder against, and Svenson wedged it securely in place and began his tentative climb, eased by the darkness—he could not exactly see how high he was, nor thus how far there was to fall. He kept his gaze resolutely above him and reached out—nerves dancing with dismay at holding on with but a single hand—to undo the bolt. He pushed back the hatch and nearly lost his balance recoiling from the chemical stench. This was a good thing, as his instinctive shrinking from the smell caused his head to duck just out of the path of a sharp wooden heel. A moment later—taking in the swinging heel and the woman swinging it—Doctor Svenson's foot slipped on the rung and dropped through it—a sudden descent of two feet until his hands caught hold (and his jaw smacked into a rung of its own). He looked up with distress, rubbing his stinging face. Looking down at him, hair in her face and a shoe in her hand, was Elöise.

"Captain Blach!"

"Have they hurt you?" he rasped, working to restore his dangling leg on the ladder.

"No . . . no, but . . ." She looked to something he could not see. She had been crying. "Please—I must come down!"

Before he could protest, she was out of the hatch and nearly on top of him. He half-caught, half-hung on to her legs as they descended, finding the floor himself just in time to help her do the same. She turned and buried her face in his shoulder, hugging him tightly, her body shaking. After a moment, he put his arms around her—timidly, without exerting any untoward pressure, though even this much contact set off a wondrous appreciation that her shoulder blades could be so small—and waited for her emotions to subside. Instead of subsiding, she began to sob, his greatcoat muffling the sounds. He looked past her, up into the open hatch. The light in the room was not from a candle or lantern—it was somehow more pale and cold, and did not flicker. Doctor Svenson took it upon himself to pat the woman's hair and whisper "It's all right now...you're all right..." into her ear. She pulled her face away from him, out of breath, swallowing, her face streaked. He looked at her seriously.

"You can breathe? The smell—the chemicals—"

She nodded. "I covered my head—I—I had to—"

Before she could erupt once more he indicated the hatch. "Is there anyone else—does anyone need help?"

She shook her head and shut her eyes, stepping away. Svenson had no idea what to think. Dreading what he would find, he climbed the ladder and looked in.

It was a narrow gabled room with the roof slanted on each side—perhaps a child of seven could have stood without stooping in the very center. Across the floor near the window were the slumped shapeless forms of two women, obviously dead. Equally clear, though he possessed no explanation, was that their bodies were the source of the unnatural blue glow animating the grisly attic. He crawled into the room. The smell was unbearable and he paused to replace the handkerchief over his face before continuing on his hands and knees. They were from the train—one was well-dressed, and the other probably a maid. Both had bled from the ears and nose, and their eyes were filmed over and opaque, but from within, as if the contents of each sphere had become scrambled and gelatinous under extreme pressure. He thought of the Comte d'Orkancz's medical interests and recalled men he had seen pulled from the winter sea, whose soft bodies had been unable to withstand the crushing tons of ice water above them. The women were of course completely dry—nothing of the kind could explain their conditions . . . nor could any disease of the arctic account for the unearthly blue glow that arose from every visible discolored inch of their skin.

Svenson bolted the hatch behind him and climbed down, laying the ladder on the floor. He coughed into his handkerchief—his throat was unpleasantly raw, he could only imagine what hers felt like—and then tucked it away. Elöise had crept to the stairs, sitting so she could look into the shadow of the floor below. He sat next to her, no longer presuming to place an arm around her, but—as a physician—scrupling to take one of her hands in both of his.

"I woke up with them. In the room," she said, her voice a whisper, ragged but under her control. "It was Miss Poole—"

"Miss Poole!"

Elöise looked up at Svenson. "Yes. She spoke to us all—there was tea, there was cake—all of us from so many places . . . come for our different reasons, for our *fortunes*—it was all so congenial."

"But Miss Poole is not in the attic—"

"No. She had the book." Elöise shook her head, covering her eyes with a hand. "I'm not making any kind of sense, I'm sorry."

Svenson looked back at the attic. "But those women—you must know them, they were on the train—"

"I don't know them any more than I know you," she said. "We were told how to get here, not to speak of it—"

Svenson squeezed her hand, fighting down each impulse of sympathy, knowing he must determine who she really was. "Elöise . . . I must ask you, for it is very important—and you must answer me truthfully—"

"I am not *lying*—the book—those women—"

"I am not asking about them. I must know about you. To whom are you a *confidante*? Whose children is it that you tutor?"

She stared at him, perhaps unsure in the face of his sudden insistence, perhaps calculating her best response, and then scoffed, bitterly and forlorn. "For some reason I thought everyone knew. The children of Charlotte and Arthur Trapping."

"There is too much to tell," she said, straightening her shoulders and pushing the loosened strands of hair from her eyes. "But you will not understand unless I explain that, upon the disappearance of Colonel Trapping"—she looked at him to see if he required more information but Svenson merely nodded for her to go on— "Mrs. Trapping had taken to her rooms, receiving the calls of no one save her brothers. I say brothers, for it is the habit of the family, but in truth the brother she wanted to hear from, to whom she sent card after card—Mr. Henry Xonck—did not once respond, and the brother with whom her relations are strained—Mr. Francis Xonck—called upon her throughout the day. On one visit, he sought me out in the house, for he is enough of a family presence to know who I am, and my relation to Mrs. Trapping." She looked up again at Svenson, who opened his expression into one of gentle questioning. She shook her head, as if to gather her thoughts. "Who of course you don't know—she is a difficult woman. She has been shut out of her family business by her older brother—she gets money, understand, but not the work, the power, the sense of place. It haunts her—and it is why she was so determined her husband should rise to importance, and why his absence was so distressing . . . indeed, perhaps more than the loss of her man was the loss of her, if you will permit me . . . *engine*. In any case, Francis Xonck took me aside and asked if I should like to help her. He knows my devotion to Mrs. Trapping—as I say, he has seen her reliance on my advice, and he is a man who misses nothing—of course I said yes, even as I wondered at this sudden attention to his sister, a woman who despised him as a corrupting influence on her already corrupted husband. He told me there would be secrecy and intrigue, there would even—and here he looked into my eyes—I would not be telling this to a soul, Captain, were it not—what has occurred—" She gestured to the darkened house around her.

Svenson squeezed her hand. She smiled again, though her eyes were unchanged.

"He looked at me—looked *into* me—and whispered that I might find advantage in the affair myself, that I might find it . . . a revelation. He *chuckled.* And yet even as he played at seducing me, the story he told was very dark and horrid—he was convinced Colonel Trapping was being held against his wishes—because of scandal it was impossible to go to the authorities. Mr. Xonck had only heard rumors but was too visible himself to attend to them. It was part of a much larger set of events, he said. He informed me that I would be expected to reveal secrets—compromising information—of the Trappings, of the Xonck family—and he authorized me to do so. I refused, at least without first consulting Mrs. Trapping, but he insisted in the gravest terms that to alert her to even this much of her husband's predicament was to strain the marriage to the breaking point, to say nothing of what it must do to the poor woman's nerves. Still, it seemed shameful—what I knew, I knew only because of her trust. Again I refused, but he pressed me—flattering me as he praised my devotion, only to insinuate a deeper devotion lay in doing as he asked. Finally I agreed, telling myself I had no choice—though of course I had. We always do . . . but when someone praises us, or calls us beautiful, how easy it is to believe them." She sighed. "And then this morning instructions arrived to take the train and come here."

"Who offers sin shall brave Paradise," said Svenson. Elöise sniffed, nodding.

"The others were all like me—relations or servants or partners

or associates of the very powerful. All of us bearing secrets. One at
a time, Miss Poole led us from the parlor to another room. Several
men were there, wearing masks. When my turn came I told them
what I knew—about Henry Xonck and Arthur Trapping, about
Charlotte Trapping's hunger and ambition—I am ashamed of it,
and I am ashamed that while part of my mind did this in earnest
hope to save the missing man, another part—the truth of this is
bitter to me—was greedy to see what Paradise I'd find. And now . . .
now I cannot even recall what I said, what might have been so important—the Trappings are not scandalous people. I am a fool—"

"Do not—do not," whispered Svenson. "We are all so foolish,
believe me."

"That cannot be an excuse," she answered him flatly. "We are
all also given the chance to be strong."

"You were strong to come so far alone," he said, "and you were
even stronger . . . in the attic."

She shut her eyes and sighed. Svenson tried to speak gently. He
felt utterly convinced by her story, and yet wished he was not so
predisposed to believe it. She had been at Harschmort—with the
Trappings, as explained—but still, he needed more before he
could trust her fully.

"You said that Miss Poole had a book . . ."

"She laid it on the table, after I'd told them what I thought they
wanted to hear. It was wrapped in silk, like—like some kind of
Bible, or the Jewish Torah—and when she revealed it—"

"It was made of blue glass."

She gasped at the word. "It was! And you had mentioned glass
on the train—and I hadn't known, but then—I thought of you—
and I knew I did not understand my situation—and just at that
moment I had the most vivid recollection of the chill of Mr.
Francis Xonck's eyes—and then Miss Poole opened the glass
book . . . and I read . . . or should I say that it read me. That makes
no sense—but *it* made no sense at all. I fell into it like a pool, like
falling into another person's body, only it was more than one—

there were dreams, desires, such thrills that I blush to recall them—and such visions...of power...and then—Miss Poole—she must have placed my hand on the book, for I remember her laughing...and then...I cannot convey it...I was deep...so deep, and so cold, drowning—holding my breath but finally I had to breathe and gulped in—I don't know what—freezing liquid glass. It...felt like dying." She paused and wiped her eyes and glanced back at the hatch. "I woke up there. I am lucky—I know that I am lucky. I know I should have perished like the others, my skin glowing blue."

"Can you walk?" he asked.

"I can." She stood, and smoothed out her dress, still holding his hand, and reached down to replace her shoes. "After all the trouble to gather me here they have cast me aside without a care, with so little thought! If you had not come, Captain Blach—I shudder to think—"

"Do not," said Svenson. "We must leave this house. Come... the next floors are dark—the house seems to be abandoned, at least for now. I have followed the party of men, who I believe went elsewhere on the estate. Perhaps Miss Poole and the other ladies have gone to join them."

"Captain Blach—"

He stopped her. "My name is Svenson. Abelard Svenson, Captain-Surgeon of the Macklenburg Navy, attached to the service of a very foolish young Prince whom I, also a fool, yet retain a hope of saving. As you say, there is not enough time to tell the necessary tale. Arthur Trapping is dead. Earlier this morning Francis Xonck tried to sink me in the river, in the same iron casket as Colonel Trapping's corpse. It may well be that he schemes to undo both of his siblings as his own part of these machinations—and indeed, damn it all, there is too much to say—we have no time—they could return. The man you sat with on the train, Mr. Coates—"

"I did not know—"

"His name, no, nor he yours—but he is dead. They have killed him for as little cause as can be imagined. They are all dangerous, without scruple. Listen to me—I do recognize you, I have seen you among them—I must say this—at Harschmort House, not two nights past—"

Her hand went to her mouth. "You! You brought word of the Prince to Lydia Vandaariff! But—but it wasn't about that at all, was it? It was Colonel Trapping—"

"Found dead, yes—murdered, for what and by whom I've no idea—but what I am saying, what—I am deciding to trust you, despite your connection to the Xonck family, despite—"

"But you have seen them try to kill me—"

"Yes—though apparently some among them are happy to kill each other—no matter, please, what I need to tell you—should we escape, as I hope we shall, but if we are separated . . . Oh, this is ridiculous—"

"What? What?"

"There are two people you may trust—though I don't know how you should find them. One is the man I described on the train—in red, dark glasses, very dangerous, a rogue—Cardinal Chang. I am to meet him tomorrow at noon under the clock at Stropping Station."

"But why—"

"Because . . . Elöise . . . if the last days have taught me anything it is that I do not know where I shall be tomorrow at noon. Perhaps you will be there instead . . . perhaps we have met one another for just that purpose."

She nodded. "And the other? You said two people."

"Her name is Celeste Temple. A young woman, very . . . *determined,* chestnut hair, of small stature—she is the ex-fiancée of Roger Bascombe—a Ministry official who figures in this—who owns this house! Oh, this is foolish, there is no time. We must be off."

*   *   *

Svenson led her by the hand down the successive flights, a nagging anxiety rising along his spine. They had taken too long. And even if they escaped the house—where to go? The two men knew he was at the King Crow—it could not be safe if they were part of the Cabal, as of course they must be—but the train was not until next morning. Could he sleep in someone's shed? Could Elöise? He flushed at the very idea, and squeezed her hand in instinctive assurance that the thoughts in his head would not be succumbed to—a certainty challenged by her squeeze of his own hand in return.

At the top of the last staircase—leading down to the brightly lit first floor and the parlor where he'd left the Bascombe woman—he stopped again, indicating they should be especially silent. Svenson listened . . . the house was still. They crept down one stair at a time until Svenson could step to the parlor door itself and peer in. It was empty, the dishes still there (but not the cake). He looked the other direction—another parlor, also empty. He turned back to Elöise and whispered.

"No one. Which way is the door?"

She finished descending the stairs and crossed to him, standing close and leaning past his chest to look for herself. She stepped back, still quite close, and whispered in return. "I believe it is through that room and one other, not far at all."

Svenson barely took in her words. In her exertions in the attic, her dress had opened another button. Looking down at her—she was not so very short, but still his was a lovely view—he could see the determination in her face and eyes, the naked skin of her throat and then, through the opened collar of her dress, the join of her clavicles to her sternum—bones that always made him think with a strange sensual stirring of bird skeletons. She looked up at him. Without moving her eyes he knew she saw him looking at her body. She said nothing. Around Doctor Svenson time had slowed—perhaps it was all this talk of ice and freezing—and he drank in the sight of her and her acceptance of his gaze equally. He was as helpless as he had been before the Contessa. He swallowed and attempted to speak.

"This afternoon...do you know...on the train...I had... such a dream..."

"Did you?"

"I did...goodness, yes..."

"Do you remember it?"

"I do..."

He had no idea what lay behind her eyes. He was about to kiss her when they heard the screaming.

It was a woman, somewhere in the house. Svenson spun his head toward either parlor but could not tell in which direction to go. The woman screamed again. Svenson snatched hold of Elöise's hand and pulled her back through the tea cups and cake plates to the corridor where he'd first arrived, his hand digging at his great-coat as they went. He quickly opened the door and thrust her into the study. She tried to protest, but her words were stopped as he placed the heavy service revolver in her hands. Her mouth opened with shock, and Svenson gently forced her fingers around the butt of the gun, so she was holding it correctly. This got her attention enough that he could whisper and know she would understand him. Behind them the woman screamed again.

"This is Lord Tarr's study. The garden door"—he pointed to it—"is open, and the stone wall is low enough to climb. I will be right back. If I am not, go—do not hesitate. There is a train at eight o'clock tomorrow morning to the city. If anyone accosts you—anyone who is not a man in red or a woman wearing green shoes—shoot them dead."

She nodded. Doctor Svenson leaned forward and placed his lips on hers. She responded fervently, emitting the softest small

moan of encouragement and regret and delight and despair all together. He stepped back and pulled the door closed. He walked
down the hallway to the other end, passed through a small service
room. Svenson availed himself of a heavy candlestick, twisting it in
his hand to get a firm grip. The woman was no longer screaming.
He strode forward to his best estimate of where the sound had
been with five pounds of brass in his hand.

Another hallway fed Svenson into a large carpeted dining room,
the high walls covered with oil paintings, the floor dominated by
an enormous table surrounded by perhaps twenty high-backed
chairs. At the far end stood a knot of men in black coats. Curled
into a ball on her side, on top of the table, was the Bascombe
woman, her shoulders heaving. As he walked toward them—the
carpet absorbing the sound of his step—Svenson saw the man in
the middle take hold of her jaw and bend her head so she must
face him. Her eyes were screwed shut and her wig dislodged,
revealing the poignantly thin, lank, dull hair beneath. The man
was tall, with iron grey hair worn down to his collar—and Svenson
saw with alarm the medals on the chest of his tailcoat and the scarlet sash that crossed his shoulder, signs of the highest levels of nobility. If he were a native he felt sure he would have known the
man...could he be *Royal*? To his left were the two men from the
tavern. To his right was Harald Crabbé, who—pricked by some
presentiment—looked up, eyes widening, at Svenson's grim-faced
approach.

"Get away from her," Svenson called coldly. No one moved.

"It is Doctor Svenson," said Crabbé, for the benefit of his
superior.

Svenson saw that the Royal's other gloved hand held a lozenge
of blue glass above the struggling woman's mouth. At Svenson's
call she had opened her eyes. She saw the lozenge and her throat
gurgled in protest.

"Like this?" the man idly asked Crabbé, taking the lozenge between two fingers.

"Indeed, Highness," replied the Deputy Minister, with all deference, his widening eyes on Svenson's approach.

"Get away from her!" Svenson cried again. He was perhaps ten feet away and approaching fast.

"Doctor Svenson is the Macklenburg *rebel*..." intoned Crabbé.

The man shrugged with indifference and stuffed the glass into her mouth, snapping the woman's jaw between his two hands, holding it tight, her voice rising to a muted scream as the effects within intensified. He met Svenson's hot gaze with disdain and did not move. Svenson raised the candlestick—for the first time the others saw it—fully intending to dash the fellow's brains out, no matter who he was, never breaking stride.

"Phelps!" Crabbé snapped, a sudden, desperate imperative in his voice. The shorter of the two men—with the Empire hairstyle—rushed forward, a hand out toward Svenson in reasonable supplication, but the Doctor was already swinging and the candlestick caught the man across the forearm, snapping both bones. He screamed and dropped to the side with the momentum of the blow. Svenson kept coming and now Crabbé was between him and the Royal—who still had not moved.

"Starck! Stop it! Stop him! *Starck!*" Crabbé barked, backing up, exerting his full authority. Over his shoulder dove the other man from the tavern—Mr. Starck—reaching for Svenson with both hands. Svenson met him with his own outstretched left arm. For a moment they grappled at such arm's length, which left Svenson's other hand, with the candlestick, free to swing. The blow caught Starck squarely on the ear with a sickening, pumpkin-thwacking thud, dropping him like a stone. Crabbé stumbled into the Royal personage, who was finally taking note of the mayhem around him. He had released the woman's jaw—the bubbles at her mouth a foaming mix of blue and pink. Svenson prepared to strike over

the shorter diplomat's head directly at the offending aristocrat—
Prince, Duke, whoever—and realized, somewhere in the periphery
of his mind, that he was acting just like Chang. He was astonished
at how *good* it felt, and how much *better* it would feel as soon as
he'd broken the face of this monster into pulp...but it was just
then that the ceiling of the room—he did not know, as he fell,
what else could have been so heavy—collapsed without warning
on the back of Doctor Svenson's head.

He opened his eyes with the distinct memory of having been in
this exact lamentable situation before, only this time he was not in
a moving horse-cart. The back of his head throbbed mercilessly
and the muscles of his neck and right shoulder felt as if they'd been
set aflame. His right arm was numb. Svenson looked over to see it
shackled above his head to a wooden post. He was sitting in the
dirt, leaning against the side of a wooden staircase. He squinted his
eyes, trying to focus through the pain in his head. The staircase
wound back and forth many times above him, climbing close to a
hundred feet. Finally the truth dawned on his dimmed intelligence. He was in the quarry.

He struggled to his feet, desperately craving a cigarette despite
the bitter dryness of his throat. Doctor Svenson squinted and
shaded his eyes against the glaring torchlight and the quite oppressive heat. He had awoken into a very hive of activity. He fished for
his monocle and attempted to take it all in.

The quarry itself was deeply excavated, its sheer orange stone
walls betraying an even higher concentration of iron than he had
seen from the train. The density of the reddish color made his scattered mind wonder if he had been transported in secret to the
Macklenburg mountains. The floor was a flattened bed of gravel
and clay, and around him he could see piles of different mineral
substances—sand, bricks, rocks, slag heaps of melted dross. On
the far side was a series of chutes and grates and sluices—the

quarry must have some supply of water, native or pumped in—and what might have been a shaftway descending underground. Near this—far away but still close enough to bring sweat to Svenson's collar—was a great bricked kiln with a metal hatch. At the hatch crouched Doctor Lorenz, intent as a wicked gnome, once again wearing his goggles and gauntlets, a small knot of similarly garbed assistants clustered around him. Opposite these actual mining works of the quarry, and sitting on a series of wooden benches that reminded Svenson of an open-air schoolroom, were the men and women from the train. Facing them and giving some sort of low-voiced instruction was a short, curvaceous woman in a pale dress—it could only be Miss Poole. Installed alone on the backmost bench, Svenson was startled to see the Bascombe woman, her wig restored and her face—if perhaps a little pale and drawn—almost ceramically composed.

He heard a noise and looked up. Directly above him on the wide, first landing of the staircase, which made a balcony from which to overlook the quarry, stood the party of black-coated men: the Royal personage, Crabbé, and to the side, his complexion the color of dried paste, Mr. Phelps, his arm in a sling. Behind them all, smoking a cheroot, stood a tall man with cropped hair in the red uniform of the 4th Dragoons, the rank of a colonel at his throat. It was Aspiche. Svenson had not attracted their notice. He looked elsewhere in the quarry—not daring to hope that Elöise had escaped—scanning for any sign of her capture. On the other side of the stairs was an enormous, stitched-together amalgamation of tarps, covering something twice the size of a rail car and taller, some kind of advanced digging apparatus? Could its being covered mean they were *done* with digging, that the seam of indigo clay was exhausted? He looked back to the kiln for a better sense of what Lorenz was actually doing, but his eyes were stopped by another single tarp, thrown over a small heap, near the large stacks of wood used to stoke the oven. Svenson swallowed uncomfortably. Sticking out from the tarp was a woman's foot.

*   *   *

"Ah . . . he has awakened," said a voice from above.

He looked up to see Harald Crabbé leaning over the rail with a cold, vengeful gaze. A moment later he was joined by the Royal, whose expression was that of a man examining livestock he had no intention to buy. "Excuse me for a moment, Highness—I suggest you keep your attention on Doctor Lorenz, who will no doubt have something of great interest to demonstrate momentarily." He bowed and then snapped his fingers to Phelps, who slunk after his master down the stairs. After another taste of his cheroot, Aspiche ambled after them, allowing his saber to bang on each step as he went. Svenson wiped his mouth with his free left hand, did his best to hawk the phlegm from his throat and spat. He turned to face them as Crabbé stepped from the stairs.

"We did not know if you would revive, Doctor," he called. "Not that we cared overmuch, you understand, but if you did it seemed advantageous to try and speak with you about your actions and your confederates. Where are the others—Chang and the girl? Who do you all serve in this persistently foolish attempt to spoil things you don't comprehend?"

"Our conscience, Minister," answered Svenson, his voice thicker than he'd expected. He wanted very much to sleep. Blood was creeping into his arm, and he knew abstractly that he was going to be in agony very soon as the nerves flooded back to life. "I cannot be plainer than that."

Crabbé studied him as if Svenson could not possibly have meant what he said, and therefore must be speaking in some kind of code.

"Where are Chang and the girl?" he repeated.

"I do not know where they are. I don't know if they're alive."

"Why are you here?"

"And how's the back of your head?" chortled Aspiche.

Svenson ignored him, answering the Minister. "Why do you

think? Looking for Bascombe. Looking for you. Looking for my Prince so I can shoot him in the head and save my country the shame of his ascending its throne."

Crabbé twitched the corners of his mouth in a sketch of a smile.

"You seem to have broken this man's arm. Can you set the bones? You *are* a doctor, yes?"

Svenson looked at Phelps and met his pleading eyes. How long had it been? Hours at least, with the raw fractures cruelly jarred with each step the poor fellow took. Svenson raised his shackled wrist. "I will need out of this, but yes, certainly I can do something. Do you have wood for a splint?"

"We have plaster, actually—or something like it, Lorenz tells me—they use it for mining, or for shoring up crumbling walls. Colonel, will you escort the Doctor and Phelps? If Doctor Svenson diverges from his task in the slightest, I'll be obliged if you would hack off his head directly."

They walked across the quarry, past the impromptu schoolroom, toward Lorenz. As they passed, Svenson could not help but glance at Miss Poole, who met his eyes with a dazzling smile. She said something to her listeners to excuse herself and a moment later was walking quickly to catch him.

"Doctor!" she called. "I did not think to meet you again, or not so soon—and certainly not here. I am *told*"—she glanced wickedly at Aspiche—"that you have made yourself a most deadly nuisance, and have nearly slain our guest of honor!" She shook her head as if he were a charmingly disobedient boy. "They say that enemies are often closest in character—what separates them is but an attitude of mind, and as I think we all must see, those are eminently flexible. Why not join us, Doctor Svenson? Forgive me for being blunt, but when I first saw you in the St. Royale, I had no idea of your status as an adventurer—your legend grows by the day, even to the heights of your unfortunate friend Cardinal Chang, who I am led to understand is, well, no longer your competition in heroic endeavors."

Svenson could not help it, but at her words he flinched. To the obvious anger of Colonel Aspiche, Miss Poole draped her arm in Svenson's and clucked her tongue, leaning in to his face. Her perfume was sandalwood, like Mrs. Marchmoor's. Her soft hands, the overwhelmingly delicate scent, the sweat around his neck, the hammering in his skull, the woman's galling *blitheness*: Doctor Svenson felt as if his brain would boil. She chuckled at his discomfort.

"*Next* of course you will tell me you are a rescuer and defender of women—I have heard as much this very evening. But look"— she turned and waved to the Bascombe woman, sitting on the bench, who immediately waved back with the hopeful vigor of a whipped dog's wagging tail—"there is Pamela Hawsthorne, the present Lady of Tarr Manor, and happy as can be, despite the unpleasant *misunderstanding*."

"She has undergone your Process?"

"Not yet, but I'm sure she will. No, she has merely been exposed to our powerful science. Because it *is* science, Doctor, which I hope as a scientific man you will credit. Science advances, you know, just as must the moral fiber of our society. Sometimes it is dragged forward by the actions of those more knowledgeable, like a recalcitrant child. You *do* understand."

He wanted to offend her, call her a whore, to crassly violate this pretense of companionable flirtation, but he lacked the presence of mind to form the appropriate insult. Perhaps he could vomit from dizziness. Instead, he tried to smile.

"You are very persuasive, Miss Poole. May I ask you a question—as I am a foreigner?"

"Of course."

"Who *is* that man?"

Svenson turned and nodded to the tall figure next to Crabbé

on the stair landing, looking over the quarry as if he were a Borgia Pope sneering down from a Vatican balcony. Miss Poole chuckled again and patted his arm indulgently. It occurred to him that she had not possessed this sort of power before the Process, and still searched for its proper expression—was he a child to her, a pupil, an ignorant tool, or a trainable dog?

"Why, that is the Duke of Stäelmaere. He is the old Queen's natural brother, you know."

"I did not know."

"Oh yes. If the Queen and her children were to perish—heaven forbid—the Duke would inherit the throne."

"That's a lot of perishing."

"Please don't misunderstand me. The Duke is Her Majesty's most trusted sibling. As such he works most *intimately* with the present government."

"He seems intimate with Mr. Crabbé."

She laughed and was about to make a witticism when she was brusquely interrupted by Aspiche.

"That's enough. He's here to fix this man's arm. And then he's going to die."

She bore the intrusion gracefully and turned to Svenson.

"Not much of a prospect, Doctor. I would consider a switch in alliances, if I were you. You truly do not know what you are missing. And if you never do, well . . . won't that be too sad?"

Miss Poole gave him a smiling, teasing nod of her head and returned to her benches. Svenson glanced at Aspiche, who watched her with evident relish. Had she been groping Aspiche or Lorenz in the private dining room at the St. Royale? Lorenz, he was fairly sure—though it looked as if Lorenz was quite occupied with his smelting and could not be bothered. Svenson saw the man empty one of the bandolier flasks into a metal cup that his assistants were preparing to stuff into the raging kiln. He wondered what the chemical process really was—there seemed to be several distinct steps of refinement . . . were these for different purposes, to convert the indigo clay to distinct uses? He looked back at Miss Poole, and wondered where her glass book was now. If he could manage to capture that...

He was interrupted again by Aspiche, tugging his tingling arm toward Mr. Phelps, who was painfully attempting to take off his black coat. Svenson looked up at Aspiche, to ask for splints and for some brandy at least for the man's pain, when he saw, looming in the orange kiln-light like the tattoos of an island savage, the looping scars of the Process scored across his face. How had he not noticed them before? Svenson could not help it. He laughed aloud.

"What?" snarled the Colonel.

"You," answered Svenson boldly. "Your face looks like a clown's. Do you know that last time I saw Arthur Trapping—which was in his coffin, mind you—his face was the same? Do you think, just because they have expanded your *mind,* that you are any less their contingent tool?"

"Be quiet before I kill you!" Aspiche shoved him toward Phelps, who began to move out of the way and then flinched with pain.

"You'll kill me anyway. Listen—Trapping was a man with powerful friends, he was someone they needed. You can't pretend to that—you're just the man with the soldiers, and your own elevation should demonstrate how easily you too could be replaced. You mind the hounds when they need to hunt—it's servitude, Colonel, and your expanded mind ought to be *broad* enough to see it."

Aspiche backhanded Doctor Svenson viciously across the jaw. Svenson sprawled in a heap, his face stinging. He blinked and shook his head. He saw that Lorenz had heard the sound and turned to them, his expression hidden behind the black goggles.

"Fix his arm," said Aspiche.

*   *   *

In fact the "plaster" was some kind of seal for the kiln, but Svenson thought it would work well enough. The breaks were clean, and to his credit Phelps did not pass out—though to Svenson this always seemed a dubious credit indeed. For, if he *had* passed out it certainly would have gone easier for them all. As it was, the man was left trembling and spent, sitting on the ground with his arm swathed in his cast. Svenson had curtly apologized for the inconvenience of breaking his arm—assuring him that it was the Duke he had wanted to strike—and Phelps had answered that, of course, given the circumstances, it was entirely understandable.

"Your companion...," Svenson began, wiping his hands on a rag.

"I'm afraid you have done for him," replied Phelps, his voice somehow distant for all the pain, with the delicate, whispered quality of dried rice paper. He nodded to the tarp. Now that they were closer, Svenson saw that in addition to the woman's foot, there was also a man's black shoe. What had been his name— Starck? The weight of the killing settled heavily on the Doctor's shoulders. He looked to Phelps, as if he should say something, and saw the man's eyes had already drifted elsewhere, biting his lip against the grinding of his broken bones.

"It's what happens in war," Aspiche sneered with contempt. "When you made the choice to fight, you made the choice to die."

Svenson's gaze returned to the hidden stack of bodies, trying desperately to recall Elöise's shoes. Could that be her foot? How many people—dear God—were under the tarp? It had to be at least four, judging by the height, perhaps more. He hoped that, with him captured, they would not bother to search the inn or the train platform in the morning, that she might somehow get away.

"Is he going to live?" This was the arch, mocking call of Doctor Lorenz, walking over from the kiln, the goggles pulled down around his neck. He was looking at Phelps, but did not even wait for an answer. His eyes roamed over Svenson once, a professional estimation that revealed nothing save an equally professional depth of suspicion, and then moved on to Aspiche. Lorenz gestured to his assistants, who had followed him over from the kiln.

"If we're to dispose of this evidence, then now is the time. The kiln is at its hottest, and will only burn lower from this point on— for all that we wait, the remains shall be more legible."

Aspiche looked across the quarry and raised his arm, getting the attention of Crabbé. Svenson saw the Minister peer, then realize what the Colonel was pointing to and give him an answering wave of approval. Aspiche called to Lorenz's men.

"Go ahead."

The tarp was whipped away and the men stepped to either side, each pair picking up a body between them. Svenson staggered back. On top of the pile were the two women from the attic room, their flesh still glowing blue. Beneath them were Coates and Starck and another man whom he recalled but vaguely from the train, his skin also aglow (apparently the men had been shown the book as well). He watched in horror as the first two bodies were taken to the kiln and the wider stoking panel kicked open, revealing a white-hot blaze within. Svenson turned away. At the smell of burning hair his stomach heaved. Aspiche grabbed his shoulder and shoved him back across the quarry to Crabbé. He was dimly aware of Phelps stumbling along behind. At least Elöise had not been there . . . at least she'd been spared that. . . .

As they again passed Miss Poole and her charges, he saw her amongst the benches, handing out books—these with a red leather cover instead of black, whispering something to each person. He assumed it was a new code, and the key for new messages. She saw him looking and smiled. To either side of Miss Poole were the man and woman he'd first sat with on the train. He barely recognized them. Though their garments had changed—his were smeared with grease and soot, and hers were noticeably loosened—it was more for the transformation of their faces. Where before had been tension and suspicion, now Svenson saw ease and confidence—it truly was as if they were different people entirely. They nodded to him as well, smiling brightly. He wondered who they were in the world, who in their lives they had just betrayed, and what they had found in the glass book to be so altered.

Svenson tried to make sense of it all, to force his tired brain to think. He ought to be drawing one conclusion after another, but nothing followed in his dulled condition. What was the difference between the glass book and the Process? The book could obviously kill—though this seemed almost cruelly arbitrary, like a toxic reaction to shellfish, as he doubted the deaths were intentional or planned. But what did the book *do*? Elöise spoke of falling into it, of visions. He thought of the compelling nature of the blue glass card, and then extrapolated that to the experience of a *book*...but what else...he felt near to something... *writing*...a book must be written in, the thoughts must be recorded...was that what they were doing? He recalled Chang's description of the Institute, the man dropping the book as it was being made—made somehow *from* Angelique—the same man from Crabbé's kitchen. What was the difference between using a person to *make* the book, and then using these people here to *write* in it...or be drawn into its clutches like a spider's web? And what of the Process? That was simple conversion, he felt—a chemical-electric process using the properties of the refined indigo clay—indigo clay melted somehow into glass—to affect the character: to lower inhibitions and shift loyalties. Did it merely erase moral objections? Or did it rewrite them? He thought how much a person could accomplish in life without scruples, or one hundred such people working together, their numbers growing by the day. Svenson rubbed his eyes as he walked—he was getting confused again, which merely returned him to the first question: what was the difference between the Process and the book? He looked back at Miss Poole and her little schoolroom in the slag heaps. It was a question of direction,

he realized. In the Process, the energy went *into* the subject, eras-
ing inhibitions and converting them to the cause. With the glass
book, the energy was sucked *out* of the subject—along with (or in
the form of—was memory energy?) specific experiences in their
lives. Undoubtedly this was the blackmail: the secrets these bitter
underlings had to tell were now *secreted* within Miss Poole's book,
and that book—like the cards—would allow anyone else to *experi-*
ence those shameful episodes. There would be no denial, and no
end to the Cabal's power over those so implicated.

It was making more sense to him now—the books were tools
and could, like any other book, be used for a variety of purposes,
depending on what was in them. Furthermore, it might be that
they were constructed in different ways, for different reasons,
some written whole and some with a different number of empty
pages. He could not but recall the vivid, disturbing paintings of
Oskar Veilandt—the compositions explicitly depicting the
Process, the reverse of each canvas scrawled with alchemical symbols. Did that man's work lie at the root of the books as well? If
only he was still alive! Was it possible that the Comte—clearly the
master within the Cabal of this twisted science—had pillaged
Veilandt's secrets and then had him killed? As he thought of books
and purposes, Svenson suddenly wondered if d'Orkancz had been
intending to make a book of Angelique alone—the vast adventures of a lady of pleasure. It would be a most persuasive entice-
ment for his cause, offering the detailed experience of a thousand
nights in the brothel without ever leaving one's room. Yet that
would be but one example... the limit was sensation itself—what
adventures or travels or thrills that one person had known could
not be imprinted onto one of these books for anyone to consume,
which was to say, to experience *bodily* for themselves? What sumptuous banquets? What quantities of wine? What battles, caresses,
what witty conversations... there truly was no end... and no end
to what people would pay for such oblivion.

He looked back to Miss Poole and the smiling couple. What

had changed them? What had killed the others, but spared these two? It was somehow important to know—for this was a wrinkle, something that did not flow cleanly. If there was only a way to find out—yet any idea of who those people were or what might have killed them was even now disappearing into ash. Svenson snorted with anger—perhaps there was enough after all. Their skin had been infused with blue—this hadn't happened to the ones who had survived. He thought of the couple, changed from suspicious resentment to open amity...Svenson stumbled with the sudden impact of his thoughts. Aspiche took hold of his shoulder and shoved him forward.

"Get along there! You'll be resting soon enough!"

Doctor Svenson barely heard him. He was recalling Elöise—how she could not remember what scandals she might have revealed about the Trappings or Henry Xonck. She had said it in a way to mean there had been nothing to reveal...but Svenson knew the memories had been *taken* from her, just as the memories of spite and injustice and envy had been taken from the venal young couple—all to be inscribed in the book. And the ones who had died...what had d'Orkancz said about Angelique? That the energy had "regrettably" gone the other direction...this must have happened here too...the book's energy must have entered deeper into the people who died, leaving its mark as it drained them utterly. But why them and not the others? He looked back at the smiling people around Miss Poole. None of them could remember exactly what they had revealed—indeed, did they even know why they were here? He shook his head at the beauty of it, for each could be safely sent back to their life, lacking any knowledge of what had been done, aside from a trip to the country and a few strange deaths. But when was there not a way to explain deaths of those considered to be insignificant? Who would protest—who would even remember those killed?

For a moment Svenson's thoughts stabbed toward Corinna—the degree to which her true memory was retained in his breast

alone—and he felt within him a sharpening rage. The death of
Starck weighed heavily, but he took the words of the simpleton
Aspiche (why must such men always reduce the complexity of the
world to single-syllable thinking—an empire of grunts?) as a re-
minder of who his enemies truly were. He was not Chang—he
could not feel good about killing, nor kill well enough to preserve
his life—but he was Abelard Svenson. He knew what these villains
were doing, and which of them were truly doing it: above him on
the platform balcony, Harald Crabbé and the Duke of Stäelmaere.
If he could kill them, then Lorenz and Aspiche and Miss Poole did
not matter—whatever mischief they made in the world would be
limited to the reach of their own two arms and would land them in
the same undoubted discontent they knew before their glorious redemption in the Process. The Process depended on the organization of the Cabal—on these two, on d'Orkancz, Lacquer-Sforza,
and Xonck. And Robert Vandaariff... he must be the leader.
Doctor Svenson suddenly knew that even if he did escape he
would not be meeting Chang or Miss Temple at Stropping
Station. Either they were dead, or they would be at Harschmort.

But what could he hope to do? Aspiche was tall, strong, armed,
and vicious—perhaps even a match for Chang. Doctor Svenson
was unarmed and spent. He looked back to the kiln. Lorenz
walked toward them, shucking his gauntlets as he came. Above,
Crabbé and the Duke chatted quietly—or Crabbé was chatting
and the Duke nodding at what he heard, his face glacially impassive. Svenson counted fifteen wooden steps to their platform. If he
could make a dash for it, reach them ahead of Aspiche—Crabbé
would again throw himself in front of the Duke... Svenson
thought of his pockets—was there any kind of weapon? He
scoffed—a pencil stub, a cigarette case, the glass card... the card,
perhaps if he could snap it in his hands as he ran, and use the
jagged edge, one sharp cut into Crabbé's throat, and then to take
the Duke hostage—to drag him up the steps, somehow—would
he have his coach above?—making it back to the train, or all the

way to the city. Lorenz was nearing them. It was the perfect distraction. He casually slipped a hand into his pocket and groped for the card. He shifted his feet, ready to run.

"Colonel Aspiche," called Doctor Lorenz, "we are nearly—"

Aspiche swung his forearm savagely across the back of Svenson's head, knocking him to his knees, his skull near to bursting with pain, his stomach heaving, tasting the vomit in his throat, blinking tears from his eyes. Somewhere behind him—it seemed miles away—he could hear Lorenz's thin laughter and then the dark hiss of Aspiche at his ear.

"Don't even *think* of it."

Svenson knew he would probably die, but he also knew that if he did not get off his knees he would lose whatever infinitesimal chance he had. He spat and wiped his mouth on his sleeve, noticing with vague surprise that his hand held the blue card still. With a terrible effort he braced his other arm on the grimy clay and raised one knee. He pushed off, wobbled, and then felt Aspiche take hold of his greatcoat collar and yank him up to his feet. He let go and Svenson staggered, nearly falling again. Again he heard Lorenz laugh, and then Crabbé call out from above.

"Doctor Svenson! Any new thoughts about the location of your comrades?"

"I am told they are dead," he called back, his voice hoarse and weak.

"Perhaps they are," responded Crabbé. "Perhaps we have taken enough of your time."

Behind him he heard the metal swish of Colonel Aspiche drawing his saber. He must turn and face him. He must snap the card and drive the sharp edge into his neck, or his eyes, or . . . he could not turn. He could only look up at Crabbé's satisfied face, leaning over the railing. Svenson pointed to the quarry walls and called up to the Deputy Minister.

"Macklenburg."

"I beg your pardon?"

"Macklenburg. This quarry. I understand the connection, your indigo clay. This can only be a small deposit. The Macklenburg mountains must be full of it. If you control its Duke, there is no end to your power . . . is that your plan?"

"*Plan,* Doctor Svenson? I'm afraid that is already the *case.* The *plan* is what to do with the power we've managed to achieve. With the help of wise men like the Duke here—"

Svenson spat. Crabbé stopped mid-sentence.

"Such *vulgarity*—"

"You've insulted my country," called Svenson. "You've insulted this one. You're going to pay, each arrogant one of you—"

Crabbé looked past Svenson's shoulder to Colonel Aspiche. "Kill him."

The shot took him by surprise, as he was expecting a blow from a saber—and it took him another moment to realize that it wasn't he who had been hit by the bullet. He heard the scream—again, wondering that it wasn't coming from his own mouth—and then saw the Duke of Stäelmaere reel into the railing, clutching his right shoulder, quite cleanly punctured, blood pouring through his long white fingers clutching the wound. Crabbé wheeled, his mouth working, as the Duke dropped to his knees, his head slipping through the rails. Above and behind them, both hands tightly gripping the smoking service revolver, stood Elöise.

"God be damned, Madame!" shouted Crabbé. "Do you know who you have shot? It is a capital offense! It is treason!" She fired again, and this time Svenson saw the shot blow out through the Duke's chest, a thick quick fountain of blood. Stäelmaere's mouth opened with surprise at the impact, at the shocking scope of his agony, and he collapsed to the planking.

Svenson whirled, drawing new energy from his rescue, and—recalling something he'd once seen in a wharf-side bar—stomped on Colonel Aspiche's boot in the same moment he shoved the man straight back sharply with both hands. As the Colonel fell back, Svenson's weight fixed his foot to the ground so that he was both unable to rebalance himself and to prevent his own weight from being thrown against his pinned ankle. Svenson heard the cracking bones as the Colonel landed with a cry of rage and pain. He leapt away—Aspiche, even so down, was swinging the saber, face reddened, tears at the corners of his eyes—and dashed to the stairs. Elöise fired again—apparently missing Crabbé, who had retreated into the corner of the landing, arms over his face, hunched away from the gun. Svenson charged and struck him in his exposed stomach. Crabbé doubled forward with a grunt, his hands clutching his belly. Svenson swung again at the Deputy Minister's now-exposed face, and the man went down in a heap. Svenson gasped—he had no idea how such a blow would hurt his hand—and staggered toward his rescuer.

"Bless you, my dear," he breathed, "for you have saved my life. Let us climb—"

"They are coming!" she said, her voice rising with fear. He looked back down to see Lorenz's assistants and the gang of men from the benches all running. Lorenz had helped Aspiche to his feet and the limping, hopping Colonel was waving his saber and bawling orders.

"Kill them! Kill them! They have murdered the Duke!"

"The Duke?" whispered Elöise.

"You did right," Svenson assured her. "If I may, for there are many of them—"

He reached for the pistol and took it, pulling back the hammer, and jumped down to the cowering Crabbé. The men charged up the stairs as Svenson took the Minister by his collar and raised him to his knees, grinding the gun barrel against Crabbé's ear. They surged to the very edge of the platform, eyeing Svenson and Elöise with hatred. Svenson looked over the rail to the quarry floor to where Lorenz stood supporting Aspiche. He shouted down to them.

"I will kill him! You know I will do it! Call your fellows off!"

He looked back to the crowd and saw it part to allow Miss Poole to pass through. She stepped onto the platform, smiling icily.

"Are you quite all right, Minister?" she asked.

"I am alive," muttered Crabbé. "Has Doctor Lorenz finished his work?"

"He has."

"And your charges?"

"As you can see, quite well—enthusiastic to protect you and avenge the Duke."

Crabbé sighed. "Perhaps it is best this way, perhaps it can be better worked. You will need to prepare his body."

Miss Poole nodded, and then looked up beyond Svenson to Elöise. "It seems we have underestimated you, Mrs. Dujong!"

"You left me to die!" shouted Elöise.

"Of course she did," called Crabbé, rubbing his jaw. "You failed your test—it seemed as if you *would* die, like the others. It cannot be helped—you are wrong to place blame with Elspeth. Besides, look at you now—so bold!"

"Do you think we were hasty with our decision, Minister?" asked Miss Poole.

"Indeed I do. Perhaps Mrs. Dujong will be joining our efforts after all."

"Join you?" cried Elöise. "*Join* you? After—after all—"

"You forget," called Miss Poole. "Even if you do not remember why you came, *I* remember it quite well—every noisome little secret you offered up in exchange for your *advancement*."

Elöise stood, her mouth open, looking to Svenson, then back at Miss Poole. "I did not—I cannot—"

"You wanted it before," said Miss Poole. "And you want it still. You've proven yourself quite bold."

"There's barely a choice, my dear," observed Crabbé with a sigh.

Svenson saw the confusion on Elöise's face and jabbed the gun hard into Crabbé's ear, stopping the man's speech. "Did you not hear what I said? We will be going at once!"

"O yes, Doctor Svenson, you were heard quite clearly," Crabbé muttered, wincing. He looked up at Miss Poole. "Elspeth?"

The woman retained her icy smile. "Such *chivalry*, Doctor. First it is Miss Temple, and now Mrs. Dujong—a veritable collector of hearts you seem, I never would have thought it."

Svenson ignored her, and yanked Crabbé back toward the stairs.

"We will be taking our leave—"

"Elspeth!" the Deputy Minister croaked.

"You will not," Miss Poole announced.

"I beg your pardon?" asked Svenson.

"You will not. How many shots remain in your gun?"

Aspiche called back to her from below, a disembodied voice. "She fired three times, and it is a six-shot cylinder."

"So there you are," continued Miss Poole, indicating the crowd of men around her. "Three shots. We are at least ten, and you at the very most can shoot three. We will take you."

"But the first I shoot shall be Minister Crabbé."

"It is more important that our work proceed, and your escape may endanger it. Do you agree, Minister?"

"Unfortunately, Svenson, the woman is correct—"

Svenson cracked him sharply on the head with the gun butt. "Stop talking!"

Miss Poole spoke to the gang of men behind her. "Doctor Svenson is a *German* agent. He has succeeded in causing the death of the Queen's own noble brother—"

Doctor Svenson looked up at Elöise, whose eyes were wide with fear. "Run now," he told her. "Escape—I will hold them off—"

"Do not bother, Mrs. Dujong," called Miss Poole. "We cannot allow either of you to leave—really we can't. And I do promise,

Doctor, however much time your bravery does buy your ally, she will not in that dress outrun these gentlemen across three miles of open road."

Svenson was at a loss. He did not believe they would sacrifice Crabbé so easily—yet could he risk Elöise's life on the chance? But, if he were to surrender—impossible, surely—what hope would they have of surviving? None! They'd be ash in Lorenz's oven—it was an appalling thought, unconscionable—

"Doctor...Abelard..." Elöise whispered to him from above. He looked up at her, helpless, sputtering.

"You will not join them—you will not stay—"

"What if she wants to stay?" asked Miss Poole, wickedly.

"She does not—she cannot—be quiet!"

"Doctor Svenson!" It was Lorenz, shouting from below. Svenson edged closer to the rail—pulling his hostage with him—and looked down. The man had walked over to the large conglomeration of tarps, covering the hidden train car. "Perhaps this will convince you of our great purpose!"

Lorenz pulled on a rope line and the tarps were released. At once the great shape beneath them rose some twenty feet in a lurch, thrusting up clear of the covering. It was an enormous cylindrical gasbag, an airship, a dirigible. As it ascended to the limits of its tethering cables, he could see propellers, engines, and the large cabin underneath. The entire thing was even larger than he'd thought, expanding like an insect coming out of its cocoon, an iron skeleton of supporting struts snapping into place as it rose—and the whole painted to perfectly match the deepest midnight sky. Traveling at night the craft would be near invisible.

Before Svenson could say a word, Elöise screamed. He wheeled to see her off balance, a man's hand incongruously holding onto her leg through the gap in the stairs—an arm in a red sleeve, Aspiche, reaching up from below while he'd been distracted by

Lorenz's spectacle like a gullible fool. Svenson watched helplessly as she tried to pull herself free, to step on his wrist with her other foot—it was all that was needed for the spell to be broken. The men around Miss Poole surged forward, cutting Svenson off from Elöise. Crabbé dropped into a ball on the planking, pulling Svenson off balance. Before he could re-position the pistol the men were upon him—a fist across his jaw, a forearm clubbing him across the head and he staggered back into the rail. Elöise screamed again—they were all around her—he had failed her completely. The men scooped him up bodily and threw him over the rail.

He came to his senses with the cloudless black night sky in motion above him and the steady bumping of gravel and dirt beneath his skull. He was being dragged by his feet. It took the Doctor a moment to realize that his arms were over his head and his greatcoat tangled up behind, scooping up loose earth like a rake as he was pulled along. Toward the oven, he knew. He craned his head and saw a man at each leg, two of Lorenz's fellows. Where was Elöise? He felt the pain in his neck and aches everywhere, but nowhere the sharp jarring agony that must mean a broken bone—and the way they carried his legs and his arms dragged, he would certainly know. His hands were empty—what had happened to his revolver? He cursed his pathetic attempts at heroism. Rescued by a woman only to betray her trust with incompetence. As soon as the men saw he was awake they would simply dash his brains out with a brick. And what could he possibly do, unarmed, against both of them? He thought of everyone he had failed . . . how would this be any different?

The men dropped his legs without ceremony. Svenson blinked, still groggy, as one of them looked back at him with a knowing smile, and the other stepped to the oven.

"He's awake," said the smiling one.

"Hit him with the shovel," called the other.

"I will at that," said the first, and began to look around him for it.

Svenson tried to sit up, to run, but his body—awkward, aching, stiff—did not respond. He rolled onto his side and forced his knees up beneath him, pushing off and then up into a stumbling tottering attempt to walk away.

"Where do you think you're going, then?" called the laughing voice behind him. Svenson flinched, fearing any moment to feel the shovel slicing across the back of his skull. His eyes searched for some answer, some idea—but only saw the dirigible hovering across the quarry and above it a pitiless black sky. Could this be the finish? So pedestrian and brutal, cut down like a beast in a farmyard? With a sudden impulse Svenson spun around to face the man, extending his open hand.

"A moment, I beg of you."

The man had indeed picked up the shovel and held it ready to swing. His companion stood some feet behind him, with a metal hook he'd clearly just used to pry open the oven hatch—even this far from the glowing furnace Svenson could feel the increase in heat. They smiled at him.

"Will he offer us money, do you reckon?" said the one with the hook.

"I will not," said the Doctor. "First, because I have none, and second, because whatever money I have will be yours in any case, once you knock me on the head."

At this the men nodded, grinning that he had guessed their unstoppable plan.

"I cannot offer you anything. But I can ask you—while I have breath—for I know you will be curious, and it would pain me to leave such honest fellows—for I know you merely do what you must—in such very, very grave danger."

They stared at him for just a moment. Svenson swallowed.

"What danger's that?" asked the man with the shovel, shifting his grip in anticipation of swinging it rather hard into Svenson's face.

"Of course—of course, no one has told you. Never mind—I'm not one to interfere—but if you would, for the sake of my conscience—promise to throw this, this *article* straight into the oven after—well, after *me*—" His hand reached into a pocket and pulled forth his remaining blue card—he'd no idea which—and held it out for them to see. "It seems a mere bit of glass, I know—but you must, for your own safety, put it straight into the fire. Do it now—or let me do it—"

Before he could say another word the one with the shovel stepped forward and snatched the card from Svenson's hand. He took two steps back, eyeing the Doctor with a sullen suspicion, and then looked down into the card. The man went still. His companion looked at him, then at Svenson, and then lunged over the other man's shoulder to look at the card, reaching for it with a large callused hand. Then he stopped as well, his own attention hooked into place.

Svenson watched with disbelief. Could it be so simple? He took a gentle step forward, but as he extended his hands to take the shovel the card came to the end of its cycle and both men emitted a small sigh that stopped his movement cold. Then they sank into the next repetition, jaws slack, eyes dull. With a brutal determination, Svenson snatched the shovel cleanly away and swept it down twice, slamming the flat blade across each man's head, one after the other, as they looked up at him, still dazed. He dropped the shovel, collected the blue glass card, and turned away as quickly as he could. He had not used the edge—with luck each man would live.

A chopping roar echoed off the stone walls—such an encompassing din that he'd barely noticed it, assuming it was inside his battered skull. It must be the dirigible—its engine and propellers!

What would drive such a thing, he wondered—coal? steam? The iron-framed cabin had looked woefully fragile. Had anyone heard his conversation with the men? Had anyone seen? He looked up, squinting—what had happened to his monocle?—at the demonic airship. It had risen to the height of the iron-red stone walls, tethered to the quarry bed only by a few small cables. There were figures in the window of the gondola, too far away to see clearly. He didn't care about them—what had happened to Elöise? If she had not been taken to the oven with him—if she was not dead—then what had they done with her?

The tall staircase seemed empty save at the very top, where a cluster of figures had gathered on a level equal to the suspended dirigible's cabin. On the quarry floor he saw only three men minding the last ropes, their attention focused upwards. Doctor Svenson limped toward the stairs, his right leg dragging, his neck and shoulders and head feeling as if they'd been wrapped in plaster and then set aflame. He wiped his mouth on his filthy sleeve and spat, having put more dust into his mouth than he'd wiped away. There was blood on his face—his own? He'd no idea. The figures on the giant staircase had to be the men and women from the train. Would Miss Poole be with them? No, he reasoned—no one would be with them. They'd served their purpose. Miss Poole would be waving from the gondola, off to Harschmort with the others. Where was Elöise?

Svenson walked more quickly, pushing against the objections of his body. His fingers dug into his coat and came out with his cigarette case. There were three left, and he stuffed one into his bloody face as he hobbled forward, and then exclaimed with pain when he tried to strike a match on a split thumbnail. He changed hands, lit the cigarette, and drew in an exquisitely taxing lungful of smoke, shaking the pain out of his hand, dragging his right foot forward, and finally heaving a thick bolus of phlegm and blood and dust from the back of his throat. His eyes were watering but the smoke pleased him nevertheless, somehow recalling himself to his task. He was becoming relentless, unstoppable, an adversary of legend. He spat again and in another stroke of luck happened to glance down at where he was spitting—to see if there was any visible blood—and saw something in the dirt catching the light. It was glass—it was his monocle! The chain had snapped when he was being dragged, but the glass was whole! He wiped it off as best he could, smiling stupidly, then pulled out his shirt-tail to wipe it again, his sleeve having hopelessly smeared things. He screwed it in place.

Crabbé stood framed in the small opened window, shouting to someone on the stairs. It was Phelps, evidently enough recovered to travel on his own. Next to Crabbé in the window was indeed Miss Poole, waving away. He did not see Lorenz—perhaps Lorenz was flying the craft. Doctor Svenson knew absolutely nothing about how these things worked, indeed, how they stayed in the air at all. Aspiche had to be inside. Where was the body of the Duke? Would that be in a cart, going back to the city with Phelps? Would that be where he found Elöise—dead or alive? It seemed likely—he would need to climb the stairs and follow them into Tarr Village.

He was half-way across the quarry, the airship looming larger above him with each step. Still no one had seen him, not even to look for the two stupefied men. Someone would have to turn—the fellows minding the cable would release it any moment. He'd never make the stairs—he couldn't outrun a child. He needed to hide. Svenson stopped and looked around for some niche in the rock when something fell in the dirt some ten yards away. He looked at it—couldn't tell what it was—and then turned his gaze to where it might have possibly come from. Above him, through the back window of the dirigible's gondola, he saw a hand against the glass and a pale, half-obscured face. He looked again at what had fallen. It was a book…a black book…leather-bound…he looked up again. It was Elöise. He was an idiot.

*   *   *

The Doctor charged forward just as the nearest of the men minding the cables finally happened to look his way, but his cry of alarm at the strange, running figure emerged as an inarticulate shout. Svenson lowered his shoulder and cannoned into his midsection, knocking them both sprawling and the cable loose from the grounded spike that had held it. The rope began to snake around them as the dirigible surged against its moorings. The other two men released their own lines, thinking this had been the signal—only realizing their error once the lines had actually been slipped. Svenson struggled to his feet and dove for the whipping cable—he was insane, nearly gibbering with terror—and thrust his arm through the knotted loop at its end. The dirigible lurched upwards and with a shriek Svenson was pulled off his feet, some three feet in the air. The craft surged into the black sky, Doctor Svenson kicking his legs and holding to the rope more tightly than he ever imagined human beings could do. He swept past the crowd on the steps, swinging like a human pendulum. At once he was out of the quarry and over a meadow, the soft grass close beneath him for a sudden tempting moment. Could he drop and survive? His hand was tangled in the rope. Fear had made his grip hard as steel and before he could push another thought through his paralyzed mind the craft rose again, the meadow spiraling farther and farther away.

Black night above and around him, mocked by a chilling wind, Doctor Svenson looked helplessly at the impossibly distant gondola and began to climb, hand over bloodied hand, gasping, sobbing, all the terrors of hell screaming below his feet, his eyes now screwed shut in agony.

About the Author

Playwright Gordon Dahlquist was born in the Pacific Northwest and lives in New York City. His second novel, *The Dark Volume,* will be available from Bantam Books in spring 2009.

If you enjoyed Gordon Dahlquist's
internationally bestselling

THE GLASS BOOKS
of the
DREAM EATERS

✦ VOLUME ONE ✦

you won't want to miss

THE GLASS BOOKS
of the
DREAM EATERS

✦ VOLUME TWO ✦

coming in trade paperback
from Bantam Books
in February 2009.

And look for

THE DARK VOLUME

which continues the adventures of

THE GLASS BOOKS
of the DREAM EATERS.

It will be available in hardcover
from Bantam Books
in April 2009.